About the Authors

Carol Marinelli recently filled in a form asking for her job title. Thrilled to be able to put down her answer, she put writer. Then it asked what Carol did for relaxation and she put down the truth – writing. The third question asked for her hobbies. Well, not wanting to look obsessed she crossed the fingers on her hand and answered swimming but, given that the chlorine in the pool does terrible things to her highlights – I'm sure you can guess the real answer.

After completing a degree in journalism, then working in advertising and mothering her kids, **Robin Gianna** had what she calls her awakening. She decided she wanted to write the romance novels she'd loved since her teens, and now enjoys pushing her characters toward their own happily-ever-afters. When she's not writing, Robin's life is filled with a happily messy kitchen, a needy garden, a wonderful husband, three great kids, a drooling bulldog and one grouchy Siamese cat.

Melanie Milburne read her first Mills & Boon at age seventeen in between studying for her final exams. After completing a Masters Degree in Education she decided to write a novel and thus her career as a romance author was born. Melanie is an ambassador for the Australian Childhood Foundation and is a keen dog lover and trainer and enjoys long walks in the Tasmanian bush. Melanie won the HOLT Medallion, a presti... literary talent.

Spanish Scandals

Spanish Scandals:
A Private Affair

CAROL MARINELLI

ROBIN GIANNA

MELANIE MILBURNE

MILLS & BOON

First Published in Great Britain 2020
By Mills & Boon, an imprint of HarperCollins*Publishers*
1 London Bridge Street, London, SE1 9GF

SPANISH SCANDALS: A PRIVATE AFFAIR © 2020 Harlequin
Books S.A.

The Baby of Their Dreams © 2015 Carol Marinelli
The Spanish Duke's Holiday Proposal © 2017 Harlequin Books S.A.
The Mélendez Forgotten Marriage © 2010 Melanie Milburne

Special thanks and acknowledgement are given to Robin Gianna
for her contribution to the *Christmas in Manhattan* series.

ISBN: 978-0-263-29855-0

MIX
Paper from
responsible sources
FSC™ C007454

This book is produced from independently certified FSC™ paper
to ensure responsible forest management.

For more information visit: www.harpercollins.co.uk/green

Printed and bound in Spain
by CPI, Barcelona

THE BABY OF
THEIR DREAMS

CAROL MARINELLI

PROLOGUE

THIS WASN'T HOW July was supposed to be.

'Hey, Cat!'

Catriona Hayes stood as her friend came out of her office but she was unable to return Gemma's smile. 'I've just got to go up to Maternity to see a patient and then we can…' Gemma didn't finish her sentence. Now she was closer she could see that her friend was barely holding it together—Cat's green eyes were brimming with tears, her long curly black hair looked as if it had been whipped up by the wind and she was a touch breathless, as if she'd been running. It quickly became clear to Gemma that Cat was not here at the London Royal for their shopping date.

She wasn't.

Cat had walked out of her antenatal appointment at the hospital where she worked and, like a homing beacon, had taken the underground to the Royal, where Gemma was an obstetrics registrar. She had sat in panicked silence on the tube and, despite being twenty weeks pregnant and wearing a flimsy wraparound dress and heels, she had been one of those people running up the escalator rather than standing and letting it take them to the top.

'You're not here for our shopping date, are you?' Gemma checked, and Cat vaguely recalled a date that they had made a couple of weeks ago. They were both supposed to finish at four today and the plan had been to hit the shops, given that Cat would know by now if she was having a boy or girl.

They had had it all planned—they were going to head off for a late afternoon tea and Cat would reveal the news about the sex of her baby. Then they would shop for baby things in the appropriate colours and choose shoes for Cat and Mike's wedding, which was just over three weeks away.

That was how it was supposed to be.

This was how it was.

'You know how we discussed keeping things separate?' Cat felt as if her voice didn't belong to her as she spoke to her closest friend. 'Can I change my mind about that?'

And, because she and Gemma had been friends since way back in medical school, she didn't have to explain what she meant.

'Of course you can,' Gemma said, battling a feeling of dread. 'Let's go into my office.'

When Cat had found out that she was pregnant she had discussed with her family doctor, and also her fiancé, the potential pitfalls of having your closest friend as your obstetrician.

Against her own gut instinct, an esteemed colleague of Mike's was now overseeing her pregnancy.

She had walked out on both of them today.

Now Cat walked into her friend's office on shaky legs and, for the first time as Gemma's patient, took a seat, wondering how best to explain what had been going on in her life. The past two weeks she had dodged speaking with Gemma as best she could.

Gemma poured her a glass of water and Cat took a long drink as her friend waited patiently. Finally she caught her breath enough to speak.

'I had an ultrasound a couple of weeks ago,' she started. 'There were some problems... I know I could have spoken to you but Mike wanted to wait for all the test results to be in before we told anyone. *If* we told anyone...' Tears were now falling thick and fast but she had run out of sobs and so was able to continue. 'The results are not good, Gemma. They're not good at all. I had an amnio and the baby has Edwards syndrome...' Cat elaborated further. 'Full-form Edwards syndrome.' She looked at her friend and saw Gemma's small swallow as she took in the diagnosis.

'What does Mike say?'

Not only had Cat found out her baby was terribly sick, but also in these past two weeks her relationship had crumbled.

'Mike says that it's not part of the plan... Well, he didn't have the guts to say it like that. He said that as a paediatrician he knows better than most what the baby would be up against and what we'd be up against—the anomalies are very severe. There really isn't much hope that it will survive the birth and if it does it's likely to live only for a few hours.' Her voice was starting to rise. 'He says that it's not our fault, that we've every chance of a healthy baby and so we should put it behind us and try again...' Cat's eyes flashed in anger. 'He's a paediatrician, for God's sake, and he wants me to have a late abortion...'

'What do you want, Cat?' her friend gently broke in. 'Do you even know what you want?'

'A healthy baby.'

Gemma just looked.

'And that's not going to happen,' Cat said.

Finally she had accepted it.

She sat there in silence. It was the first glimpse of peace she had had in two weeks. Since the first ultrasound, at Mike's strong suggestion, they had kept the findings to themselves and so she had been holding it all in—somehow working as an emergency registrar, as well as carrying on with their wedding plans and doing her best to avoid catching up with Gemma.

At first Cat had woken in tears and dread for her baby each morning. Today, though, she had woken in anger and, looking at the back of her fiancé's head and seeing him deeply asleep, instead of waiting for him to wake up, she had dug him in the ribs.

'What's wrong?' Mike had turned to her rage and she had told him they were through. That even if, by some miracle, the amnio came back as normal today, there was nothing left of them.

The amnio hadn't come back as normal.

Cat had known that it wouldn't; she'd seen the ultrasound and nothing could magic the problems away.

It had been confirmation, that was all.

Now Gemma gave her the gift of a pause and Cat sat, feeling the little kicks of her baby inside her as well as the rapid thud of her own heart. Finally both settled down as she came to the decision she had been reaching towards since the news had first hit.

'I understand that it's different for everyone. Maybe

if I'd found out sooner I'd have had a termination.' She truly didn't know what she might have done then; she could only deal with her feelings now. 'But I'm twenty weeks pregnant. I know it's a boy and I can feel him move. He's moving right now.' She put a hand on her stomach and felt him, in there and alive and safe. 'Mike keeps saying it would be kinder but I'm starting to wonder, kinder for whom?'

Gemma was patient and Cat waited as she rang through to the hospital where Cat was being seen and all the results were transferred.

Gemma went through them carefully.

And she didn't leave it there; instead, she made a phone call to a colleague and Cat underwent yet another ultrasound.

Her baby was imperfect, from his too-little head to his tiny curved feet, but all Cat could see was her son. Gently Gemma told her that the condition was very severe, as she'd been told, and she concurred that if the baby survived birth he would live only for a little while.

'I want whatever time I have with him,' Cat said.

'I'll be there with you,' Gemma said. 'Mike might—'

'I'm not discussing it further with Mike,' Cat said. 'I'll tell him what I've decided and it's up to him what he does, but as a couple we're finished.'

'You don't have to make any rash decisions about your relationship. It's a lot for any couple to take in...'

'We're not a couple any more,' Cat said. 'I told him that this morning—as soon as things started to go wrong with the pregnancy, even before things went wrong, I felt as if I didn't have a voice. Well, I do and I'm having my baby.'

* * *

It was a long month, a difficult month but a very precious one.

Cat cancelled the wedding while knowing soon she would be arranging a funeral but she pushed that thought aside as best she could.

Her parents were little help. Her mother agreed with Mike; her father just disappeared into his study if ever Cat came round. But she had Greg, her brother, who cleared out all her things from Mike's house.

He didn't hit him, much to Cat's relief.

Almost, though!

And, of course, she had Gemma.

At the end of July and at twenty-five weeks gestation Cat went into spontaneous labour and Gemma delivered her a little son. Thomas Gregory Hayes. Thomas because she loved the name. Gregory, after her brother. Hayes because it was her surname.

Cat would treasure every minute of the two precious days and one night that Thomas lived.

Most of them.

His severe cleft palate meant she couldn't feed him, though she ached to. She would never get out of her mind the image of her mother's grimace when she'd seen her grandson and his deformities—Cat had asked her to leave.

For two days she had closed the door to her room on the maternity ward and had let only love enter.

Her brother, Gemma and her new boyfriend, Nigel, a couple of other lifelong friends, along with the medical staff helped her care for him—and all played their part.

When Cat had no choice but to sleep, Greg, Gemma

or Nigel nursed him and Thomas wasn't once, apart from having his nappy changed, put down.

His whole life Thomas knew only love.

After the funeral, when her parents and some other family members had tried to tell her that maybe Thomas's passing was a blessing, it was Gemma who held Cat's hand as she bit back a caustic response.

Instead of doing as suggested and putting it all behind her and attempting a new normal, Cat took all her maternity leave and hid for a while to grieve. But as her return-to-work date approached she felt less and less inclined to go back, especially as Mike still worked there.

She applied for a position in the accident and emergency department at the London Royal, where her baby had been born and where Gemma worked.

Four months to the day that she'd lost her son Cat stepped back out into the world… Only, she wasn't the same.

Instead, she was a far tougher version of her old self.

CHAPTER ONE

Seven years later

'YOU'RE FAR TOO cynical about men, Cat.'

'I don't think that I am,' Cat answered, 'though admittedly I'd love to be proven wrong. But, no, I'm taking a full year off men.'

Cat was busy packing. Just out of the shower she was wearing a dressing gown and her long, curly black hair was wrapped in a towel. As she pulled clothes out of her wardrobe she chatted to her close friend Gemma, who was lying on Cat's bed and answering emails on her phone.

They were two very busy women but they usually managed to catch up a couple of times a week, whether at the hospital canteen, a coffee shop or wine bar, or just a quick drop-in at the other's home.

This evening Cat was heading to Barcelona for an international emergency medicine conference, where she was going to be giving a talk the following morning. She had got off early from her shift at the hospital to pack and Gemma had popped around to finalise a few details for the following weekend. Gemma and

Nigel's twin boys, Rory and Marcus, were being christened and Cat was to be godmother to Rory.

They were used to catching up on the run. Any plans they made were all too often cancelled at the last minute thanks to Cat's position as an accident and emergency consultant and Gemma juggling being a mother to two eighteen-month-old boys as well as a full-time obstetrician.

Their lives were similar in many ways and very different in others.

'So you and Rick have definitely broken up?' Gemma checked that Cat's latest relationship was really over.

'He's been gone a month, so I'd say so!'

'You're not even going to think about it?'

'Why would I consider moving to Yorkshire when I'm happy here?'

'Because that's what couples do.'

'Oh, so if Nigel suddenly decided that he wanted to move to…' Cat thought for a moment and then remembered that Nigel was taking French lessons. 'If he wanted to move to France, you're telling me that you'd go?'

'Not without consideration,' Gemma said. 'Given that I'm the breadwinner there would have to be a good reason, but if Nigel really wanted to, then, of course, I'd give it some thought. Relationships are about compromise.'

'And it's always the woman who has to be the one to compromise,' Cat said, but Gemma shook her head.

'I don't agree.'

'You've never played the dating game in your thirties.'

'Yes, I have—Nigel and I only married last year.'

'Ah, but the two of you had been going out for ever before then. It's different at our age, Gemma. Men might say that they don't mind independent working women and, of course, they don't—just as long as you're home before them and have the dinner on.'

'Rubbish!' Gemma responded from her happily married vantage point. 'Look at Nigel—I work, he gave up teaching and stays home and looks after the children, and the house and me...'

'Yes.' Cat smiled. 'Well, you and Nigel are a very rare exception to my well-proven theory.'

But Gemma suddenly had other things on her mind when she saw what Cat was about to add to her case. 'Please don't take them,' Gemma said, referring to Cat's running shoes. 'They're ugly.'

'They're practical,' Cat said. 'And they are also very comfortable. I'm hoping to squeeze in a little bit of sightseeing on Sunday afternoon once the conference wraps up. There's a modern art museum, hopefully I'll get some inspiration for this room...'

She looked around at the disgusting beige walls and beige carpet and beige curtains and wished she knew what she wanted to do with the room.

Gemma got off the bed and went to Cat's wardrobe and took out some espadrilles.

'Take these instead.'

'For walking?'

'Yes, Cat, for walking, not striding...' She peered into her friend's luggage. 'Talk about shades of grey—that's the saddest case I've ever seen. You're going to Spain!'

'I'm going to Spain for two nights to catch the end of a conference. I'm not going on a holiday. I shan't even see the beach,' Cat pointed out. 'I wish that I *was* flying off for a holiday,' she said, and then sat on the bed. 'I hate July so much.'

'I know you do.'

It had been seven years since Thomas had died.

She didn't lug her grief around all the time but on days like today it hurt. Gemma smiled as her friend went into her bedside drawer and took out his photo. Cat kept it there; it was close enough that she could look at it any time and removed enough not to move her to tears. The drawer also meant she didn't have to explain the most vital piece of her past to any lovers until she was ready to.

She simply found it too painful.

'Rick asked how likely I was to have another one like him,' Cat admitted. It was what had really caused the end of her latest relationship. 'I told him about Thomas and then I showed him his photo…'

'He's not a doctor, Cat,' Gemma said. 'It's a normal question to ask. It's one you've asked.'

'I know that. It was more the way…' She was so hypersensitive to people's reactions when they saw her son but she smiled when Gemma spoke on.

'I loved how he smiled if you touched his little feet,' Gemma said, and her words confirmed to Cat that she was very blessed to have such a wonderful friend. 'He's so beautiful.'

He was.

Not to others perhaps but they had both seen his lovely eyes and felt his little fingers curve around theirs and they had felt his soft skin and heard his little cries.

And this was the hard part.

It was late July and she'd be away on *those* days.

The day of Thomas's birth and also the day that he had died.

'Do I take his photo with me?' Cat asked, and Gemma thought for a moment.

'I don't think you need his photo to remember him,' she said.

'But I feel guilty leaving him in the drawer.'

'Leave him with me, then,' Gemma said. 'I'll have a long gaze.'

Yes, she had the very best friend in the world, Cat thought as she handed over her most precious possession, and because she was going to start crying Cat changed the subject. 'Hey, did you have any luck tracking down that dress for the christening?'

'Nope.'

Gemma shook her head as she put the photo in her bag. 'I knew that I should have just bought it when I saw it. It was perfect.'

'It was very nice, but…' Cat didn't continue. A white broderie anglaise halter-neck with a flowing skirt was a bit over the top for Cat's tastes but, then, that was Gemma.

And this was her.

She pulled on some white linen pants and a coloured top *and* added the espadrilles.

'Am I girlie enough for you now?'

'You look great.' Gemma laughed. 'It's once you get there that worries me. With those clothes you'll just blend in with all the others…'

'Which is exactly my intention,' Cat said. 'I have to go soon.'

'But your flight's not till nine.'

'I know but I've booked in to get my hair blow-dried on the way.'

Her long black curls would be straightened, just as

they were twice a week. Cat always washed it herself before she went to the hairdresser's, though.

It saved time.

They headed downstairs, chatting as Cat did a few last-minute things. 'You're speaking in the morning?' Gemma checked.

'At nine.' Cat nodded. 'I'd have loved to have flown last night but I couldn't get away. Hamish isn't back till tomorrow and Andrew is covering me this weekend. Same old. It would have been nice to stay on for a bit and spend a few days in Barcelona…'

'Are you ever going to take some time off?'

'I'm off in October for three weeks.' Cat smiled. 'My exams will be done and I'm going to celebrate by decorating my bedroom. I can't wait to turn it into something that doesn't make me want to sleep downstairs on the sofa.'

'You've done an amazing job with the house.'

Last year, after a year of looking, Cat had bought a small two-bedroom home in a leafy London suburb. It was a twenty-minute drive to work at night, which meant, if Cat was on call, that she had to stay at the hospital. Yes, perhaps she could have bought somewhere just a little bit closer but the drive did mean that when she left the hospital, she really left the building.

Here, she could pull on tatty shorts and a T-shirt and get on with her second love—knocking down walls, plastering and painting. The house had been a real renovator's delight and Cat had delighted in renovating it.

The ghastly purple carpet had been ripped up to expose floorboards that, once sanded and oiled, brought a warmth to the house. A false wall in the lounge had been removed to reveal a fireplace and the once-purple-themed bathroom was now tiled white with dark wood fittings and had a gorgeous claw-foot bath.

'Will you sell it once you've decorated the bedroom?'

'I really don't know,' Cat admitted, tipping milk down the sink. 'Initially that was the plan, but now I love the place and want to simply enjoy it, but...'

'But?'

'I've really enjoyed doing it up bit by bit. I'm going to miss that.'

'After your bedroom you've still got the garden to make over.'

'Oh, no!' Cat shook her head. 'I'll get someone in to do that.'

As they headed out, Cat locked up and Gemma looked at the small front garden.

'It's the size of a stamp,' Gemma pointed out. There was just a rickety path and two neglected flower beds, and the back garden, Gemma knew, was a small strip of grass and an old wooden shed. 'You could have it sorted in a few days...'

'Nope!' Cat smiled. 'I have black thumbs.'

They said goodbye on the street.

'We'll catch up properly soon,' Cat promised. Both women knew that they wouldn't get much of a chance to gossip at the christening. 'I'll come over to yours after the conference. I haven't seen the twins for ages. I'll bring them a stuffed donkey each back from Spain.'

'Please, don't!' Gemma winced and glanced at her phone to check the time. 'Ooh, I might make it home in time to give them their bath before bed. Nigel's cooking a romantic dinner for the two of us tonight...'

'Lovely.'

'Enjoy Spain,' Gemma called. 'You might find your-self some sexy Spanish flamenco dancer or matador...'

'At an emergency medicine conference?' Cat laughed. 'I don't think there's much chance of that.'

'Well, a gorgeous waiter, with come-to-bed eyes and—'

'Oh, please!'

'Why not?' Gemma winked. 'If you can't manage a love life, then pencil a few flings into that overcrowded diary of yours.'

'There's another conference in Spain the following week that *you* might want to consider attending,' Cat said in a dry voice. 'Sexual health. You, as an obstetrician, better than anyone must know the perils of casual sex.'

'Of course I do, but sex *is* healthy.' Gemma grinned and then she looked at Cat. She wanted to pick up an imaginary sledgehammer of her own and knock down the wall that had gone up around her friend since her baby's death.

'Do you know what's brilliant about a one-night stand, Cat?'

'Gemma...' Cat shook her head. She really didn't have time to stand and chat but her friend persisted.

Gemma loved to talk about sex! 'He doesn't have to be perfect, you don't have to worry how you might slot into each other's lives and whether he leaves the toilet seat up or is going to support you in your career and all that stuff, because you're not looking for a potential Mr Right. He can be Mr Wrong, Mr Bad, Mr Whatever-It-Is-You-Fancy. God, but I miss one-night stands.'

'Does Nigel know your theory?'

'Of course he doesn't.' Gemma grinned. 'Nigel still thinks he was my second...' They both laughed for a moment but then Gemma stood firm. 'It's time for you to have some fun, Cat. Doctor's orders—you're to buy some condoms at the airport.'

Cat laughed and waved and got into her car and headed for the hairdresser's.

She adored Gemma.

And Nigel.

But…

What she hadn't said to her very good friend was that, as much as it might work for Gemma, she really didn't want a Nigel of her own. She didn't want someone asking what was for dinner every night, but nor did she want to be the one coming in after work and doing the 'Hi, honey, I'm home' thing.

Still, there wasn't time to dwell on it all.

She parked her car in her usual spot behind the church and grabbed her bag and walked quickly to the hairdresser's. She pushed on the door but it didn't open and she frowned and then she saw the 'Closed' sign.

'Don't do this to me, Glynn…'

He never forgot her appointments and Cat had been very specific about the time for today when she had seen him on Monday. Glynn knew that she had a plane to catch and that she would be pushed for time.

'Breathe,' Cat mumbled as she accepted that no amount of rattling the door was going to make Glynn suddenly appear.

It's a hair appointment, that's all, she told herself. There would be a hairdresser at the hotel. Only, her presentation was at nine in the morning and she'd wanted to have a leisurely breakfast in her room and calm herself down before that.

And it was Thomas's birthday tomorrow.

She was not going to cry over a missed hair appointment.

Cat wasn't crying over that as she drove to the airport. Instead, she was wishing the boot was full of presents and wrapping paper and that she was dashing to pick up a birthday cake...

Why was it still so hard?

So, as she could not get her thick curly hair smoothed into long, glossy and straight, she bought some hair serum at the airport, then checked in her luggage and headed through with ages to spare.

She went to the loos and sorted her hair as best she could, deciding she would straighten it tonight and again in the morning, but for now she tied it back and headed out.

She took a seat and read through her talk on her tablet. It was about palliative care and its place in the emergency department and, really, she knew it back to front and inside out. She had done hours of research and all her meticulous notes and patient studies now came down to one talk.

And then what?

Exams.

And then?

Cat blew out a breath.

Her career was a little like her house renovation.

The day she'd moved in Cat had stared at the purple carpet and the purple tiles that would take for ever to get off. It had seemed unlikely, near impossible, that she would ever get there and yet here she was, just a bedroom and a garden away from completion.

She had, through high school, always wanted to be a surgeon yet as a medical student she had stepped into the emergency department and had been quickly ushered into Resus to observe the treatment of a patient who had just come in.

A cyclist had lain there unconscious with a massive head injury. Cat had watched in silent awe as the staff had brought his dire condition under control. His heart, which hadn't been beating, had been restarted. His airway had been secured and the seizures that had then started to rack his body had been halted with drugs.

She had been sure at first that he would die and yet he had made it to Theatre and then on to Intensive Care.

She had followed him up and found out a week later that he had been transferred to a ward. She had gone in to see him, expecting what, she hadn't known. Certainly not a young man sitting up in bed, laughing and talking with his girlfriend, who was sitting by his side.

He should be dead, Cat had thought, though, of course, she didn't say that. Instead, she'd chatted to him for a few moments, unable to truly comprehend that here he was, not just alive but laughing and living.

Emergency medicine had become her passion right there and then. Yes, at twenty years old she had known she was a long way off being as skilled as the staff who had attended the cyclist that day.

Slowly she had got there, though.

And now here she was, coming to the top of her game.

So why the restlessness?

Cat glanced up at the board and rolled her eyes when she saw that her flight was delayed, and decided to wander around the shops.

Oh, there was Gemma's dress!

She was sure that it was, though looking at the price tag, not quite sure enough to buy it without checking, so she took a photo and fired a quick text to her friend.

Is this it?

It was, and Gemma promised to love her for ever and forgive any stuffed donkeys she might bring home for the twins if Cat would buy it for her.

She bought some duty-free perfume too, as well as her favourite lip gloss and…no—no condoms.

Finally the plane was boarding and Cat, along with her purchases, was on her way.

She didn't read through her talk again. She dozed most of the way, trying to drown out the sound of over-excited children and their parents. As they disembarked she almost forgot the dress but luckily she grabbed it at the last minute.

Very luckily, as it turned out.

Having spent hours watching an empty baggage carousel, seeing the shutters go down on all the airport shops and filling in numerous forms, she was doing her level best to hold it together as she climbed out of the taxi and walked into the hotel. It was close to midnight.

Her luggage was lost, her hair was a joke.

And tomorrow, at nine, she had to deliver the most important presentation of her life.

CHAPTER TWO

CAT WOKE BEFORE her breakfast was delivered and lay there.

She remembered a day seven years ago and wished, how she wished, that there was a seven-year-old waiting to open his birthday presents and to sing 'Happy Birthday' to.

It was a hard picture to paint and each year it got harder.

Was Mike in this happy family picture and did Thomas have brothers and sisters now?

No, she didn't miss Mike and the perfect world they had been building. She missed, on Thomas's behalf, all that he had been denied.

She couldn't afford to cry, especially given the fact she had no make-up with her and so she headed to the bathroom to set to work with the little she had.

With her heavy-duty hair straighteners neatly packed in her lost luggage, she was very grateful for the hair serum she had bought and applied an awful lot in an attempt to tame her long, wild curly hair.

When her breakfast was delivered she walked out onto the balcony and tried to calm herself with the spectacular view of the Mediterranean. It was just after seven but already the air was warm. The coffee was hot and strong and Cat tried to focus on her speech. *It will be fine,* she told herself, refusing to fall apart because she didn't have the perfect, *perfect* pale grey suit and the pale ballet pumps in the softest buttery leather to wear.

They were here to hear her words, Cat reminded herself.

Yet she couldn't quite convince herself that it didn't matter what she wore or how she looked.

Neutral.

That was how she always tried to appear.

There was nothing neutral about her today, she thought as she slipped on Gemma's dress.

Her rather ample bust was accentuated by the lace, the halter-neck showed far too much of her brown back—the tan was from painting the window frames on her last lot of days off, rather than lying on the beach. Her hair she tied back with the little white band that came with the shower cap in the bathroom and then she covered it with a thick strand of black hair.

A squirt of duty-free perfume, a slick of lip gloss and she would simply have to do.

Yet, she thought, having tied up her espadrilles, as she stood and looked in the mirror, while never in a million years would she have chosen this outfit for anything related to work, she liked how it looked. She wouldn't even have chosen it for anything out of work either. Generally she was in shorts or jeans when sorting out the renovations. Yes, she liked how she looked today. It reminded her of how she had looked before she'd had…

Cat halted herself right there.

She simply could not afford the luxury of breaking down.

Tonight, Cat told herself. Tonight she would order room service and a bottle of wine and reminisce.

Today she had to get on.

She had one last flick through her notes and then she headed out to register for the conference and also to check that everything was in place for her talk.

She was just putting her swipe card in her bag when the elevator doors opened and she looked up to an empty lift, bar one occupant.

Bar One was tall and unshaven with grey eyes and his dark hair was a touch too long yet he looked effortlessly smart in dark pants and a white shirt. All this she noted as she stood there and briefly wondered if she should simply let this lift go.

For some bizarre reason that seemed far easier than stepping in.

'Buenos días,' Bar One said, and then frowned at her indecision as to whether or not to enter.

'Buenos días,' Cat replied, gave him a brisk smile and stepped in. The floor number for the function rooms had already been pressed and as she glanced to the side and down, anywhere other than his eyes, she noted he too was an owner of the softest buttery leather shoes.

His luggage clearly hadn't been lost.

And neither was he wearing socks.

Three, Cat thought as his cologne met her nostrils and she found herself doing a very quick audit as to the number of garments that would remain on his lovely body once he'd kicked off those shoes.

Talk about thinking like a man!

She blamed Gemma, of course. It was her fault for

putting such ideas in her head, Cat decided as the lift opened at the next floor and unfortunately no one got in.

He said something else in Spanish and Cat shook her head. 'Actually, *buenos días* is as far as my Spanish goes.'

'Oh,' he said. 'I thought you were a local.'

His accent was English and he had just delivered a compliment indeed, because the locals, Cat had worked out during her prolonged time at the airport last night, were a pretty stunning lot.

'Nope.' She shook her head.

The lift doors opened and he wished her a good day as he went to step out.

'And you,' she offered.

'Sadly not,' he replied, and nodded to the gathering crowd outside the elevators. 'I'm working.'

'So am I,' she said, and he stood there a little taken aback as he let her out first.

Oh!

Dominic had thought she was on her way to some… Well, he'd had no idea really where she might have been on her way to but talk about a sight for sore eyes.

She had a very, very nice back, he decided as he followed her over to the registration desk, where there was a small line-up.

A very tense back, he noted as she reached into her bag and pulled out her phone.

'I'm Dominic…'

Cat had just had a text from the airline to say her luggage had been found. At Gatwick! It *should* be with her later this afternoon and could she confirm that she was still at the same hotel. She barely turned around as she fired back a text and told him her name. 'Cat.'

'Short for?'

She really didn't have time for small talk and she knew, just knew, because her back was scalding from his eyes, that it was more than small talk he was offering. 'I'm actually a bit busy at the moment...'

'Well, that's some name—no wonder you have to shorten it.'

Her fingers hesitated over the text she was typing and she gave a small, presumably unseen smile.

Dominic, even if he couldn't see her mouth, knew from behind that she'd smiled.

He watched as that rigid spinal column very briefly relaxed a notch and those tense shoulders dropped a fraction.

Still, he left things there. He certainly wasn't going to pursue a conversation that had been so swiftly shut down.

Instead, he looked at the brochure with only mild interest. He loathed this type of thing. He'd only put his hand up because he'd needed the update hours and because his parents and sister lived nearby—it would be a good chance to catch up. As well as that, he was seriously considering moving here.

He kept himself up to date and found these presentations pointless, or rather bullet-pointed—most speakers had everything on slides and it was rather like being read a bedtime story out loud. At thirty-two years of age, he would rather read for himself.

'Dominic!'

He glanced over at the sound of his name and gave a smile when he saw that it was someone he had studied with in London.

'How are you, Hugh?'

Cat stood there, trying not to notice the delicious depth to his voice. Not that he spoke much; it was his friend who did most of the talking.

She registered and was told that one of the organisers would be with her shortly to take her to where her talk was being held.

'This way, Dr Hayes...'

Dominic stopped in mid-sentence as Cat was led away. She must be speaking, he realised, and, quite shamelessly, he glanced through the list of speakers and found out her name for himself.

Catriona Hayes.

And then he saw the topic of her talk.

Palliative Care and its Place in the Emergency Department.

Absolutely *not* what he needed.

So, instead of hearing her speak, he took himself off to listen to a disaster management panel but his mind wasn't really there. Half an hour later he slipped out unnoticed and slipped into where she was talking.

She noticed him come in.

There was a tiny pause in her talk as she glanced at the opening door and saw *him* enter.

He didn't take a seat but leant against the back wall with arms folded. There was a small falter in her flawless talk as he took his place but then she continued where she'd left off.

'Of course, it's great for the patient when they receive a terminal diagnosis to take that break, that trek, that overseas trip. It can just be a touch inconvenient for us when they present, minus notes, diagnosis, information and family. And so, because that's what we do, we leap in and do our best to save them.' She looked out at the room. 'Of course, it's not so great for the patient either when they come around to our smiling faces... It's hard on the staff when a four-year-old presents on Christmas Eve. It's our instinct to do all that we can. There isn't always time to speak at length with the family when they come rushing in with their child but listen we must...'

It wasn't like a bedtime story with everything spelt out. Yes, there were bullet points, but they were only brief outlines and, for Dominic, a lot of her words felt like bullets as she filled in the gaps.

Brusque was her delivery as she covered things such as legalities, next of kin, patient rights. For good measure, staff, relative and patient guilt was thrown in too.

He listened, he felt, yet his face never moved a muscle.

As she finished, he left the room and went off to lunch but, even if it smelt fantastic, food didn't appeal and instead he took some water and went out onto a large balcony.

Unlike others who had been at her talk Dominic didn't go up and congratulate her. Neither did he tell her that her talk had touched a nerve.

He could have walked over and said how his wife had got up in the night and wandered off. He could have said how angry she had been to wake up two days later in ICU and that he could still see the reproach in her eyes, as if Dominic had somehow failed her because she'd lived.

No, he didn't need or want *that* look from Cat and he was tired, so tired of women who gave out sympathy and understanding.

He'd prefer something lighter.

Or darker, perhaps! Hopefully, Dominic thought, heading back in, so too would she.

CHAPTER THREE

IT WOULD BE an absolute lie to say the attraction hadn't been as instant as it was mutual.

All through the lunch break there was a knot high in Cat's stomach and tension in her muscles and she knew that she was bracing herself for him to come over.

Except he didn't.

Ouch!

She wasn't sure if she even wanted him to.

There was an arrogance to him, not that she couldn't handle arrogant men; she'd dealt with more than her share of them.

No, it was something else about Dominic that had her seriously rattled—the presumption of sex.

From the briefest conversation she had gleaned that much. From the roam of his eyes on the bare skin of her back, from the sullen, one-sided conversation with his friend that had told her his mind was on her.

From the corner of her eye she watched as he came in from the balcony and then went over and chatted to a group.

She was incredibly aware of his presence and it had been a long time since she had felt anything close to that.

Not that it mattered.

She was being ignored.

Funny, but she knew that it was deliberate and what was stranger still it made her smile. 'Excellent talk...' A middle-aged blond man came over and introduced himself. 'Gordon.' He smiled.

'Cat.'

It was a very long thirty minutes.

Gordon simply didn't let up and Cat couldn't really make her excuses and leave because he was talking about his wife who had died and the total hash that had been made in the emergency department.

It was a busman's holiday for Cat as she lined up for the lovely buffet lunch and Gordon followed her with his plate.

'Two hours, we waited, Cat,' he said, and she glanced up and met those gorgeous grey eyes and saw that Dominic was now unashamedly watching her.

Rescue me, her green ones said, but he looked away.

'And then...' Gordon continued to tell her about his wife's IV coming out and the drugs that didn't go in. Yes, it was a sad story, but it was a story she dealt with every day and it was her lunch break.

'Paella, please.' Cat held out her plate to the waiter but he shook his head.

'We're waiting for some more...'

Cat chose some odd noodle salad, just to get away, but Gordon chose the same and he was off again. He sat next to her at a high table and droned on and on.

She met Dominic's eyes again and this time he smiled.

You missed your chance, his eyes said.

I've changed my mind, was her silent plea.

Well, you're too late!

He yawned and pulled out his pamphlet and with a very small smirk walked off.

What a bastard.

Cat laughed and then turned to Gordon's confused expression.

'I said, then she died…'

'Sorry, I thought you said then she…' Cat let out a breath. 'What a terrible time you had.'

She just didn't need to hear about it today of all days.

She didn't see Dominic again all afternoon, not that it mattered by then. At 5:00 p.m. when she got back to her room to find that her luggage still hadn't arrived, it wasn't the Spanish-speaking English doctor who was on her mind.

It was Thomas.

She didn't want to go down for dinner in an hour and be sociable.

Room service seemed a far better idea.

A huge plate of paella.

A bottle of wine.

She wished she'd brought his photo.

But there had been too many sad birthdays and, suddenly realising that she had a very small window if she didn't want to spend tomorrow dressed in Gemma's dress or linen pants that were more suitable for travel, she headed out.

She found herself in a large department store, explaining to an orange woman that, apart from a lipstick, she had no make-up with her.

'My luggage was lost,' she said.

The woman was so horrified on her behalf that Cat actually smiled. 'It's fine…'

It was.

So much so that instead of buying loads of make-up and then heading upstairs to the *ropa de señora* section to purchase a chic Spanish outfit Cat wandered out and found herself drawn to a busy market. There were gorgeous dresses blowing in the late-afternoon breeze and they were nothing like what she usually wore.

If she walked into work dressed as she was today, it would draw comment. Here, apart from a couple of vaguely familiar faces from conferences of long ago, no one knew her.

It was incredibly freeing—she could be whoever she chose to be.

Cat took her time with her purchases. She chose a loose long dress in lilac and shorts that were very short, along with a top and a stringy-looking bikini. And, she decided, instead of the museum on Sunday afternoon she was going to the beach.

She liked Barcelona.

Far more than she had expected to.

It was cosmopolitan, busy yet friendly, colourful and hot.

Walking back into the hotel, she was about to take her purchases up and get changed and, instead of hiding in her room, perhaps head out for dinner by herself when she saw him.

Dominic.

'I was wondering where you were,' he said by way of greeting, and Cat liked it that he was direct.

'I went shopping…' She was about to explain that her luggage was lost but then decided she didn't have to explain anything.

'Cat!' a voice boomed, and she turned and saw that

Gordon was bearing down on her. 'There's a group of us heading to the hotel restaurant. Why don't you join us?'

'Oh, I'd love to but I can't,' Cat said. 'I'm expecting a call. A conference call. I—'

'Maybe after?' Gordon checked.

'I'll try.'

Gordon smiled over to Dominic. 'Do you have plans or would you like to join us?'

Dominic dealt with things far more effortlessly than Cat. 'I've already got plans, but thank you for asking.'

As the group walked off they were left standing.

'Liar,' Dominic said. 'You don't have a conference call you have to get to.'

'Was it obvious?' she groaned.

'To me it was.' Dominic nodded. 'Liars always have a need to elaborate. You'd know that, working in Emergency.'

'I know,' she said. 'So would Gordon.'

'Is he a friend?'

Cat shook her head.

'A colleague?'

'No.'

'So why not just say no if it's something that you don't want to do?'

'I know that I should. I just feel bad...'

'Well, don't—he's far too busy banging on about his late wife to notice what others are feeling.'

She felt her nostrils tighten. 'That was mean.'

'No,' Dominic refuted. 'He tried to run the whole sorry story by me yesterday. What's mean is buttonholing a relative stranger and completely ruining their lunch.'

He shrugged.

He was dismissive.

She didn't like that and she was about to head off when he halted her in her tracks.

'Do you want dinner away from the hotel?'

'I've got a conference call to make,' she said, and gave him a tight smile.

'Sure?' he said.

Usually, yes.

She didn't like his dismissal of Gordon but, apart from that, he was, well, deliciously overwhelming.

Gemma's words were ringing in her ears. He didn't have to be perfect, he didn't have to be anything other than…

God, but she fancied him.

She could have left it there, just walked off and it would have been over. There were no games, no pretence, just his question, which she now answered truthfully. 'Dinner away from the hotel sounds great,' she said. 'I'll just…' She held up her bags and was about to suggest that she take them up and meet him back here in…half an hour, or however long it took to get showered and dressed.

But by then she'd have changed her mind, she knew.

Half an hour from now she'd be calling Reception to pass on a message to him.

Or she could just go with how she felt now.

'I'll just ask Reception if they can take my bags up.'

The streets were noisy and he navigated them easily and took her to a place that Cat would never have found had she explored on her own—a few streets along from the strip the hotel was on. They walked down a stone stairwell and to an *asado* restaurant that was noisy and smoky, even with the open area out the back.

'So, are you pleased your talk is over?' he asked when they were tucked away at a table.

'Very,' Cat said. 'I can relax now.'

And relax she did, admitting she had no clue about Spanish wine and letting him choose.

'Are you staying till Monday?' he asked, and she shook her head.

'No, I fly out tomorrow evening—I'm back at work on Monday. I wish...'

'Wish what?'

'Well, I was really only thinking of my talk when I booked the flights. I wasn't actually expecting to like Barcelona so much. I should have tagged on a couple of days' annual leave and done a bit of exploring.'

'You always could.'

It sounded very tempting but it was a little too late for that now. 'We're pretty short on staff at the moment. My colleague Andrew is going on leave and Hamish, he's the other consultant...' She rolled her eyes. 'I'm sure you know how it is.'

'Remind me,' he said.

'Remind you?' she checked. 'Where do you work?'

'Scotland.'

She waited for him to elaborate, which he did but it was vague rather than specific. 'I work a little bit here and a longer bit there,' Dominic said, and Cat then felt the scrutiny of his gaze and the message behind his words as he spoke on. 'I don't like to be tied to one place.' And then he elaborated properly. 'Or one person.'

Well, that certainly told her.

In part, Cat was tempted to simply get up and leave. It wasn't a meal, they both knew that. This wasn't two like-minded colleagues sharing a dinner after a busy day at a conference.

This was exactly what the dear Dr Gemma had ordered.

Cat was old enough to know it.

Their knees were nudging and suddenly her lips felt too big for her face without the resting place of his mouth.

She felt his eyes glance down as she reached for her drink and from the sudden weight in her breasts she knew where his glance had been. Only, it wasn't sleazy. Or, if it was, it came from both of them because she'd been doing the same to his bum a little earlier as he'd walked down the stairs.

No, this wasn't just dinner.

'Do you have a problem with that?' he said, and she blinked as she tried to remember the conversation. Oh, yes, the not-tied-to-one-person thing, he was asking if she had a problem with that.

Did she?

Yes, a part of her did.

Very much so.

A part of her wanted to tell him where he could shove his arrogant, presumptuous offer and head back to her hotel room and bury herself in the grief of today.

Yet the other part of Cat thrummed in suspense. Could she simply let loose and enjoy a night of passion with a very beautiful man with the cast-iron guarantee of no future?

It was refreshingly tempting.

He was seriously beautiful. Far more so than she was used to.

He was also rather more brusque and arrogant than she would choose, just rather too alpha for her.

She was tired, so tired of the inevitable let-down in relationships, the starting gun of hope, the numerous false starts and then the sprint that turned into an exhausting jog, and then standing bent, hands on thighs, and admitting defeat, because the two of you were just not going to make it to the finish line.

She was surprised at the ease of her decision.

'No.' Cat finally smiled. 'I have no problem with that.'

'Good.'

Housekeeping sorted, she tried to focus on the menu but, at thirty-four, she felt she'd just passed her driving test and been given the keys but was far from skilled enough to drive.

'Están listos para ordenar?'

The waiter came over and presumably asked if they were ready to order.

'I'll have paella.' She handed back the menu.

'The chicken here,' Dominic said, 'is the best you'll ever taste…'

Her eyes narrowed. Usually she'd say that she'd like the paella, thank you for interfering. She certainly didn't need a man choosing her food and yet as she glanced around, sure enough, the locals were eating the chicken.

Oh, he was so far from her usual fare but, no, he didn't need to be perfect tonight.

'When in Spain…' She shrugged.

She had the chicken and, as he had promised, it was amazing.

'Lemony, herby and so fat and juicy,' Cat commented on her second mouthful.

'And salty,' Dominic said. 'We'll be up all night, guzzling water…'

He was presumptuous.

She knew, though, that he was right.

The rest of the world, the past, the future, was like rain as they huddled, as if under some imaginary umbrella, and enjoyed now—the spectacular food, the music that filled the restaurant.

They barely talked about work. She said something about being the only female consultant and how they gave every gynae patient to her. He mentioned how he'd lived in London till a couple of years ago, just half an hour or so away from her.

But then work got left behind and she found out how he loved the architecture in Edinburgh but was fast falling in love with Spain.

And she told him about her passion for renovation, and her obsession with wallpaper, how she could spend hours leafing through sample books but, even then, you could never quite know how it would look once up.

Usually she never got to that part as eyes had long since glazed over with boredom.

His glazed with lust.

'Do you put it up yourself?' Dominic asked.

'I do.' She smiled.

'I feel emasculated.'

'Oh, I doubt you could ever be that.'

It was Dominic who then smiled.

Was it wrong? she wondered as they danced.

Was it wrong to be dancing and happy on his birthday?

Tonight it felt right.

A sexy flamenco dancer was kicking his heels and strumming away and then, when he slowed things down,

Cat felt her cheeks blaze with fire for sins not yet committed as Dominic pulled her into him.

His fingers ran lightly down her bare back and it felt utterly blissful.

'Fourteen hours later than I'd have preferred,' Dominic said into her ear, because that was how long it had been since he'd first itched for the feel of that sexy spine beneath his fingers.

'Well, I'm glad for your sake that you waited,' she said, imagining her reaction had he been so bold.

His touch didn't feel bold now; it felt right.

When the music ended they made it back to their table and when the bill came Cat did her usual and put her card down.

'We can go halves,' she said as he picked up the card to hand it back to her.

'Don't do that, Cat.'

'What?'

'Ruin a perfectly good night.'

If she were setting the ground rules for the future, she'd have insisted on paying her way.

Instead, they were setting the ground rules for tonight and she shivered in the warm night air as they headed for the hotel.

They walked back along the beach. It was after eleven but not really dark thanks to a near full moon and, despite the hour, the beach was far from deserted.

'There are some gorgeous beaches not far from here,' he said. 'Are you still determined to head back without seeing the place?'

'I am, though I wish I'd known just how much I'd like it,' she admitted. 'I'm going to come again but next time for a holiday. You're here a lot, then?'

'Quite a bit,' Dominic said. 'I have family here.'

'Oh.'

She ached to know more about him but Reticent was possibly his middle name because, apart from long conversations about everything and nothing, he gave away little.

The only thing she was sure of was their attraction.

'Which is why,' he continued, 'when I saw the conference was being held this year in Barcelona I decided to combine both. I'm very glad now that I did.' He turned her around and she looked into his dark eyes and his face. He was unreadable. 'I wish you had got here on Thursday.'

'Why?' she asked, her brain a bit sluggish with his mouth so close. She was far too used to focusing on work and she assumed that she must have missed some spectacular talk, or some cutting-edge revelation. The answer was far more basic than that.

'We could have had three nights instead of one.'

Still, he didn't kiss her, though she ached, *ached* for him to do so, but he just smiled in the dark like a beautiful devil and then they walked on.

Back at the hotel Cat was breathless, though not from walking, as they stepped into the foyer. They went through Reception and there was a lot of noise coming from the bar from their fellow attendees.

'Did you want to go to the bar?' Dominic offered.

'Yes.'

'Again,' he said, 'she lies.'

Cat smiled. 'She does.'

They headed for the elevators.

No, he didn't ask her for her floor.

He pressed his.

They stood backs against opposite walls facing each other as the lift groaned its way up, letting people in, letting people out.

And his eyes never left her face.

With three floors remaining they were finally alone and still he did not beckon.

Stay, Cat told herself, though she felt like a Labrador waiting for Christmas dinner.

Ping!

She walked slowly only because he did.

And his very steady hand swiped the card and opened the door to his room.

Would he offer her a drink? Cat wondered as she looked around.

The room was the same as hers, except it smelt of his cologne and there was a suitcase on the floor.

And then there was no time for further observation because he turned her to him and finally there was the bliss of his mouth. It was the roughest ever kiss and tasted divine. His tongue, his lips, his hands, the hunger in him was so consuming that there was no room for thought. She hadn't been kissed like this since—well, since for ever. His tongue was wicked, his hands pressing into her head and his body just primed and ready, because she could feel him.

She ached to feel him, so much so that the three garments of clothing she'd assumed he was wearing—was it only this morning?—were being unbuttoned and unzipped by Cat as his mouth never left her face.

He halted her briefly, long enough to retrieve his wallet, because of course he carried condoms, and she watched as he deftly put one on and so thick and hard was he that she played with him for a moment as he removed her dress.

She heard a brief tear and knew she would be up all week sewing Gemma's dress as it was now a white puddle on the floor.

She'd think about that later. Right now she was concentrating on him as his tongue met with her ear and she just about came in midair at the thought of him inside her.

Her bra was gone. She knew that because his mouth was on her breast as his hands slid her panties down.

And then she felt herself being lifted.

Not just onto him, but lifted out herself.

Out of grief, out of control, out of everything she knew.

Her shoulders met the wall and then he entered her and filled her, so rapidly and completely that it hurt enough to shout.

'Yes,' he said, and his mouth moved under her hair and his fingers met the back of her neck as he ground into her.

Cat wasn't used to being so thoroughly taken. A bit of foreplay might have been nice, but then she'd never been so close to coming in her life.

She was thoroughly rattled in the nicest of ways. He just kept thrusting in and she held on to her own hands behind his neck and then of her own accord was grinding down.

It felt amazing.

Just that.

It felt so amazing that he knew, more than she did herself, about what she liked.

Oh, she liked it rough.

She liked the intensity of him and the deep, rapid

thrusts and the way he stopped kissing her and stared her down.

He felt the tension and thank God for that because he was past consideration. He could feel the clamp of her thighs around him and the heat of her centre and had moved to the point of no return just as she started to pulse.

He loved orgasms, he met them regularly, but there was something so intense about hers, something so intrinsically matched to his, that she drove him on to more.

To get back to her mouth and rougher kisses and deeper thrusts and then he felt it, the slight collapse of her spinal column and the slump of her shoulders as she rested her head on his and he knew she was smiling.

Even as he shot the last of himself into her, he knew she was smiling and somehow that made him smile too.

No guilt, no regret, they met each other's eyes and kissed again but without haste this time.

Then he took her to bed and they lay there a moment before she was back to his mouth, down to his hips, and they did it all over again.

And again.

CHAPTER FOUR

DESPITE HAVING SLEPT for all of an hour, Dominic woke before sunrise.

Just as he always did.

Even if he went back to sleep afterwards, his body clock still dictated that he watch the sun come in.

He glanced at the clock and it was just after four and he knew where he needed to be.

Where they needed to be.

'Cat,' he said. 'Cat…' He watched her slowly stretch like her namesake. 'Get dressed…'

She could have, given the circumstances, assumed her use-by date had expired and she was being thrown out, but he gave her a kiss to awaken her and told her to hurry as he picked up the phone.

Her Spanish was…well, it wasn't, but she knew the word 'coffee' when she heard it in any language.

'Where are we going?' she asked as, doing up her espadrilles in the elevator, they made their way down.

'You need to see more of this city.'

'At 4:30 a.m.?'

'We could do it tomorrow if you'd stay another night.'

He hoped she would stay another night but they both knew that that wasn't happening.

Cat blinked as the doorman handed them two take-out coffees and Dominic took her hand and they walked to a car.

'You've hired a car.'

He didn't answer and when she got in she realised that it wasn't a hire car because there were coffee cups and papers and it looked pretty much like the inside of hers.

'Just how long are you here for?' she started to ask.

'Ask no questions,' he said.

Yes, she reminded herself, that was what they were about—fun, freedom...

And yet he intrigued her.

He spoke Spanish and he drove like a local through the dim city streets and she drank her coffee and tried to get her brain into gear.

'Come on.' He parked the car and took her hand and she was happy to just go with the adventure.

Without him she'd still be asleep.

Instead, she was wide-awake, walking up a hill and wondering just what the hell was going on, and then she remembered it was one of *those* days.

There was a tiny fracture to her mind, an angry inward curse that she could have made it through almost forty minutes of being awake without remembering the day that it was.

'This is Collserola,' Dominic explained. 'It is a national park—the green jewel of Barcelona...'

And it wasn't exclusively here for them because, as they climbed the hill, Cat found herself behind a group of tourists and it became clear as they chose their spot and sat on mossy ground that this was the place to be at sunrise.

And it was.

The city twinkled its night lights, the cars weaved in orange lines and beyond that, slowly, the dark ocean started to turn to blue as around them woodland came to life.

'It's amazing,' she said, and then turned to him but Dominic didn't answer.

He sat watching and tried to tell himself that he shouldn't have brought her, that he should feel guilt. Oh, there it was, this clutch of guilt in his chest had arrived. He had no issues with last night; it was the morning he was wrestling with.

And Cat didn't notice his lack of answer because as the world came to light she was on the edge of crying.

I miss you every single day.

I miss you this very second.

Just not every second.

Not every moment.

And sometimes moments run into hours but I still miss you every single day and will for ever.

How can that be? both wondered.

When did the seconds start to join up? When did that first full minute devoid of grief arrive and your leaving go unthought-of for an hour?

At what point did a cruel world start to turn beautiful again?

'To think I could have left without seeing this.' Cat broke the strange silence they were wrapped in and he turned then and looked at her.

And the clutch of guilt in his chest released.

It just went.

He would regret it later, Dominic decided.

Right now they shared a kiss.

A deep kiss that chased her softly to the ground and she could feel damp grass beneath bare shoulders and for them both all was right with the world.

It was a kiss unlike last night's, soft and tender, and she opened her eyes in the middle and saw his closed and wondered how it might be to be loved by this man.

It felt as if she was, it was the strangest glimpse of it. Her hands were in his hair and his mouth was still over hers, and if there hadn't been a lot of tourists present and two hundred cameras clicking, he would have made love to her, Cat knew.

He would have peeled off her dress and just slipped inside her.

She'd never come to a kiss, but the deep, sensual press of his mouth persisted. The roam of his hands was gentle, pressing into the side of her. In public, somehow shielded, she just came to private thoughts that she dared not examine and he nearly did too just feeling her slight rise and then the stillness in his arms.

It was a long, lingering kiss that had to stop and as his lips left hers she looked up into his eyes and she wished she could stay here for ever.

So did he.

Of course they couldn't.

'We have to get back,' he said, and waited for the clutch of guilt to return but it had escaped.

'We do.'

It was rather odd to step back into normality.

This time she pressed the lift button for her floor and there were others in there with them. When they arrived at her floor they shared a sort of odd wave as Cat got out.

Oh, my, she thought as she saw the damage to Gemma's dress. There were grass stains up the back, a tear near the bust, and then she looked at her face.

Yikes.

She looked as if she had spent the night having torrid sex with a stranger.

She had!

It was this morning that disconcerted her, though in the very nicest of ways.

She had a shower, wearing a shower cap, and then got out and picked half a forest out of her hair.

She had love bites on her breasts and she remembered his mouth there and suddenly she wanted him all over again.

She put on her lilac dress and went downstairs and took her seat in a talk she had been very much looking forward to.

But how did you concentrate on extracorporeal membrane oxygenation? Cat thought. Dominic was off doing whatever he was doing but he might as well have been sitting next to her because that's where her thoughts were.

She felt the buzz of her phone in her bag and she sneakily pulled it out.

Of course it couldn't be him, suggesting they sneak away, she reminded herself.

He didn't even know her number.

It just felt as if he should.

Instead, it was Gemma.

Are you okay?

Yes, but your dress isn't, Cat was tempted to reply. She thought of the tear he had made in it last night and the grass stains today.

She just hoped they had another one at Gatwick.

All good, Cat answered without thought, and then she guiltily fired another text.

It seems wrong to say that today.

She smiled when Gemma replied.

You awful person. Go to your room and be miserable this very minute. xxx

No, Cat didn't want to go to her room and cry away the day.

She closed her eyes.

She flew at seven and it seemed far, far too soon.

He wasn't around at lunchtime and thankfully Gordon was telling his story to someone else. There was a sag of disappointment in Cat, though, as she lined up for lunch, for the few remaining hours they were missing out on.

Still, there was always something to smile about and smile she did when she saw a lovely full silver platter of delectable paella and she held out her plate to the waiter.

'My room, now...'

She hadn't even heard him come up behind her and the low whisper in her ear was like an audible hallucination.

'I'm not going to get my paella, am I?' she said, but he'd gone.

No, she wasn't going to get her paella.

Two minutes later, with only sixteen minutes to spare before the afternoon session started, she was kneeling on the floor, hands splayed on his bed as he took her from behind.

He wasn't a considerate lover, just a very, very good one.

If they'd had time, Cat would have turned her head to tell him that usually she wouldn't...

Wouldn't what?

She did turn, though, and she saw his look of intense concentration, felt his fingers on her clitoris, urging her to come, and then she didn't even bother thinking. She just closed her eyes to the pleasure of being taken.

Her head was on her forearm and he was pounding her from behind and, Cat thought as she started to come, it was blissful to be that woman, even if just for a little while.

His.

They skipped the afternoon sessions.

Like bunking off school, they took his car again and drove for half an hour to a beach and sat there, eating ice cream and then rubbing suntan lotion into each other with sticky hands.

And on one of the saddest days in her calendar year she found bliss.

'So your parents are both doctors?' Dominic said as they lay on towels and stared at each other, and she nodded.

'Were they high achievers?'

'God, yes. They still are. It's easier to ring their secretaries to schedule lunch than try to do it myself.'

'You are joking?' he checked.

'Half.' She smiled. 'What about yours?'

He seemed to think before answering.

He was.

They really hadn't spoken about anything other than themselves but it felt quite normal to have her ask.

'I don't really know where to start,' he admitted. 'Well, my mother never worked. Her sole job was to look beautiful for my father. He was an arrogant bastard. Growing up, I hardly ever saw him—he worked on the stock market and would bring his stress home, worrying about the yen or the pound dropping a quarter of a percentage point.' Her eyes were so patient, Dominic thought. She didn't ask questions; she just lay there, staring.

Because she loved his voice.

Because anything he said she wanted to hear.

'Anyway, then he had the absolute fortune of collapsing with a heart attack and going into full cardiac arrest.'

'Fortune?'

'We always joke now that he had a personality transplant because, while his illness made me switch from physics to biology and suddenly become very interested in medicine and saving the world, my father completely changed. He was very depressed at first and he had to see a psychologist and things but then he completely turned his life around. He sold up, got out of the money game, and he and my mother fell in love all over again, and now...'

He hesitated. He didn't want to give too many specifics. He didn't want to say that he was looking forward to Monday and heading over to see his slightly eccentric parents or rather, disconcertingly, he did want to tell her just that.

There was a part of Dominic that wanted to extend this conversation, which meant extending them, and that wasn't what this weekend was about so he kept things light.

'They started an internet dating service. Or rather it wasn't by internet initially, it was more a word-of-mouth thing. They used to set up their friends and anyone coming over to Spain…'

'Stop!' Cat laughed.

'It's true, though. Now they run this very exclusive dating site for the over fifties…'

To hear this rather detached man talking about his crazy parents made Cat start to *really* laugh.

Oh, she laughed at times, of course she did.

Just not like this.

They lay then in silence and Dominic thought about the six months after Heather had died.

After the funeral, instead of throwing himself into work, as had been his initial plan, he had accepted his parents' suggestion to come and stay in Spain with them.

At first they had infuriated him with their calm acceptance of the terrible facts. Of course they had been upset but not once had they matched his anger.

As he had raged and paced around the villa, or slept in well past midday, they had simply accepted him and whatever place he was in—providing conversation when needed and meals that appeared whether he felt he needed them or not.

And finally, when the anger had gone, Dominic had been very grateful for their presence and calm, which had allowed him to heal in his own time.

He had spent days walking and watching the ocean as he slowly come back to join a world that had altered for ever. Yet move on he had, catching himself the first time he'd found himself laughing along at a joke or smiling at a thought that had popped into his head.

And a smile stretched his lips as he thought of them now.

'They're amazing people,' he admitted. 'So, yes, what seemed like the most terrible disaster at the time turned out to be a blessing.'

They stared at each other, they found each other, right there in that moment.

'Don't leave tonight…' he said, but even before the words were out he was changing his mind and even as she heard them there was confusion in her eyes because it was supposed to be a one-night stand.

'Come on,' he said. 'Let's go in the water.'

There they could be apart and think.

There she could work out how to articulate the million reasons that she had to go back. How did she tell him that the woman he had met this weekend didn't actually exist, that she wasn't floaty and feminine and spontaneous?

She was rigid and brittle and meticulous.

And Dominic too, as they ran to the water, was wondering what had possessed him to ask her to stay.

But not even the sea could keep them apart because ten strides in they were waist deep in water, limbs around each other, kissing in the sun, out on display, and there was no reason in the world why she should leave.

The water was idyllic, just a shade cooler than the temperature of skin, and she could feel the sun beating on her shoulders.

She'd heard about the magical seven. Seven waves in, seven out, seven years since love had died and today it felt as if it was being born again.

They said nothing but their kisses were deep and tender but whatever they were finding was invaded, whatever the moment had meant it was gone.

'Ayuda!'

No, Cat didn't know Spanish, but a cry for help she was familiar with and she swung around.

'Necesito ayuda...'

Dominic was already swimming over to an elderly man who was waving his arms. Beside him on a pedalo there was a woman who was sitting up but even from here Cat could see she was in trouble. She was clutching her chest and leaning forward.

Others were coming over to assist and Dominic was calling out to a woman standing on the beach to call for an ambulance.

He called for Cat to go to shore. 'In my backpack!' he shouted. 'There's a pack...'

At least someone was organised today.

Cat raced up the beach as a group of men steered the pedalo in and then carried the woman to the shore.

She was still sitting up, Cat noted as she shook the contents of his backpack out.

There it was, a small pack, but as she went to stuff the contents she had tipped out back inside, her hand closed on a small bump in his wallet.

A circular bump.

She shook her head and ran back towards the gathered crowd.

'Thanks...'

She opened the pack. There were gloves, a mouthguard and airway... There was even a small kit for IV access and she watched his very steady hands slip a needle in, all the while reassuring the woman, who was clammy and sweaty, that she would be okay.

It should feel very different to be out in the middle of nowhere rather than in the calm efficiency of the emergency department, yet he had everything under control—a few beachgoers were holding their towels to shade the woman from the fierce afternoon sun and Dominic wiped her face with a cloth soaked in bottled water and spoke calming words in Spanish.

Cat noticed he was holding the woman's wrist as he spoke, keeping a constant watch on her pulse. As she glanced down at Dominic's hand Cat wondered if she had been blind or simply not looked, because now she could see the slight pinkness of a ring mark on his suntanned skin.

She felt a bit sick.

In the distance she could hear sirens and, even if the worst happened now and the lady went into cardiac arrest, assistance and equipment were just a few moments away.

The paramedics were just as efficient as they were back home and rather more used to retrieving heavy patients from a sun-drenched sandy beach than they would be in London.

They spoke at length with Dominic as they did the ECG tracing and administered analgesia and generally made the woman more comfortable before transferring her onto the stretcher.

The men all carried the stretcher up the beach until they let the legs down on the stony ground.

Her heart was racing, not from the mild drama but from what she had thought she had felt.

A wedding ring?

Surely not, Cat thought.

But why not? another voice in her head asked.

Why the hell not?

'Let's grab our things and head back,' Dominic said, and she nodded and tried not to shrug him off as his arm went around her waist.

She didn't know what to say to him. She just didn't know how to speak.

'You've caught the sun,' he commented as they drove back to the hotel.

'I know,' she said. Her shoulders were stinging but not as much as her thoughts.

'Are you okay?' Dominic checked.

'Of course.' She cleared her throat. 'It was just a bit upsetting.'

'What?' He glanced over. 'She had chest pain.'

Oh, that's right. Cat remembered the man she had disliked before she had completely fallen under his spell. He was arrogant, dismissive and rather mean.

'It's different without all the equipment...'

He didn't comment. Chest pain was such a routine part of his day and he'd assumed it was the same for her.

'She'll be fine,' he said, but she couldn't answer.

They were back in the elevators and she went to push the button for her floor but his hand stopped her and he pushed his.

Arrogant bastard, Cat thought this time.

Still, she wanted to be sure so she went with him to his hotel room and, completely at ease, he dropped his clothes and headed for the shower.

She didn't join him.

He washed off the sand and was glad that she hadn't come in. He needed to think.

Was he going to ask again that she stay awhile longer?

And if she couldn't, was he going to ask to see her again?

'What time is your flight?' he called from the shower.

'Seven,' she answered, and then she did something most uncharacteristic for her. She wasn't a nosy person yet she was about this.

She went into his bag and pulled out his wallet and opened it, and she didn't need to dig for the ring to find her answer. She pulled out a photo instead.

Cat knew her fashion and, yep, this was pretty recent.

Dominic made a lovely groom.

He also made a very dark lover because she jumped when she heard his voice.

'I wish you hadn't done that, Cat.'

He stood with a towel around his waist, watching as she tucked the photo back in. In his mind he was conflicted.

Tell her.

No.

Because then the bubble burst and everything they had found this weekend dispersed.

Yes, he could explain.

He simply wasn't ready to.

If he was going to tell her, then it would be in his own time.

And their time had run out.

He didn't like a snoop.

'Do you know what, Dominic?' She looked up at him. The delicious scent of him, fresh from the shower, was reaching her now and she practically held her breath as she gave a grim smile. 'I wish I hadn't done that either.'

She tossed the wallet on the bed and walked past him.

And he held open the door and let her out.

CHAPTER FIVE

CAT ARRIVED BACK at Gatwick Airport and, of course, because she didn't need it now, her suitcase was amongst the first to come out.

Instead of driving home, though, she found herself on a search of the shops and thankfully found Gemma's dress.

They met in the canteen on Monday morning and Cat got back her photo while Gemma received the second version of the white dress.

'Thank you so much for this.' Gemma beamed as she peered into the bag. 'It's beautiful, isn't it? I know I probably shouldn't wear white for the christening...'

'It's not a wedding,' Cat said. 'You don't have to worry about offending the bride.'

She looked at the dress as Gemma pulled out a corner and she felt her throat go tight. Hers, she knew, should have been thrown straight into the garbage but instead she'd thrown it into the back of her wardrobe.

No, she wanted to say to Gemma, *I did not have sexual relations with that married man.*

Oh, help.

She most certainly had.

'So how was it?' Gemma asked.

'It was great,' Cat said. 'Very informative.'

'About what?'

'Well,' Cat attempted, 'about things.'

'And how was your talk?'

'It went really well,' she said, but all she could really remember of it was the moment Dominic had walked into the room and how he had stood with his arms folded at the back.

'And how was the museum?'

Cat frowned.

'You said you were going to do some sightseeing and go to the museum, maybe get a bit of inspiration for your bedroom.'

As Cat's cheeks burned pink, she wondered if her friend was a witch.

'Well, did you?'

'Did I what?'

'Get inspiration for the bedroom?'

'No.'

'Oh.'

'And no shopping for stuffed donkeys, I see.'

'I was working, Gemma.'

'Of course you were.' Gemma smirked.

She knew, Cat was quite sure.

Had she examined things more carefully at the time, some flags might have been raised. Perhaps it should have been obvious, Cat thought, that he was married. Yet his reluctance to share personal information hadn't been an issue at the time; instead, it had felt as if they were chasing the same thing—fun, pleasure, grabbing the moment and running with it.

It had started to feel different at Collserola, though.

Cat couldn't properly explain it but there she had

started to want more than just the weekend. There, watching the sunrise, there had been a shift and she had felt him pensive beside her and for a moment, just a moment, she had felt as if time might not have been running out for them.

And that night, her second without him, Cat did what she'd tried not to because it hurt too much—she recalled their kiss in the sea. For a while there she'd thought she'd be staying.

Not for ever.

Just that something had been starting.

Something far bigger than either had expected to find.

Yet, as guilty as she felt about the weekend, Cat didn't feel used—after all, she had gone along with the anonymity that had been offered. She had enjoyed embracing her femininity, going out and doing things she never would have done had Dominic not been there.

And, even though she did her level best to forget him, their time together could not be undone and it was as if he had set off a little chain reaction, because colour started coming back into her life.

The following Sunday Cat wore another new dress to the twins' christening, a burnt orange and red paisley wraparound dress, and her hair was worn down and curly.

Glynn had rung to apologise and explain that his mother had been taken ill and Cat had had a difficult time explaining to him that, no, she wasn't not coming to see him because of what had happened. 'I like it curly, Glynn,' Cat said. 'Of course I'll be in again...'

Just not yet.

For now she enjoyed having those two extra hours a week not having her hair yanked and blown smooth.

She stood at the font, looking at Gemma's dress as she and Nigel juggled the twins, and wondering who on earth she was to offer guidance as a godmother, while knowing if that day ever came, then she would.

Oh, she doubted she would ever marry but she did believe in the sanctity of it and to think about what had happened made a curl of shame inside her that meant it was something she wouldn't be discussing with Gemma.

She loved Gemma and Nigel and their little family and she remembered Thomas's christening and when they had been there for her.

Gemma must have been thinking of it too, because she gave her friend the nicest smile and later pulled her aside.

'My parents are driving me crazy,' Gemma said. 'They want to know when we're having the cake. I'm sure they want to go home.'

Cat smiled. Gemma's parents loathed any change to their routine.

'Are you okay, Cat?'

'Of course.'

They told each other everything and she could have come up with some airy excuse, that today was hard because…

Only, she wouldn't use Thomas as an excuse for not being able to meet her friend's eyes.

'What are you up to, Cat?'

'I'm not up to anything.'

'Is there something you're not telling me?'

For the first time since they'd been teenagers she lied properly to her friend.

'Don't be daft.'

And she got on with smiling and enjoying this very special day.

But over the next few weeks Cat threw herself into her work and studying for her exams, which were tough but no tougher than expected. It meant there was no time to catch up with Gemma.

And even when three weeks' annual leave stretched ahead of her, she still avoided her friend.

Though she was starting to realise that she wouldn't be able to avoid her for long.

Gemma texted.

Is everything okay?

Cat didn't answer.
Gemma persisted.

Did we have an argument that I didn't notice?

Finally Cat texted back.

Can I tell you when I'm ready?

Because she wasn't just yet.

Of course.

No, she wasn't quite ready, so she stripped walls and sanded back a mantelpiece and tried to face something she was avoiding.

When it proved too hard, she took herself to her

favourite shop and spent a morning turning pages of wallpaper samples.

'I think a silver grey,' Cat said to Veronica, the owner, who was as obsessed with wallpaper as she was. 'Perhaps with one wall in silver and the rest in a matt finish...'

Silver moonlight hues had appealed but as Veronica went to clear some space so they could put together samples she moved a book and suddenly it wasn't those colours that Cat wanted.

'I haven't seen this,' she said.

'It's only just in...'

'Oh, my,' Cat said. She could almost feel the pulse from the sample book as she turned the pages. It was like being walked blindfolded and then having it removed and finding herself standing in a spring park. Birds, butterflies and tree branches that stretched and flowers, endless flowers...

It reminded her of Collserola and that one magical morning and she certainly didn't need such a constant reminder, except...

'Would this be a feature wall?' Cat checked, and then almost winced when the assistant pulled up some images on her computer screen.

Every wall was covered. In some of the images even the ceilings were papered. It was a sort of cross between a cheap Paris hotel and an enchanted wood.

'This is so far removed from what I was planning,' Cat said, and Veronica nodded.

'You don't want to know the price.'

'I don't,' Cat said, and tried to get back to silver grey. 'Have you got it in?'

'I do, though it's incredibly hard to get hold of. It

was on a special order but the buyer couldn't wait and went for something less…'

'Less what?' Cat asked. 'Less migraine inducing, less…?' She let out a breath. 'Less sexy…?'

Yes, somehow it was sexy.

'Just less,' Veronica said.

It was sold to the guilty conscience that just wanted to revisit that gorgeous morning over and over again.

A time when the world had been absolutely beautiful.

Magical even.

The strange thing, Cat thought as she stepped back a full week later and surveyed her handiwork, the world still was.

Magical.

Instead of the muted tones for the bedroom she had chosen colour. And now, in autumn, she stood in the middle of summer and imagined this being her haven when winter came in.

Yes, that weekend had changed her in a way she was finally accepting.

'Hey, Gemma.' Cat called her friend, who had so patiently waited for the morose mood to pass by. 'The bedroom's finished.'

Gemma really was a brilliant friend. She came over within an hour, clutching a bottle of champagne and two glasses, and they did a walk through the house. Cat had a photo in each room of what it had looked like before she'd set to work and it was hard to believe now just how bad it had once been.

As she opened the bedroom door she watched her friend's jaw drop in absolute amazement as she stepped in.

'I want to live in your bedroom for ever,' Gemma said.

'Nigel might not be too pleased.'

'He can come too,' Gemma said. 'Oh, my, it is beautiful. It's just stunning. I can't believe you've finished the house.'

'I haven't yet.'

'Well, it looks pretty perfect to me. What do you still have left to do—the garden?'

'No.'

Gemma followed Cat out of the master bedroom and down the hallway that no longer creaked when you walked, and she frowned as Cat opened up the guest bedroom.

It had a dark wooden bed that was dressed in white linen. There was a gorgeous bookcase next to the open fire. On the mantelpiece were beautiful ornaments. Every last piece had been chosen with care.

'But it's already perfect,' Gemma said.

'I'm going to make it into a nursery.

'Will it sell better if you do?

'No, I've decided against selling.'

'So why are you making it into…?' The penny was slowly dropping and a rather stunned Gemma halted and turned to her friend.

Yes, there was magic in nature.

'You're pregnant?'

There was a long stretch of silence.

Gemma was an obstetrician and she was used to women finding themselves rather unexpectedly pregnant.

It seemed today, though, that it was the doctor who was more surprised.

She was.

Cat had spent the past few weeks fighting the idea and then getting used to it. A private person, she revealed only when she was ready.

And tonight she was.

'How long have you known?' Gemma asked.

'A couple of weeks after the twins were christened,' Cat said. 'I tried to put it out of my mind, what with my exams and everything. I decided to work out how I felt when I was on leave.'

'And how do you feel?' Gemma asked, struggling to put back on her obstetrician's hat.

'Well, I'm going to be terrified until I have the tests and get all the results back…'

'The chances of it happening again are minimal,' Gemma said.

'I know they are.'

'But you shan't relax till they're in.' Gemma smiled gently and Cat nodded. 'Apart from that, how do you feel?'

'I still don't know,' Cat admitted. 'I don't know if I'm happy or worried or anything really.'

'You know that I'm here for you, whatever you decide.'

'I do and even if I haven't been ready to speak about it till now, it's helped a lot to know that.'

Gemma opened the champagne.

For herself.

She didn't even bother with a glass!

'What about Rick? How did he take it?'

'It isn't Rick's.'

'Then who—'

'I don't want to discuss that.'

'Now, hold on a minute,' Gemma said. 'You're not my patient yet—you're my friend so we *are* going to discuss that. What happened in Spain?'

'How do you know that it was in Spain?'

'Because you've been different since then, and also you don't top up your tan by sitting in a hotel room.'

'Yes, it was then,' Cat admitted. 'I met someone but it was never going to be going anywhere. It was supposed to be a bit of fun, a weekend of no consequence...' She gave a wry smile. 'We were careful...'

'You have no idea how many times I hear that a day,' Gemma said.

'We used condoms.'

'Note the plural,' Gemma said. 'Was it a sex-fest, then?'

'I guess.'

'You dirty girl.' Gemma grinned.

'Okay, I can tell you what happened now.' And so she told Gemma all about the hair appointment that hadn't happened and the missing luggage. 'I ended up wearing your dress for the presentation,' Cat explained. 'I felt like a fish out of water at first but then I started to enjoy myself. I felt a bit like my old self. Anyway, he made it very clear from the start that he was only interested in the weekend and nothing more...' Cat thought about the moment when he had asked her to stay on for longer but she shoved that aside. It didn't matter now. 'At first I was going to tell him to get lost, he's not my usual type at all, but then...' She shrugged. 'I decided that a weekend of no-strings fun was better than six months of starting out all hopeful and then slowly finding out that a relationship wasn't working.'

'And was it?'

'For a while,' Cat said.

'So, what's his name?'

'Dominic,' she replied.

'And have you told him about the baby?' Gemma asked.

'He's married.' Cat made herself say it. They stood

in the spare room that would soon be a nursery in silence. It was Cat who broke it. 'I'm sorry, Gemma...'

'You don't have to say sorry to me,' Gemma said. 'After all, it wasn't Nigel who you slept with.'

'I know, but even so.' There were tears in Cat's eyes. She still couldn't quite believe how careless she'd been. 'I didn't know that he was married right until the end— the bastard had taken off his ring and tucked it in his wallet. I probably didn't ask enough questions,' she admitted. 'He seemed very direct to me. He didn't seem the sort of person who would cheat, which says a lot about my gauge for guys...'

'Well, whether he's married or not,' Gemma said, and Cat knew that her friend's doctor's hat was firmly on now, 'Dominic still has a responsibility towards the baby...'

Cat shook her head. 'It might be a bit late to be thinking of it but I'm not tearing a family apart. I'm not going to contact him just yet. I don't even know where he works, I don't even know his surname...'

'Come off it, Cat.'

'Okay, I looked up the conference attendees and I do know his surname but I can manage—'

'It's actually not about you and whether or not you can manage,' Gemma said. 'And it's not about his wife and how she'll react. It's about the baby, Cat.' Gemma was as firm as Cat had known she would be. The very questions that she had been wrestling with for weeks were now being voiced by her friend. 'It's about your baby, who will grow up and will want to know, and has a right to know, who their father is. Whether or not you want him to be, Dominic has a right to be involved, or not, in his baby's life.'

'I know all of that,' Cat said. 'And I shall tell him, just not yet. Gemma, I'm eleven weeks pregnant. I'm doing my very best to simply get used to that fact. I'm not going to upend his life while I'm still in my first trimester…'

'Oh, but you'll upend yours. Why the hell should he get away with a few weeks of stress—'

'I'm not stressed,' Cat said. 'I was at first but I'm not now. I want this baby and I'm going to do the very best that I can by it. I shall look up Dominic at some point but not now. Not now while I'm still trying to work things out. I need to find out the test results before I tell anyone. I need to know that it's not going to be happening again…'

Cat knew she had Gemma's support and, yes, she could tell her most things but there was something she couldn't explain to her friend just yet because she didn't actually understand it herself.

She missed Dominic.

Yes, it had been but one weekend and, yes, she was angry, not just with him but herself.

It was how she would react when she saw him that terrified Cat.

She knew that she wouldn't cry and break down if he told her he wanted nothing to do with them—it would come as a relief, in fact.

And she didn't want a penny from him either.

There were two things that terrified her—how he might react to the news if their baby was less than perfect, which was understandable given all that had gone on.

And how she might react if he took the news well.

Or, rather, how she might react when she saw him again.

What if that spark blew all her scruples away?

The mere thought of his kisses terrified her.

His smooth talk too.

She had this awful glimpse of life as a mistress.

Tucked away in England with her baby.

And she'd never be that.

If he was to be in their baby's life, then it would be without lies.

Which meant someone was going to get hurt.

CHAPTER SIX

CAT DID LOOK him up.

At twenty weeks gestation, when her scan and amnio had come through as clear, Gemma told her that she had no excuse not to.

It really had been an excuse because whatever the outcome of the tests it wouldn't have changed the course of the pregnancy for Cat.

But the results came in before Christmas and Cat had visions of Dominic and his fraught wife and the triplets she had now assigned to him, and decided she couldn't ruin Christmas for them.

Or New Year.

Still, she had looked him up and it had taken about fifteen minutes to find out where he worked.

She recalled him saying that he liked the architecture in Edinburgh and after a few false starts she found someone who knew him and was told he was now working at a large teaching hospital in Glasgow.

Ah, that's right, Cat remembered, he didn't like to be tied to one place for too long.

Or one person.

And so Cat had sat on that knowledge for another month.

Her second pregnancy threw up so many memories

of her first. There were so many thoughts and fears and she wanted to get past the milestone she had reached with Thomas.

Finally, though, she plucked up the courage to make the call.

'You're looking for Mr Edwards?' A cheery female voice, with a heavy Glaswegian accent, checked.

'Dominic Edwards—he's an emergency consultant.'

'Oh, you mean Dom!' There was a long pause. 'No, he was only here for a couple of months… Sorry, I've no idea where he is now.'

And that ended that.

Though, not quite, of course.

Now into February and thirty weeks pregnant Cat and Gemma caught up one Monday morning for breakfast in the canteen. They were interviewing for Cat's maternity leave position and she didn't want to be around for that.

Pregnancy suited her and she was enjoying this one. Colour had continued to come back into her life since that weekend and she was wearing the paisley dress that she had bought for the twins' christening, along with chocolate-brown high-heeled boots. Her hair hadn't been straightened since and hung over her shoulder in a thick, long ponytail.

'I really don't want to see who's replacing me,' she admitted as she peeled the lid of her yoghurt and, having licked it, added, 'Temporarily, of course! I'll be back.'

'Full-time?' Gemma checked.

'That was the plan,' Cat admitted, 'and I've told Andrew that I shall be returning full-time but I'm starting to really wonder how on earth I'm going to manage it.'

'Have they had many applicants for the role?' Gemma asked.

'There have been a few, but only two standouts—two women who are looking at job share,' Cat said.

'You could think about doing that,' Gemma suggested.

'I don't like sharing at the best of times and especially not my job,' Cat said. 'Still, I'm going to have to work something out. I can't believe how quickly my due date is coming up.'

Cat had always heard women saying that their pregnancy seemed to drag on for ever, yet hers seemed to be galloping along at breakneck speed.

Work was as unrelenting as ever and she did her level best not to bring any aches and pains with her, but by the end of the day she was exhausted. The nursery hadn't been sorted out; instead, her days off were spent looking at child-care centres. All to no avail. Even the crèche at the hospital wasn't geared to a baby whose single parent worked such erratic hours.

'If I'm going to work, then I'm going to have to get a nanny,' Cat conceded as she added sugar to her tea. 'But even that comes with its own set of problems.'

'Such as?'

'I have a two-bedroom home.' She sighed. 'A small two-bedroom home.'

'And you don't like sharing.' Gemma smiled. 'Can't you get somewhere bigger?'

'I'm going to have to at some stage but the thing is, I love my home. I've just got it exactly how I want it but, yes, I guess I'm going to have to look at moving. Not yet, though,' she said. 'I think I'll stay put for now and once I've had the baby I'll think about putting the house on the market. I'll have six months to move...'

'So you're planning to have your house on the market, find another one *and* move, all with a new baby?'

'It's a baby,' Cat said. 'I'm not going to be working...' She let out a sigh. 'I haven't got a clue, have I?'

'Well, if anyone could do it all, then it would be you,' Gemma said. 'Though I just can't imagine how I'd have managed when the twins were tiny. Just having people viewing the house when you're trying to feed or you've just got...' Gemma hesitated '...*it* off to sleep...'

'You were about to say *him*.' Cat smiled.

'No, I wasn't,' Gemma refuted. 'What I'm actually trying to say is that I wouldn't count on getting too much done during those six months of maternity leave. It's isn't an extended holiday, Cat. If you are considering moving to somewhere bigger, it might be a good idea to start that ball rolling now...'

'I guess.' She sighed. 'Even if the new place does need some work, I could do that while I'm...' She stopped when she saw Gemma's small eyebrow rise and then laughed. 'Okay, I'm going to accept that I have no real idea as to the disruption this small person is going to make to my life when *he* arrives.' Cat waited for Gemma to comment but she didn't. 'I want to find out what I'm having.'

'Well, then, it's good that you've got an appointment to see me this evening.'

'Gemma!' Cat protested, because now that she had made up her mind, she wanted to know straight away. 'Tell me.'

'No, I won't tell you here and I'm serious about that. We agreed that catch-ups were for friend talk and my office was for official baby talk...'

'Fair enough,' she grumbled.

'And speaking as a friend and not a doctor, have you—'

'I need to get back,' Cat interrupted. She didn't want to get into that conversation with Gemma *again*, and explain that she still hadn't spoken with Dominic.

She knew, though, that she needed to contact him.

Tonight, she decided, she'd deal with it tonight but almost immediately she changed her mind.

It was surely better to ring around hospitals during the day. It would sound far more professional to any of his colleagues than calling at night, and she certainly didn't want to create gossip for him.

Gemma started to head to Outpatients, where she was holding antenatal clinics all day, and Cat would be her last patient. 'I'll see you at five. Hopefully I shan't be running late. Come and have dinner after,' she suggested. 'We might even make it in time to see the twins before they go down for the night.'

'I'd love that. I honestly don't know how you do it,' Cat admitted. 'Do you feel like you're missing out?'

'Sometimes.' Gemma nodded. 'I worry more, though, that they're missing out on me and so I completely overcompensate when I do see them and rot up all of Nigel's routines. I know I'm lucky, though. I don't have to worry about them while I'm here and I can concentrate on work, knowing that they're at home with their dad.' She gave her friend a smile. 'You need your own Nigel.'

Cat smiled back but the thing was, she didn't want her own Nigel.

She wanted... Cat halted her thoughts right there. Dominic wasn't the man she thought she had met. And even if he was, it was supposed to have been a one-night stand. He had said to her face that he didn't want to be tied to any one person or place. She couldn't really imagine his reaction when he found out that she was having his baby.

She didn't want his reaction.

Cat slowed down her walking. There was a flutter of panic in her chest as she remembered her last pregnancy and the disappointment of Thomas's father, the silent suggestion of blame for daring to mess up his perfect life.

She didn't want that for herself again and she couldn't stand it for her baby.

Yet she had to.

She was tired of the guilt that came with putting it off and she decided that, bar an emergency coming into the department, she wasn't leaving her office until she had found out where he was working and had contacted him.

Did she tell him outright? Cat wondered.

Suggest that they meet?

So deep in her thoughts was she that at first she didn't notice the tall suited man walking alongside Andrew.

He noticed her, though.

In fact, at first sight she barely looked pregnant.

She was wearing a tight dress and high boots and looked somehow sexy and elegant but then she turned to speak with one of the nurses and he saw the tight, round swell of her stomach and, attempting a detached professional guess, he would put her at…

Yes, there was something that they needed to discuss. That was why he was here after all.

He watched as she turned from the conversation she was having and startled as she glanced towards him, but then she gave a small shake of her head and strode on.

Then she looked over towards him again and he watched as not only did her face pale but she stood frozen to the spot.

Frozen.

For a foolish moment Cat considered darting into a cubicle—it would be a futile game of hide-and-seek, though, because it would appear that she'd already been found.

And so, as Andrew called her over, somehow she did her best to pretend that the walls of the emergency department weren't shaking and that the ground wasn't opening up between her feet.

She walked towards him.

Dominic.

Her one-night stand.

The father of her child.

'Cat.' Andrew beamed. 'Did you have nice days off?'

'I did.'

'Excellent! I tried not to worry you, but on Friday one of the job share applicants pulled out and the other wasn't interested in pursuing the position if she couldn't be guaranteed regular part-time hours.'

'I see,' Cat said, even though she didn't.

'I've still got two more interviews to complete,' Andrew went on, although Cat knew those two were really more of a formality and would be a rather poor choice. 'However,' Andrew said, 'we had a late applicant. Cat, this is Dominic Edwards. He's been working in Scotland for the last two years but we're hoping to lure him back south of the border.'

For now, Cat knew, she would simply have to go along with the polite small talk. Whatever the reason Dominic was here, whatever the outcome when she told him her news, at the first opportunity she would have a quiet word with Andrew. Hopefully she wouldn't have to reveal to her colleague that Dominic was her baby's father, but if she had to, then she would. There was no way this could happen.

No way!

Thankfully there was a call for help from one of the cubicles and Cat was just about to flee in relief and go and assist when Andrew halted her. 'I'll go,' he said. 'If you could carry on showing Dominic around.'

'I can deal with the patient,' Cat said. 'You're in the middle of conducting an interview.'

'I know, but the patient happens to be my mother-in-law.' Andrew rolled his eyes. 'The interview has already been interrupted twice. My apologies again, Dominic…'

'It's no problem at all,' Dominic said. 'Take your time.'

As Andrew walked off Cat stood there and she truly didn't know what to say.

She kept praying that the alarm clock would buzz, or that there would be a knock on the door to the on-call room and she'd find out she was having a bad dream.

A vaguely sexy bad dream, though, because rather inappropriately, given the circumstances, she couldn't help but notice how amazing he looked.

When in Spain, the times that he'd had clothes on, Dominic had dressed smartly, though somewhat more casually than he was now. Today, on a Monday morning, he seemed too beautiful for the rather scruffy emergency department. Dressed in a dark grey suit and tie, his hair was shorter than she remembered but it still had enough length that it fell forward. Clean shaven, he smelt as he had the last time she had seen him, the moment he had stepped out of the shower.

The moment she had walked away and he hadn't stopped her—in fact, he had held the door open.

And, just like that day, she could feel his contained anger.

'Has the cat got your tongue, Cat?' he asked as she stood in silence.

It would seem that it had because still she said nothing.

'Well, I'll make this very simple for you, then,' he pushed on. 'A, B or C?'

Cat could feel her eyelashes blink rapidly as he sped through the multi-choice he had created just for her.

'A—mine, B—not mine, or C—not sure.'

'Dominic...' she said, and how strange it felt to be saying his name while looking at him again. How odd it felt that he was here, terribly beautiful, terribly cross. 'It's not that simple...' Cat attempted. But it was to him.

'A, B or C, Cat?'

She couldn't meet his eyes as she delivered the answer. 'A.'

'Mine.'

Yours.

His.

Dominic said nothing at first. He tried to stare her down but she refused to look at him as she now attempted to speak.

'I was going to try to find out where you were working. Today, in fact,' Cat said.

'I don't believe you for a moment.'

She couldn't blame him for that.

'What time to do you finish work?' Dominic asked.

'I've got plans tonight,' Cat said to his shoulder, because she still couldn't meet his eyes.

'Tough,' he said. 'Cancel them.'

'I've actually got a doctor's appointment.'

He hesitated but he refused to be fobbed off. 'What time is your appointment?'

'Five,' Cat said. 'But my obstetrician is a friend of mine and I'm going there for dinner afterwards…' She was floundering for excuses. She would far prefer to have had this conversation over the phone or via email. There at least she could have hidden from his angry gaze.

And, yes, he was angry—even if she was doing her best not to see it, she could feel it from his stance and she could hear it in his terse voice.

'I'm quite sure that your obstetrician friend will understand that you can't make dinner because you're going to be having a long overdue conversation with your baby's…' He halted and glanced over her shoulder, and Cat guessed that Andrew was making his way back.

'Name somewhere,' Dominic said, 'and I'll be there.'

She hesitated a beat too long for his impatient mood.

'Name somewhere,' he said again, 'or I'll just keep right on talking until you do and your boss will quickly realise that I have a rather vested interest in this maternity leave position.'

'Oliver's,' Cat said, referring to a small wine bar that a lot of staff at the hospital frequented. 'It's just down the—'

'I'm sure that I'm capable of working it out.'

The conversation ended as Andrew joined them again.

'How's your mother-in-law?' Dominic asked politely.

'Thankfully, she's about to head off to the ward.' Andrew gave a sigh of relief. 'Would you like to come and take a look at the radiology department, Dominic?'

'I'd love to,' he said, and then he addressed Cat. 'It was nice to meet you.'

'And you.' She gave him a tight smile.

For the next couple of hours Dominic remained in the department, being shown around, observing a clinic and being introduced to staff. It was clear to Cat that Andrew had decided that he had the role.

She was busy enough to avoid him and Dominic seemed fine with that for he made no attempt to catch her eye or talk.

He did let her know, though, when he was leaving. She was sitting on a high stool, trying to write up some notes, but had just put her hands on her hips to curve her aching back and stretch it when he came in.

'I'm heading off,' he said, and Cat glanced around and saw that they were alone.

'You don't have to tell me your movements,' she responded in a very crisp voice. Now that the shock of seeing him was starting to wear off, her own anger with him was making itself known and she let a little of it out. 'You knew full well that I worked here. What on earth were you thinking?'

'We'll speak tonight,' he said. 'Take as long as you need for your appointment but don't even think of not showing up afterwards. I want this sorted before we start working together.'

'Working together?' she checked. 'I thought you were applying for the maternity leave position.'

'I am but Andrew mentioned that you were short-staffed and wanted to know how I'd feel about doing a few locum shifts prior to commencing full-time.'

'*If* you get the job.'

'Why wouldn't I get it? The interview went very

well,' he said. 'I happen to be very good at what I do. Andrew seems to think I'd be an asset…'

He'd be an emotional liability, though, Cat thought. Well, she'd soon see about him working here, she decided as Dominic stalked off, though she didn't get a chance to speak to Andrew for the rest of the day.

Instead, she sat in Gemma's office at a quarter to six, having her blood pressure taken. Given who had just arrived on the scene, neither Gemma nor Cat were surprised to find that it was a smudge high.

'I can't believe that he'd just show up like that,' Cat said as her friend undid the cuff.

'Well, I think it's a good thing that it's all being brought to a head,' Gemma said. 'Go and lie down so I can have a feel.'

They carried on chatting as Cat did so and she opened up her wrap-over dress.

'Ooh,' Gemma said as Cat's stomach danced away while she lay there. 'Someone's wide-awake.'

'I just grabbed a glass of orange juice,' Cat said. 'I think it's woken him up.'

Gemma examined her bump as they chatted and this evening she made an exception to their rule and was both doctor and friend.

'He's furious.' Cat sighed.

'Which makes two of you,' Gemma said. 'Ask him if he's told his wife yet! That might knock him off his high horse a touch…' Then she was kind. 'Cat, you had many reasons for not telling Dominic. Given all you've been through and Mike's reaction to the bad news, of course you're protective of this baby…'

'I just wanted to know it was okay before I said anything to Dominic.' Cat admitted what Gemma already had guessed. 'Then I wanted to get further along than I had with Thomas…' She closed her eyes for a moment because tears were on the verge of spilling out. Getting past twenty-five weeks had been a huge milestone. 'The last few weeks I've had no excuse, though.'

'So why didn't you tell him?'

'It was supposed to be a one-night stand. I don't want to discuss Thomas with a man I spent one night with. Do you know, I didn't even particularly like him? I thought he was a bit mean and dismissive.'

Gemma said nothing.

'Arrogant,' Cat said. 'Chauvinist… He wouldn't let me pay half for dinner.' She mimicked a deep voice. '"Why would you ruin a perfectly good night?" He's all the things I don't want in a man.'

Cat frowned as a blob of warm jelly was squirted onto her stomach. 'What are you doing?'

'An ultrasound.'

'I'm not due for one. Is there a problem?'

'No problem at all,' Gemma said, 'I just thought it might be nice for you to have a peek at your gorgeous baby. I'm recording it,' she added. 'Maybe Dominic might want to see it too.'

'Do you think?' Cat frowned. She loved having Gemma doing her ultrasounds—all her ultrasounds with Thomas had been fraught affairs. Mike had actually taken the probe out of the radiologist's hand once in an attempt to take over.

'I think that it might be a very nice olive branch,' Gemma said. 'It must be a shock for him and this might help him get used to the idea. When things get tense between the two of you, this might serve as a little reminder that it's your baby you're discussing…'

Cat nodded and looked over at the screen.

It was a fun ultrasound. Gemma wasn't taking measurements, just a brief check that all was okay, which it was, and then they took a lovely long look.

There it was, opening its little mouth like a fish, and it was the most beautiful thing Cat had ever seen. 'What am I having?'

'You're sure you want to know?'

'I already know,' Cat said. 'I just want to hear it.'

'You're having a little girl,' Gemma said, and Cat felt as if the examination couch had dropped from beneath her, a little like turbulence on a plane.

'I was convinced it was a boy!'

'I know that you were,' Gemma said. 'She's beautiful. Look at those cheeks…'

It felt so different to look at the screen and to know it was her daughter that she was seeing. There she was, wiggling, waving and content in her own little world.

'Happy?' Gemma asked as Cat lay there.

Yes, she was dreading facing Dominic, yes, her life had been turned upside down and inside out but 'happy' was the right word.

Here, now, seeing her little girl, Cat was exactly that—happy.

'You're going to be a brilliant mum,' Gemma said, 'and, no matter how awkward things are between you and Dominic, I'm sure that you'll sort it out as best you can.'

After Cat had stood up and done up her dress, Gemma handed her the recording of the ultrasound and Cat put it in her bag.

'Good luck.' Gemma smiled.

'I'll need it.' She glanced at the clock. 'He's going to think I've stood him up.'

'He knows you've got an antenatal appointment?' Gemma checked, and Cat nodded. 'Well, surely he knows they don't run like clockwork…'

'Mike was always—'

'That was Mike,' Gemma said.

And this was Dominic.

'Hey, Cat,' Gemma said as she went to go. 'When you saw him again, did you still fancy him?'

'Moot point—I don't fancy married men.'

'Did you still fancy him?' Gemma persisted.

'Yes,' she admitted, 'but that's for this office only. The day I sit crying to my friend about whether or not I sleep with him because, of course, he and his wife never do it, or I start saying, he's going to leave his wife after Christmas…you have my permission to shoot me.'

'I shall and can you tell him from me that he's an utter bastard,' Gemma said.

'Oh, I shall.'

Trust Gemma to make her laugh, Cat thought as she walked the short distance to Oliver's. She was calmer than she'd expected to be as she stepped inside.

There was Dominic, sitting with a glass of wine and looking rather more rumpled than he had that morning. His tie was off, the top button of his shirt undone and his eyes were black with loathing as Cat made her way over.

She didn't expect him to stand for her.

Very deliberately he didn't.

It was a bit like walking into the headmaster's office, Cat thought, but refused to be rattled. She shook off her coat and put it on the low bench opposite him and then took a seat.

'Sorry, I'm a bit late. Gemma was running—'

'It's fine.'

Cat blinked at the ease of his acceptance.

It wasn't her timekeeping that was Dominic's concern!

'How was the appointment?'

'All's well,' Cat said.

'She's a good friend?' Dominic asked, and Cat nodded as she bristled in instant defence.

'Are you going to ask if that's wise?' she checked.

Dominic said nothing and she continued.

'Everybody seems to question whether or not I'm sensible to be seeing a friend, but—' Only then did he interrupt.

'You're a consultant and, from everything I heard at my interview and everything I've seen, you're meticulous and thorough, possibly a bit obsessive about certain details. I'm quite sure you've given your choice of obstetrician very careful thought. I'm sure your friend and you both discussed the pros and the cons of having her. I don't think there's anything I can add that you haven't already thought through.'

Cat felt the little bubble of indignation that she had around that topic deflate a touch.

'She's excellent.'

'I'm sure she is.'

'Have you heard from Andrew?' Cat asked.

'Nope,' Dominic said. 'I'm not really expecting to hear positive news. I'm quite sure you've had, or will be having, a quiet word in his ear…' He watched the colour mount on her cheeks as a waiter poured Cat some water and gave them menus. 'Though, if you haven't already, please think long and hard before you do. I assume you live close to work?'

'Sorry?'

'I'm just thinking for handovers and things.'

'Handovers?'

'Access visits, or whatever they're called.' Then he raised his voice just a fraction and the pink on her cheeks moved to a burning red. 'If we work at the same place, then it might make it a little easier when I want to spend time with *my* child!'

'I was going to tell you—' Cat attempted, but she didn't get very far.

'When it turned eighteen?' He shook his head. He clearly didn't believe her and she couldn't really blame him a bit for that. 'I don't think for a moment that you were going to tell me. In fact, I'm quite sure you'd already got what you needed from me that weekend.'

Cat's mouth gaped open. 'You think I deliberately got pregnant? What? That I'm some psycho going around pricking holes in condoms?' She shook her head and then met his eyes. 'I shouldn't be surprised. My mother thinks the same. Well, not quite that scenario but she seems to think I got bored one weekend and popped off to the sperm bank.' She dragged her eyes from his and looked at the menu as she spoke.

'I never set out to get pregnant.'

Dominic sat there and images of them making love danced before him—her hand rolling on a condom, another time, about to take her from behind, it had been Cat who had grabbed one and handed it to him.

If anything, it had been he who had been about to be careless, so ready had he been to take her.

It wasn't the best thought to be having right now and he reached for a wine and gave a small nod.

'Fair enough.

'And I did try to contact you. I spoke to some cheery woman in Glasgow who said that Dom had moved on…'

'It would have taken an hour tops to find me if you'd really wanted to,' he said.

'Have you told your wife yet?' She smirked as she read through the menu. 'Or were you hoping it wasn't yours?'

'Well, given my wife is all seeing and knowing now, I'd assume that she already knows.' He watched her frown. 'She's dead.'

Cat looked up.

'She's been dead for more than two years.'

'And you didn't think to tell me?'

'Don't even go there, Cat. You're the one keeping the big secret. Anyway, I *chose* not to tell you.'

'Why?'

'Because I didn't want *that* look.'

He didn't get to elaborate—the waiter was back and Cat ordered steak and a tomato salad and rolled her eyes because she really wanted seafood but it was on the list of noes that Gemma had given her. 'I'm never going to get my paella.'

'I'll have it for you,' he said, and ordered it.

'Bastard,' Cat said, even if she managed a small smile, but it soon faded as they got back to the serious talk once the waiter had gone.

'I didn't tell you at first because I wanted to make sure all the tests were okay…' The water she took a sip of seemed to burn as it went down. 'They were.'

'That's a poor excuse, Cat, because if they hadn't been

okay, a bit of notice that I'd be arranging my life around a special-needs child would have been appreciated.'

Again, his reaction surprised her. He didn't jump on results or demand facts. He had but one question.

'When's your due date?'

'The nineteenth of April.'

'Cat, I nearly bought a house in Spain last month. I was offered a job and that was going to be the starting date.'

'You can still take it,' Cat said, but rather quickly wished that she hadn't as his finger pointed in her direction and he shot out one word.

'Don't!'

He was doing his very best to stay level and calm but that she'd happily wave him off to Spain incensed him. 'I was pointing out how bloody late you've left it. I know!' Dominic said. 'How about you have the baby, I take it to Spain and you can see it during your annual leave?' He watched as her pink tongue bobbed out and she licked nervous lips. 'Yeah, not a nice thought, is it, Cat, so don't suggest the same for me. You need to get used to the idea that I'm not going to be some distant figure in my child's life. I'm going to be there, not just for Christmas and birthdays. I'm going to be doing the school pick-up and homework and I'll be there each and every parent-teacher night. You might not want me there and I fully get that we can't stand each other, so we can do it through lawyers if you prefer...'

'When did we get to not being able to stand each other?'

'Oh, about the time you started snooping through my wallet, about the time I found out that you'd deny me knowledge of my own child...'

'I thought you had a wife, maybe a family...'

'Even if I had, I still should have been told.'

Their food came then and she stared at his rather than hers.

'That was really horrible of me,' he admitted as he looked at his large plate of paella, especially as it looked seriously nice.

'Hopefully you'll have a massive allergic reaction.' Cat, less than sweetly, smiled.

'Yes, and no doubt you'll take ages to find the adrenaline pen so I'll be dead and that will take care of that...'

There was a tiny silence.

'When you said you didn't want to tell me you were a widower because of *that* look,' Cat said as she cut her steak. 'What did you mean?'

'Things change when you tell people that you're a widower...' He scooped out a mussel and then pulled a misty-eyed face that made her smile reluctantly. 'I can't really explain it. Honestly, since Heather died I've had more offers for sex than a rock star. Which sounds good but women seem to think I want to make love, or that I'm comparing them to my poor late wife, or even that I must want a wife... They don't get I just want to get down and dirty.'

'So we weren't making love?' Cat pouted and he smiled. 'Dominic, it was supposed to be a one-night stand.'

'And now we have to deal with the consequences.' He got back to his food. 'Did you find out what *we're* having?'

The 'we're' was very deliberate.

'I only just found that out now,' she said. 'A girl.'

She watched as his fork paused midway to his mouth and then he put it down.

The past ten days, since he had seen the maternity cover position being advertised, since he'd started to suspect she might be pregnant, had been spent in a whir of fury and concern. Now, in the midst of anger and change, he got a moment in the quiet centre of the storm.

A girl.

A daughter.

He just sat there as the news sank in and somehow, he had no idea how, it changed things, because, in that moment, he went from none to having not just one but two ladies to take care of and he looked at the bump of the little one and then into the eyes of her mum.

'Oh.'

'I know,' Cat said. 'I thought I was having a…' She was about to say *another boy* but she quickly changed. 'A boy.'

Yes, she understood Dominic a little better than he knew because she didn't want to be the recipient of *that* look.

Baby two after such a turbulent baby one was a private pain, one she could barely share with Gemma, let alone a man whose bed she'd been in for a single night.

No, he didn't need to know all about her.

There was a lot to talk about but they finished their meal in silence, lost in their own private thoughts.

'Have you thought of names?' Dominic asked as they put their cutlery down.

'I was leaning towards Harry till tonight.'

'I never thought I'd be running through baby names,' Dominic said.

'Didn't you and…?' She hesitated. It was none of her business whether or not he and his wife had planned on having children.

Dominic was grateful that she didn't finish the question. No, he and Heather hadn't got around to thinking of children. And he didn't want to share his wife with this virtual stranger.

'Do you want a quick coffee? Then I'm going to have to go,' he said, 'if I want to make my flight.'

'You're going back to Scotland tonight?'

'No, I'm going to Spain for a few days. As I said, I'm in the middle of relocating there and I've been looking at homes. Given that the baby is mine, there's a lot to do there. I'll have to withdraw my application and I'd like to do that in person, and I want to tell my parents face-to-face what's happening.'

'Will they be disappointed that you're not moving there now?'

'I don't think so. I wasn't exactly going to be living next door to them or anything. I expect they'll be surprised about the baby and then pleased.'

'Where are you flying out from?'

'Gatwick.'

'Good luck with your luggage,' Cat said, and gave a low laugh. 'I'll drive you.'

'I can take a taxi.'

'You're the one banging on about how we need to talk.'

He conceded with a nod.

'And no coffee for me, unfortunately.' Cat sighed. 'It gives me hiccoughs. I'm stuck with tea. I miss champagne, I miss coffee, I miss seafood…'

'I'll buy you the biggest bottle of champagne and have paella delivered to your hospital bed once the baby is here.'

It was a very nice thing to say, Cat thought. It was a nice thought to have because, even if they were the odd couple and doing this on the run, at least they weren't at each other's throats now.

'How did you find out about the baby?' Cat asked a little later as they walked to her car.

'Well, I keep an eye on jobs and things and I saw one come up in your department. I remembered something you said about being the only female consultant...'

She flashed the lights of her car and they walked over to it.

'I told myself that I was being ridiculous. You could have been married or anything...'

'Would you have cared if I was married that weekend?' she asked.

'No,' he admitted.

'I don't like you,' Cat said, but he just laughed.

'You don't have to like me. Anyway, I'd never have cheated on my wife, but that weekend, had you been cheating...' Dominic shrugged. 'Anyway, it's all hypothetical.'

'But very telling.'

'Do you want me to lie to you, Cat, just say the right thing?'

'No.'

'Anyway, back to how I tracked you down—the dates for the leave all added up and...' They stopped talking as they got in but once they were pulling out of the car park the conversation resumed. 'I was going to call you but then I decided to surprise you.'

'That wasn't very nice.'

'No, I know that it wasn't,' he said. 'I wasn't feeling very nice at the time, but...' He didn't continue, they just drove in silence, but as the airport came into view conversation started again. 'You haven't chosen badly, Cat. I might have been a bit of a bastard the way I landed on you and some of the things I've said tonight but I'm not going to be a negative in your baby's life. And,' he added, 'I'm sure you don't need my opinion of you but when I think of some of the women that I could have been having this conversation with, I'm very happy that it's you. I think you'll be a brilliant mum and I'm quite sure we'll do this right. We've still got a couple of months to work things out...'

'We do,' Cat said.

He went into his wallet, pulled out a business card and wrote a few things on the back and Cat frowned when she read them.

'Why would I need your social network details? I'm not going to be checking up on you...' Then she went pink when she recalled how he'd caught her going through his wallet.

'Or me you,' Dominic said. 'But if you update about the baby and things...'

'I'll call you if there's a problem.'

'I meant for day-to-day stuff,' he said. 'I don't need formal emails and progress updates. Soon you might want the same...'

'Sorry?'

'Well, she won't stay a baby. My family lives in Spain.'

'You'd take her on holiday? No.'

She was adamant, her response was instant. 'You're not taking her out of the country.'

And Dominic was about to respond that his lawyer would see to it but he held that in. He could see the conflict in her eyes and he knew that she was struggling with the concept.

Cat was. She had glimpsed the future.

There would be pictures of her child with her father in houses she never set foot in. Holidays spent apart.

'I just sent a friend request,' Dominic said. 'Up to you whether or not you accept it.'

'Here…' She went into her bag and wrote down her number, then she remembered the recording.

'What's this?'

'I had an ultrasound today. If you want to see her…'

'Thanks.'

He went to get out of the car. 'I am sorry for not telling you, Dominic.'

He gave her a grim smile. 'Yeah, well, I don't accept your apology—I'm not that magnanimous. Call me when you need to…'

'I shan't.'

'Oh, I'm sure you'll have questions.'

'I won't.'

But even before she got home Cat had found several.

Would he want to be at the birth?

The very thought filled her with horror!

Cat did her best to stay in control and the one place she was guaranteed to lose it was in the labour ward.

No, she did not want arrogant, surly Dominic seeing her swearing like a sailor and breaking down.

No way!

And what were they going to tell people at work?

Her mind was darting as she stepped back into her home.

She put some washing on and, completely wrecked from a long and difficult day, wrestled off her boots, which was very hard with a stomach like a basketball, and then had a very quick bath and went to bed.

Except, though tired, she couldn't sleep and she picked up her phone and, sure enough, there was his friend request, which she accepted.

His status was given as single and Cat frowned, wondering why he didn't say he was widowed.

Oh, that's right, he loathed *that* look.

Then she smiled when she read his status. A little cryptic note that she was sure was aimed at her.

You can run but you can't hide.

She carried on reading and looking at photos of his eccentric parents and terribly beautiful sister and then there she was.

Heather.

She knew it was her from the photo she had glimpsed in the hotel.

Now she felt as if she was snooping, so she went back to Dominic and saw a picture of him all wet and gorgeous coming out of a swimming pool. At thirty weeks pregnant and not wanting to be, she was terribly, terribly turned on.

'So not happening,' she said, and turned off her phone.

His body was still there, goading her to have another glimpse, at six the next morning when she drank her tea and switched her phone back on.

But then she smiled when she saw what he had changed his relationship status to.

It's complicated.

It most certainly was but, the funniest thing was that as she dressed for work and headed out to face the day, even if they weren't together, they were on the same side—her baby had a father and that sat right with Cat. She didn't feel quite so alone.

CHAPTER SEVEN

DOMINIC'S PARENTS WERE, though initially surprised, completely delighted with the news.

There was too much wine drunk and they spoke late into the night, and they kept making the most ridiculous suggestions.

'Why don't you bring her here so we can get to know her and she can have a little holiday?'

'She's thirty weeks pregnant,' Dominic said, and looked over at Kelly for some help.

'Mum, they're not a couple,' his sister said.

'Perhaps, but I'd still like to meet her. We could come over.' His mother, Anna, was warming to the idea. 'We could fly over for the birth. I'd love to see my granddaughter being born.'

Dominic swore under his breath before answering. 'I don't even know if I'm going to be present at the birth...'

'You could film it,' Anna said. 'Live-stream it.'

'And then you could set it to music and forward it to your hippy friends...' Dominic sarcastically responded, and when his father nodded this time Dominic swore out loud. 'You weren't even there when we...' he gestured to Kelly '...were born.'

'And I regret it to this day,' James said. 'That's the beauty of being a grandparent, you get to do things right the second time around.'

What planet were they from? Dominic wondered.

Even if they made him laugh, they drove him mad at times, and this was one of those times. He could only imagine how well that suggestion would go down with the cool and rather distant Cat.

Yes, they made him laugh, because he was doing that now as he pictured her shocked expression as he told her he wanted to film the birth.

'Cat and I are going to sort things out between us.' Dominic told his parents how it would be. 'Preferably without lawyers. You guys need to stay back.'

'From our grandchild?'

He closed his eyes for a brief moment. He'd never considered having a baby but now that he was he wanted his parents in his child's life, so he thought long and hard before answering.

'From Cat and me,' he said. 'We've got two months to work things out. You're to stay out of things.'

Anna didn't answer. In fact, Dominic was sure she shook her head.

After his parents had gone to bed, he sat, listening to the trickle from the pool filter and enjoying sitting with his sister outside. It was cool and they had the gas heaters on but after a cold Scottish winter it was blissful.

'I love it here,' Dominic said.

'Would Cat?'

'Oh, we are so far from that, Kelly,' he said. 'It was a one-night stand, a weekend conference...'

'That's completely changed your life,' Kelly said. 'You were all set to move here.'

'I was *almost* all set,' he said.

'Almost?'

'I don't want to talk about it.'

He didn't.

He didn't want to tell his sister that, despite the seriousness of his plans, since August they had started to change. Unable to get that night out of his mind, and furious at how the weekend had ended, he had considered calling Cat to explain things. And if he was thinking about calling her, it had seemed a bit nonsensical to be considering moving further away than he was already.

Yes, he hadn't been idly flicking through jobs in London.

He'd been wondering how he could ask her to give them a chance.

'Is there any hope for the two of you?' Kelly asked. 'You obviously fancied each other and you said things went well when you saw her again…'

'Kelly, the stakes are a lot higher now. Surely we should be concentrating on how we're best going to be as parents rather than trying to establish a relationship.'

'I guess.'

'What if it doesn't work? What if we give it a go and one of us wants to end it? God, we don't need hurt feelings and resentment added to the mix. I hardly know anything about her.'

'Does she know about Heather?'

'I told her tonight that I was a widower.'

'Tonight?' Kelly checked.

'Yep.'

'So what were you two talking about that weekend?' Dominic rolled his eyes. 'We weren't really talking.'

Except that wasn't entirely true.

They had talked, they had shared more than sex. That was the reason he had wanted to look her up.

'I took her to Collserola Park,' Dominic said. 'We watched the sun come up. You know how Heather had a thing about sunrise?' he asked, and Kelly nodded. 'Not once, when I've been with someone, have I felt guilty. It's always just been sex and I knew Heather would get that but that morning, sitting watching the sun come up with someone who wasn't Heather, was the most unfaithful I'd ever felt.'

'It sounds like you two have something to build on...'

'Maybe,' he said. 'But it would be foolish at best to rush this. I've had one brilliant marriage, Kelly. I'm not downgrading for the second one. Right now Cat and I need to sort out how we're going to be for the baby. The two of us as a couple will just have to wait. I'm not going to see her for another three weeks and that's if I even get the job.'

'Won't she see to it that you do?'

Dominic managed a wry laugh. 'You have a far sweeter mind than I do, or Cat come to that. I'm quite sure she'll be seeing to it that I don't.'

They said goodnight and as he lay in bed he took out his laptop and plugged in the recording and saw for the first time the life they had made.

She was beautiful, so beautiful that it actually brought tears to his eyes.

It should feel like a mistake—surely this was something he should have been doing with Heather—and yet, seeing his baby on the screen, thinking of Cat...

It didn't feel like a mistake.

It felt right.

Was there a chance for them?

Could strangers who had shared just a night have got it so right that they could spend the rest of their lives together?

Cautious with his emotions, it had taken years to get around to getting engaged to Heather.

They had gone out for more than two years before they'd moved in together.

Another three years before they'd got married.

And they hadn't been ready to even start trying for a baby before Heather had been taken ill.

He flicked on his social media site and saw that Cat had accepted his friend request and it was Dominic who snooped.

She had the most boring page ever.

He found out nothing new about her, other than that her star sign was Virgo and that her friends wrote on her wall more than she did.

No mention of Spain, no lovers' names.

Nothing.

He wanted to know more, though, and even if they needed to be concentrating on the baby, somehow they had to make time for them, and that was why he changed his status.

Not single.

Not in a relationship.

It's complicated sounded about right, so that, for now, would do.

CHAPTER EIGHT

'You sound out of breath,' Dominic commented.

It was Thursday night, a few days since they'd met, and Cat had only just arrived home when she answered her phone and it was him.

'That's because I just took my boots off.' She sighed. 'Which is no mean feat these days.'

'I'm just calling to let you know what you probably do already—Andrew called this afternoon while I was flying back from Spain and left a cheery message, asking me to call him. So it sounds like I got the job.'

'You did,' Cat said, flicking on the kettle.

'Do you have an issue with that?'

'I did,' she admitted, 'but I don't now.'

'He's also asked if I can start a couple of weeks before I officially take up your position. Do you have an issue with that?'

'A bit,' she admitted, 'but I'll get over it. How was Spain?'

'Still beautiful.'

'How were your parents with the news?'

'Elated.'

'Oh!'

'Invasive.'

'Okay.' She let out a laugh. 'It's not just them. Honestly, people think they can ask me the most personal questions and as for touching my bump…' She shuddered.

'I promise not to touch your bump uninvited.'

'Thank you.'

'I'm coming down this weekend and I'll be looking at houses. I'm just checking you're not planning on moving in the near future…'

Cat was silent. He really had meant it when he'd said he wanted to be around for his child.

'No, I have no plans to move. Well, I might need a bigger house but I shan't be leaving the area.' She thought for a moment. 'You're not going to move too close, though? I mean…'

'I don't want to be your neighbour, Cat. Just close enough to make things easier on both of us. I was going to rent but I've been doing that for a couple of years. I want to give her a proper base.'

'Sounds good. While I've got you on the phone I actually do have a couple of questions,' she said.

She had quite a list actually.

'Can they keep till the weekend?' he asked. 'I'm a bit swamped right now.'

'Sure.'

'We can go out for dinner and discuss things.'

And if he could be so brusque and direct, without apology, then so too could she.

'I don't want to go out,' she said, because she'd had to swap to get this weekend off and there was a lot to be done. By evening all she would be ready for was a night flopped on the sofa. 'I don't want to discuss my private life in a restaurant. You can come here.'

'Okay, don't worry about cooking, though.'

'Oh, I shan't.'

'Saturday, about six?' Dominic checked. 'I'll come when I've finished looking through houses.'

'Whenever,' Cat said.

She heard a voice in the background.

A female voice.

'I have to go.'

He was probably at work, she told herself as she ended the call.

And even if he wasn't, it was none of her business.

Cat really didn't have time to dwell on her feelings, if she even had feelings for Dominic. Aware she was only going to get bigger and that there weren't too many days off between now and her maternity leave starting, when Saturday came she found herself back in the wallpaper shop. This time she had Gemma in tow and her brother's offer to come and help this afternoon when the cot was being delivered.

'We have the softest pink,' Veronica said. 'It actually feels like candy floss…'

'The last time I ate candy floss I vomited,' Cat said to Gemma.

'It's gorgeous,' Gemma insisted as she ran her hands over it, but Cat shook her head as she opened up another sample book.

'That,' Cat said, 'is what I call gorgeous.'

'It's blue!'

It was *so* blue, the paper was every shade of night and brushed with dandelions that looked as if they could blow away in the night wind.

And so Cat found herself up a ladder as her brother, Greg, hovered nervously. He had no idea how to hang wallpaper so he held the ladder instead and handed her the glued sheets to put up.

'It's very dark,' Greg offered, when she was done.

'It's supposed to be for sleeping,' Cat said. 'You don't like it?'

'I don't know,' Greg admitted. 'Maybe when the cot's in and you've got the right furniture and light fittings…'

'You have no imagination, Greg.'

'I'm an accountant,' Greg said. 'What time's the cot arriving?'

'It's a p.m. delivery, that's all they'd say.' A knock at the door had Cat smiling. 'You can help set it up while I go and get changed.'

'Help?'

Cat laughed as Greg went down to get the door and then she looked around the bedroom. 'A brave choice' had been Veronica's words when she had made her selection. Gemma had looked worried and Greg was sitting on the fence…

'Cat!' Greg called. 'The cot's here and so is the reason for its purchase.'

Dominic gave a wry grin as Cat's brother announced his early arrival.

He had surprised himself with his own reaction when he had seen a man waiting for the delivery of the cot.

A good-looking man around Cat's age.

It had taken only a moment to work out it was probably her brother, and as he introduced himself the same green eyes had confirmed that fact.

Dominic, though, was unsettled by his brief two-bulls-in-one-paddock moment.

Another thing that needed to be discussed, he thought.

No, he wasn't particularly looking forward to tonight.

Then he changed his mind because, wearing khaki trousers and with a vest top on, Cat came down the stairs and he noticed that between now and earlier this week her belly button had poked out.

'Dominic.' Cat gave a wary smile at the strange air of hostility in her hallway. 'This is my brother, Greg.'

'We've already introduced ourselves,' Greg said as the delivery man dragged cardboard boxes up her stairs. 'Right, I'm off.' Greg gave his sister a brief kiss on the cheek.

'I thought you were going to stay and help with the cot.'

'Er…Cat,' Greg said, 'I'm sure Dominic can manage that much at least…so long as it's not too much responsibility for him…'

Oh, no!

She groaned inwardly as Greg got all big brother and angry and tried to somehow equate putting up a cot with men who impregnated helpless virgins and left them heavy with child.

'I've got this, thanks, Greg,' she said, but only as her brother shot Dominic a filthy look and then stalked off did it dawn on her what the problem was.

'Oh, God,' she said to Dominic. 'I forgot to tell him you weren't married.'

'Remind me never to take over a multi-trauma patient from you,' he said.

'What?'

'Well, you're not very good at passing on pertinent information.' He smiled. 'Anyway, the mood he's in, it wouldn't have made a difference. I'm still the one-night stand who left his precious little sister pregnant.'

'He hasn't been like that…' she was about to say,

since she'd broken down on Greg about Mike, but now wasn't the time and anyway she had to sign for the delivery, so she finished with a lame '…in ages.'

He waited till she'd signed for the cot and the door was closed before he continued speaking.

'Well, next time you're talking, if you could slip into the conversation that I'm not cheating on my wife, it would be appreciated.'

'I shall.'

Dominic doubted it.

He assumed he was way down on her list of topics of conversation.

He assumed rightly.

But he was up at the top of her thoughts.

Inappropriate thoughts for a heavily pregnant woman about a man she didn't particularly like.

'Lovely hallway,' he said.

'Come through.' She opened the door to the lounge and Dominic stood there for a moment.

'This is such a sight for sore eyes after some of the dumps I've seen today.'

'Did you find anything you liked?'

'One that I liked.' He told her the address and it was close but not too close. 'It needs far too much work, though.'

'Ooh,' Cat said. 'Tell me.'

And so he told her about the dodgy plumbing, the ancient kitchen, fireplaces, cornices and the disgusting bathroom with green carpet and a study that was completely covered in cork tiles.

'That sounds like my idea of heaven,' Cat said, and she went to her perfect mantelpiece and took down a photo. 'This was what this room looked like when I bought the place.'

'Oh, my God, it's worse than the one I saw today.'

'We can do a tour if you like,' she said. 'I love showing off my handiwork.'

'You renovated it?'

'Every last bit of it.'

'Oh, my...' he said as they walked down her hallway and to the kitchen. 'We could swap houses,' he said. 'You could renovate mine while you're on maternity leave...'

'I might be a bit busy, Dominic,' she said.

'I'm sure you could fit it in,' he teased, and yet it made Cat smile because everyone else told her how zoned out and incapable she was going to be once the baby was here.

He seemed to know her better than everyone else.

It was strange, it was nice.

It was unexpected.

She took down a picture from the fridge and showed Dominic the absolute disaster the kitchen had once been.

'I didn't have a sink for the first three months. I had to do my dishes in the purple room of pain upstairs.'

'Show me your purple room of pain, Cat...'

Whoops, were they flirting?

Up the stairway they went, admiring the wooden bannister as they did so. 'There were about twenty layers of gloss paint,' Cat told him, and then she opened the bathroom door and took a photo from a small dark wooden chest so he might understand just how painful purple could be.

'Everything was purple,' Cat said, 'even the toilet seat cover...'

'But it's like something you'd find at a yoga retreat now,' he said. 'Not that I frequent them, but if I did...' he looked at the rolled white towels on the dark wood and the gorgeous claw-foot bath '...well, I'd demand a bathroom like this.'

'It's fabulous, isn't it?' she said. 'But the place is tiny. No room for a nanny.'

'A nanny?'

'I'm going to be working full-time, Dominic.' She didn't look to see his expression. 'Do you want to see her room?'

'The nanny's?'

'The baby's.'

'I would.'

She was a little nervous about opening the door, she wasn't sure why, but as she did and he stepped in, she found she was holding her breath. Dominic looked around.

'It's like...' he started, and she braced herself for 'a brave choice' or to be told how dark it was, or for Dominic to point out that it was dark blue when they were having a little girl. 'It's like a magical night-time,' Dominic said. 'It's amazing. You just want to...'

'Say it!'

'Sleep!'

'Yes.' Cat was delighted. 'That's what I thought. It's just so dark and peaceful and once the curtains are in and the light fittings...'

'And the cot,' he said, looking at it all piled against the wall. 'Do I have to do that?'

'You'd look a right bastard if you left it for me to do.'

'Fair call,' Dominic said. 'Right, shall I go and get dinner?'

Cat nodded.

'Anything in particular?'

'I'd love a hot curry,' she said. 'And mango chutney...'

'How hot?'

'Very hot.'

'Okay.' Dominic frowned. 'But I thought pregnant women would avoid curries...'

'What's the population of India?' Cat asked as they walked back down the hall. 'I'd like a beef curry and lots of naan. You get dinner and I'm going to have a bath and get changed.'

'What's in there?' Dominic asked, fully knowing they were passing her bedroom door.

'Something you'll never see.' She smirked as he headed off.

But as Dominic got into the car and Cat stripped for the bath, she wondered if she should just run it cold to put out the fire down below. They'd both known she was lying.

Her bedroom was *yet* to be seen.

Which was a problem.

A very real one.

Sex would only make things complicated.

And they were complicated enough already.

CHAPTER NINE

HE WAS GONE for ages.

Ages.

So much so that when Cat came out of the bath and peered out of her bedroom window and saw that there was no car coming down the street, instead of quickly dressing, she took a few minutes to put on moisturiser. As she rubbed it into her stomach she wondered just how much bigger she could get.

She put on a long grey tube dress and then combed through her hair.

Still no car.

Was he shopping for ingredients? she wondered.

She didn't bother with make-up.

Instead, she poured a nice big glass of iced water, her latest favourite drink, and then she put the door on the latch and went back upstairs and started taking the cardboard off the cot.

'It's open,' she called, when he finally arrived. 'I'll be down soon.'

Dominic was serving up dinner when she came down five or so minutes later, carrying a pile of cardboard.

'Come and eat.'

She did so, but first she poured herself a small glass

of antacid for her inevitable heartburn and he smiled
as she took a seat on the floor at the coffee table, where
he had set up.

'If I'm going to get heartburn, I want it to be worth it,'
she said. 'It smells fantastic. Where did you go?'

'About fifteen minutes away. I worked near here
a few years ago and I was guessing this curry house
wouldn't have closed down.'

She could see why it hadn't when she tasted the
curry.

'We can put the cot up after dinner,' he suggested,
and Cat nodded.

'It will be good to have that room done.'

'You had some questions for me.'

'I do,' she agreed, and took a breath. 'Are you going
to tell people at work that, well, that you're going to
be a father?'

'I don't know.'

'And if you do, are you going to say that the mother
is me?'

Dominic pondered for a moment. He hadn't thought
this through properly. 'I guess not. Well, not at first.
Maybe once you've gone on leave, or you've had the
baby. Has anyone actually asked who the father is?'

'Not at work,' Cat said. 'Well, not directly. I keep
my personal life to myself pretty much.'

'Okay,' he said. 'Well, you don't have to worry about
me saying anything. What else?'

She was rather nervous to ask the next one. 'Are you
going to want to be there at the birth?'

This question Dominic had thought about. 'I think
that depends on what you want, and I would guess that

you might not want me there…' He gave a tight shrug and then he looked at Cat for her response.

'I don't want to rob you of anything, but…'

'Just the first six months of the pregnancy,' he sniped, and then he stopped trying to score points. 'Sorry, go on.'

She didn't really know how best to say it. 'If you add it all up, we've probably spent less than forty-eight hours together.'

'I get that.'

'And I just think I'd do better on my own.'

'Fair enough.'

She was grateful for his words but she knew that it wasn't completely fine with him, that she was denying him being present at the birth of his daughter.

Well, tough, she thought, scooping some curry onto her naan. Surely some things were better unseen!

'My parents both want to be there, though,' Dominic said suddenly, and she nearly choked on the water she was drinking. She looked at his expressionless face and she had no idea if he was joking. 'I pointed out that I didn't even know whether I'd be there and they suggested that you film it…'

'For them?' she croaked, and he nodded. 'I know we don't know each other very well,' she said, 'but I trust we know each other enough that you said an emphatic no.'

'I did,' he said. 'While I wouldn't normally presume to speak on your behalf I delivered that no for you and reminded my father that he was away on business when I was born and didn't see me till I was six weeks old.'

'Really?'

'This apple fell very far from that tree. I'll be seeing her very soon after she's born.'

'Of course.'

He got up then and Cat waited as he went out to the car and when he came back he handed her a bag. 'I wasn't going to give this to you.'

'What is it?'

'My mother's been shopping.'

She most certainly had. Wow, the Spanish had amazing taste in baby clothes. There were tiny little sleepsuits and little hats and cute socks and a thick envelope, which Cat opened with a frown.

'I've no idea…' Dominic said.

'They just wanted to say congratulations,' she said as she read the letter, 'and to let me know that whatever goes on between us two, I'm welcome any time in their home.'

'Too much?' he checked.

'No,' she admitted. 'That's actually very nice of them.' She thought for a moment—it really was. Suddenly her baby had a whole other family and, aside from Dominic, they included her.

'Don't expect the same from my family,' Cat warned.

'Oh, I don't.' Dominic smiled. 'Next question.'

'I'm hoping to breastfeed. I know that you'll want to see her and have her stay over, but…'

'Not till she's old enough,' he said. 'I understand that she'll need her mum. Maybe we play that one by ear, trust that we'll work out what's right for her.'

'Okay.'

It sounded a lot better than trying to work out some neat arrangement with a lawyer.

'Any more questions?'

'I think that's it,' she said. She'd had loads but, really, now that he'd said they'd play things by ear she felt soothed by that.

'You're sure?' he said, as if he expected there to be more, but Cat nodded.

'Do you?' she asked.

'Well, I guess that I do… Are you seeing anyone at the moment? I mean, is there someone who's going to…?' He couldn't really admit that he didn't like the idea of another man being more of a constant in his child's life than he was but Cat had started to laugh.

'I have no idea why, Dominic,' she said, 'but I can't seem to pull lately. It's like I've got two heads or something.' Then she was serious. 'No, I'm not seeing anyone.'

It didn't fully answer the sudden questions that filled both their minds, how they'd feel about the other dating, but they decided to drop that hot coal for now.

After dinner they headed upstairs and between them they put up the cot.

'This is about as far as my DIY skills go,' Dominic warned. 'I only know how to use a drill from my orthopaedic rotation.'

It was more a fiddly job than a difficult one, though it was easier with two, but after a few attempts it was up. Cat put in the mattress and then Dominic checked that the side slid up and down.

'Do you think,' Dominic asked as they surveyed their handiwork, 'that I should maybe get the same wallpaper for her room at my place?'

'I think that would be really nice for her.'

For the first time she glimpsed the two of them getting this right, not just able to manage but that their daughter's future would be better for having him in her life.

'I'm sorry I didn't let you know,' she said. 'I had my reasons.'

'You thought I was married,' he said. 'I really wish you hadn't gone snooping that day. I don't like snoops.'

'I don't usually. Remember on the beach, when I went to get the mouthguard?'

He frowned in recall as Cat spoke on.

'I saw a ridge in your wallet that felt like a ring and then I kept seeing a pink line on your ring finger, and the more you stayed out in the sun the pinker it got. When you were having a shower I let curiosity get the better of me.'

'Fair enough,' he said. 'I'd only just started to take the ring off.'

'Why didn't you tell me you were widowed?'

'I wasn't ready to share her with you,' Dominic said. 'That might sound odd…'

'No, no, I get it.'

That part Cat did, because she still wasn't ready to share Thomas.

'Heather had several brain tumours and that's all I want to say about it.'

'Okay,' she said, and she glanced over and saw how uncomfortable he was with the topic. 'We didn't sign up for this, did we?'

He understood what she was trying to say. 'The baby's actually the easy part.'

It was opening up and sharing your life with another person that was the difficult bit.

He looked down at her stomach and the mini-gymnast within, because in her tight dress you could see the baby moving. Cat did the right thing.

She took his hand and he felt the solid bulge of their child's head trying to climb into Cat's ribs, and then she guided his hand down past her belly button to a foot, and then she left him free to roam.

And that lump of hot coal that they had dodged was back, it had to be, because she was terribly hot and for once it had nothing to do with the extra person she was carrying.

It had more to do with the reason her baby was there.

'Haven't you got another question, Cat?'

Her cheeks were pink and she wondered how to broach the most difficult question of all.

'Us.' Dominic did it for her. 'Dating.'

She swallowed.

'My parents and sister all seem to think we should give us a go,' he said. 'I've told them that it's the most terrible idea I've ever heard.'

'Terrible?'

'Well, we know the sex part would be fine...'

'You assume it would be fine,' Cat corrected.

'I know it would be fine for me,' he said. 'I've never found a pregnant woman attractive till now...' His hand was on her stomach and it wanted to move up to the thick nipple and stroke it, he wanted that dress off, and from the loaded silence between them he guessed that she did too. 'From my perspective,' he said with a low, sexy huskiness, 'I'd have no problem doing you on the floor right now.'

'You could,' she admitted.

'But then what?' He looked at her and met eyes that glittered with lust. 'What if we break up? What if it doesn't work out between us?'

'I don't know.'

'So,' he said, when he'd far rather not, 'no sex for

us, none of the easy part. What I'm proposing is six months…'

'Of what?'

'No dating anyone else…just us, getting to know each other, working out how we can be friends, concentrating on the baby…'

It was the most sensible thing she had ever heard.

She should be cheering really.

No pressure, no stepping on the roller-coaster, no promises made that might prove impossible to keep.

No sex.

It was the last part she was wrestling with.

'Sure.' She smiled. 'Can you remove your hand, please?'

'Yep.' He did so. 'I'm going to go,' he said.

'Where are you staying?'

He didn't answer her question. 'I start work in three weeks on Monday…'

'Where will you stay? I mean, even if you put in an offer on the house…'

'Not your problem, Cat,' he said, though he said it nicely. 'You worry about yourself and the baby. I'll sort out things at my end.'

He did.

The next day he had another look at the house before heading for home. It was a ten-minute walk from Cat's.

Two weeks later, driving home, Cat found herself slowing the car down as she always did when she drove past it.

Actually, she had no need at all to be driving past.

She just did these days.

SOLD.

She tried to imagine the future.

Stopping the car at this very spot and getting her baby and its bags out and handing her heart over to him.

She couldn't.

And it was even harder to imagine driving off.

Going home alone to an empty house when the people she loved were in another one.

No, Cat corrected, the baby she loved…

No, a little voice told her, *you are crazy about him and have been since the moment you met him.*

They just didn't know each other at all.

CHAPTER TEN

THERE WASN'T REALLY the chance to get to know each other.

Cat's pregnancy continued to gallop along at breakneck speed and for Dominic, seeing the bank, sorting out the purchase of his house, working his notice and arranging to move his stuff to England had his blood boiling about how hard Cat had made it by not telling him.

Then he'd remember the reason he was moving his life several hundred miles and *not* in the planned direction of Spain and he chose to let it go.

He didn't move in on the weekend before he started working at the Royal. Cat knew that because, after a long weekend on call, she drove home on the Monday morning and the house was still untouched.

And even if their paths didn't cross during those first few days at work she certainly knew that he had started because she heard the nurses discussing the sexy new doctor.

'Is he seeing someone?' Cat heard Marcia asking Julia on their coffee break early one evening. 'He doesn't have a ring.'

'I don't know,' Julia said. 'I'm going to ask him when

he comes on.' She smiled at Cat, who was taking a seat. 'How many weeks now?'

'Thirty-four,' Cat said.

'When do you finish up?' Marcia asked.

'Just next week to go.'

If she lasted that long.

She ached, her stomach was huge and she felt as if she was wearing some awful fake pregnancy outfit. She was all boobs and belly and even though it was cold and just coming into spring, she was permanently too hot and felt as if she was wrapped in a blanket.

She was dressed in her grey tube dress with her hair worn up just to keep it off her neck and a small cotton cardigan to stop people asking her if she was cold. 'You're on nights next week, aren't you?' Julia groaned in sympathy. 'I am too. I can wheel you around in one of the wheelchairs.'

Cat smiled. 'I might just take you up on that!'

They'd all tried to subtly prise out of her who the father was but had accepted that she didn't want to tell. Apart from that, though, she was getting on better with everyone. Yes, she was more than back to her old, pre-Mike self.

Cat was sipping on iced water and trying not to fan herself when Dominic walked in and Marcia and Julia perked up.

'How's the move?' Julia asked.

'Not happening till the weekend,' Dominic said, and took a seat and nodded to Cat.

'Are you on tonight?' Cat checked, and glanced at the clock. It was only seven and he wasn't due to start till nine.

'I am. I'm here now if you want to finish up.'

Cat shot him a warning look. She did not need him babysitting her and so she said nothing.

She didn't need to; Julia took care of that.

'So, is it just you moving in?' she fished. 'Or have your whole family relocated?'

'Just me,' Dominic said.

'So you're not married?'

'No.'

'Girlfriend?' Marcia asked.

'Nope.'

'So you're single!' Julia beamed.

She wasn't smiling for long.

'Julia?' Dominic asked. 'Why would you assume that just because I haven't got a girlfriend that I'm not in a relationship?'

She watched Julia frown as she tried to work it out and Dominic got up and left.

'Does that mean he's gay?' Marcia asked. 'Does that mean…?'

Cat left them to it but she did have to smother her smile as she tapped him on the shoulder in the kitchen. 'Don't start coming in early so you can cover for me. If I need help…'

'Oh, for God's sake,' he said. 'I'm staying with friends at the moment and they've got three children all under five. Believe me, I would far rather be at work.'

'Oh.'

'So stay if you want to, go home if you like…'

She stayed, but it was only on principle.

By 8:00 p.m. the department was quiet and the few patients they had were all either waiting to go to the ward or waiting for their lab work to come back.

'So you're moving at the weekend?' she asked.

'Yep.' Dominic rolled his eyes. 'I knew I was buying a bomb but when I got the keys… You should see it.'

She'd like to see it. Only, he didn't offer.

The only solace she had was the exclusion zone he'd put around dating, so she knew he wasn't busy with someone else.

She just sensed his dark mood.

'I'm going home,' she said.

''Night.'

Yes, his mood was dark.

It was two years to the day since Heather had died.

Last year at this time he had realised he had to move on.

He'd just never expected his life to head in this direction, and moving in at the weekend was going to be hell.

It was.

All the furniture he'd had brought down proved to be an expensive mistake, because it ended up being donated. He watched the charity truck drive off with half of his life on board and as he took delivery of a cot he felt as if he were on Pluto.

He was back in London minus a wife.

And about to become a father by a woman he barely knew.

It was time to rectify that.

Cat came in from work on Sunday evening and there was a note on her door, inviting her to dinner.

She stopped at the supermarket and bought flowers, which was very back to front, but, then, every part of them was back to front. Seeing her standing there, holding a bunch of daffodils, made him smile when he opened the door.

'I was lying to Marcia and Julia. I'm not gay.'

'Yes, well, I'd worked that one out. You can still like flowers, though.'

Spring had sprung and he looked in a box to find a glass because he didn't own a suitable vase.

He chose not to explain that he had once owned a heavy crystal vase that had been a wedding present but he'd got rid of it and there was a little hand-blown glass one they'd bought on their honeymoon. He couldn't bear to part with it or put Cat's flowers in it.

Then he chose to open up a little.

'It was Heather's two-year anniversary the other day...'

'I'm sorry.'

'And I've just got rid of a truckload of our stuff. Not everything, but...' Yes, he was bad at sharing and so the daffodils got a beer mug, which felt a whole lot better than placing them in *their* vase.

She knew there was nothing she could say and Dominic was very glad that she didn't try.

'Do you want a tour?' he offered.

'I thought you'd never ask.'

He saw disaster, Cat saw potential.

'This house is going to be amazing,' she said as she walked through.

'It smells,' Dominic said. 'It didn't the last time I walked through it.'

'They'd have sprayed something.' Cat laughed. 'You've got damp...'

He knew that from the surveyor's report.

'Not much, though,' she said. 'And you could just get rid of this wall...'

'Sure you don't want to swap houses?'

'I'm very sure.' She smiled. 'I've got enough to do

at mine. I think I'm nesting. I keep washing things and folding things—it's really disconcerting.'

'Here.' He opened up a cupboard and pulled out a jumble of laundry. 'If you feel the need.'

'I shan't.'

Dinner was nice.

A lovely lamb roast he had made, better than the frozen meal Cat would have managed before falling into bed.

'I start nights tomorrow,' she said. 'Four of them, and then I'm out of that place.'

'Are you looking forward to stopping work?'

'Now I am,' she admitted. 'At first I wanted to work right up to the last minute but not now.'

She was now thirty-five weeks, soon to be thirty-six, and the thought of four weeks or more of this was daunting, to say the least.

'I got a cot,' Dominic said.

'I saw.'

'I'm quite sure you don't want to put up another one…'

Actually, she did.

'I know she won't be here much at first, but if she is, it's better she has somewhere she can sleep,' Dominic said. 'I'll get around to decorating it…' He looked at the woman who wasn't the woman he was supposed to have been doing this with and then he looked away.

'I'm really sorry you're hurting,' she said.

'It's not your fault. It just is what it is. Tomorrow's the anniversary of her funeral. There are just all these bloody dates in March…'

July was her horrible month.

This one would be as hard as the first for she'd be

telling Thomas that he was a big brother now. She'd be at her happiest and saddest at the very same time and she didn't quite know how she'd deal with it.

And, yes, perhaps then she could have told him but she found it impossible to share that most painful part of herself.

She didn't trust his reaction.

The death of a child was agony.

The death of a child, when it was suggested by the people you love most, even her own parents, that it might be a blessing, made it a place you chose not to go with others.

One wrong word from Dominic, she knew, would kill her inside.

'I'm going to go,' Cat said, because they were too new to be too close. 'Give you some time.'

He nodded and saw her downstairs and to the door.

'I want to be there, Cat.' He said what was on his mind. 'For the birth.'

'I know you do.'

'I'm not going to push it. I'm not going to demand or anything, I'm just telling you how I feel. I know I said that it didn't matter but it's starting to matter more and more to me. I don't think I'll be having any more children. I think this little one will be it.'

He went to touch her stomach and then remembered he couldn't, uninvited.

'You can,' Cat said, and he felt the little life when he was so cold today on the inside. Guilt dimmed a touch because how could this be wrong?

How could falling in love be wrong?

If, indeed, that was what he was doing.

'Go,' Dominic said. 'I need to think.'

And so too did she.

CHAPTER ELEVEN

'DOMINIC WANTS TO be at the birth,' Cat said as Gemma finished examining her.

'What do you want?' Gemma asked.

'I don't know,' she admitted. 'I wish we had longer to work this all out…'

'You'd have had longer if you'd told him sooner.'

'Yes, well, I'm sure Dominic is thinking the same. I nearly told him about Thomas,' Cat admitted. 'And I know that at some point I'll have to. I'm just missing him more and more with each passing day. I'm missing all the things he missed out on and I know if I tell Dominic I'm going to start howling.' She looked up and she'd thought Gemma might be cross but her lovely friend had tears in her eyes.

She hadn't just delivered Thomas; Gemma had been his godmother. She had held him and loved him when Mike hadn't. Nigel too had been there, cuddling her baby and not grimacing at his imperfections, the way even her own mother had.

'I'm here for you, Cat,' Gemma said. 'As I am for all my mothers. If you don't want Dominic to be there, you can just say no and I'll see that it's enforced. If he is going to be there, he has to know you're going to be very emotional.' She gave her a smile. 'You finish up work this week?'

Cat nodded. 'Yes, I'm back here tonight for four nights and then I hang up my stethoscope for six months.'

'Are you okay to work?' Gemma checked.

'Is there a problem?'

'No,' Gemma said. 'If you feel up to it, that's fine. Your blood pressure is normal, everything looks good. You just look tired, Cat. I mean, really tired. I'm more than happy to sign you off for these last few nights.'

It was incredibly tempting but Cat shook her head.

'I don't think it's just the pregnancy that's causing sleepless nights,' she admitted. 'I'll see these nights through and then I'll concentrate on Dominic and me and try to decide what the hell I'm going to do about the birth.'

'Come on, then,' Gemma said. 'Let's get out of here. You're my last patient today and I need to get home. Nigel's got his French class tonight.'

'He's still learning French?'

'He is.' Gemma smiled as she put on her jacket. 'You know how we had to cancel the honeymoon because of my blood pressure with the twins? Well, he's determined we're going to have one. Though why he has to learn French to take me to Paris is beyond me.'

Cat waited as Gemma handed all the files over to the receptionist and wished her goodnight and then popped in to thank the midwife who had worked with her in the antenatal clinic today. They were out in the corridor and heading for home when Gemma stopped walking and turned to her. 'Friends now,' she said.

'Of course.' Cat frowned and then realised she was about to get a lecture.

'Let him in.'

'I don't know how,' Cat said. 'It's not just me. He never talks about Heather, or rarely. All I know is that she had a brain tumour, or rather tumours.'

'Why don't the two of you go away for a couple of days and talk things out while you're still able to?' Gemma suggested. 'You're thirty-five weeks now. There's still time. The best day of Nigel's life was seeing the twins being born. He cut the cords, he held them first...'

'I know,' Cat said, and then she smiled. 'Dominic's parents asked him to film it.' She thought Gemma would laugh but she just rolled her eyes.

'Tell me about it! I had a father ask if I could move a little to the left the other week so he could get a better shot.' They both laughed for a moment but then they were serious.

'If Dominic is going to be there at the birth, then he has to know about Thomas. If he's in the delivery room, he needs to be told that this baby isn't your first. He'll find out as soon as you get there.'

Gemma was right, Cat knew as she got ready to go to work that night.

She had a shower to wake her up and, thank goodness, Cat thought, she no longer had to worry about straightening her hair.

She massaged conditioner into the ends and then stood there for a good ten minutes, letting the water wash over her, holding her big fat belly and loving the life within.

He didn't get to do that, Cat thought as she looked down at the little foot or knee that pressed her taut stomach out.

Dominic didn't get to enjoy this simple, beautiful treasure of a moment.

Perhaps they should go away for a couple of days.

Talk.

Or not.

Just find out a little more about each other before the baby arrived and they attempt to co-parent. They were pretty much on opposite shifts at work, so they didn't really see each other there. Dominic was busy trying to get the house sorted on his days off and Cat was busy trying to catch up on sleep on hers.

She got out of the shower and combed through her hair. Everything was an effort and she wondered if she shouldn't have taken Gemma up on her offer to take these last nights off.

Despite it having been a nice clear day, it was cool and drizzling outside and the house was cold. She shivered as she crossed the hall and went into her bedroom. Turning on the light, she let out a small curse as the light bulb popped. Yes, she loved her high ceilings but it would be foolish to attempt to get out a ladder in the dark and climb it.

She'd ask Greg to come and change it for her.

She needed a Nigel, Cat thought, and then sat on her bed in the dark and surprised herself by bursting into tears.

No, she didn't want her own Nigel and she didn't want her brother dragging himself here on his way home from work just to sort out her light.

She wanted Dominic.

Cat laughed at herself, sitting there crying over a light bulb, but it was the very simple things that rammed the big things home.

She wanted the ease of asking him and didn't know whether she could or not.

It was time to find out.

She used the flashlight on her phone to choose what to wear, knowing that when she got to work she would be changing into scrubs and flat shoes. For now she grabbed her boots. She pulled out a small cami and the now well-worn paisley dress and went downstairs to put them on.

As she went to pull on her boots she remembered the hell of getting them off, but she'd deal with that later. Right now she couldn't be bothered to trudge back upstairs and rummage through her wardrobe in the dark.

Stop crying, Cat told herself as she drove to work, but the tears kept trickling out.

What the hell is wrong with you? she scolded herself. She parked in her usual spot and walked into Emergency.

There was Dominic, coming out of a cubicle, and he gave her a brief nod.

A colleague's nod.

Well, what did you want him to do? Cat asked herself. *You told him to stay back at work.*

But then he called her back.

'How come you're here?' he checked. 'You're not due to start till ten.'

'Oh!' That's right, she was on ten till eight instead of the more usual nine till seven. Her brain was so scrambled she kept forgetting the littlest thing.

Not at work.

At work she was fine but in all things domestic and mundane her memory was like a sieve.

She didn't tell him she'd mixed up her shifts. Instead, she just shrugged and walked into the changing room.

There was a knock at the door and Cat frowned and opened it.

'You've been crying.'

'Yes.'

'Can I come in?'

'It might look a bit odd if you're seen in the female changing rooms.'

'Not really. I'm checking on a heavily pregnant colleague who's clearly been crying.'

Cat went and sat on the bench as he came in and he stood against the closed door, like a security guard.

'So?'

She sat there for a moment. 'Can't I just be having a bad day?'

'Of course,' he said. 'How did the appointment go?'

Ah, that's right, Cat thought, he was worried about the baby, not her. 'All good,' she said. 'Head down. Gemma offered to sign me off work but only because I'm tired. Everything else is fine.'

'But you're here.'

'Yes.'

'And tired and teary.'

'My light bulb blew in my bedroom,' she said.

'You didn't try to change it?'

'I'm not stupid,' she answered quickly. 'No, I didn't try to change it.'

She looked up at him and he smiled, then spoke. 'You won't ask, will you?'

'I don't know if I can.'

'For God's sake, Cat, do you really think you can't even ask me that?'

'I know I can but what happens next time one blows? I mean, do I call you…?'

'Well,' Dominic said, 'from my light-bulb experience, when one goes the others tend to follow, so for the
next few weeks I will be on light-bulb duty.'

'Thank you.'

'Give me your key and I'll go and do it on the way
home and then drop the key back to you when I come
on in the morning.'

She looked in her bag to get it.

'Is there anything else?'

Say it, Cat.

She took a big breath.

'Do you want to go away?'

'Sorry?' Dominic's eyes widened, clearly taken back
by her suggestion.

'Well, I'm finishing up this week and I presume
you'll get some days off. I thought it might be nice to
get away before the baby comes along, sort out a few
things…'

'Separate rooms?' he asked, and she laughed.

'I haven't thought that far ahead.'

'I have,' he said, and came over. She thought it was
to take the key but having pocketed it he bent down.

'What are you doing?' she asked as he lifted one of
her legs.

'Helping you off with your boots,' he said. 'And it's
no to separate rooms.'

God, he was sexy. He lifted one leg and his eyes never
left her face as, far more easily than she ever could, he
pulled the boot off. 'But you said—'

'I know that I did but, as you know, I'm prone to
changing my mind.' He had her other leg up and was
pulling off the other boot, and if there had been a lock
on the door he'd have turned it.

'I think,' Dominic said, 'we should celebrate the one uncomplicated thing about us and have loads and loads of sex and then, maybe then, it might be a bit easier to talk…'

'Easier?'

'I can't think very straight at the moment.'

'Sounds like a plan,' she said. He was holding one leg and she was possibly in the least flattering position. Her dress gaped open, and she glanced down and thanked the sock gods that she'd lost them in the washing machine and her feet were bare.

She could see his erection and she was just as ready.

'I'll book somewhere nice,' she said, but Dominic wasn't waiting till next week.

'I could always arrange to come in late to work tomorrow,' he said. 'I'm on with Andrew,' he clarified, because she was frowning. 'Maybe I might need a little lie-down in your bed after I exert myself changing your bulb.'

'I might be a bit tired in the morning.'

'You won't be too tired, Cat.'

No, she wouldn't be.

Exhausted perhaps but as his hand stroked her calf she imagined it higher and she needed that now.

His pager was going off and it was possibly just as well, or they might be found in the most compromising of situations and their cover would be well and truly blown.

He leant over and gave her a kiss, a rough, wet one, and then pulled her to standing. Her stomach was hard and his hands were wild with possession but then his pager went again.

'You need to go,' she said.

'I need to come.' He grinned and gave her the briefest kiss but then he did the right thing and went to work.

Cat was way too early for her shift.

She could have let Dominic go early but was quite sure that he'd say no. Anyway, the thought of sitting down for an hour was terribly appealing so she made a mug of tea, took herself off to the break room and started to watch the news.

Her tea remained untouched, and within two minutes of sitting down she was out for the count.

Dominic popped in once to speak to one of the nurses about a patient he had in cubicle two and saw her there, dozing, and the dark smudges under her eyes.

He felt a bastard that in a few minutes he'd be waking her so that he could go home.

'Hey, Dominic.' Julia popped her head around the door. 'We've got a guy found unconscious outside a pub. He's talking now, but very confused...'

'Okay, I'll come now.'

His patent was in cubicle five.

'Hello, sir,' he said. 'I'm Dominic, one of the doctors on tonight.'

He was told, far from politely, where he could go.

'Okay, what's your name?' Dominic asked.

It was a swear word, apparently.

Dominic saw that the patient's blood pressure was high and when he checked it again, it was even higher.

'Does he have any ID with him?' Dominic asked, and Julia gave a worried shake of her head.

'He's got no phone, no wallet, nothing. I think he might have been mugged.'

Dominic couldn't smell alcohol on the patient, and while he had all the signs of being a belligerent drunk,

Dominic was very relieved to have been called promptly. He was growing increasingly sure that this man was suffering from a serious head injury.

'Come on, sir...' He tried to calm the man down and then glanced over to Julia. 'Can you call Radiology for me? And Mr Dawson.'

The patient spat.

'And an anaesthetist. I think we'll have to sedate him.'

Thank God Cat wasn't dealing with this, Dominic thought as he blocked a punch from the irate man.

He just wanted her safe at home.

CHAPTER TWELVE

CAT WOKE AND stretched and went to take a sip of her tea, then pulled a face when she realised it was stone cold.

She gave a small yelp when she saw that it was a quarter past ten.

Yes, she might need help with a light bulb but she didn't need help with her shifts at work. She had a long drink of water in the kitchen and then walked quickly to the department, retying her long hair as she did so and trying to convince herself that she wasn't too tired to work.

She heard a raised voice coming from a cubicle and frowned as somebody told Dominic incredibly inappropriately just where he could go and to please get away from him. Cat had this sinking feeling in her stomach as she recognised the voice.

'Sir.' Dominic's voice was crisp and calm. 'I'm very concerned about you. I want you to lie down. I'm going to get you a scan now. I believe that you have a serious head injury.'

He looked up as Cat came into the cubicle and she realised he hadn't been covering for her. He'd been busy trying to calm a very agitated patient.

'Nigel.' Cat went over and she knew instantly just

how serious this was. She was grateful that Dominic had recognised this wasn't a drunken man. This was gentle, kind Nigel, who at first didn't recognise even her.

'Nigel, it's Cat, you're at the hospital.'

He told her what she could do with that information and then he frowned as the familiar face came near him and he started to cry, angry, frustrated tears.

'Cat, what the hell is going on?' Nigel begged. 'Cat, help me.'

'We're going to help you, Nigel,' she said, and he finally lay down. She glanced up at Dominic. 'What happened?'

'We think he was mugged,' Dominic told her. 'We're just taking him to be scanned now. You know him?'

Cat nodded. She was trying not to cry herself as she held Nigel's heaving shoulders. 'This is my friend Gemma's husband. Nigel Anderson,' Cat said. 'He's thirty-two.'

'Any medical history?'

'I don't think so,' Cat said. 'This is nothing like him.'

'I get that,' Dominic said, his voice grim.

Nigel had given up fighting now. He had finally lain down but then he suddenly sat up and started vomiting.

'I'm going to go with him,' Dominic said. 'The neurosurgeon and on-call anaesthetist are meeting me there.' Joe, the porter, was running over.

Everything was under control, Cat realised. No, Dominic hadn't been covering for her. He'd been busy trying to give Nigel the acute care he needed.

'Call his wife,' Dominic said as he headed off with the patient.

For a moment Cat stood there, simply stunned, but

then she went to the nurses' station and pulled out her own phone.

She had made many difficult calls in her life, it was part of her job, but this would be, by far, the hardest she had made.

'Hey, Gemma,' Cat said.

'Cat!' Gemma answered, and then she must have realised the time, or perhaps heard the distress in her friend's voice, even though Cat was doing her best to sound calm. 'Is everything okay?'

'Gemma…' She took a breath.

'Is the baby…?'

Oh, poor Gemma, she was busy putting her doctor's hat on and now Cat had to put on hers. 'I've just started my shift. Nigel's been brought in.'

Gemma gave a shocked gasp. 'He's at his French lesson.'

'He was found in the street, Gemma. He has a head injury and is having a CT scan now.'

'Is he unconscious?'

'No,' Cat said, but she didn't want to offer too much reassurance because Cat knew that Nigel's condition was serious. 'He's very confused, Gemma.'

'How confused?'

'He was agitated.'

'Yes, well, he hates hospitals.' Gemma pushed out a nervous laugh. 'He doesn't even like coming in to have lunch with me and—'

'Aggressive,' Cat broke in, and she knew that in saying that Gemma would understand just how serious this was.

'How long will the scan take?'

'Not long at all,' Cat said. Fortunately, they had one

of the newest machines and the results would be in very quickly, though she was quite sure that Nigel wouldn't be returning to the department. He would, she guessed, be going straight up to either Theatre or ICU. 'Can you get someone to watch the twins and come here?'

'I'll call my parents.'

Cat looked up and saw that the light that meant there was an emergency in the radiology department was going off.

'Ask Gill to come in and watch them,' Cat said, referring to Gemma's neighbour. 'Andy can drive you in. I have to go now, Gemma.'

She loathed leaving her friend hanging. She knew the panicked state she had placed her friend in, but there wasn't time to wait for Gemma's parents. They were slow and annoying and would ask five hundred questions before they even started to reach for their car keys.

She rushed to the radiology department but the anaesthetist had arrived already and was intubating Nigel.

'He's got a small subdural,' Dominic explained. 'He started seizing and has just blown a pupil. We're going to race him up to Theatre.'

Nigel was now sedated and Dominic told her that the neurosurgeon had gone ahead to scrub as they started to move Nigel out. It was calm and controlled, the only panic in the room internal, and Cat looked at her friend's husband, perhaps the kindest man she knew, lying there fighting for his life.

She held his hand as they ran along the corridor. 'I'll look after Gemma and the twins,' she said to him, and at the elevators she gave an unconscious Nigel a very brief kiss as they went to move him in. 'You look after you and get well.'

She was breathless from her brief run and wanted to sit down on the cold tiled floor and cry but instead she pushed herself to turn around and head back down.

She could only guess at what was about to greet her.

'Where is he?' Gemma was frantic, running towards Cat just as she got back to the emergency department. 'I've asked at Reception...'

'Come in here,' Cat said, leading her to a small interview room.

'I want to see him now.'

'He's in Theatre, Gemma.'

Her friend simply crumpled. She just lost it.

She stood there and folded over and it dawned on Cat she had never seen Gemma anything other than calm before. Even when there had been a scare about the twins Gemma had remained upbeat and positive. Now, though, she couldn't even make it to a chair and it was Cat who held her up.

Thankfully, Dominic, back from taking Nigel to Theatre, came in and took over. He explained what was going on.

'They're operating on him now. He has a small subdural haematoma.' Dominic explained that Nigel was bleeding on his brain and that he had been rushed to Theatre to evacuate the bleed and relieve the pressure that was building. 'Mr Dawson is the one doing the surgery and he's one of the best.'

'He's brilliant,' Cat said.

'I don't understand what happened, though,' Gemma wept. 'He was at his French class.'

'It would seem he got jumped,' Dominic said. 'He had no wallet with him, no phone or ID. A passer-by found him lying down outside a pub. Luckily they called for an ambulance instead of just assuming he was drunk.'

'Nigel doesn't drink.'

'When he arrived here he was confused, he said that he needed to get home. His blood pressure was high and I arranged for an urgent CT scan. At that point Cat came on duty and of course she knew who he was. It all happened that quickly. He was drowsy during the CT and only at the last minute did he become unconscious.'

All poor Gemma could do now was wait.

'Cat will go with you to wait,' Dominic said, and Cat gave a grateful nod.

It was only as she walked out of the department that she started to realise she wouldn't be coming back to work until she was a mother.

Just as Nigel and Gemma had dropped everything for her when she'd had Thomas, it was time for Cat to do the same.

'Will you speak with Andrew and explain I won't be able to come in?' Cat said to Dominic.

'Of course,' he said. 'Just take care of your friend.'

She did.

It was the longest night.

Nigel came through Theatre and Mr Dawson was cautiously optimistic but he explained that Nigel would remain in an induced coma for the next forty-eight hours at least.

'I can't believe someone would do this for a wallet.' Gemma sat, holding his hand. 'He's got two little boys who need him. I need him.'

And Cat, who had sworn she'd never need anybody, knew what she meant.

She needed the breakfast that Dominic bought them

when he dropped in in the morning, having finished his shift.

She needed his support and she got it.

Her shifts were covered, Gemma's parents moved in to take over the twins and Cat went home at lunchtime and packed a bag for herself, then went to Gemma's and did the same for her friend.

When she got back to the hospital, they holed up as the world went on.

Just as Thomas had never been left alone, she and Gemma took turns to sit by Nigel's bed while the other slept. Even when his parents and brother visited, either Cat or Gemma were there.

Gemma trusted Cat to notice things she wasn't sure anyone else would, and it was the only way she'd consider getting some rest herself.

'How is he?' Dominic came into Cat's line of vision late on the second afternoon.

'The same,' Cat said. 'It's just a matter of waiting.'

'How's Gemma?'

'She's just gone home to check in on the twins. She's all upbeat and positive now. She's talking as if he's just had his wisdom teeth out.'

'How are you?'

Cat shrugged.

'Are you getting any sleep?'

'Some. Gemma and I have taken over one of the on-call rooms.' She looked up and smiled as her friend came back and Dominic spoke for a moment with Gemma and then left.

'How were the twins?' Cat asked.

'Teary and clingy. Mum and Dad keep asking when

I'll be back. I know that the twins are too much for them but what else can I do?'

'I can look after them,' Cat offered.

'I need you here, though.'

'Have you managed to get hold of your sister?' Cat asked. Gemma's sister was in the army and not immediately accessible.

'Finally, and she's asking for urgent leave and should be back in a couple of days.'

It was another long night and as Gemma slept through the morning part of it Cat sat with Nigel.

They were going to try to extubate him later and it was scary, to say the least.

'You have to be okay, Nigel,' Cat said. 'Your family needs you.'

'They do,' Gemma said, and Cat looked up and smiled at her friend. 'Thanks for being here.'

'Where else would I be?'

'And I must thank Dominic.'

'For what?'

'Covering all your shifts, bringing me decent coffee. He's gorgeous,' Gemma said, and took her seat by Nigel. 'I don't blame him for not saying he's a widower.' She took Nigel's hand. 'See, Nigel, you have to get well or I'm going to be getting loads of offers for sympathy sex…seriously,' she said to her comatose husband. 'I'll have all the single dads lining up to fix the car or the leaky roof. I'll have to fend them off.' She turned to Cat and smiled. 'Go and have a sleep. I'm going to talk dirty to my husband and remind him of all he'll be missing out on if he dares to leave.'

Cat slept.

The very second she lay down in the on-call room

she fell asleep and awoke with a jolt only when the door opened and there was Dominic.

'What's happened?'

'Good news, well, cautiously good.' He was holding a large mug and he waited for her to sit up, which was rather difficult to achieve, and then he handed it to her and brought her up to date.

'He was fighting the tube and they've extubated him.'

'Is he speaking?'

'No.'

'Has he opened his eyes?'

'No, but he responds to voices and is moving all limbs.'

'I should go…' Cat went to get out of the bed but he took her shoulder and pushed her back.

'No, no. Gemma's in with him. I've just come from speaking with her. Her mum's not well. Well, she's got a cold…'

'They're useless,' Cat hissed.

'I said that you'd go and watch the twins.'

'What did Gemma say?'

'She was relieved, I think.'

Cat let out her own sigh of relief. If Gemma was happy for her to go, then, really, things must be starting to look better for Nigel.

'I thought he was going to die,' she admitted.

'I know you did.'

For the past couple of days, since the moment she'd heard Nigel swearing and cursing, she had honestly thought he would die, or that the Nigel she'd known was gone.

Now there was hope that he was on his way back.

'Have your tea, then I'll drive you. There's no need to rush.'

'Are you working?'

'Just till five. Hamish worked last night and again tonight. I'm back in at nine tomorrow, but I can take half an hour to drop you at Gemma's.'

Cat nodded. She was way too tired to drive.

He sat on the edge of the bed and she looked at him—unshaven and exhausted—and she could see the strain in his features, and whether or not she was allowed to ask, she did.

'Is this hard on you too?' They both knew she was referring to his late wife.

'Yep.' He took a drink of her tea and then handed it back to her.

'Heather ended up in ICU and she hated me for it. She never said it, of course, but it was something she dreaded and not how she wanted it to be...' He didn't tell her any more and Cat sat there, not feeling slighted in the least. The sharing part was so incredibly hard at times. They'd been sort of thrust on each other by the baby.

That hurt Cat.

It was a niggle in her heart, a wound that gnawed.

That day when she'd thought he was cheating, instead of correcting her he had simply let her go—that was how much she had meant to him then, which made it hard to confide in him now.

'I'm going to see Nigel,' she said, 'and get Gemma's keys and things.' She looked around the room—in two days she'd accumulated quite a lot of stuff. Toiletries, clothes, towels...

'I'll pack it up,' he offered.

'Thanks.'

She buzzed and was let into ICU, where Gemma sat with Nigel's mum, but she stood up and gave Cat a hug.

'How is he?' Cat asked.

'Well, he didn't exactly open his eyes but he did sort of screw them up when I spoke to him,' Gemma said. 'He knows we're all here.'

Cat went over and gave Nigel a kiss. 'Hurry up and wake up,' she whispered into his ear, 'or she'll start talking dirty to you again.'

'He moved his eyes,' Gemma said. 'What did you just say?'

Cat laughed but she gave Nigel's hand a big squeeze. 'You keep getting better, okay?' She turned to her friend. 'Right, I'll go and watch the twins…'

'I feel awful, asking,' Gemma said, because she could see how exhausted Cat was.

'Please, don't,' Cat said.

'My sister will be here tomorrow, I hope.'

'It's fine. Just stay with Nigel and don't worry about anything else.' She smiled at Nigel's mum and headed out to where Dominic was waiting for her.

'How old are the twins?' Dominic asked as they walked to his car.

'Two,' Cat said.

'Good luck!' He smiled.

It felt strange, getting into a car with him again.

It was a different car from the one in Spain but there were coffee cups and papers and she looked around for a moment, remembering him taking her to Collserola and that morning.

She hadn't known him then.

She didn't really know him much better now.

Maybe Dominic was thinking the same thing, because

he turned on the engine and reversed out of his parking space and, just when she was least expecting him to, he told her about the very moment his world had fallen apart, the split second that he'd known everything was about to change.

CHAPTER THIRTEEN

'HEATHER WAS A VET,' Dominic said, and Cat turned and looked at him but didn't respond, and he remembered that he liked that about her—she didn't butt in or say unnecessary words.

'We met at university. She was crazy about animals. Horses, dogs, cats, cows…but mainly horses. She was a staunch vegetarian. She'd given up trying to get me to be one. Almost. Really, I think she would have been vegan by now.'

Still, Cat said nothing.

'We went out for years before we got engaged and it was a couple of years after that before we got married. I knew her very well, that's the point I'm making.'

He turned briefly and Cat nodded.

'One night she got up and, I don't know why, I came downstairs and I found her eating a steak sandwich. It was one of my steaks that I'd cooked and was taking for lunch the next day.' He managed a small laugh at the odd detail, yet it had been so very strange, just so completely out of character that he could remember to this day his confusion. 'Heather got all cross when I pointed out that she was eating steak, and said she was starving and she'd just fancied it and when she saw it in the fridge she couldn't resist it. I got that but it was bizarre, so unlike Heather. I thought maybe she had some sort of iron deficiency, or even that she was pregnant, perhaps. It was just a tiny thing that didn't make sense but then there started to be more and more tiny things. A couple of days later we had an argument that came from nowhere. She was furious about something and to this day I can't remember how it started. I just know that I had never seen her more angry. I knew then there was something very wrong.'

He gave a wry smile. 'It's very hard to say in the middle of an argument that I thought there might be something wrong with her... It would be like asking if she'd got PMT. But I knew that I wasn't arguing with her. I could reason with Heather but she was suddenly like a stranger. Anyway, she huffed off to bed and went for a sleep and woke up and was back to being Heather.'

The satnav announced they had reached their destination and Cat looked up and realised they were outside Gemma's, but she made no move to go in.

He'd told her more than she needed to know, but it was what he'd needed to tell her, so she understood.

'The row scared me and it must have scared her enough that she went to a doctor, who took her seriously. She called me at work and said she was about to have a head CT and would I come down.' He turned and looked at Cat. 'I knew,' Dominic said. 'I knew even before she had the scan and so did Heather. We went from normal to dying in one week.'

'No treatment?'

'Chemo,' Dominic said. 'But it was dire and really with little prospect, so after four rounds she pulled the plug. She always said we treated animals with more dignity than humans and she was very clear about what she wanted.'

Bizarrely, Cat thought, even though she wanted to know, she also wanted to tell him to stop.

She wanted to put up her hand and say, 'She died, I get it. I don't need the details. I cannot bear your pain,' but she sat there and looked at him and there wasn't a tear on his face, just a depth in his voice, and she understood now his quip about Gordon.

He wasn't mean at all—he was in agony and trying to hold on as he did what he had to.

Talk.

'Well,' Dominic said, and he reminded her a bit of Gemma, chatting away, as if she wasn't dying inside. 'We went on holiday, we thought we had a couple of months' grace. She wanted to go to Stonehenge. I don't know if it was a tumour making her wacky or just the way people go when they're dying—you know, the universe, God and living in the moment—but Heather got obsessed with sunrises. We were staying in a little cottage and I woke up one morning and she wasn't in bed. At first I thought she must have gone to get a drink or to the toilet but then I went looking for her. The front door was open. I drove around the streets and I met some guy who said he'd seen a woman being taken off in an ambulance...' He stopped talking then because there was a tap at the window and it was Gemma's mother, so cheery that the cavalry had arrived and she could go home.

Cat pressed open the window.

'Not now!' she snapped, and closed it again. 'Sorry about that,' she said to Dominic as Gemma's mum did an indignant, affronted walk back inside.

'The ambulance...' Cat said, and Dominic nodded, very glad Cat had told the woman to go. He just had to tell this story all in one hit.

'I called the local emergency department as I drove there but I never told them that she didn't want any active resuscitation.' He took a very big breath and his eyes silently begged her to say something.

'I doubt they'd have listened to someone calling in over the phone. I wouldn't have,' Cat said. 'I mean, I'd have listened and taken it in, but...' She shook her head.

'I didn't even tell them, though. I still feel like I let her down there.'

'You just weren't ready for her to die.'

'No, but I wish for her sake she had that morning. She got another three weeks and they were hell.' He gave her a grim smile. 'I could have told you all this at that lunch, nailed you to a wall like Gordon did...'

'You couldn't, though,' Cat said. 'I get why.'

Did she say it now?

Did she say, 'Well, guess what happened to me!'

Of course she couldn't. Anyway, Gemma's dad was heading towards them.

'I want to tell him to...' Dominic said, and that made her smile.

'So do I,' Cat said. 'But we won't.'

'No, we won't. I'm going to go back to work,' Dominic said. 'You're going to look after the twins and when you have time I'd like you to look up somewhere amazing for us to escape to the very second Nigel gets the all-clear.'

'I shall.'

'Go,' he said, 'and don't give me *that* look.'

'I shan't,' she said, and gave him a kiss on the cheek instead and then headed inside.

'Sorry about that.' Cat smiled at Gemma's very offended mum. 'That was a colleague from work and he'd just had some difficult news.'

Gemma's parents were already putting on their coats.

Cat soon understood that possibly it wasn't because she'd caused offence that they practically ran out of the house.

Two two-year-olds missing their parents and their routines.

Two two-year-olds who threw down their sandwiches because they didn't know how to say they liked them cut in squares, not triangles.

Two two-year-olds who were like wriggling eels in the bath as Cat knelt on the floor beside them that night.

Yes, they *all* needed Nigel, Cat thought as she got them into pyjamas and started to shepherd them down the stairs for some milk.

She wasn't a very good shepherd. One would go down, the other up, and she was too aching to carry them again.

'Daddy!' Rory squealed, when the key turned in the door.

'Mummy!' Marcus shouted, and the three of them stood there in slightly stunned surprise as Gemma came through the door.

'Gemma!'

Cat's heart just about stopped in terror as the twins thundered down the stairs and into their mum's arms. Gemma burst into tears and dropped to her knees and cuddled them.

'Is he...?'

'He's fine!' Dominic came in, carrying an awful lot of bags, only to look up and see Cat frozen on the stairs.

'Sorry,' Gemma said. 'I didn't meant to scare you. I just lost it when I saw the boys.'

'I wasn't expecting you,' she managed.

'Nigel told me to come and get some rest.'

'He's talking?'

'A bit.' Gemma nodded. 'Really, he's asleep most of the time but he's managing a few words and they've moved him out of Intensive Care.' Gemma, after her little meltdown, was trying to sound all calm in front of the boys but Cat could hear the wobble in her friend's voice. 'It's all looking good.'

'Thank God.'

'My sister should be here soon,' Gemma said. 'She's in a taxi on her way from the airport, so I thought I'd have a night to settle these two a bit before I head back there again.'

Cat stayed and helped her with the boys and Dominic sat half-asleep in a chair. Finally the twins looked as if they might be ready to crash.

Gemma and Cat carried them up and put them in their little beds and stood watching them for a while.

'I don't know how I could do this without Nigel,' Gemma said.

'Well, you're not going to have to find out.'

They went back down the stairs and Gemma told Cat to go home.

'You'll call me if you need me, though,' Cat said, her hands on her back, trying to stretch her spine.

'I shall, but once Angela gets here I should be fine. Thank you so much, Cat, and you too, Dominic.' As they went to head out Gemma called into the night, 'You'll call me if you need me, won't you, Cat?'

'I shan't be needing you for a while yet.' Cat laughed but Dominic saw the slight frown on Gemma's face.

'Cat…' Gemma strode towards them. 'You and Dominic need to sort this out.'

'Gemma!' Cat warned.

'No!' Gemma was practically shouting. Wrung out, emotional, she just spilled out her thoughts right there on the street. 'I just about lost my husband, and I'm telling you that there are moments in life that you can never get back, and if you don't let him in—'

'Gemma!' Cat broke in. 'We've got this, okay?'

'Well, make sure you have,' Gemma said, 'because life changes in a second.'

Then she burst into tears again and Cat and Dominic saw her back to the house.

'Sorry, sorry,' she kept saying.

'It's fine.'

Cat just about drooped in relief when she saw the taxi pull up and Angela get out.

Finally they got into the car and Cat let out a tense breath. 'God…'

'She's upset, she's tired,' Dominic said.

'She's interfering.'

And she knew she had to talk to him.

Just not tonight.

'Are you coming in?' she asked as they pulled up at her house.

'Well, if I do, it's for the night,' he warned, 'but that's only because if I sit down I won't get up again.'

'And me.'

'No wild sex,' he said. 'Because I don't want you to be disappointed.'

'You're safe.'

They were so tired they didn't even bother going through the motions of sitting down or making a drink. Instead, they scaled the stairs as if it were Everest.

'Is your back sore?'

'It's killing me,' Cat said. 'The twins wanted to be carried all the time, they were so clingy...'

They got to the bedroom and she went to turn on the light but, of course, it didn't work.

'You had one job to do,' she said, and they both laughed.

It would keep.

She went for a shower and came back into her dark bedroom, where Dominic was already in bed. The street-light cast a slight orange glow and it was nice, so nice, to drop her towel and to get into her own bed, and she let out a lovely moan.

'That feels good,' she said.

'You have a very comfortable bed,' he commented.

'I know.' She sighed. Only, it didn't feel very comfortable tonight. She lay on her back and then turned and faced away from him.

'Rub my back.'

'I'm too tired,' he said, but he rolled over and obliged.

It wasn't sexual. It was intimate and blissful.

His fingers got right into the ache at the bottom of her spine and then moved up to the tight shoulders and then into her neck, and he remembered the spine that had greeted him on the day they'd met. He spoiled the thoughtful massage thing by getting a huge erection.

Cat kept feeling it, even as she tried to pretend not

to notice the brush of it against the back of her thigh now and then.

Then it stopped being a massage and his mouth came onto her shoulders and she closed her eyes at the bliss.

Not too tired at all, as it turned out.

His fingers came around the front as he kissed her neck and explored breasts that were twice as large as the last time he'd felt them.

He examined the changes. The thick, ripe nipples and then down to the taut swell of her naked stomach, and he got to feel the baby move and kick into his palm. It was a treasured moment.

Then his hand moved down to the curve of fuller hips and Cat let out a moan.

She wasn't too tired to move; she simply didn't want to. She liked it that all she had to do was nudge her bottom back a fraction to deliver her consent and he slipped in and his own moan told her it was bliss for him as he was drawn into that wet warmth.

'When I think of all those condoms I wasted on you,' Dominic said. They had deep, lazy sex and she turned her head and their tongues mingled for a very long moment. Then he got back to the easy task of making her come.

Very easy, because with each measured thrust she felt him tense more, and pressing back on him, giving in to him, the pleasure meant Cat was over and about to be done with. He came very deep inside her and she gripped him back and dragged out more. All tension left them.

'Now I'm comfortable,' Cat said.

'And me.'

They'd worked hard these past days for that long sleep.

But Dominic woke, as he once used to, just before sunrise.

He hadn't done that in months.

On this morning, though, Cat's long exhalation of breath and stirring of discomfort moved him from deeply asleep to half-awake and he lay there, feeling her stomach, which had been hard beneath his hand, soften.

Okay.

Light was starting to filter into the bedroom as he recalled Gemma's slightly odd demand that Cat ring her if needed, and he knew he was going to be a father today.

He already was, he thought.

From the moment in Oliver's when Cat had told him they were having a daughter he had become a father in his mind.

Soon he'd officially be one.

Thin rays started to stretch and strengthen and the black turned to grey and the room started to emerge. A chest of drawers, a large bookshelf and then grey dispersed and colour came in.

It was like waking up in some enchanted woodland.

There were trees, flowers, knotted wooden trunks and branches holding nests, and he half expected ivy to sneak across the bed and coil around them. He felt Cat's stomach tighten again beneath his hand and she stirred in discomfort.

'I lied to you,' he said.

Cat woke to those words and his kiss on her shoulder. 'When?'

'The second time we met,' Dominic admitted. 'I

didn't just happen to see the maternity leave position. I was already thinking of moving to London.'

'Not Spain?' Cat's brain was all foggy.

'I was thinking of moving to Spain, I almost was moving to Spain, but I couldn't quite get that weekend out of my head and I was wondering, before I cut all ties here, whether it might be worth...'

Cat lay there in silence as he continued.

'I regretted how it ended and I wondered if we stood a chance. I kept waiting to get over you but I didn't so I was looking at jobs in London. I was thinking of taking a temporary one before I moved to Spain and catching up with you to see...'

'See what?'

'If what we'd found that weekend still existed.'

Cat felt his hand stroking her stomach and his lovely long body melded with hers and, yes, what they'd found still existed.

'I haven't been honest with you,' Cat said, but tears tripped her words and he kissed the back of her head.

'That's okay,' Dominic said. 'You were stepping into my hotel room, not a confessional.'

Her stomach tightened and Cat stretched her legs out because it hurt, not just in her stomach but her back too and right down to her toes. 'Oh...' Cat breathed her way out of it. 'I think...'

'You are,' Dominic said. Her contractions were coming about five minutes apart.

'It's too soon.'

'You're thirty-six weeks, it's fine.'

'I mean, it's too soon for us,' she said, and started to cry. 'I was going to talk to you. I wanted to tell you things when we went away.'

'We've got ages to talk,' Dominic said. 'First labours take…' And he stopped then, halted at his own presumption as realisation hit.

'Second.'

She started to really cry.

It wasn't supposed to be like this.

They should be sitting in some lovely mansion, having afternoon tea, and she would be selecting a cupcake and mention Thomas, and Mike, oh, so casually and bypass the agony it had been. Instead, her stomach was in spasm and her knees were coming up and, ready or not, this baby was coming today.

'I want a bath,' she said. 'Oh, my God, we had sex…'

She was frantic for her bath and to arrive all clean and shiny in the labour ward.

No, it wasn't supposed to be like this.

He ran the bath, she rang the hospital and it was just as well she'd told him because the tired midwife asked if it was her first.

'No, it's my second.'

Dominic closed his eyes as he checked the water and then Cat came in.

'They said to come straight in.'

'Have your bath,' Dominic said. 'Your waters haven't broken…'

He helped her in and she got another contraction and from the strength and speed of them now she wasn't going to be sitting in the bath for very long. She looked at Dominic sitting on the toilet lid and there would be no Gemma delivering her. It would be a stranger. She had no choice but to confess how scared she was today.

And so she told him a little, about the happy person

she had once been and the baby and husband-to-be she'd had, and he sat, as she had for him, quietly.

She told him about the ultrasound and the Edwards syndrome and he didn't start demanding if she'd been thoroughly tested this time around, he just sat. And he didn't insist that it was unlikely to happen again and that his brilliant sperm couldn't possibly be at fault, he just sat.

'Thomas,' Cat said. 'Thomas Gregory Hayes.'

And he wanted to put his hand up and tell her to stop. *You had a baby, I get it.*

But they had to share themselves.

'Thomas, because I love the name. Gregory, after my brother, and Hayes because I didn't want Mike to be attached to him. He didn't want him…'

And still he sat there as Cat, angry, pregnant, lay in the bathtub.

'He's in the drawer.'

Dominic gave a slightly startled look as if she was telling him to go and fetch a dead baby or an urn of ashes from her bedside.

'His photo,' Cat said.

He went and fetched it and came back.

And, no, it wasn't how it was supposed to be. Where were her cupcakes, where was her cup of tea and something to distract her as he looked closely at her child.

Dominic sat on the loo seat as she breathed through another contraction, and when she finally opened her eyes it was to see the man who had told her with little emotion about the death of his wife crying.

He did not recoil in horror. He was looking at her son and then he looked at her and finally, only then, he spoke.

'A few weeks ago I couldn't imagine having a baby and now I'm sitting here trying to imagine how I'd feel if I lost one.'

Oh, my God! Cat was stunned. *He's crying!*

'Sorry, Cat.'

'It's fine.'

'No, I'm really sorry. I should be…'

What?

Stronger?

A touch more dismissive?

That he cried for her son and her loss meant the world.

'I wanted to get to twenty-five weeks,' Cat said. 'And then…' She told the truth. 'I didn't trust you enough to tell you about him.'

'I understand why you didn't.'

They trusted each other now. Their hearts always had but finally their minds had caught up.

'We need to get to the hospital,' she said, and as she stood her waters broke.

'Some one-night stand you turned out to be,' he said as he helped her out of the bath.

A drive that took twenty minutes at night was mark-edly longer at 7:00 a.m. and Cat was having visions of delivering at the kerb when thankfully the hospital came into view.

'Argh, I'm supposed to be working,' Dominic said, and made a very rapid call but then started to laugh.

'Poor Julia, she's really confused now. I just told her my partner's about to deliver a baby.'

They walked down the long corridor and gathered a few double takes along the way as some of the staff saw that snooty Cat was in her dressing gown *and* with the new sexy doctor.

That this was Cat's second pregnancy was on her chart, mentioned in every phone call made, and then the lovely doctor who came asked about Thomas as he went through Cat's notes.

'You had him at twenty-five weeks?'

Cat nodded.

'Normal vaginal delivery?'

'Yes,' Cat said. 'Well, it didn't feel very normal at the time.'

'Okay, I'm just going to take a look…' The doctor's voice trailed off as the doors opened and Gemma walked in.

'Thanks, Chand.' She smiled. 'This special delivery is mine.' And then she gave Cat a very severe frown. 'I told you to call me…'

'So you did,' Cat said. 'How did you find out I was here?'

'I told the ward that if you came in they were to let me know.'

'You knew I was going to have her.'

'Sort of,' Gemma said. 'But I was here anyway.' She started to pull on gloves. 'I couldn't sleep, I wanted to see Nigel.' Gemma looked over at Dominic and tested the water. 'Can you step out while I examine her, please?'

'He's staying.'

'I can have him removed.' Gemma grinned, delighted by the turn of events.

'There's no need for that,' Cat said.

'Has she finally told you?' Gemma asked, looking up at Cat's puffy face.

'Yep.'

'And so you know that this going to be very emotional for her,' Gemma checked. 'I mean, above and beyond.'

'I do.'

'How's Nigel?' Cat asked as Gemma pulled the sheet back.

'Talking,' Gemma said. 'He knows who I am, he knows the year we're in if not the month…he's doing really well,' she said as she examined her friend. 'As are you.'

Cat found out then that she was already fully dilated.

'Can you give me a push…?'

'I don't want to push.'

Oh, maybe she did.

'I'm not ready to push.'

'Yes, Cat, you are,' Gemma said, and nodded to the midwife, who was busily getting equipment out.

'Come on, Cat,' Gemma urged, when she lay there, fighting her own body and refusing to bear down.

'I can't.' She was starting to lose it. The lights were too bright, the voices too loud, and she'd never known pain like it. She wanted ten minutes to get used to the idea that her baby was on the way and when Gemma told her to push, right down into her bottom, she told her just what she could do with that notion.

'Come on, Cat…' Gemma's voice, Cat noticed for the first time, was really annoying. 'You can do this…'

'I can't,' she said.

She was scared to push, as scared as she had been the last time, but then Dominic spoke.

'Yes, you can,' he said, and she was about to argue when his lovely deep voice spoke on. 'You've done this before, Cat, you know what to do.'

He let Thomas in.

All the fear she'd had the last time, fear she still held on to, left, and she started to push her baby into the world.

She'd done this before, she had been a mother for seven years, just a lost one, but now the world was turning that around.

Gemma moved one leg back and Dominic the other. 'Just getting a better angle for the live-stream to my parents,' Dominic said, and that made her laugh.

'Come on, Cat...' Gemma said, and her voice wasn't annoying any more. 'Hold it...'

And there was a silence, a pause, and then she arrived. A little scrawny thing, very red and with a mass of black hair, she lay on Cat's stomach too stunned to cry, her little mouth open, her eyes screwed closed.

'Hey, kitten,' Dominic said.

'Don't,' Cat said. 'That's cheesy...'

But Cat and Dominic's kitten she was. Tiny and mewing and there, ready or not.

Dominic cut the cord and Cat just lay there, gazing down at her tiny, perfect baby and her funny-shaped head, little dark red lips. She had never been happier or sadder at the same time, because this was how it should be.

'It's okay...' Gemma was there when Cat folded. She'd known it was coming and she wrapped up her daughter and handed her to her dad, who had to juggle the two loves of his life. One arm full of baby, the other full of Cat as she cried for Thomas.

It was such a cry, one she had been dreading and the reason she hadn't wanted him near her for the birth. The midwife took away their daughter for a little while and

Gemma disappeared and she was alone with her heart and with him until the grief that would be present for ever faded enough to let life in.

Somehow they coexisted.

'Thank God I told you,' Cat said, because she couldn't imagine him not being here, not just for himself or their baby but for her.

'That's how I felt when I told you,' he admitted. 'Just relief.'

'Where is she?' Cat asked, when she peered out from the shield he had provided and wanted her little girl.

'Do you want her back in?'

She did.

Cat fed her for the first time and it soothed not just the baby but the baby's mum.

The midwife left and Gemma went to write up her notes and then it was the three of them.

'What are we going to call her?' Cat asked.

'I've no idea,' Dominic said.

For now she was Baby Hayes.

He didn't much like that.

When she finished feeding Cat handed their little daughter to her dad and she watched as he held her. She saw his expression falter and she knew that Heather was on his mind.

It didn't threaten her, not a bit. She knew he wasn't thinking that he wished Cat was Heather, more that Heather should have got to know this bliss.

'She'd be so proud of you,' Cat said, and let the other love in his life in, just as he had with Thomas.

'She would be,' he agreed, because Heather had known what a closed-off bastard he was and how long it had taken him to even commit to getting engaged. Yet here he was a dad and in love, not just with his baby but with the woman who'd given birth to her. Yes, she'd be so proud of him for pushing through, for showing up to each day and having the guts to fall in love again while knowing more than most just how much it could hurt.

Gemma came back in for a last-minute check before she headed back to visit Nigel.

'She's beautiful,' Gemma said. 'Just so gorgeous. I think I need to have another baby.'

'Don't tell Nigel that yet.' Cat smiled as her best friend got to hold her tiny daughter. 'You want to keep his blood pressure down.'

'I went over and told him you'd had a little girl and he smiled and said, "That's good." I'm starting to really think that he'll be okay.'

'Go and be with him,' Cat said. 'Thank you for being here today.'

'I couldn't not be,' Gemma said. 'I'm hardly going to miss out on delivering my own goddaughter…'

'Er…Gemma…' Cat said, and looked at Dominic. 'We haven't quite got around to discussing religion yet.'

'I don't even know how old Cat is,' Dominic said, and peered at Cat's observation chart and saw her date of birth. 'You're two years older than me!'

'Oh.' Gemma pouted, her doctor's hat clearly well and truly off. 'Well, bear me in mind when you do get around to it.'

'Tell you what,' Dominic said, 'if you can't be godmother, how about you be bridesmaid?'

'Really?' Gemma beamed.

'Well, I have to ask her,' Dominic said, 'and then she has to say yes…'

'You'd better,' Gemma said, and handed back the baby, and when she'd gone Cat turned to Dominic.

'You don't have to marry me.'

'I know that I don't but I want to.'

'She can have your surname if that's what you want.' But, no, from the way Dominic was looking at her Cat was starting to realise that he loved her.

'I want you to have my name.'

'Not professionally, though,' Cat checked.

'Oh, yes,' Dominic said. 'I want my name on everything.'

'You are so completely not my type.'

'Well, you're not mine either,' he admitted. 'You stood outside that elevator in your lovely floaty dress, with your girlie curly hair, all blushing, shy and nervous...'

'Is that your type?'

'It was for a while.'

'Well, for your information, I wasn't shy and I wasn't nervous.'

'I know that now,' he said. 'You were turned on.' But then he was the most serious he had ever been. 'I never thought I'd do this again, Cat. I never thought I could get so lucky twice, but I have. So you're going to marry me, Gemma's going to be the bridesmaid and that's settled. Now all we have to do is choose a name for our baby.'

It was the best day ever.

And made more so by Dominic going out while Cat slept at lunchtime and returning with a very big ring. He then scratched out 'Baby Hayes' and changed it to 'Baby Edwards'.

'I don't think she's old enough to know,' Cat said.

'I know.'

They still couldn't decide on her name.

Her parents came, and then Greg and his wife and children.

A little later in the afternoon Eloisa was dressed in a little Spanish sleepsuit that had been bought a few weeks ago and had been sent along with a letter without judgment, just offering love.

And so they did live-stream with his barking-mad parents, though thankfully not the birth, and showed off their daughter to them and his sister, Kelly, as well as Cat's ring.

'She's beautiful,' Anna said.

'I know.' Dominic smiled. 'I think she looks like me.'

'I was talking about Cat!'

They were gorgeous!

And then a rather bemused Andrew popped in for a visit and did a double take when he saw Dominic sitting there by the bed and holding Cat's hand.

'I thought it was just a coincidence that your partner had gone into labour, Dominic. Then the rumours started flying and it would seem that they're true.' He just stood there bemused. 'You two?'

'Yep,' Dominic said.

'But why did you go to such lengths to hide it? You could have said at the interview.' Andrew frowned. 'Cat, you know it wouldn't have affected his chance at the role.'

Cat just smiled and chose not to tell Andrew that even she hadn't known he'd applied for the job and Dominic decided not to reveal he hadn't known for sure then if it was even his baby.

'I wonder,' Dominic said, when Andrew had left,

'what he'd have to say if he knew just what went on at the conference that the department sent you to.'

It was exhausting, being so happy.

So much so that when she'd fed her tiny baby again and put her down for a sleep Cat chose to take the midwife's advice to rest when the baby did. She didn't even notice that Dominic left, but awoke to the sound of the meals trolley. It rolled past her door.

'You're nil by mouth,' the midwife said, when Cat buzzed her to ask where her food was.

'Why?' Cat asked, but the midwife had gone.

She was starving and there was absolutely no reason for her to be nil by mouth, but then the midwife came back smiling, holding the door for Dominic, who was carrying a tray along with a big bucket holding champagne.

'Paella.' Cat licked her lips as he removed the lid and she saw the saffron rice and gorgeous seafood.

'Oh, and coffee…' She picked up the cup and inhaled. 'You remembered.'

'Of course,' Dominic said. 'I might not know an awful lot about you but I remember the little I do.'

Dinner in bed, her baby sleeping by her side and Dominic pouring champagne. It was time to get to know each other a whole lot more.

From the luxurious place of love.

EPILOGUE

They were possibly the most frazzled bride- and groom-to-be ever.

On the plane the five of them took up a full aisle.

There was Cat on one end, Dominic on the other, Eloisa in her bassinet and Rory and Marcus creating havoc between them.

Nigel and Gemma were on a delayed honeymoon and were, about now, taking a leisurely drive from Paris to Barcelona. They would be there to meet them at the airport.

'Did you pack your pills?' Dominic checked, when they finally got off the plane. 'Because I'm not coming near you otherwise.'

'Oh, yes.' Cat nodded, very happy to have only one child.

The twins were adorable but, absolutely, Dominic agreed, they all needed Nigel.

And there he was with Gemma, smiling and waving. Cat's friend was very happy to see the twins and relaxed after a full week away from her beloved terrors.

She was also ready for a girls' night out before the big day, she told Cat as they walked to the car.

Cat and Gemma had a room booked for the night, her hen night, but for now Gemma was with Nigel, unsettling the twins and his routines, while Cat was in Dominic's room, sneaking in one last feed with Eloisa.

She was gorgeous, a smiley, happy baby who had her father's dark eyes and her mother's thick black hair.

'I *can* give a bottle,' Dominic said, holding his hands out to take her.

'I know,' Cat said. 'I just feel guilty,'

'Why would you feel guilty?' came Dominic's sarcastic response. 'I get the family buffet with Nigel and co. and you get to eat wherever you choose with adults and get as drunk as you please.'

'I know, I can't wait,' Cat said.

'Again she lies,' Dominic said. 'I assume it's not me and the family buffet you're feeling guilty about?'

'No.'

She *was* looking forward to her night out, she really was. She'd managed to breastfeed for only six weeks and now, at three months old, Eloisa happily took her bottle and Dominic often got up to feed her at night.

It was just…

'It's just…' Cat said. 'It's not just one night that I'm leaving her but two.'

'Cat.' Dominic was firm. 'If we hadn't got our problems sorted then about now, I might be having Eloisa to stay at my house for the night. And when you went back to work, there would have been no nanny, it would have been me.'

'I know.'

'And,' Dominic added, 'if you're worried about leaving her with my parents tomorrow, don't be. They are a bit odd but they will look after her as if she's made of glass.'

'I know all that.'

Cat loved his parents. She and Dominic had taken Eloisa to Spain when she was six weeks old and had stayed at the villa. Anna had been brilliant when Cat had been upset that her milk had dried up. She had been far more understanding about Cat's tears than her own mum would have been. Now they were back again just a few weeks later. Cat was looking forward to the next couple of weeks. After their wedding night they would stay at the villa again and she would get to know his parents better.

'I'd have brought her here without you,' Dominic pointed out. 'Not just yet, of course, but I always wanted her to be close to my parents. So just thank God we grew up and spoke to each other and that you're not crying your eyes out, driving back from Gatwick Airport, having just waved her goodbye.'

'Okay.'

'So go and enjoy your night out.' He smiled. 'And I'll see you tomorrow.'

She had the best night with her friend and her family. They went to the restaurant Dominic had first taken her to, and though she would tell him she'd had the paella he'd know she was lying.

'This chicken,' Gemma said, 'is amazing.'

'There's a lot of salt,' Cat's mum replied, and reached for a glass of water.

They laughed a lot, drank a bit much and danced into the small hours.

Well, Cat's mum and dad went off to bed but the two best friends had a brilliant time.

And then it was back to the hotel and she stayed up late into the night, chatting with Gemma.

'It was bliss,' Gemma said about their honeymoon. 'It was so nice to be able to talk to each other without being interrupted and to go for a walk without having to sort out hundreds of shoes.' She turned and looked over at Cat, who lay on her side in bed, listening to Gemma. 'I've got something to tell you.'

Cat both smiled and frowned. 'Well, I hope you're not pregnant, given the amount of champagne consumed tonight.'

'No, and I know both Nigel and I said never again when I had the twins, but we are going to try for another,' Gemma said.

'Yes!' Cat grinned. 'I knew you would.'

But that wasn't all.

'Remember when you joked about Nigel moving to France? Well, as it turns out, he wants to move there for a while and teach English.'

Cat's jaw gaped. 'And?'

'I want to take some time off with the next baby. Some real time off. I've loved working but before I know it the twins will be at school and I want some mummy time with them... So home might be France for a while.'

'It sounds brilliant,' Cat said, though she held on to news of her own until she could run it by Dominic.

'It does.' Gemma sighed. 'Though it's a terrible shame I did German at school! You know, a few months ago, as much as I said I'd give it every consideration, I'd still have freaked. We probably can't afford it, but...'

'You can't afford not to?'

Gemma nodded. 'Things were a bit tense between Nigel and I for a while,' she admitted. 'Nothing terrible but I was tired of working and felt I was missing out on the twins. But then his head injury happened and I thought I was going to lose him and, believe me, that changed an awful lot of things.'

Cat lay there remembering being with Dominic on the beach and his words—*'What seemed like the most terrible disaster at the time turned out to be a blessing.'*

There were so many blessings to be had.

'Spa day tomorrow.' Gemma broke the silence. 'I do love late weddings. There's ages to get ready and none of that hanging around between the service and party.' She looked at her friend. 'How come you chose sunset instead of sunrise, if that's when you two knew it was serious?'

'We just thought it would be easier to get everyone there in the evening,' Cat said. 'Greg isn't arriving till tomorrow.'

Gemma frowned but Cat changed the subject.

Just as Gemma hadn't told her till now about tense times with Nigel, she too didn't tell Gemma everything.

As she drifted off to sleep Cat thought about what sunrise had meant for Dominic and Heather, how she was quite sure that it had been that morning at Collserola that Heather had handed him over to Cat.

And sunrise was, for Cat, one of those times when you lay in bed with your baby feeding, and sometimes shed a tear for the one that you never got to feed.

Sunsets belonged to them, sitting outside in the garden, as Cat liked to now she had finally done it up. Sunsets were the time when she thought about Dominic driving home from work and the night to come, which was always precious.

Their wedding day dawned and Cat and Gemma awoke to breakfast in bed and then shared a spa day, getting massaged and oiled. Cat's hair was done and make-up applied and then late afternoon Gemma headed off to get Eloisa.

She was all smiles, blowing bubbles, happy to see

her mother, and together Cat and Gemma dressed her in her little outfit and Cat's dad knocked on the hotel room door and July was about to become beautiful again.

Oh, there were sad days in it but there were very happy ones too.

They drove the short distance to Collserola.

'How far is it?' Gemma asked, once they were out of the car and walking up the hillside, with Cat's dad puffing behind.

'Nearly there,' Cat said, and then she saw her tribe all waiting and she saw Dominic's smile when he noticed how they were dressed.

The bride and the bridesmaid both wore white.

Two broderie anglaise dresses. Cat's one had spent three days at the dry cleaner's having grass stains removed, and two being expertly repaired, but she refused to wear anything else for this very special wedding.

And, no, Gemma did not outshine the bride. No one could for her smile was so wide as they stood at sunset at Collserola Park, with their families beside them.

Gemma held Eloisa, who was dressed in white broderie anglaise too, and at three months of age was going to spend her second night away from Mummy.

She was going to get to know her rather eccentric grandparents on her father's side, of course.

Her rigid maternal grandparents were flying back to England at the crack of dawn.

Still, they were here tonight and that was all that mattered for now.

Or rather she and Dominic were all that mattered right now.

He put a ring on her finger and Cat's eyes filled with tears as he told her how much he loved her.

And then she put a ring on his finger, a finger that had worn one before, and Cat's eyes filled up again.

'I love you,' she said.

'I know you do.'

Their vows were said as the sun went down and life together carried on.

They had a party at his parents' villa.

Greg's children swam in the pool and Nigel took the twins inside for a sleep.

Cat dived into the paella and looked up to see Anna holding her granddaughter and smiling down. Kelly asked her something and Anna stood and handed little Eloisa over to her husband, who took the baby with a smile.

It reminded her of that precious time with Thomas when he had never been put down and had been surrounded only by love.

'She'll be fine,' Anna said, bringing out a tray of desserts and placing them on the table.

'I know she will.'

They had their priorities right, Cat thought, glancing at her own parents, who were both checking their phones.

She thought about the letter James and Anna had sent her, inviting her, with or without Dominic, into their home. Cat understood better now why Dominic would have fought, legally if he'd had to, to have his parents in his daughter's life.

It hadn't come to that, though.

They partied into the night and then it was time to head back to the conference hotel for Dominic and Cat, though to the luxury suite this time.

'She's sound asleep,' Dominic said as they crept in to whisper goodnight to their daughter.

'How lucky are we?' Cat said, remembering how it might have been.

Dropping the baby off.

Picking her up.

Doing this apart, instead of together.

'Come on,' he said. 'I guess we have to go and do what newlyweds do now.'

'I suppose.' Cat sighed.

They couldn't wait!

They left the people they loved and were driven to the hotel.

They walked through the foyer. 'Do you want a quick drink at the bar?' Dominic nudged.

'No.'

The elevator door opened and together they stepped in and this time there was no hugging the wall and wondering where the night might lead.

It was straight to his arms and a blistering kiss and it would be straight to bed, except Cat had something on her mind.

'I've been thinking,' Cat said as they stepped into the suite and Dominic poured champagne.

'Have you?'

'How's my job?'

'Do we have to talk about work tonight?'

'Please.'

'It's busy,' Dominic said. 'Are you still thinking about job-sharing with me?'

Cat shook her head. It was something they'd both considered but Cat had other plans.

She loved him.

No question.

'I was thinking of selling my house,' Cat said, which made sense, given they spent most of their time at his.

'I'm going to make a nice profit. Enough to maybe take a year off work.'

'What are you going to do?' Dominic asked. 'Renovate mine?'

'No.' Cat laughed at the hope in his voice and she closed her eyes at his kiss and his hands that were, more tenderly this time, removing her dress. 'I think I want to learn Spanish.'

Dominic stopped in mid-kiss.

'Er…why?'

'I'd like to be able to speak with the locals,' Cat said. 'You said you wanted to spend some time here.'

'I did.'

'Then do,' Cat said. 'You've already upended my life, so why not a little bit more?'

'When did you decide this?'

'I started thinking about it last time we were here. I can see how much you love it and I think it would be amazing to live here for a while, and then…' She thought of life here with him and smiled when she thought of her best friend just a leisurely drive to Paris away, and she gave a small shrug. 'Who knows?'

She loved him and love deserved careful consideration at times.

He had made her so happy, had given her back her dreams, and she wanted to make all his come true too.

She had been far too cynical about men, about love, about hope.

'You're sure?' he checked.

She was now.

Absolutely, Cat was sure of this love.

* * * * *

THE SPANISH DUKE'S
HOLIDAY PROPOSAL

ROBIN GIANNA

I'd like to dedicate this book to wonderful, fellow medical author Amalie Berlin, who helped me brainstorm parts of this story and was always there when I needed to wail about struggles I had pulling it together. Thanks for always being there, Amalie! Xoxo

A big thanks to Dr. Meta Carroll for helping me with the medical scenes in this book, per usual! Meta, you are the best! xoxo

CHAPTER ONE

FOR HEAVEN'S SAKE, can't you go any faster?

Since it was obvious the massive traffic jam made that impossible, Miranda Davenport bit her lip to keep from exclaiming exactly that. Her cab driver seemed as frustrated as she was, not being able to move more than a few feet at a time as the minutes ticked by, and no amount of impatience by either one of them was going to help her get to the hospital sooner. Even from several blocks away, the blue and red strobe-like flashes from multiple emergency vehicles covered the street, jammed so heavily with cars that could only inch along every five minutes or so.

"Subway tunnel collapse must be bad. Hope it isn't a terrorist attack," her cab driver said.

"Yeah. Me, too." The thought of the subway tunnel collapse being done by terrorists made Miranda shiver, but she also knew that sometimes things like that happened from structural decay, and prayed that was the case this time. She also prayed there wouldn't be too many casualties, and she clenched her teeth with impatience because it might be critically important for her to get to the hospital ASAP. Excruciatingly long minutes ticked by until she couldn't stand sitting there any longer.

"Listen, I think I'm going to get out and walk from here." It was still quite a few blocks to the hospital and her trek home had proved that winter had decided to arrive in New York City with a vengeance. But sitting here barely moving felt torturous when the Manhattan Mercy ER might well be swamped with patients, and they'd called her back, anticipating the worst.

"Hang on a few more minutes, lady. Let me see what I can do."

Like so many of the drivers whose vehicles filled the street, her cabbie honked his horn, and Miranda nearly clamped her hands to her ears at the cacophony. Growing up in Chicago then living in New York City for the past thirteen years meant the sound of car horns usually faded into the background. But after being stuck in the middle of this traffic mess for the past half-hour, it was starting to give her the mother of all headaches. Or maybe her headache was from not enough sleep after the twelve-hour shift she'd just worked in the ER, not expecting a catastrophe to bring her back before she was even home.

The cab managed to move a couple feet before the driver laid on the horn again, and Miranda knew the poor guy was going to be creeping along in this traffic for a long time. "Sorry, but I've got to get to the hospital. Thanks for bringing me this far. Here's extra for your trouble." Never having had that "extra" in her younger life was something she'd never forget, and even after all this time it felt good to be able to share the wealth. She shoved a fold of cash through the window to the front seat, then opened her door to exit right in the middle of the street. Not that dodging between stopped cars to the sidewalk brought any risk to life and limb at that moment.

The frigid air sneaking down her neck felt practically sub-zero, and she grabbed her coat collar, ducked her head down against the wind, and hurried toward the hospital. Good thing she had on the comfortable shoes she always wore to work, and her strides ate up the pavement fairly quickly until she came to the dust particles filling the air. Then she stared in shock at the yawning hole where the pavement had collapsed in the street, the subway tracks clearly visible below. Her heart tripped into double-time as she watched numerous firefighters and paramedics running in and out of the tunnel. Then she yanked herself out of her shocked stupor, moving closer to see if she could assist.

"You have any patients that need help?" she shouted above the chaos. "I'm—"

"You need to move to the other side of the street!" a paramedic yelled back. "It's not safe here."

"I'm an ER doctor, heading to the hospital. Wondering if you need any help here."

"No. We're doing okay. Thanks, but you need to move on."

"Can you tell me how many injured the hospital might be dealing with?"

"Right now, looks like not a lot. The collapse was only in a small area, and not many people were waiting for the train there." He swiped a grimy gloved hand against his forehead. "Unless something else happens, we're hoping for minimal victims. Right now we're focusing on shoring up the tunnel as we search to see who else might be down there."

The air Miranda sucked into her lungs in cautious relief was cold and full of the nasty dust, and she coughed. "Okay. Good luck, and be careful in there."

She pulled her scarf up over her mouth and moved away from the hole to hurry on to the hospital, only to be stopped by police officers who were setting up orange barriers on the sidewalk, insisting she cross over to the other side of the street.

About to argue and tell them her mission, she decided to just do as they asked. There were hardly any pedestrians on the other sidewalk to impede her progress, so she'd be able to walk faster anyway. As she moved across the barricaded street, a sound caught her ears. Something that sounded like someone crying out in the distance, and she stopped, straining to hear. Another faint cry had her heart pumping faster, and she hurried around the barricade in the street to see what was making the sound, abruptly stopping at the sight. Had no one seen this other, small collapse in the pavement? Dust swirled up from a virtual stepping stone of concrete and asphalt, leading down into the darkness.

Had the first responders been so focused on the large collapse that they hadn't discovered it yet? Did they know someone was in there?

She swung around to get the attention of one of the police officers, but they'd moved too far away to hear her. Heart beating in triple-time, she windmilled her arms to get the attention of the firefighters and paramedics, but in the midst of everything going on, nobody noticed a lone woman in a black coat waving at them. It probably didn't help that this hole was a good block away from them now.

Would she lose precious time trying to get help? Her heart jerked at the thought of going down into that tunnel, but she had to do something, right? Whoever was in there might be injured, and surely the paramedics would see this small hole any minute. The question was, would they arrive too late, when she was there right now?

Miranda battled down the fear that rose in her throat as she fished in her purse for the small but bright flashlight she always kept there. Stumbling a little, she picked her way through chunks of asphalt and concrete as quickly as she could, leaning over to place her free hand on the jagged lumps to steady herself as she descended beneath the street. The farther down she went, the harder her heart pounded, finally leaving the light of day completely behind her as she headed into the flat darkness.

She peered through the dark, fighting a slightly panicky feeling of claustrophobia. But she was here now, and she'd never forgive herself for being cowardly and climbing back up when, for all she knew, someone could be dying down here.

"Hello? Anyone there? Are you okay? Do you need help?"

A moan and a shout she couldn't understand came back, which sent adrenaline surging through her blood.

"Hang on! I'm a doctor. I can help if you're hurt."

No answer this time. Moving through the rubble wasn't easy, and she felt beyond frustrated at how hard it was to see through the fine silt filling the tunnel beneath the street, swirling up as occasional small bits of rubble fell from the ceiling. Where were the victims in this mess, and how far inside could they be?

The dust made it hard to breathe, and she coughed, pulling the scarf looped around her neck up to cover her mouth again. Not to mention that she was short of breath from the worry of who might be trapped and if she could help at all. And, oh, yeah, the idea that the whole street might come crashing down was just a tad unnerving. She tripped a few times, until a second beam of light from farther inside the tunnel slashed across her, illuminating the way a little more.

"What the hell are you doing in here? Get out!"

Taken aback by the angry male voice, Miranda stopped in her tracks for a second and didn't answer. Then she gathered her wits and sent her own flashlight toward the voice as she fired back, "I'm here to see if I can help."

"Not if this tunnel collapses on you. Get out of here.

Right now. Can't you see it's dangerous down here? There's only one injured person, and I'm taking care of him. Last thing I need is someone else getting hurt through her own stupidity."

Anger joined the adrenaline heating her veins. Who did this guy think he was? Being told what to do was something she'd hated for years, let alone when it was coming from some hero wannabe. She moved forward again, trying to see through the dust and rubble.

"There's nothing stupid about helping injured people. Where…?" Her flashlight finally landed on two men. One was on the ground, bleeding from his forehead and lying awkwardly on one arm. Even with the lack of light, his pallor told her he was going into shock. The other man was crouched over him, his fingers on the man's neck, apparently trying to get his pulse rate.

"I'm not going to say it again—you need to leave! For all I know, this could be the work of terrorists, with a chemical attack to follow. I've got this guy, and responders will be here any minute."

The thought of a chemical attack sent a shiver down Miranda's back, for both herself and anyone else nearby, but she wasn't going to leave until she knew survivors were taken care of. "Have you seen anyone besides this victim?"

He yanked off his coat, completely ignoring her question. His tone changed so completely when he spoke to the man, its gentle quietness surprised her. "I'm going to move you so I can look at your arm. Try to relax, and don't help, okay?" He slowly rolled the victim to his back with extreme care, wadding his coat up under the man's feet to elevate them, obviously knowing how to treat someone going into shock. Then in one fluid movement he pulled his shirt over his head before ripping it into pieces, pressing one section against the man's forehead. "You hold this against your head wound while I look at your arm."

"My dog," the man said on a moan. "Do you see my dog?"

"Remember? I said I'll look for him after I check you out. And I will, but it's not going to do your dog any favors to have you go into shock, is it?"

The patient nodded in response. Miranda finally reached them and crouched down. "I'm a doctor. I can help."

The bossy man paused to look up at her, his eyes meeting hers in an intense stare before he gave her a quick nod. "All right. Hold his arm steady as I get this off." He pulled a knife from his coat pocket, flipped open the blade, then began quickly and efficiently cutting away the victim's coat sleeve.

"Got it." She briefly flashed her light over the victim's arm, noting the navy-blue sleeve was dark with what was probably blood. She put her flashlight down on the rubble, trying to direct the light toward the man's arm, before she reached to gently but firmly hold it in place as the rest of the sleeve was cut away.

He paused in his cutting to clamp his flashlight between his teeth so he could use both hands and see at the same time he worked, which made Miranda look more carefully at his shadowed and dirty face. His ridiculously handsome face, which she now realized with a start she'd seen before, and that always made her take an involuntary second and third look. A face that belonged to an EMT she'd often seen in the hospital, bringing in patients.

Trying to remember his name, she was filled with a short rush of relief that she wasn't alone in this place, trying to deal with this serious injury before figuring out how to get him to the hospital. That the man working on the patient knew what he was doing, and that they could work together as a team.

The way he was leaning over the patient made it hard to see the man, so she stared at the medic's head instead, tipped downward as he cut away the cloth. She knew his short hair was normally black, but right now gray powder covered both it and his dark brows. More of the silt filtered down onto all three of them, and she swallowed hard, shoving down the fear that skittered down her back again at the thought of being buried alive.

The last of the coat and clothing was cut off, and they were both finally able to see the jaggedly ripped and bleeding flesh of the victim's forearm. While she couldn't see the bone beneath it, there was no doubt this was a compound fracture. Which meant the bleeding had to be stopped and the arm stabilized while trying not to jar the broken pieces in the process.

The medic's eyes met hers, and what she saw there telegraphed loud and clear that he knew as well as she did that if the bones got moved the wrong way, they risked an artery being torn, which would turn a bad situation worse.

He took the flashlight from his teeth and tucked it under his chin. "You still got his arm steady? I'm going to wrap it."

"Yes. You can let go. I have a book in my purse. We can use it as a splint."

He glanced up, his intense eyes meeting hers again. "I have a magazine folded in my coat pocket. I'll use both to stabilize the arm after I get the bleeding stopped, so leave the book, then go."

Ignoring his comment the way he'd ignored hers earlier, she watched him carefully lay a piece of his shirt on top of the bleeding wound, then lift his hand, apparently planning to press down on it.

"Don't do that, you'll dislodge the bones!" she said. "We need to be as careful as possible not to cause further damage. Putting pressure on it isn't a good idea. A tourniquet is a better option to try first."

"I realize that a lowly EMT knows little compared to you, Dr. Davenport," he drawled, emphasizing the word *doctor* as he continued to work quickly, wrapping a strip of torn shirt around either end of the cloth bandage. "But I know a lot more about field medicine than you do and I have the technique down pat."

Surprise that he knew her name was quickly replaced by serious annoyance as his nearly amused tone started to really tick her off. She opened her mouth to retort that an ER doctor was fully trained in all kinds of emergencies. Until that emotion and her words dried up fast as she watched the remarkable efficiency and competency he showed as he tied off a makeshift tourniquet, then held the victim's legs up with one arm as he grabbed his now filthy coat from the ground to pull out a magazine.

All right, she had to admit it, but not to this autocratic male. While she worked hard to be the best doctor she could be, this guy had her beat when it came to this kind of emergency, working without all kinds of medical supplies and the equipment she always had available at her fingertips.

"This is probably going to hurt, so hang on," he said to the patient. "You doing okay?"

"O-Okay," the man said on a gasp that turned into a groan as the medic slowly and carefully straightened his arm. He then curved the magazine beneath the man's elbow.

"Can you—?"

"Yes." She reached to cup her hands underneath to hold it in place as he worked to secure it with strips of his shirt. The patient moaned, and Miranda leaned closer. "I'm sorry, sir. I know it hurts, but the hospital's close by. As soon as we get the wound secured, we'll get you out of here. You're going to be fine, and getting meds to help with the pain really soon."

"Where's that book?" the medic asked, never pausing as he knotted the strips and reached for another.

"Here." With one hand, she slid her bag from her shoulder and reached in to fish out the book. "I'll place it under his wrist when you're done."

A quick nod as he finished up with the magazine, then suddenly lifted his eyes to hers. The quick grin he sent, along with a smile in that brown gaze, took her totally by surprise, and for some ridiculous reason made her heart beat little harder. Apparently helping him had taken her off his list of highly irritating things. For the moment, at least.

"I'm sorry, I should know, but what's your name?" she heard herself ask, suddenly needing to know.

"Mateo Alves. This is John, and his dog, Benny, ran in here after the collapse, which is why John came down here in the first place. He's a fast one for a shorty dog, but I'll find him. And I already know you're Miranda Davenport. I'd say it's nice to meet you, except you shouldn't have come in here to begin with."

"Too bad. There's nothing falling now, so we're probably safe." She knew she sounded a little breathless, which was probably due to the silt in the air and not at all to the fact that she'd fantasized about the über-handsome EMT more than once in the ER. During those times, they'd all been busy treating patients, so there hadn't been time to spend more than a brief moment staring at him, and now wasn't a good time either. Except she found that, for what felt like a long moment of connection between them, she was staring at him anyway.

"Yeah, well, that could change in one second."

She glanced up, gulping at that reality. To cover her worries, she threw out a tart response. "Aren't you going to admit that both of us working on John's arm has been faster than you doing it alone, and better for him?"

"Maybe." Another quick flash of teeth.

"I'm going to put the book under his forearm now."

"Wait. I want to cover the wound better first."

Her rapt attention on his handsome features was interrupted when he frowned and paused in his work on the wrist splint. She looked down and saw that he'd used every scrap of fabric from his torn shirt.

"Give me your scarf."

"Oh. That's a good idea," she said, wishing she'd thought of it. She slipped it from her neck and handed it to him. "And I can cut the bottoms off my pants, too, if we need them."

That flash of grin. "What do you think, John? How often do you have a woman offering to rip her clothes off for you?"

"Not often enough." A weak smile accompanied his words, then disappeared again. "My dog. My Benny. I haven't heard him bark."

"Probably too scared to bark. But I have a surefire way to call dogs—you'll see. Right now, though, we have to get you out of here without jostling your arm any more than necessary. Dr. Davenport?"

"Yes?"

"I'm afraid I'm going to have to take you up on the offer of your pants. Don't worry, I won't cut any above your knees." That sexy smile again. "But that fabric is a lot better than my jeans to finish securing the splint, since I'm going to use your scarf as a sling to keep it still."

"That makes sense." Of course he'd need a sling, and

she thrashed herself that it hadn't occurred to her. Thank God none of her siblings or father could see her. She'd spent the last thirteen years trying to make them proud of her, to earn their respect, and right now she felt totally inept.

She reached for the knife and pushed the point into the knit material. It went in easily, even as she inwardly cringed at the thought of accidentally jabbing herself in her own calf. And being that kind of wimp proved even more that Mateo was absolutely right—he was definitely better at this field medicine stuff than she was, and she vowed to study it again, maybe even go on some runs with the EMTs to refresh her skills.

But not with Mateo Alves. She'd find someone whose sexy face and body wouldn't distract her from her training mission.

"Careful. Don't cut yourself."

"I know how to use a knife."

"Do you cut clothes off yourself on a regular basis? Pretty sure that's harder than cutting a sandwich."

"Funny." She struggled to move the knife down through the pants leg without gouging herself in the process, and as she did so heard an impatient sound come from Mateo.

"Let me."

"I'm doing fine."

"Yeah? Well, every second is time John isn't at the hospital for pain meds and treatment, and we're all still down here."

"There hasn't been any debris for a while. Right?" She paused in her cutting to look up at the dark tunnel ceiling again, wishing he'd stop pointing out the possibility of impending collapse.

A snorting *humph* was his only response as he tugged the knife from her hand and took over, getting it through the cloth in mere seconds, then hacking it off from around her knee before tearing it into strips. For some reason, having the blade so close to her skin didn't worry her when it was Mateo doing the cutting. Maybe it was because the touch of his fingers on her skin as he moved them down her leg distracted her from being scared. "Rule number one is to get the hell out of any collapsed building ASAP. Which you're going to do right now, to get a crew down here with a stretcher. I'm surprised someone hasn't already come in here."

"Okay." She knew he was right, that trying to move John, even with his injury splinted and in a sling, would be painful and dangerous if he had to try to walk, especially after all the blood he'd lost. "I'll be right back."

"Back?" His focus was on finishing tying the last strip over the book then fashioning a sling from her scarf, but his scowl was most definitely directly at her. "Don't be stupid. Just tell them where we are."

And again he was right. Why she was feeling this weird need to actually see both of them make it out, she didn't know. But she wasn't needed here, and might well be needed at the hospital. "Okay," she repeated as she stood, ridiculously feeling a need to brush some of the powdery dirt from her coat. "Since I definitely am not stupid, I'll see you at—"

"Anybody in here?"

Miranda sagged in relief at the voices and the sight of two bobbing flashlights.

"Back here! About thirty feet. Bring a stretcher," Mateo called. "Just one victim. No access to the subway platform. He came in because he was trying to get his dog out."

"Got a stretcher right outside." In mere moments two medics were there, Mateo helping them get John settled on the stretcher as he shared details of the patient's condition and treatment. They wore full gear—reflective coats, hard hats, gloves, and various tools dangled from their belts. Which made Miranda wonder, for the first time, why Mateo was in street clothes. Or, actually, at that moment, very few clothes, with his shirt destroyed and his coat still off, and she found herself staring at his wide, muscled chest and broad shoulders.

"Are you off duty?" she asked.

"Yes. I was on my way to the main collapse when I saw John run in after Benny, then get hit by a chunk of concrete."

"My little dog…" The two men picked up the stretcher, ready to carry him out, and John's words were bitten off as he moaned.

"You get out of here too, Mateo," one of the rescuers said. "You're not equipped. I'll send some guys in to check for anyone else, just in case, but the good news is that it looks like a structural collapse, nothing else. We've got plenty of crew on the scene and if no one else is in here, that means everyone's out and clear both places. So you can go on home."

"I have make sure a certain stubborn doctor gets to the hospital first."

"Tough job you have," one said, laughing, as they made their way toward daylight.

Miranda bent to casually retrieve her purse and flashlight from the ground, not wanting to show him how eager she was to get the heck out of there now that John was taken care of. Not wanting him to see how she'd been staring at his beautiful body. "You know, I'm not stubborn. It just seemed like I should help if I could, just like you did."

"It's my job to run into harm's way when necessary. Don't think that's in your job description. Come on."

He slid the filthy coat back on over his naked torso,

then reached for her elbow. As they stepped over chunks of concrete, Miranda suddenly longed to be outside in the cold air and out of the dark gloom. Which she wouldn't admit to Mateo for the world. "You don't need to hold me up. I'm perfectly capable—"

"I just want to get outside, and if you fall and gash open your head we'll be stuck in here all that much longer."

"I'm sorry if I've made the situation more difficult," she said, her stomach churning a little that he seemed to still think she'd done exactly that, and what did that make her? A pain in the neck, that's what, just like her stepmother had told her for years. "I should have thought it through better and gotten a firefighter instead of coming in here myself."

"Yes, you should've. But I have to admire how brave you are. And you were a big help, even though I hate to admit it."

Even in the darkness she could see the smile in his eyes, which put a warm little glow in her chest and had her smiling back.

"That's much better than telling me I'm annoying and stubborn," she said. "You—"

A deep, ground-shaking rumble was followed instantly by sharp cracks and the thud of chunks of concrete hitting the ground. Miranda gasped, instinctively covering her head with her arms, as though that flimsy barrier could protect her in any way, when a heavy weight slammed straight into her.

CHAPTER TWO

MATEO'S HARD BODY took her down like a football line-backer, as he somehow managed to wrap his arms around her before they hit the earth. The sharp pebbles they landed on stabbed and scraped her one bare leg, a bigger chunk of concrete jabbed into her ribs, and her face landed on the hard pillow of Mateo's muscled forearm before sliding off it into a pile of silty debris.

His weight smashed her down so hard she couldn't get her mouth clear to breathe, and his body jerked at the same time as he grunted loudly in her ear. Lifting her head half an inch to suck in a chokingly dusty breath, she twisted and pushed at him, blinded by the dirt in her eyes, which sent tears streaming down her cheeks. "Get off! Can't breathe…"

He didn't move, and she jabbed her elbow into his ribs, which sent another low grunt into her ear. "Hold still a minute," he said. "I just took a boulder for you and you're trying to hurt me more?"

"What?" His weight lifted slightly off her, and she twisted around fully to lie on her back, sucking in deep breaths as she stared up at his grim face. Her hands decided on their own to grab at him, landing inside his coat on his shoulders, clinging, pulling him close. Somehow, she wriggled enough to move her spine off whatever was currently lodged there.

"You okay?"

"I— I'm okay." She realized that was true, she was fine, possibly only because she had a two-hundred-pound blanket of bone and muscle covering her. "You?"

"Bleeding, but okay. And see? Seems to be all finished," he said in a ridiculously calm voice. He lifted his gaze to scan the tunnel. "Let's give this a few more seconds to make sure it's done, then we'll get the hell out of here."

Light silt still showering down in intermittent swishes mingled with his heavy breaths against her lips, and her own fast breathing against his. Their eyes met and held, and she was suddenly acutely aware of the feel of his skin against her palms, the strength of his muscles, the movement of his naked chest against her. The grip she had on his warm shoulders loosened, and her hands moved down his pectorals, smoothing across the soft hair covering them before she realized with dismay what she was doing. Making herself let go, she curled her fingers into her palms to keep from touching him again. Fought the peculiar combination of sensations swirling around her belly that didn't seem connected to the fear that had consumed her just moments before.

She pulled in another deep breath. What in the world? The two of them were lying in a collapsed tunnel, for heaven's sake, and it was long past time to get safe.

"I'm… I'm ready," she said unsteadily. "To leave."

"Finally?" His lips curved just a little. "Let's go."

His big body lifted from hers, and his hands grasped her waist, effortlessly swinging her to her feet. His arm wrapped around her shoulders as they moved quickly out of the tunnel toward the light. Miranda blinked at the brightness of the sky—how had it seemed so gray and gloomy before? The fresh, cold air filled her lungs, sharp and stinging and wonderful. Trembling a little now that the whole thing was over, she tried not to think about how bad it could have turned out, and turned to see Mateo watching her with an odd expression on his face.

"You sure you're okay?"

Probably, she looked pale and shaken, her pretense of bravery through the situation now shot to heck. "Yes, okay. Thanks for, you know, crushing me with your body so I didn't get crushed worse by flying debris."

"You're welcome. Except I didn't completely succeed. Your coat is torn."

She followed his gaze to the large rip in the shoulder seam of her coat, and couldn't help the little dismayed sound that came from her lips. "Oh, no! I just bought this last month! Must have happened when you tackled me."

"Better a torn coat than a broken head. Which you would have deserved for not leaving when I asked you to."

"Not even I deserve a broken head."

That statement made his lips quirk as he reached out to brush his finger across her dusty eyelids. "You'd better get washed up."

"Me? You look like a gray-haired old man right now." Which couldn't be further from the truth, since no old man had the kind of wide, muscular chest that was mostly bare right in front of her, or flat, rippling abs, or such a chiseled jaw. And because she couldn't stop looking at him and was enjoying their banter far too much, she forced herself to look away up the sidewalk, pretending to focus on all the emergency equipment and personnel. Then her peripheral vision caught bright red drops of blood splattering on the sidewalk behind his feet.

Wide-eyed, she jerked her attention back to him. "You're bleeding! Oh, my God."

"I can tell it's just a scrape. Maybe a gouge, too, but nothing worse than that."

"Take off your coat so I can see."

"I'll freeze."

"Better to freeze than die from blood loss." She pushed at the shoulders of his open coat and, shaking his head and grumbling, he finally slid it off. She turned him around, then stared in dismay at the swollen, raw scrape and shallow puncture wound that was the source of the drops of blood. "For heaven's sake, you really did take a boulder for me!"

"I'll live."

"Does it hurt anywhere else?" She ran her hands across his shoulders and back, wiping off the dusty debris from when he'd had his coat off earlier, looking for other injuries that might not be obvious. "I feel just terrible that I was pushing and jabbing you to get off me when you really were hurt."

"Like I said, just a scrape. And I'm tough."

He tried to turn around, but she stopped him. "And you call me stubborn! Just be still a minute." With her scarf gone, the best she could do to staunch the trickle of blood was a pathetic wad of tissue she scrounged from her coat pocket, pressing it firmly against the bruised indentation as her left hand continued to roam his hard contours and smooth skin.

Abruptly and without warning, he surprised her by turning, her hands moving along with him, and the sight of that manly chest and the feel of his skin and soft hair on her palms had her mesmerized again, touching him the same way she'd touched his back, slowly and thoroughly, though there was clearly no injury on this side of his body.

"You about finished examining me, Doctor?"

Oh, my God. His low rumble made her realize exactly

what she'd been doing. Dropping the tissue and yanking her hands back like she'd touched a hot furnace, horrified that she'd practically been fondling the man, she stared up at amused brown eyes.

"I'm sorry... I didn't mean to, you know, run my hands all over you like that, I was just, um, checking for more injuries, but you seem..." She cleared her throat, utterly mortified. "Fine."

He gave her a slow smile that said he knew exactly why she'd been touching him, which had been way too softly and leisurely to be considered a medical necessity. Heat flooded her face because, yes, the man was very, very fine and she'd just made an utter fool of herself.

Beyond relieved that he slid his coat back on, she wished with all her heart that he'd button it up, too, so she wouldn't have to keep finding other things to look at. Like his gorgeous face.

"Thanks for the first aid." He reached out to gently smooth a finger down her dirty cheek. "You're a mess. Do you live nearby?"

"No, I live in Brooklyn. But I'll go to the hospital and use the showers there."

"Be careful walking—looks like some of the sidewalk has heaved in the collapse."

He turned and, astonishingly, it looked like he was about to head back inside the collapsed street they'd just come from. "What are you doing?"

"I've got to find John's dog."

"What? Surely you're not going back in there! Or at least get the safety equipment and hard hat on before you do."

"Unless he somehow got out, it won't take long. The space beyond where John was injured ends just another thirty-five feet or so back."

And with that, he disappeared, leaving her with her hands clutched to her chest and her mouth gaping open after him.

What should she do now? Go on to the hospital like she didn't know the crazy man had gone back into harm's way? Go tell the first responders that one of their men was insane? She felt bad about John's poor dog and understood why he'd gone back in for it, but what if the whole ceiling collapsed and neither one of them survived? He should have gotten help before going back in to look for him, and protected himself somehow.

She stood there with various horrible scenarios running through her mind, each worse than the last, making her feel a little woozy. After several minutes ticked by she decided, nearly hyperventilating, that she had to tell someone so that he wouldn't be in there alone, knocked unconscious by a slab of concrete or buried under a shower of rubble, and just as she was about to rush to one of the fire trucks, an even more dusty Mateo trudged up out of the wreckage. A small dog was tucked into the crook of his elbow like a football, and Miranda wasn't sure if she wanted to laugh or yell at him.

She planted her hands on her hips and sucked in a shaky breath. "Are you out of your mind? You had me worried to death!"

"Unnecessary. But when a beautiful woman worries about me, it's appreciated nonetheless." He held up what she could now see was a rather chubby dachshund that was probably brown, though it was hard to tell for sure. "Benny likes it, too, don't you, buddy?" Mateo scratched beneath the dog's chin, who managed to feebly wag his tail despite his ordeal.

Miranda smoothed her hand across the pup's back, smearing the dust around, and her fear and desire to yell at Mateo faded into a smile of her own. "He's so cute. John will be very glad. How in the world did you find him?"

He stuck two fingers into his mouth, and the shrill whistle was so loud it made Benny squirm and Miranda cover her ears.

"Oh, my gosh! That would make me run instead of come to you. And you do realize your hands are filthy."

"Eating a little dirt is good for one's immune system, which you surely know, Dr. Davenport."

"Yes. Well, I already ate my quota of dirt for the day." Aware of a ridiculous desire to just stand there and talk with him for hours, filthy and cold or not, she managed to remember that she had to see if the hospital had a big patient load after the collapse. "Gotta go. You want me to find John and tell him? What are you going to do with the dog?"

"Take him home. I'll call the hospital and have them tell John, and he can find someone to come pick him up."

"That's...nice of you." In spite of her best intentions, her eyes kept wandering from the dog to Mateo's naked chest beneath his coat, remembering how his skin and body had felt, and she decided she'd better get out of there before he could see exactly what she was thinking. "Well..."

Fixated as she was on his handsome face and beautiful physique, she didn't even hear the chime of her cellphone announcing a text until his finger pointed to her purse. "That your phone?"

"Oh! Yes. Thanks." Lord, had he noticed her distractedly, ridiculously, staring at his body? Again? She quickly fished in her bag and read the message. "The hospital says they don't need me. That there aren't too many injured, they're sure it wasn't a terrorist event, and everything's under control. So that's good news."

"It is."

She lifted her eyes to his brown ones, and something

about the way he was looking at her made her chest suddenly feel oddly buoyant. The thought of going to her apartment and being all alone for the rest of the day pushed that air right back out, but she shook it off. When she wasn't working, didn't she spend most of her time alone anyway?

"Well, good luck with the dog and all." She cleared her throat. "See you at the hospital sometime."

She turned away from that mesmerizing brown gaze and started walking, then realized she'd have to rethink her route, since the subway she usually rode might be out of commission. She pulled up the subway updates on her phone to check which ones were running and which weren't, when a large, dirty hand rested on her forearm to stop her in her tracks.

"So where are you going?" Mateo asked.

"Brooklyn. My subway might be open but if not, I'll just take a taxi."

"In this mess? It'll take you hours."

And wasn't that the truth? The clogged-up traffic looked even worse than when she'd left the taxi. "Then I'll go to the hospital after all."

"Do you have a friend or boyfriend who lives close enough to walk to their place?"

"No boyfriend, and most of my family live on the Upper East Side."

"I live just a couple of blocks from here. You might as well come with me and Benny and get cleaned up there. I probably have pants that'll fit you that you could wear home."

She'd hardly be surprised if a man as hunky as Mateo Alves had clothes women had left at his place, but she wasn't about to wear any of them. "Thanks, but no. I'll be fine."

"Suit yourself. Walking ten blocks to the hospital, covered with dirt, wearing a torn coat and pants with one bare leg exposed in this cold, is going to feel very uncomfortable." An indifferent shrug made her wonder why he was even asking. "And if you can ride the subway, people will think you're homeless and want to sit far away from the strangely dusty woman with ripped clothes. Or offer you money."

She had to laugh at that, but as she looked down at herself, she realized he was right. Not to mention that her leg already felt a little numb from the cold wind. And what if she ran into someone she knew, or a former patient, and had to answer a gazillion questions and have people think she was crazy to run into a collapsed tunnel, just like Mateo had?

She thought about how her sister Penny always accused her of doing everything in her life as safely as possible, and today she'd proved that wasn't always true. And taking Mateo up on his offer would definitely not be the quiet, boring route either, would it?

"Fine." Her pulse quickened as she agreed. "I appreciate it."

"I have a secret reason for asking, you realize."

Her heart lurched at the wicked glint that suddenly appeared in his eyes, and a whole lot of possibilities swirled through her head. Was she out of her mind to actually go with him? Her eyes glued to his, she breathlessly asked, "What?"

"Benny can't be returned in his current condition." He held out the little dog. "I'm hoping you'll take him in the shower with you to get him washed up as well."

Miranda felt warm from head to toe as she shoved her arms into the oversized white robe Mateo had given her before her shower. She had a bad feeling that the heat pumping from her pores was from more than just the hot shower. That it might have something to do with feeling embarrassed that she was naked in Mateo Alves's bathroom, and that she'd been thinking thoughts that should not have formed in her brain at all.

Thoughts of Mateo coming into the small space while she was in the shower, which of course would be horrifying and creepy in real life. But in her fantasy world, safe behind a locked bathroom door? Very, very exciting. And what woman wouldn't think about that for at least a second, when the man was the most gorgeous male specimen she'd ever laid eyes on?

Not to mention that there was something about him that made her feel utterly safe. Had even felt absurdly safe in that tunnel with debris showering down on them, which was ridiculous. His body, big though it was, couldn't have fully shielded her if the entire street had collapsed on them. But that he'd thrown himself on her to protect her the best he could made her feel a little warm glow, even though she knew it was part of his job and he'd been angry with her for even being there in the first place.

She stared into the mirror and finger-combed her damp hair, glad she'd decided to cut it into a bob a couple of years ago. With her work schedule it was easier to take care of now, and after today's crazy events it would have been a tangled mess if it had been longer. She shook her head at the sudden wish that she had more than just lipstick, making a mental note to put some makeup in her purse for next time.

As though there'd be another time she'd rush into danger, be yelled at by the world's most handsome paramedic, then insistently brought to his home to get cleaned up. No, this was a once-in-a-lifetime moment, and she needed to get her clothes dried fast and get out of there before she embarrassed herself again by ogling him. Before he remembered he'd been annoyed about her getting in his way today. The kind of annoyance she'd gotten all too used to once Vanessa Davenport had grudgingly allowed her to live with her father and half-siblings.

"Thanks again for your robe," she said as she walked into his small but comfortable living room, tying the attached terrycloth belt of the over-large robe even tighter. She stared at him lounging on his sofa and licked her dry lips, trying to sound calm and normal instead of absurdly nervous. Which was obviously a ridiculous way for a mature woman to feel, but boyfriends had been few and far between in her life, mostly because she'd quickly learned that none of them had been interested in her, just in her name and the Davenport money and connections. "Are my…are my clothes almost dry?"

"They need maybe ten more minutes." Unfolding his body from the deep leather sofa, he moved toward the bathroom with Benny, now wrapped in a towel to keep the dust from getting everywhere, tucked under his arm again. "I hope you left some hot water for us."

Her mouth went even dryer. "You're…going to shower? Now?"

Dark eyebrows lifted at her as he paused. "Do you object to me using my own shower? I believe I'm covered in even more silt than you were. And I can't exactly pass Benny on in his current state, since you refused to take him in with you."

"Of course I don't object." Which was a lie, because she really wanted to say, *Yes! I'd really rather you wait to take off your clothes until after I'm gone!* "And I didn't refuse, you said you'd take care of washing him."

"Because I'm an excellent dog washer, and I suspect you don't have much experience with canines."

It was true, but the way he said it seemed to imply he thought she was a prima donna or something. "You sure do claim to be excellent at everything. And I'm sure I could handle washing a little dog."

"I have no doubt you handle all kinds of things with aplomb, Dr. Davenport." That quick grin of his flashed before he disappeared into the only bedroom.

Apparently, she'd fooled him pretty well, because there was only one thing she was really good at, and that was being a doctor. Something she'd worked hard to do, trying to live up to the Davenport name. The family she only sort of belonged to, and would probably never be worthy of.

The sound of the bathroom door clicking behind him sent Miranda to perch on the end of the sofa, looking around his small apartment. His decor could be described as minimalist, but the furniture was obviously expensive, and the few pieces of art unusual and eclectic. Not posters from a cheap store but beautifully framed originals hung on the walls, and several excellent sculptures were placed on the modern tables.

She ran her finger across a bronze with fluid lines. Interesting and unexpected that an EMT would have the financial resources for art like this. Maybe he was the kind of man who bought very little, but when he did, it was only the best.

Pondering the man, she absently picked up a magazine, surprised to see that it was about horses and horse-breeding, and flicked through the photos of beautiful animals, hoping for a distraction from her nerves. Until the sound of the shower put a completely different image in her head. Picturing a naked, muscular Mateo with water streaming down the dark hair on his chest shortened her breath and did other things to her body that embarrassed her all over again, reminding her of exactly how she'd felt in that tunnel when he'd been lying on top of her.

Lord, this was ridiculous. What in the world was wrong with her? She was twenty-nine years old, for heaven's sake, and a doctor who'd seen plenty of naked men in her career. Naked men were in her life every day!

Except Mateo wasn't a patient, and she couldn't remember a single man she'd ever known, patient or otherwise, who'd been even close to as gorgeous as he was.

She blew out a breath, and just as she was about to go to the small laundry closet to check on her clothes and throw them on, damp or not, a loud knock sounded at the door to his apartment.

She stared, frozen. Should she answer? The distant sound of the shower told her Mateo wasn't even close to being done, and if she hadn't been there, he wouldn't be answering anyway, right? Besides, what if it was a girlfriend or something? How could she explain being in his apartment in his robe? Then she remembered it might be whoever was coming to get Benny, and decided she'd better answer before they left, assuming no one was home. She moved toward the door as a man's voice boomed through it.

"Mateo! Are you there?"

To Miranda's surprise, she heard the keypad beep just before the doorknob turned. The door opened to reveal an older couple, probably in their early sixties. The petite woman had dark hair with streaks of gray, coiffed into an elegant chignon, and the man was tall and unusually slender. He held a cane and was walking slowly, a step behind the woman as they came into the apartment. Both stared at her with raised eyebrows as their gazes took in her wet hair and the fact that she was standing there naked except for Mateo's robe.

The embarrassment she'd felt before flamed another hundred degrees, and if there'd been anywhere she could have run, she would have torn right out of there.

"Is Mateo here?" the woman asked, her eyes remarkably cold-looking for being a warm, velvety brown.

"Um, yes. He's...he's in the shower. See, there was an accident today, part of the subway tunnel collapsed, you might have seen it on the news, or gotten stuck in all the traffic? So I went to help and Mateo was in there rescuing a man and his dog, and we got all dirty, and then..." Her voice faded away. Lord, she must sound like a raving lunatic. "Um, come in. I'm sure he'll be out in—"

"Mother. Father. What are you doing here? I thought you'd already left for home."

Miranda turned to see Mateo standing in the doorway to his bedroom, and what little breath she had left backed up in her lungs. Because he was wearing a towel around his waist and nothing else, with a sheen of water droplets in relief on his wide shoulders and athletic chest, a few dripping down the dark hair on his taut stomach just as she'd visualized earlier. Only even better.

She gulped. Obviously, he'd heard voices and hadn't taken the time to fully dry off, and between the vision in front of her and her embarrassment that these two people were his *parents*, she thought she just might go into a swoon.

"Our plane is ready to go, but we decided to come here before we left, hoping to convince you to come home with us now, instead of waiting. But apparently you are otherwise engaged."

His mother turned those cold eyes to Miranda, and they reminded her so much of the way her stepmother had always looked at her, it made her heart constrict oddly. Made her feel as unwelcome as she had in her teens when she'd first shown up at the Davenport mansion, which was absurd. She didn't even know these people, but she couldn't help feeling like she'd somehow shoved herself somewhere she was unwelcome anyway.

Mateo folded his arms across his damp chest, his features stony. "I told you I'd be coming home soon. And I will."

"It must be very soon. There are things we need to address right away. You are the heir now!" His father pulled a sheaf of papers from his coat pocket and held them out to Mateo, his hand shaking with what looked to be a tremor as he did so. "Your mother and I are trying to manage until you arrive, but it is difficult for us to attend to everything. Too many people are relying on me, on you, to be ignored."

Miranda looked from Mateo to his parents, and back. What in the world were they talking about? Unlike his mother, his father's attention was focused exclusively on Mateo, who made no effort to introduce her to them. Which shouldn't have bothered her, except it made her feel even more like the lowly interloper that Vanessa Davenport had clearly viewed her as thirteen years ago. And still did.

"I understand. I'll let you know when I'm going to arrive, which I promise will be in just a few days." Mateo's biceps bulged as he lifted his arm to squeeze the back of his neck, his expression grim. A now clean, tail-wagging Benny ran from the bedroom to stand next to Mateo's feet, looking up at him adoringly as Mateo dropped his arm back to his side. "However, as you can see, I'm rather busy right now."

"You have a dog? In this ridiculously tiny apartment you insist on living in?" his mother asked in an incredulous voice.

"It's not my dog."

A man of few words. Miranda had to wonder about the

odd exchange between Mateo and his parents, with him obviously not wanting to share anything about the events of the day. It was also obvious they weren't going to be sharing warm and fuzzy hugs. She knew how it felt to have a strained relationship with your own family, and hoped it didn't bother him the way her own situation always had.

"Well. We will see you at home, then, and look forward to your arrival."

His mother's eyes rested on Miranda one more time before she turned and swept out into the hallway without another word, her husband slowly following. It struck Miranda that their bearing was remarkably regal, their clothes obviously expensive. It was somehow surprising that these two unusually elegant people had a son whose chosen profession was that of a paramedic. But as she watched Mateo move to close the door behind them, it struck her that there was something intangibly noble about his bearing too.

He turned, his face impassive. "Sorry about that. Probably your clothes are ready."

His words reminded her that she was still standing there in his robe, otherwise naked, and that he was practically naked, too. She found herself staring again at the beyond sexy contours of his torso, the beautiful golden shade of his skin, and the dark hair covering his pectorals and hard stomach, which she knew felt soft to the touch. Jerking her eyes up to his didn't help the breathless feeling that came over her, as they only managed to land on his chiseled jaw and the beautiful shape of his unsmiling mouth, and her own lips parted to suck in a much-needed breath.

What was it about Mateo Alves that had her feeling so peculiarly stirred up and uncomfortable and embarrassingly aroused whenever he was near?

One hand lifted to clutch her robe tighter to her throat before he turned to get her clothes from his small laundry closet. Eyeing the wound on his back as he opened the dryer, she nearly offered to bandage it for him in case it started bleeding again, but decided she needed to keep her hands off his body. Getting dressed and out of there as soon as possible was the best plan, and she practically snatched the warm clothes he brought from the dryer.

"There are a pair of women's sweatpants on my bed for you. It's the best I could do."

"Anything is better than walking down the street with only one pants leg," she said, feeling a little strange about wearing pants that had presumably belonged to a lover of his, but she didn't have much choice. "I'll get dressed, then out of your hair."

Finally respectably covered up, she swiped on a little lipstick, still feeling oddly jittery as she went back to his living room.

"Thanks again for letting me get pulled together here. I guess I'll see you around the hospital sometime."

"Are you feeling all right?" The way he was carefully looking at her made her wonder what he was seeing. "Not stressed or odd about having concrete showering down on you, wondering if it was going to get worse? It's okay if you do. Even after regularly being in harm's way, plenty of people suffer emotional aftereffects from it."

"Well, as you pointed out, it's pretty much my own fault for going in there to begin with. Makes you think about how quickly things can happen, doesn't it? I see the results of bad accidents in the hospital every day, but somehow I never think about it happening to me."

"So next time promise you'll stay put and get someone trained in search and rescue."

"I'm hoping there's no 'next time.' But I can't promise—I took an oath to help sick or injured people, and if I have to put myself in harm's way, I'm going to do it."

"Yep, a very stubborn woman." A small smile curved his lips even as he shook his head in exasperation. "Just be sure to take care of yourself, and if you start to have bad dreams or flashbacks, talk to someone about it."

"Don't worry, I really am fine. But thanks." Maybe he thought she sounded stubborn and brave, but the truth was, she fervently hoped she never came across another situation like that in her life. "I do have vacation time coming up this week. I'm planning to get out of the city, do something fun."

"Like what?"

"Still figuring that out." The main reason to go away was so she didn't have to be at the big Thanksgiving family gathering at the Davenports'. She shoved her hand toward his, and his warm one engulfed hers. "Goodbye, and thanks again."

The way she rushed out of his apartment probably made him wonder if she really did have some post-traumatic stress going on, but she couldn't worry about that. She had enough to worry about.

Like what she was going to do with her week off, and why she'd had a sudden, astonishing urge to ask Mateo Alves to join her.

CHAPTER THREE

THE CHILD'S PIERCING shrieks would have unnerved even the most hardened EMT, and Mateo stepped up the pace to get her into the ER fast. Based on what the father had told him when he'd picked the wailing child up off the sidewalk, it seemed unlikely she had an internal injury. No blood, no visible head injury, no misshapen limb told him it probably wasn't extremely serious. But because he couldn't know for sure, that's why they were heading to the hospital—to check out the possibilities then go from there.

The anxious father had agitatedly told him the story of how the three-year-old girl had been sitting on his shoulders as they'd walked through the crowds. The dad hadn't expected his daughter to suddenly lunge sideways to get a better look at a toy store's glittering Christmas window display, and he'd lost his grip on her legs.

"I just couldn't catch her all the way, you know?" the father repeated as Mateo and the other EMT lifted the stretcher out of the ambulance. "I partially broke her fall to the sidewalk, but I'm so scared she might be really hurt."

"I know it's scary," Mateo said in a calm voice he hoped would keep the poor guy from hyperventilating. "But Manhattan Mercy's ER docs are the best so, whatever's going on, they'll figure it out. Try not to worry."

The man nodded and gulped in some air, and Mateo

turned to his patient. "Almost there, Emily," he said, giving the girl an encouraging smile. "Soon the doctors will figure out why you're hurting and get you something for your pain, okay?"

"What do you think is wrong?" the girl's father asked. Apparently, Mateo's attempts to reassure him weren't working. His voice was panicky, and his knuckles were white as he hung onto the gurney Mateo propelled through the ER's doorway. "It…it didn't look like she hit her head, but I couldn't tell for sure, you know?"

"Her vital signs are normal, other than an accelerated heart rate, probably caused by pain. I'm guessing it's not anything major, but we'll have the doctor take a look." Hopefully, whoever the doctor was would do a better job calming the dad than he'd managed to accomplish.

A nurse sent them to an exam room, and when a white-coated doctor with chin-length brown hair appeared in Mateo's peripheral vision, he knew it was Miranda Davenport before he'd even looked up. As if he'd somehow sensed it was her, and how strange was that? Also strange that he couldn't help the smile that formed on his face just from seeing her again.

"Hi," Miranda said with a sweet smile as she came to lean over the child and give her a comforting pat. "What's going on?"

"Three-year-old girl fell from her dad's shoulders onto the sidewalk." Mateo began his report as he unbuckled her from the gurney. Being careful to not jostle her, he gently moved her to the bed. "Ambulatory at the scene. Heart rate one twenty, BP ninety over fifty. Her name is Emily, and this is her father."

"What do you think, Doctor?"

The man's anxious eyes stared at Miranda, and Mateo decided that the professional but still warm smile she gave him would have had anyone breathing slightly easier. "We're about to find out," Miranda said as she turned that smile to Emily. "I know you're hurting, but can you be brave for me? Just like the princess here always is?"

Miranda tapped the sticker of a glittery cartoon princess she had attached to her name badge, and, remarkably, the child nodded and hiccupped as her crying lessened a little.

"Wow, you really are brave, like her! So, can you tell me where you hurt?"

The child waved her left hand toward the right side of her body, and Miranda moved her hands gently over Emily's head, then her arms and torso. Her careful fingers slowly went to touch Emily's neck, and Mateo instantly saw the swelling forming there. The child shrieked again, and Miranda lifted her head, her gaze meeting Mateo's for a long moment before moving on to the child's father.

"It looks like she has a fractured clavicle. See the bulge here on her collar bone? That might not sound like good news since she's hurting so much, but it's a comparatively simple injury that will heal well on its own. We'll get her pain meds right away to make her comfortable, then an X-ray to confirm the diagnosis. But I'm sure that's what the problem is."

That smile, her quick diagnosis, her ability to calm the child and her father, and the utter confidence illuminating her amazing blue eyes, all wrapped up in what Mateo knew was a hell of an attractive body, were one irresistible package.

"Thank God it's nothing super-bad," Emily's father said, swiping his hand across his brow. "What can you do for it? My wife is probably gonna kill me. I really need to know what to tell her when she calls me back."

"We'll get her a sling called a clavicle strap to keep her arm and shoulder from moving as it heals. And you can tell your wife that it's very common for young children to fracture their clavicles, sometimes even from a simple fall in their own homes. So she's actually a pretty tough cookie, aren't you, Emily?"

The child sniffled between whimpering cries and nodded as Miranda pulled one of the princess stickers from her coat pocket and handed it to Emily. "I hope this will always remind you how brave you were today. Your mom and dad should be proud of you."

Another nod, and as Emily even managed to smile through her sniffles this time, Mateo realized that Miranda had a special gift for soothing little ones.

"You don't put a cast or anything on it?" the father asked.

"If the two ends of the broken clavicle are in the same state, I promise it will heal on its own." Miranda sent the man another encouraging smile before giving instructions to the nurse about not moving Emily's arm or shoulder, and what pain medication to give her.

Mateo's job was done here, and though he would have liked to stay a little longer to watch Miranda work her magic, he figured he should get the ambulance back to the station. He pushed the gurney from the room, but as he passed Miranda in the hallway, she paused in typing her instructions into the computer chart and turned to look at him.

"Busy day?"

"Not too bad. No collapsed tunnels with crazy doctors running inside."

"Or dusty dogs to deal with." Her lips curved. "Did John's family come and get Benny?"

"Yes. My apartment seemed quiet after the little guy was gone."

"So getting a dog might be on your to-do list?"

"Probably not." He had other things on that list. Like being forced to move back home when he didn't want to, despite being needed there, and the guilt of his feelings about all that gnawed at his gut. He couldn't tell his parents he didn't deserve to step into his brother's shoes to take over the family's estate full-time. That his not being there for Emilio, for not doing more to help him, might be part of the reason he wasn't alive anymore. That memories of his laughter and jokes, of their closeness and all they'd done together their whole lives, were a constant ache every moment he was back in Spain.

The weight of all that hung heavily on his shoulders, as it had for the past six months, and he didn't know what he was going to do about it. Didn't know how he could convince his parents that it would be fine for him to be home just a few months of the year, when they expected him to be there full-time now that Emilio was gone.

As he stared at Miranda's pretty face and smiling eyes and thought about the disapproving looks his parents had given her, a radical idea struck him, slowly forming fully in his mind. And the more he thought about it, the more he liked it.

Yes, it just might be brilliant, and actually work. But would she possibly agree? He had no idea. But what he did know? Trying to persuade her just became the number one thing on that to-do list.

By the end of the day, Mateo had become convinced that the idea that had developed in his head earlier was the perfect solution to his problem. If Miranda was willing to go along with it, that was.

After all, what did he have to lose by asking her? He definitely couldn't suggest it to one of the women he casually dated, because they might read more into it than he wanted them to. But since he and Miranda barely knew one another, he couldn't imagine she'd read his proposal the wrong way. Plus, she was a Davenport. Someone from a wealthy and powerful family wouldn't think his lineage was a big deal and because of that, she'd be unlikely to get excited about it, like the women back at home always had. Women who wanted nothing more than to snag a wealthy duke, live a lavish lifestyle, and lord it over everyone who worked for his family, like his sister-in-law had.

Which was just one of the reasons he liked living anonymously in a big city like New York. He could date women for a short time who didn't want anything from him. No long-term commitments offered or expected, and that's how he wanted to keep it.

Miranda had said she didn't have a boyfriend, which he found incredibly surprising, but was more than glad about. She had also said that she'd like to get out of the city for a week or so. Get away from work and the challenges of getting to her apartment while the subway was being repaired. Away from memories of the tunnel collapse and how scary he knew that had to have been for her, even though she'd put on a brave front.

He thought about that again while he waited around for her shift to end. Frustrated with her as he'd been at that moment, now that she was safe and it was over with he had to admire that she'd run in there to help. Search and rescue had been his passion since his days in the Spanish military, but she lived her life on the receiving end of casualties in the ER. Without a doubt, lots of physicians would have waited for the rescue crews to bring out any injured before they got to work taking care of them.

He leaned against the wall of the hospital corridor, his gaze on Miranda standing farther down the hall, talking to the doctor taking over her patients. Did she always take this long to tie up loose ends after her shift was over? He glanced at his watch, impressed that, unlike some of the docs in the hospital who ran out the door the second their shift was over, she obviously wanted to make sure everyone was taken care of before she left.

Restlessly squeezing the back of his neck, he wondered if there was any way she'd agree to his proposal. If she said no, he'd just be in the same situation he was in now, right? But maybe he'd get lucky and she'd say yes, which would solve his problem at least in the short term. At the same time, he'd get to look at her pretty face and enjoy her lively mind during the time they spent together.

He'd always taken a second and third look at her whenever he'd brought in a patient, never dreaming he'd have her lush body beneath his the way it had been in the tunnel, or her nearly naked in his apartment. The memories of how both those things had made his blood pump hard and his breath get short had him turning to look somewhere other than at her before his body reacted all over again.

Miranda finally headed to the locker room and emerged just a few minutes later. Mateo pushed off the wall and moved toward her, watching as her slender fingers slowly buttoned her coat. She looked deep in thought about something, and he wondered if her brain was working overtime about her patients, or if something else was on her mind.

"Miranda."

She turned, and her amazing blue eyes that had shone through the darkness in that tunnel lifted to his in surprise. "What are you doing here? I thought your shift ended quite a while ago."

"It did. I came to see if you'd like to join me for coffee. A little thank-you for doing such a great job with Emily this afternoon."

"Oh. Well." Her tongue moistened her lips, and he found

himself fixating again on how soft and full they were. "I was just doing my job, you know."

"Yes, but you do it very well." She looked so wide-eyed and shocked he couldn't help but tease her a little. "It's just coffee, Miranda. Surely your time in my apartment showed you I'm not a big, bad wolf."

A nervous little laugh left those pretty lips. "No. I mean, yes, I know. Of course, I'd love some coffee."

"Good. How about we go to the coffee house two blocks down? Pardon me for saying so, but the stuff they serve in the hospital is swill."

Another laugh, but this time it was a real one. "I don't mind it. But I suspect those of European heritage are a little more picky than those of us raised in Chicago."

He felt his eyebrows rise. He'd seen the Davenport mansion, and it was in one of the most exclusive areas in New York City. "Chicago? What do you mean? I know you live in Brooklyn now, but didn't you grow up on the Upper East Side?"

"Long story."

He wished he hadn't said anything, because the smile on her face instantly disappeared, and he hoped he hadn't ruined his chances of her going along with his proposal before he'd even had a chance to ask. He grasped her elbow and headed toward the revolving back door. "Come on. It's been a long day for both of us. I don't know about you, but I need a double shot of espresso, *pronto*."

"Espresso pronto sounds like exactly the drink I need right now." The twinkle in her beautiful eyes was new to him, as she'd been so serious during their previous interactions. But he liked it. A lot. "Let's go."

A somewhat private corner table was open, and Mateo steered them there, glad he could ask his important question without anyone overhearing. After some general hospital talk and conversation about the continuing traffic mess from the tunnel collapse, Mateo drew a breath.

It was show time.

"I have something I'd like to talk with you about," he said. "To ask you."

"All right." She looked a little concerned about that, and he wondered what his expression was, forcing himself to relax. Not a big deal, right? Nothing to stress about. She'd either give him a yes or no, and he'd go from there.

"You met my parents yesterday," he said. "They—"

"Actually, I didn't meet them," she interrupted. "You didn't introduce me."

He stared at her, then realized that was true. Their stopping by his apartment unannounced, lambasting him and trying to drag him home right then and there, had upset him so much he'd completely forgotten his manners.

"I'm very sorry. That was rude of me. I was frustrated at the situation, which is what I want to talk to you about."

Her eyes met his, serious again. She sat quietly, sipping her coffee, and something about her expression and the caring way she was looking at him helped him relax.

"I've heard your family described as New York royalty. My family is a little like yours. We have a dukedom in Spain. In Catalonia, about an hour from Barcelona."

"A...what? A dukedom?"

"Sí." He had to smile at her incredulous expression. "I know you may think I'm making up a story, but it's true. You're welcome to look us up on the internet. You'll see my father, Rafael Alves; my mother, Ana Alves; and myself listed under the Duchy of Pinero, living at the Castillo de Adelaide Fernanda. My brother, Emilio, is listed as well." Just saying his name made Mateo's chest constrict with pain and disbelief. It was probably even worse for his parents since Emilio had been the favorite, golden son, which was another reason Mateo could never take his place.

"Wow. That's real royalty, not the fake kind the Davenports enjoy." Her palm pressed against her cheek as she stared at him. "I wondered what in the world your father was saying about you being an heir or something. What made you move to New York, if you had a cushy life of back home?"

Cushy life. If only she knew the difficult dynamics of their family. "I served in the Spanish army for four years, and discovered there my love for search and rescue. For field medicine. Being part of a team. Working as an EMT is a little like that, and I enjoy the anonymity of a big city like New York."

He wouldn't go into all the reasons he'd wanted to leave home, which included despising his brother's cheating, social-climbing wife and Emilio's private pain because of it. Somehow, for as long as possible, he had to avoid being thrust back into that world. Did part of him feel bad about that attitude? Hell, yeah. He also felt horrible that his father's health continued to decline. He had to find some kind of compromise where he could be there for his parents while still living most of the year here. Away from painful memories he didn't want to be reminded of every day.

"But they want you to go back home." She said it as a statement, not a question, which wasn't a surprise, since she'd heard his parents insisting he go back right away.

"Yes. My father is ill and handed over his responsibilities to my brother a few years ago. Then, six months ago, Emilio died in an accident. I became the heir and they believe it's my responsibility to run the estate."

"Oh, Mateo, I'm so sorry. I know how hard it is to lose someone you love."

She placed her warm palm on top of his as her eyes

filled with a deep compassion. Remarkable, really, how a blue that intense could be warm and soft and brilliant all at the same time. Normally, he didn't want others' sympathy, but hers felt genuine and so full of caring for a man she barely knew that he found himself soaking it in, despite himself.

"Yes, it's been...hard. And just as hard is the thought that I have to leave my life here. We have many managers at the estate who are good at what they do. If I'm there only part-time, I believe that will be enough."

"You grew up there. Why don't you want to move back?"

"I like my job here. And there are reasons that I've been somewhat isolated from my family for a long time." Despite the question and the way her eyes focused on him in a way that showed she cared, he didn't want to go into them right then. "My father's illness puts pressure on me to step into his shoes, the way Emilio did. While I know that I have to take over for him in some capacity, I'm not going to move back to Spain full-time. I'm confident my parents will come to see that all will be okay when I'm there only part of the year. But I need some time to make that happen, for them to understand that. And that's where you come in."

"Me?"

"Yes, you." He smiled at her expression of startled surprise. "You'd said you have some vacation time and want to get out of the city for a while. I know that, as a Davenport, you have the means to travel anywhere you want, any time. But I can show you the beautiful area of Spain where my family has lived for centuries, have some fun riding our horses. Tour Catalonia and the Pyrenees. At the same time, you can help me accomplish an important goal by doing me a huge favor."

"Goal? Huge favor?" Those intense blue eyes had widened even further, and Mateo drew a fortifying breath, because her saying yes to his proposal suddenly felt much more important than it had an hour ago.

"I'd like for you to pose as my fiancée. My parents won't like me planning to marry an American who doesn't share their culture. I'll tell them you have a contract with the hospital, and can't possibly leave there for another year. You saw their disapproving expressions when you were at my apartment. I'm confident that our faking an engagement would buy me extra time and get them more used to the idea that I'll only be there a few times a year. Please, Miranda?" His heart sped up as he held her hand between his. "Will you pretend to want to marry me?"

Miranda realized her mouth had sagged open and stayed that way for a very long moment. Managing to finally close it, she stared at Mateo in utter astonishment, unable to find her voice. But who wouldn't be in total shock at his unbelievable proposal?

Pretend to be his fiancée? A fake engagement to keep his parents from insisting he move back right away, while the two of them, two people who barely knew one another, spent vacation time together in Spain? It was the most unbelievable, outrageous thing anyone had ever asked her to do.

And also crazily, absurdly, tempting.

The man was utterly gorgeous. The kind of man any woman would love to spend time with. She'd seen he was caring, too, the way he'd run into the tunnel to help John, and had even put himself in danger again to go back and find Benny. Then today he'd been so good with little Emily, and the synchronized way they'd worked together had been remarkable and impressive.

But all that was a far cry from spending a week with him. And pretending to be engaged, for heaven's sake! Impossible.

"I'm just… I…" She gulped. "I don't even know you, really. That would be too strange, pretending we're, you know, a couple. And going on a trip together. I'm sorry, but I can't."

"I can tell you that it wouldn't be hard for me to pretend to want to spend time with you, because I genuinely do. I know we'd have a good time adventuring together while we're there." He gave her a crooked smile as he squeezed her hand, speaking softly. "When was the last time you did something crazy, Miranda? Just threw caution to the wind? That's what I just did, asking you to pretend to be engaged to me. What do you say? Good or not so good, it will be a true adventure for just a week, right? When we get back, you'll go back to your regular life, as I will, taking with us some enjoyable memories."

When was the last time you did something crazy, Miranda? His words echoed in her head. Her sister Penny lived her life as a daredevil, and had often asked Miranda that question, wondering why she was okay with her life being pretty mundane outside the excitement of the ER. She could just see Penny rolling her eyes at her hesitation, which was part of what had motivated Miranda to be bold and go to Mateo's after the tunnel collapse. How often had her sister challenged her to come along on one of her adventures? Each time she'd refused, Penny had run off without her, shaking her head and grinning, to climb some mountain or abseil from a helicopter or drive a dirt bike on a race course.

When *was* the last time she'd done something crazy? Probably when she'd been sixteen years old, and had gone to see Hugo Davenport, which was a long time ago now.

Mostly, she'd lived her life carefully. Sensibly. Studying hard to become a doctor, to try to fit into the Davenport family at least a little. To make them proud of her. She'd excelled at school, and now she mostly worked, still proving herself.

If she'd been looking in a mirror, she could easily see *dull and dutiful* practically tattooed on her forehead.

So wasn't she due for something crazy? Something illogical and inappropriate and completely mad? Something ultra-exciting to do with her week off? After all, when she travelled with her family, she still sometimes felt like the outsider she'd always been. And most of her friends had boyfriends or husbands, and didn't want to vacation without them. So that left Miranda vacationing alone, as she often did.

As she'd planned to do this week. Because she knew that Vanessa Davenport only had a place setting for her at their Thanksgiving table because she was obligated to. And even though Miranda loved her siblings, and knew they cared about her, holidays always reminded her that she didn't really belong the way everyone else did. Having travel plans had become her MO in recent years to avoid that.

Suddenly, the thought of another trip all by her lonesome felt unbearable. Could she really do it? Do something insane and use her vacation time to travel with Mateo? Maybe it would be a disaster, or maybe it would be wonderful, but, no matter which, it would be something she'd never done before, right? Something not careful and sensible and dutiful. And if it turned out to be awkward, it was only one week out of her life. Seven days.

At the same time, she'd be helping Mateo with his problem, and never mind that her friends would tell her she was just being a people-pleaser as usual, which was a learned behavior she'd been trying to work on.

No, Mateo was obviously disconnected from his family, and didn't she know all about feeling that way? The pain he felt over his brother's loss? She had the power to help him during this difficult time. And she couldn't help the thought that, maybe, if she told Vanessa afterwards that she'd been briefly "engaged" to the heir of a dukedom, the woman might actually be slightly impressed.

And how pathetic was it that something like that would even cross her mind?

She drew a breath then stared at the incredibly handsome man sitting there, smiling encouragingly. "This is… this is the most outrageous thing anyone's ever suggested to me," Miranda said, and the reality of exactly how outrageous it was made her start to laugh. "But I find that, somehow, I can't resist. So my answer is yes, Mateo Alves. Yes, I will go to Spain with you and pretend we're going to get married."

CHAPTER FOUR

MIRANDA WASN'T NEW to flying in a private jet, since the Davenport family often used theirs, and she'd occasionally joined them. So it clearly wasn't the plane departing at night that was making her stomach jump up and down and her heart feel all fluttery.

No, it was the close proximity of the über-sexy man sitting across from her, his deep brown eyes focused on her during the entire take-off. It was the peculiar feeling that, despite the strangeness of the situation, it somehow felt oddly right, too. During the taxi ride to the airport and while they'd been waiting on the tarmac for clearance, he'd talked with her about his work and the ways it intersected with hers. Had shared an amusing story from his childhood that had made her laugh, putting her at ease. He had been an utter gentleman as he took pains to make sure she was comfortable on the plane. He was so proud and regal in his bearing, it struck her that she should have realized he was different from most of the EMTs who brought the injured and ill into Manhattan Mercy's ER.

Her eyes met his and the way he smiled at her had her smiling back, and at the same time her stomach felt oddly squishy, as though she'd known this man for years instead of days.

"Miranda."

His voice made her start. Probably because she'd been fixated on his handsome features and brown eyes and charismatic smile. "Yes?"

"A very small part of me feels a little guilty to have asked you to participate in the charade we are playing. But most of me is very happy that you've agreed to come with me, and I hope you know that. I'm looking forward to spending time with you, and this isn't just about my situation with my parents. So, for all those reasons, thanks for coming with me."

"No need to thank me. I came because I wanted to." And she had. Even when she'd been shocked at his proposal, deep inside she'd wanted to say yes the moment he'd asked, despite the self-protective part of her telling her she shouldn't.

Swatting down those insecure misgivings, she let the excitement of this adventure bubble up in her chest. It overflowed into a big smile she couldn't have stopped even if she'd wanted to.

"We'll be served a late meal soon, then you should try to get some sleep. I'm sure you know that, with the time change, traveling overnight is always best, arriving in the morning refreshed and ready to go."

"I'll try to sleep, but have to confess I'm not good at that."

"Not good at sleeping? What, are you in reality an android?" The corners of his lips tipped up as he raised his eyebrows. "Is this why you seem to always be at the hospital, working?"

She laughed. "No, I'm very human. I just mean I'm not good at sleeping on planes and in cars and such. I just get restless and start thinking too much and then I can't sleep."

"I hope you're not thinking too hard, and worrying, about how our week is going to go. I'll do my best to make it less awkward when dealing with my parents, and show you Catalonia when we're not with them. I can't imagine you not loving it there."

If he felt that way, why was he so determined not to return? "I'm not worrying." Well, truthfully, now that she was actually on this plane with him, she couldn't help but hear, again, those whispers that reminded her she wasn't good enough for a man like Mateo Alves. But it wasn't real, right? So she didn't have to be concerned about not measuring up.

He reached into the pocket of his sport coat, and she stared when he held out what was obviously a small jewelry box, wrapped in light blue paper with a silver ribbon. She looked up to see him giving her an encouraging smile. "Go on, open it."

Oh my gosh. Her breath catching, she carefully tore the paper and lifted open the lid to expose a ring. A ring that held a pale blue stone at its center, surrounded by small white diamonds.

"I…" Miranda swallowed and tried again. "I assume this is a ring you'd like me to wear to convince your parents that we really are engaged?"

"I hope you like it. I got the blue diamond for you to wear because it reminded me of your eyes. Though no stone could look anywhere near as vivid and beautiful."

Her heart oddly fluttered at the seeming sincerity of his words and expression, though at the same time she knew they were probably just the practiced words of a man very good at charming women. "Well, it certainly is…pretty. I'll take good care of it for you."

"Thank you. I had no idea that I'd have to search for a jeweler that would allow me to return a ring. I'd assumed that if the woman said no, that would be a given."

"Well, now you know for up the road when you're asking a woman to marry you for real."

"Trust me, that's never going to happen."

The light amusement on his face disappeared and he turned to look out the window, seeming to concentrate on the gray clouds swirling around the plane. Feeling even more awkward now, Miranda sat there wondering what to do with the ring. Should she put it on, so it was safe on her hand? Or wait until they were about to meet his parents? A part of her wanted to put the dazzling ring on her finger just to see what it would look like there, but that felt too weird. Not that the whole situation wasn't weird. What if everyone at his estate, and not just his parents, took one look at her wearing that and knew she was nowhere near good enough to be a duchess one day? Fake or not, the thought sent a feeling of panic through her lungs that made it hard to breathe.

She swallowed hard and stuck the box in her purse just as Mateo turned to her with another smile that banished his somber look. "One note of warning when it comes to the ring. We have quite a few animals at the castillo, both inside and in the barns. One mischievous Siamese cat we had named Tup Tim was always sneaking onto my mother's dressing table and taking off with any jewelry she'd put there as she was changing.

"Once he stole a diamond bracelet that had belonged to my grandmother, and all of us chased Tup Tim out of the house, all around the grounds, then into the barn, where he ran up to stand on a high beam, triumphantly staring down at us with the bracelet dangling from his mouth. I had to shimmy up a pole and stagger across the beam like a tightrope walker, finally cornering him and retrieving it, and getting bitten for my efforts. He was not happy to lose his prize, but my mother was very pleased with me when I got it back. She never left jewelry on her dressing table again."

The amusing story was just what she'd needed to relax. Had he somehow known?

"That is really funny—I can just picture the scene."

"There was a lot of anxiety on the part of various staff and stable workers as everyone tried to grab the cat, with my mother shouting orders at everyone. I was glad to be the one who succeeded."

Something about the way he'd said his mother had been pleased with him made her wonder if that had been in short supply in his life. She wanted to ask, but decided it wasn't the right time to delve further into the Alves family dynamics. "I promise not to leave the ring out anywhere, though I admit I'd like to see you tightrope walking."

"Other than getting bitten, I thought it was quite an adventure. I ended up practicing walking along that beam as fast as I could whenever nobody was around to scold me. Turned out to be a good thing. Learning how to do that has come in handy plenty of times during various rescues, believe me."

His flashing grin made her chest feel buoyant all over again. Yes, Penny had been right. Doing something crazy had been the best decision she'd made in a long time. Miranda leaned back in her seat and gave herself up to the pleasure of being on this beautiful plane with smart, gorgeous, and amusing Mateo Alves as her surprise companion for a whole week of adventure she knew would be like nothing she'd ever done before. Nothing serious. Nothing to worry about. Just seven days to enjoy some no-strings fun.

The drive to the family estate was about forty-five minutes from the airport, and now that Miranda was past feeling a little concerned at the speed with which Mateo pushed the sports car through the open, winding roads, she was enjoying every second of the drive. It was more than clear that Mateo was a confident, excellent driver, which allowed her to sit back and soak up the incredible views. Valleys, still green in November, stretched far to the mountains in the distance, only to disappear as the road wound through forested areas with gold, orange, and red leaves clinging to the trees. Farms dotted the landscape, with cattle, pigs, and sheep grazing between long, ancient-looking stone walls. Picturesque towns came and went, each with at least one church featuring a tall bell tower that reached toward the sky.

"I can't believe how beautiful it is!" Miranda exclaimed again, pointing at the mountains rising behind a distant valley, snow visible at the peaks, with the bluest of lakes shimmering in front of it. "The colors take my breath away."

"At this time of year, you won't see all the flowers that Spaniards like to grow everywhere but, yes. The fall color and green valleys are still pretty. Have you not been to Spain before?"

"No. I haven't been to Europe at all."

"What?" Stunned eyes flicked her way before he returned them to the curving road in front of them. "How is that possible? Surely the Davenports travel all over the world."

Miranda struggled with how much to say about her life, explaining when and how she'd come to live with the Davenports, but decided to settle on a basic answer. Going into the strange, sad, and upsetting truth of her past, and the rest of her family's, would put a damper on the drive she was enjoying more than she could remember enjoying anything in a long time.

"Well, I was in college, then medical school, which takes a lot of time and focus, you know? Then I went on a few medical missions to Africa and Central America before working at Manhattan Mercy. I do go on vacation but they tend to be short breaks."

"I respect the single-minded focus and dedication it takes to become a doctor. And that you worked on medical missions says good things about you, Miranda."

The admiring smile he gave her made her tummy get squishy and she could feel herself blush. "Not really. Just another way to use the skills I'd learned." And to hone them more in a place where the Davenport reputation wouldn't hang over everything she did, making her nervous that she might let the whole family down if she made some mistake. Which probably meant that working overseas had been more selfish than altruistic.

"So." She moved the subject to him, because she'd wondered a lot about who he really was since the moment they'd met. "Did you ever think about going to medical school?"

"Honestly? Yes. For just a short time." His voice held an odd tone—a smile tinged with maybe bitterness? "Since I planned to leave Spain, my parents would have appreciated that occupation much more. Something better to tell friends and family about why I was going to the U.S. I realized, though, that while I like the medical aspect of my job, my time in the army showed me that search and rescue is in my blood. Which they never understood. But I came to see that I had to live my life for me, not for them."

She could tell that figuring that out had been a major struggle for him, and part of why she was on this trip to begin with. "Lots of people never find their calling. It's wonderful that you found yours."

"It is. And I thank you for helping me keep living my

life as I want to. At least, as much as that will be possible. And now we are finally here. Welcome to the Castillo de Adelaide Fernanda."

A keypad was imbedded in a tall stone wall that seemed to surround the entire front of the property, and Mateo leaned out his window to punch in some numbers. Ornate iron gates probably ten feet high slowly swung inward as Mateo nosed the car through, then up a sloping, curved driveway, and Miranda couldn't contain a gasp at what lay at the top of the hill.

A huge, obviously very old stone house with a terra-cotta tiled roof sat nestled on lush green grass, looking nearly as though it was a natural part of the landscape. Other buildings made of stone or wood in various sizes could be seen not too far away, some surrounded by trees and others completely stark. Forests and fields seemed to stretch forever, with long stone walls dividing the spaces, and Miranda turned to stare at Mateo.

"Is…is all this your family's? It looks like it goes on for miles!"

"The estate is about one hundred and twenty-five hectares, which translates to about three hundred acres. We have livestock, farmland, and an equestrian center where show horses are bred and sometimes shown. The horses were always a big part of my and Emilio's lives when we were growing up, but when my father became too ill to manage the estate, they became my brother's passion. I… don't know what's going to happen with that part of the business now that he's not here to run it anymore. It's one of the things I'll have to talk with my parents about."

She looked at his profile, unable to read his impassive expression. "A lot of things to figure out, I'm sure. I'm sorry this is going to be a difficult trip for you."

He didn't respond, and she had to wonder if the mere

act of driving through those iron gates had brought home to him full force the challenges he'd have to deal with on this visit. Since he didn't seem to want to go into that right now, Miranda made small talk about the amazing views until he stopped the car in a wide, circular turnaround in front of the house.

"We'll go inside and see where my mother has decided to put her house guest. I didn't tell her who my guest was— we get to surprise everyone."

"You didn't warn your parents ahead of time that it's the woman from your apartment, and that we're...er... engaged?"

"What was the point of having them stew about it in advance and be ready with protests? The military tactic of surprising the enemy is always a good strategy."

"Your parents aren't the enemy, Mateo. Remember that they've had a hard time of it recently, too."

"Believe me, I remind myself of that every day. And, no, not the enemy, but hostile to my chosen way of life? Yes." He turned his dark, shadowed eyes to her as they walked up stone steps to the massive arched wooden door decorated with a large, evergreen wreath with pine cones and a red bow. "But I know they don't understand, and are dealing with their own struggles. I plan to tread lightly, I promise."

Mateo swung open the huge door, and the moment they stepped inside, a plump, friendly woman came rushing up, exclaiming in Spanish as she wrapped her arms around him in a big hug.

"*Hola*, Paula! It's good to see you." Smiling, he hugged her back, and Miranda was struck by the joyous way he was being greeted by this woman compared to his mother's interactions with him in his apartment in New York.

"I'd like you to meet Dr. Miranda Davenport. Miranda doesn't speak Spanish, so we'll stick to English, hmm?"

"*Sí, sí!* It is very nice to meet you, Dr. Davenport. Please come in." To Miranda's astonishment, Paula gave her a quick, motherly hug, too, and she wasn't sure what to do, finally giving her a hesitant hug back. Another stark contrast. Vanessa Davenport hadn't hugged her in her life, and being embraced by this woman felt uncomfortable yet oddly nice at the same time, bringing back long-ago memories of her own mother's love. "The guest house is all ready for you. Alfonso will get your luggage."

"Thank you. What I've seen of the place so far is beautiful, and I'm looking forward to my visit."

"Mr. Mateo will show you around as soon as you're settled. I have some breakfast waiting for you—after your long trip through the night, you must be hungry, *sí*?"

Right on cue, Miranda's stomach growled. "Oh, dear!" The way Paula chuckled kept her from feeling bad about that. "I didn't even know I was hungry until you mentioned it. Thank you."

She glanced at Mateo's face, and was surprised to see a scowl there, which made her flush scarlet. Had she embarrassed him?

"Paula, I don't want you to call me Mr. Mateo. You've called me Mateo my whole life."

"I must!" Paula looked shocked. "You are the heir now! You are owed that respect."

"But…" Mateo looked like he wanted to keep arguing, but sighed instead. "All right. Are Mother and Father having breakfast?"

"No. They left for a doctor appointment in Barcelona. I expect them to be gone most of the day but back to dine with you tonight."

Miranda's core relaxed a little at this news. She hadn't

even realized her belly had been tensely knotted about meeting Mateo's parents, and how they'd react to their "news." Based on what she'd seen so far, and what Mateo had said, it wouldn't be with happy, open arms, the way Paula had greeted them. But she was here to support him, right? Help him smooth the way with his family as they all moved into a new reality now that their son and brother was dead.

"Isn't Barcelona pretty far?" Miranda asked in a low tone as they were ushered back to the kitchen. "Your dad doesn't have a doctor that's close by?"

"The local doctor practiced for years, and didn't retire until he was well into his seventies. But now we have no one, and even though Barcelona is only about an hour away, it isn't very convenient for all the people who live and work on the various estates around here."

The kitchen was huge; ancient and modern at the same time. Arched stone walls and doorways met intricately tiled floors, and the cabinetry was a dark cherry wood. A cheerful fire in a large stone fireplace at one end warmed the space, as did homey touches like copper pans on the walls, a verdigris teakettle on the big, modern stove, and colorful plates and cups lined across a large wooden hutch.

"Sit, sit. I have made all your favorites, Mr. Mateo."

His lips twisted as he shook his head, guiding them to sit at the long table while Paula moved to the stove. "How am I going to get her to stop calling me that?"

"If I had to guess, you're not. Just go with it. If you're not home all that often, it'll just be here in Spain that you are 'Mr. Mateo.' Unless you'd like me to tell the other EMTs and staff at the hospital to use it when speaking to you."

"Funny."

His tight lips relaxed into a small smile, and she was

glad she'd made the joke. She gazed around at the large expanse of the kitchen, awed at how beautiful and comfortable it was. "Your home is incredible, Mateo. And I know I've barely seen any of it yet."

"It is beautiful. I admit I've taken its beauty for granted all my life. It feels strange to be here without Emilio, though. He and I wreaked a lot of havoc in this room, and the whole house, over the years."

He stared out the wide window overlooking pastureland, and Miranda's heart squeezed at the pain etched on his face. "I know how that feels. But over time the memories become ones that make you smile more than those that bring you pain."

"I know."

He turned back to her and reached for her hand, and she gave it a little squeeze before she realized he'd doubtless been giving Paula hints about their "relationship." She tugged it loose to tuck both hands in her lap. "Why is the house called the Castillo de Adelaide Fernanda?"

"Named after a great-great-, however many greats, grandmother. I'll give you a full tour after you've rested, since I know you didn't get much sleep on the plane."

"I admit I'm a little sleepy." The words sent a sudden, deep fatigue through her bones, and had her covering an unexpected yawn, which made Mateo chuckle. "Oh, dear. I'm sorry. But you put that idea in my head."

"And once you have a good meal by Paula in your stomach, you will need a nap for sure. Then when you're feeling energetic again? A little adventuring this afternoon. If you'll join me, Miranda?"

His dark, brooding eyes met hers. The man who'd seemed like he wanted nothing more than a fun adventure with her was gone, replaced by this grim-looking stranger, and her stomach bunched in knots at the reality of the situation.

Mateo was dealing with grief over the loss of his beloved brother. Also his parents' lack of appreciation and their expectations, along with those of everyone who worked here. All that was tangled up with the life he'd made for himself in New York. She understood well those kinds of awful and overwhelming feelings, and how they could affect every aspect of your life if you let them.

Then there was Paula, obviously delighted over their engagement and Mateo being the heir now, having no idea he didn't want to be, or that their relationship wasn't real. When Miranda had agreed to the fake engagement, it had seemed like such a harmless thing. Something to tell his parents to help him smooth over his wanting to stay mostly in New York. But seeing Paula's happiness drove a nasty pang of guilt straight into Miranda's gut.

Was this charade really a huge mistake, and had she done more harm than good by agreeing to it?

CHAPTER FIVE

MATEO PAUSED ON his way to the guest house, which was perched on a part of the property that overlooked the valley, below where the estate's sheep roamed. He breathed in the brisk November air and stared across the golden pastures, memories of his childhood flooding his mind and heart. Good memories of times spent with his brother, with the animals and the horses. Not so good memories of his parents always putting Emilio first, pandering to his every need as the future Duke, even when he hadn't wanted them to.

Now that he was here, he was filled with confusion about exactly what his mission needed to be.

He knew that living here full-time was the last thing he wanted to do. Flooded with constant reminders that his brother would never be here again. Being a disappointment to his parents, where they expected things from him he couldn't give. Accepting a bride of their choice, complete with providing grandchildren, which was never going to happen.

Being married at all had never been on his list of life goals. The girls and women of his youth here in Catalonia, and at college, had all seemed to care about the same things his sister-in-law cared about. Money and prestige and titles and power, and who would want to be saddled with that kind of woman? A fate worse than death, as far as he was concerned.

Or, maybe, a fate that led to one's death.

The thought made Mateo's chest ache. When he'd agreed to his brother's pleas to keep the kind of woman he was married to a secret from their parents, he'd had no idea what he was promising. That the burden of a secret like that could lead to terrible consequences.

He rubbed his hands over his eyes. Tried to remind himself that he didn't know for sure if that's why his brother had become more and more reckless. Regardless, he should have been here for him. Supported him and advised him, instead of living his life hiding far away in New York, where he could turn a blind eye to how bad things had gotten.

The same with his father's illness. Showing up once every couple of years hadn't been much help with his father's ongoing deterioration, but his excuse was that he'd known Emilio had been all the support they needed.

So, now they wanted to believe Mateo was good enough to take Emilio's place, when it had always been more than clear he never had been? Never would be?

No. There was a better solution that would be right for everyone, including his parents. He just had to figure out exactly what that was.

The depressing thoughts clouded his mind and threatened to put a damper on the afternoon he wanted to enjoy with Miranda. Why Emilio had loved the woman their parents had chosen for him, Mateo had no clue. Even more now that he'd met a woman like Miranda Davenport. Growing up privileged hadn't spoiled her—if anything, it must have been part of what had molded her into the strong, driven woman she was today. In fact, Miranda was the kind of woman who might change even the most hardened bachelor's mind when it came to ideas on marriage.

The thought startled him, and he wondered why his mind insisted on going to strange places. Must be from the stress of being home again, and he shook the discomfort from his shoulders to walk up the few stone steps and knock on the door.

No answer. He glanced at his watch to be sure it was 2 p.m., which was the time they'd agreed on. About to knock a second time, the door swung open with a sleepy-looking Miranda standing there in a robe, looking embarrassed.

"*Buenas tardes*, Dr. Davenport."

"Oh, I'm so sorry!" She ran her fingers through mussed brown hair. "I was so sound asleep I must have slept through my alarm. Come in."

She opened the door wider, and every uneasy thought Mateo had had moments ago evaporated. As his gaze touched her soft-looking hair, her full lips and slumberous eyes, all he could think about was the same thing that had filled his brain—and body—the last time he'd seen her wearing a robe. Thoughts of reaching for her and tangling his own fingers in her hair, of kissing that tempting mouth and sliding off that robe to touch her soft skin and see where it all might lead.

He forced his attention to the window, and cleared his throat. "We don't have to go out this afternoon if you're too tired."

Maybe that was a better plan. Keeping his distance for now probably made sense, since he'd been having trouble thinking of her as just a friend. A woman who was helping him out with a problem, someone to enjoy spending time with as he showed her the country of his birth.

Not a woman to have mind-blowing sex with, a tempting thought that kept appearing foremost in his mind whenever he saw her, despite telling himself he shouldn't be thinking about her that way. Not when she was his guest, and had agreed to a friendly trip, not a quick affair.

"No, I'm ready. I slept well, obviously." Her lips curved in a sweet smile. "Give me five minutes to get dressed."

It felt impossible to not watch her run up the stone steps, her slender, shapely legs and bare feet making her seem very much like any other woman, and not the skilled and accomplished doctor she was.

No, not like any other woman. Something about her attracted him, drew him in, in a way he couldn't remember happening before. Minutes ticked by as he was trying to figure out exactly why, when she trotted down again to sit on the bottom step and shove on walking boots.

"This house is like a small version of your big house. So old, yet so warm and inviting. I can't believe even this space is all decorated for Christmas."

Mateo looked around at the evergreen boughs and gold ribbon wrapping the bannister, the candles circled with greenery and pinecones, the Christmas tree in the corner covered in gilded balls, and breathed in the scent. Memories from his childhood rushed back, and he was glad all of them were pleasant ones.

"My mother loves to decorate for Christmas. Has for as long as I can remember. She's often had numerous holiday parties and church gatherings, too, which the priest always appreciates. Even winter barn parties with friends in the horse business. Christmas is always a big thing at the Castillo de Adelaide Fernanda."

Miranda didn't answer, seeming to fiercely concentrate on lacing her boots, which made him wonder about Christmas at the Davenport house. "What about your family? Is Christmas a big deal?"

"Depends on who you ask, I suppose." That seemed like an odd answer, but before he could ask her what she meant, she stood and ran her hand along the stone wall. "Tell me about this guest house. Is it the same age as the main one?"

"Yes. About three hundred years old, give or take a few."

"It must be something special to not only be a part of that, but to be a member of the nobility."

"Special? I think you already know how I feel about my family obligations, Miranda." He didn't want to talk about that right now. About the deep pain and guilt he felt over Emilio's death. The reality that he wasn't the man his brother had been. The man his parents had always trusted to be there. "Is your coat in the closet? I'd like to get going so we have all afternoon before we have to be back. I suggest we take today for one of your must-sees while you're here—the sacred mountain of Montserrat. What do you think?"

"I think I'm up for anything you suggest." Finally, he got a smile, which managed to make him smile, too. "Especially since I didn't have time to grab a travel guide and research what all you have to see and do here in Catalonia, and have no idea what Montserrat is."

"You have a travel guide, and that is me."

"Which makes me very lucky, I'm sure."

"I believe I'm the lucky one to get to show you around." He helped her slip on her coat, knowing that was beyond true. "I hope you'll be impressed and amazed by what we're going to see, Dr. Davenport."

"Those words fill me with breathless anticipation, Mr. Alves."

Twinkling blue eyes had his hand sliding down her arm to grasp her hand, because it just felt right. "Then let's get going."

The ride in the car was filled with conversation about the places they passed, and at other times a silence so comfortable it struck him as unusual for two people who didn't really know one another.

For probably the twentieth time, Mateo turned to look at the woman sitting in the passenger seat, anticipation welling in his chest at what her reaction might be to seeing Monserrat. He still remembered the first time his nanny had brought him and Emilio to this place. They'd been amazed by the soaring rocky crags and the thrill of riding the cable car up to see the amazing monastery nestled in the stone, looking almost as though it had simply grown there.

"Those mountains are incredible!" Miranda exclaimed, staring upward as he parked, then came around to her side to open her door. "I can't believe the shape of the stone, almost like a giant hand dribbled wet sand into spires, and they all stuck together that way."

"Wet sand fused into a mountain. I like that description—very apt. Just wait until you see how we're going to get up the mountain to see the basilica." He reached for her hand because he'd enjoyed holding it the first time, and why not? This trip might have a serious agenda, but he fully planned to enjoy the company of this smart and beautiful woman who had been surprising him since he'd first asked for her help. Since the moment she'd run into that tunnel.

"I hope it's not rappelling, like my sister Penny does. I'd probably faint, then fall to my death."

"No rappelling, promise. And falling to one's death only happens here maybe once a month."

She playfully swatted his arm and he started to laugh. With her hand tucked into the crook of his elbow, he found himself unable to keep from glancing into her smiling eyes as they moved toward the funicular.

Whenever he'd seen her in the hospital, she'd been all business, working efficiently, and not one of the docs who joked around sometimes with the staff and medics that came and went. When she'd come into that tunnel collapse, how unnerved she'd been afterward had surprised him, though it shouldn't have. Most people would be freaked out to have rubble falling on their heads, but, then, most people wouldn't have run in like that either. Angry as he'd been at her, and, yes, worried about her, he had to admire that she'd come to help even though he now knew she'd been scared the whole time. She didn't strike him as an act first, think later kind of person, so he had to assume she'd decided she had to go in there regardless of the risk, and that impressed the hell out of him, though he wasn't about to admit that to her.

"We're going to take the—"

He quit talking because she'd stopped dead, yanking him to a halt as she did. "Please don't tell me we're going to get in that yellow thing and go up into the sky."

"Well, we're not going up into the sky, we're going to see the basilica and museum at the monastery up there, and the Black Virgin of Montserrat. But, yes, we're getting in the funicular to do that."

"Oh, my gosh." The blue eyes staring up at him were no longer smiling, they looked beyond worried. Even panicked. "I don't know. I'm sorry, Mateo, but I don't know. I never thought I had a fear of heights, but looking at that thing now has me freaking out."

"Miranda." He turned her to him and tugged her close against him. "I would never suggest you do something that frightens you. So of course we may just stay down here, and go somewhere else if you want. But if you can face your fear the way you did in the subway tunnel, I can promise you that seeing the basilica, the Black Virgin, and the incredible views will make you glad you did."

She pressed her hands against his chest and stared at him, her eyes still wide, but looking a little less panicked now. "I'm being silly, aren't I?"

"Not silly. You know as well as I do that lots of people have a fear of heights. But I can tell you that I'm an expert at that rappelling you don't want to do. So if the cable car gets stuck, I'll hold you in my arms like Tarzan with Jane, and we'll still make it down."

She managed a weak laugh. "I can't say that really re-assures me."

"It should. I really have rescued a number of people that way, whether it was on a mountainside or a building or from a helicopter while I was in the military. But the odds of having to do that fall into the slim-to-none category, as I've never heard of the cable car getting stuck. I'm as sure as I can possibly be that it's completely safe."

"All right." A steely look of determination came to her face that reminded him of how she'd looked in the tunnel when he'd told her to leave. "Let's do it. And I apologize in advance if I hyperventilate or hold on to you too tightly."

"I can handle either scenario." He hoped she didn't hy-perventilate, but her holding on to him? Now, that he'd be more than fine with. "And I'll do what I can to make you feel more comfortable."

With that promise, he wrapped one arm around her shoulders while holding her hand with the other. Miranda squeezed it hard and, as the cable car jerked to a start, pinched her eyes shut. Mateo had to grin at her cutely scrunched-up face. Soon, though, her worried expression wasn't funny at all as the slight sway of the cable car and the chilly breeze touching their skin seemed to ratchet up her panic big time.

"Oh, God, Mateo. I don't think I can do this."

Looking like she might actually cry, she practically cut off the circulation in his hand as she gulped in breaths. "Damn it, Miranda. I feel terrible that this is making you miserable."

"I… I can do it."

"You can. You *are* doing it. Look upward at the clouds instead of down. I think that one looks a little like Benny, don't you? Except not as fat."

As he'd hoped, giving her something to think about besides how high they were seemed to calm her slightly. "Definitely not as fat." She sucked in a breath and pointed at another cloud formation. "That one looks a little like the beautiful Christmas tree in the guest house, doesn't it?"

That she was trying so hard to act brave and composed when she obviously didn't feel that way tugged at his heart. Just like when he'd realized later that the show of confidence and determination in the tunnel had been an act.

Miranda was the kind of woman who donned a persona of perfection, acting the way she expected others wanted and expected her to, even if it made her suffer.

"It does look a lot like a Christmas tree, doesn't it?" He grasped her chin and gently turned her face toward him, and the obvious anxiety there sent a sharp stab of guilt into his chest. "We'll be on solid ground soon, Miranda. Hang in there for just a few more minutes, okay?"

He pressed his cheek to hers, cupping her face in his hand as he held her close. "Just close your eyes. Think about wonderful, beautiful things you enjoy. What are those things?"

"Puppies and kittens," she whispered against his skin. "Babies. Snow. Walking in nature. Cake. Especially cake."

"Now you're talking." He smiled, hearing her relax a little, feeling the tenseness in her neck and arms fade. "What kind of cake?"

"Chocolate. Rich chocolate with chocolate icing, too, but really any kind of cake makes me happy."

"Good to know. It's also good that you like to walk in nature, because that's our next excursion, no scary heights involved. And see?" The funicular squeaked and jerked as it swung into the terminal, and Mateo found himself pressing a lingering kiss to her warm cheek before pulling back. "Here we are, safely on the mountain. You made it! And I think going down won't be as scary."

Her hands slowly slid from his shoulders as she opened her eyes and looked around. With a deep breath, her gaze turned to his. "I'm so sorry I was such a baby. Thank you for helping me get through it."

"You weren't a baby, you were expressing genuine fear, and we all have things we're afraid of, don't we? Believe me, I saw lots of men break down during training exercises in the military, even when they knew they weren't in real danger but were scared anyway. Human nature, right?"

"Right. Thank you for…for not judging me."

Did the woman often feel like she was being judged? He couldn't imagine that, considering her stellar reputation at the hospital. Then again, he knew first-hand what it felt like to be judged by people close to you.

He held her hand as they exited the car, and some of his guilt faded when a genuine smile lit her face as they walked along the wide path, looking at the scenery surrounding them.

"This is breathtaking! The mountains are like none I've ever seen before. And the monastery looks like it's almost part of the rock, you know?" Her grip on his hand loosened, and that blue gaze turned to his, a look of awe sliding over her face. "The engineering that had to go into that funicular is incredible. I wonder how they built it?"

"Impressive engineering, yes. But since it was done with modern equipment, to me, it's not as incredible as getting the monastery built. You said you haven't traveled in Europe so you haven't seen the many fortresses built high on mountains to keep the population safer from marauders, and make it easier to see enemies coming. You should plan to do a European tour soon. Even growing up here, I still marvel every time I see one of them."

"I had some chances to travel with my family, but knew I had to concentrate on college and medical school instead. All that didn't come as naturally to me as it did to my siblings, you know? They're all superstars in their own ways."

She seemed utterly serious, which Mateo couldn't believe. He might not know the Davenports personally, but being around Miranda for mere hours showed she wasn't just smart, she had street-smarts and people-smarts that not everyone with a high IQ possessed.

"I might not know you well, Miranda, but you seem like a superstar to me."

Her face turned pink and she gave him a shy smile. "Thanks, but you obviously don't know my siblings very well. And wasn't I just about to have a panic attack on the way up here?"

"Irrelevant to being a superstar. And even though you were scared, you handled it just fine."

"I think it's because you made me feel safer. Just like in the tunnel. So thank you for that. Sometimes...well, there have been a few times in my life when feeling safe was hard to come by."

The almost shy look of gratitude on her face bothered him. What had he done for her other than hold her close and tell her it would be okay? What exactly did she mean by not feeling safe at times? Did no one she knew support her?

"No thanks necessary." His voice came out a little gruff. "I'm glad I could help. So now that we're here, I can't wait for you to see why you made the effort."

The tour of the basilica and museum seemed to fascinate Miranda, and her pleasure at seeing them made him smile too. How long had it been since he'd been up here? Too long, as his parents had pointed out, and the now familiar guilt of all that pressed on his chest.

He shook off those thoughts, wanting to enjoy being alone with Miranda for the short time he had. "Quite a few monks still live here at the Montserrat Abbey, though I doubt if we'll see them. And right over here is the Black Virgin. One story says she was brought here during an eighth-century invasion for protection. She lay in hiding until being rediscovered about two hundred years later. Today, many people come to pay homage to her."

"Oh, she's so beautiful!" Miranda breathed as she looked at the statue. "I've never seen anything like this. What is she made of?"

"It's said she was carved from wood in Jerusalem. Apparently her dark color is from hundreds of years of candles being burned in front of her, though she has been painted black more than once over the centuries. Many have reported miracles after being here."

"There was a time I didn't believe in miracles, but then one happened to me. And this place is so amazing, who knows?"

"Indeed. Who knows?" Personally, Mateo didn't believe in miracles, though he'd never tell his deeply Catholic mother that. "What miracle happened to you?"

Her smile grew a little stiff. "Not important. Silly of

me to say that, really. It wasn't really a miracle. So now where do we go?"

"It's possible to climb to the cave where the Black Virgin was hidden, but that's very strenuous. We should probably just explore the area a little more then head back, to give you time to rest before having to pretend to be my adoring fiancée."

"Adoring? I don't remember that being part of our deal."

"Ah, my mother may get frustrated with me, but I think she'd expect my fiancée to think I'm wonderful."

She chuckled, obviously knowing he was teasing. But, truthfully, he was a little worried how his parents would react to his pretend engagement. Being surprised and not happy that she was an American was a given. But would they be cool with her, or possibly rude? They certainly hadn't been very cordial to her at his apartment.

His parents were normally polite, but the loss of their beloved elder son had hit them both hard. He knew they were still grieving deeply, and worried about his father's health. Weren't they all? That pain and worry, combined with feeling stressed over the future of the dukedom, had taken their toll, eating away at their innate decorum.

He sighed. If only this plan with Miranda would make his parents decide they wanted him to be there only part of the time anyway. Choosing a bride—pretending to choose—who they wouldn't deem suitable for the future Duke would hopefully give them second thoughts about their insistence that he come back permanently. He might not be able to ignore the guilt gnawing at his gut, but thinking about living here full-time made his stomach churn.

No point in fighting that argument with himself all over again. The week with Miranda here posing as his fiancée would unfold as it would, and he'd figure out the next steps as they went along.

Thankfully, their trip down the funicular didn't seem to stress Miranda as much as coming up had, and they talked like old friends on the drive back. Mateo was struck all over again at the odd connection he felt with her. Maybe it had something to do with the ruse, but he didn't think so. He'd felt that way during the very first hours they'd spent together during and after the tunnel collapse. A mysterious chemistry that just happened sometimes, he supposed, but he couldn't remember feeling so utterly relaxed and happy to be with someone, even as the dreaded first meeting with his parents loomed over them.

"Here we are, with plenty of time for you to rest before dinner." He drove straight up to the guest house. "Thank you for joining me, and for not hating me for putting you through the funicular."

"It's good for me to face my fears. Maybe that's the big lesson I'm going to get from this trip."

"I hope it won't be full of fears for you to overcome, Miranda. That it will be more about adventure and having fun together." The truth of that struck him as he remembered how scared and vulnerable she'd looked, and how protective it had made him feel. As much as he wanted her here to help him with his family problems, he knew that, even more, he wanted to help her feel more confident and appreciated, which seemed to be lacking in her life for some inexplicable reason.

With that goal now forefront in his mind, he nudged her into the guest house, slipped off her coat, and pressed a kiss to her forehead, wishing he could kiss her for real. "Get some rest. I'll be back at seven to take you to the house."

"Okay."

That uncomfortable look slipped onto her face again, and it made his chest tighten. He knew then that he had to somehow try to smooth the rough edges off the meeting with his parents ahead of time. Let them know they had to be on their best behavior without actually telling them about the engagement, because he had a feeling that if they had too much time to think about it before they met her, they'd be so upset they'd forget their manners entirely.

"They're not ogres, Miranda. It will be fine, I promise."

"I know. I'm being silly. Again. It's not even a real engagement, anyway, so there's no reason them being upset should bother me."

"Right. See you in a bit." He gave her a smile and a quick hug to hopefully reassure her before heading to the house to find his parents.

"Paula. Are Mother and Father here?"

"They got back from the doctor's about an hour ago, and are having coffee in the front room."

Seeing them sitting like they always did in their favorite chairs made him feel a warm familiarity, at the same time the knife edge of guilt stabbed his gut. His mother was reading, but his father just stared out the window.

Something about seeing them here at home was different than when they'd been in New York, and the knife twisted deeper. How had he not noticed how thin his father had gotten? How pallid and frail? Even his hair, which had always been thick and difficult to tame, seemed thinner and more gray. But grief as well as illness could age a person, and it struck him that both his parents looked about ten years older than they had at his brother's funeral.

Mateo's throat tightened, and he had to swallow before he could speak. "Madre. Padre. How did the doctor appointment go?"

"Mateo!" His mother stood and wrapped her arms around him and he held him close for a long moment, trying to remember the last time he'd done that. "Paula told us you and your friend were here, and had gone out for a bit."

"Yes, we went to Montserrat. I haven't been there for a long time."

"You haven't been home at all for a long time, other than for your brother's funeral."

And here they were, straight to familiar criticism. He bit back a negative response, instead walking to his father's chair and crouching down to grasp his bony hands. "How are you feeling?"

"Not bad."

Mateo knew his father's pride demanded that he be stoic, and he was never sure how to handle that. Whether or not he should leave it at that, or ask specific questions about his father's difficulty sleeping, or if his co-ordination was worsening, or if he was scared at the ways his body functions were deteriorating.

"Any new medications or therapies they want to try?"

"They want him to try a new medicine for his tremor, and see if it will also help him walk better," his mother answered.

Mateo nodded, making a mental note to look later at what they'd given him. He gently squeezed his father's hands, then stood. "Well, as you know, my…friend is here with me. Thank you, Madre, for having the guest house looking so beautiful. Your special Christmas touches are everywhere, which Miranda appreciates."

A smile banished the seriousness and disapproval he'd come to expect from her. "I'm glad. What time are you bringing her here?"

"Paula told me seven. Is that right?"

"Yes. We look forward to it. But remember, Mateo."

Her stern expression back, he had a feeling he knew what was coming. "Remember what?"

"We have important things to talk about privately. So be sure to leave us with plenty of time to do that before you go back to the States."

He glanced at his father, who was just looking at him with those scarily sunken eyes. When he turned back to his frowning mother, his gut tightened as he realized all over again how complicated this situation really was. How hard it was going to be to find a solution that made everyone reasonably happy. "I won't forget. And I hope that, despite that upcoming conversation, you'll be cordial and welcoming to Miranda. See you in a few hours."

CHAPTER SIX

MIRANDA CURLED HER fingers into her palms, the ring on her finger feeling strangely uncomfortable. She stared at the huge, heavy wood front door of Mateo's family home, awed by it all over again. Small evergreen trees covered with twinkling lights sat in decorative concrete pots that at each side of the wide stone porch, and the whole house looked like something out of a travel magazine during the holidays.

The door opened before they reached it, with Paula standing there, all smiles. "Welcome! Come in! Your parents are expecting you in the blue salon for drinks and appetizers before dinner."

"Thanks, Paula." Mateo took Miranda's hand and thumbed the ring as they walked into his parents' house. The feel of his hand holding hers might have eased her discomfort about their upcoming big "announcement" to his parents if he hadn't been wearing a slightly grim expression. "Thank you for wearing this. I appreciate it."

And how strange had it felt slipping it on? It wasn't as though she'd ever been in a school play to hone the minimum of acting skills required for this charade. At the same time, though, she couldn't deny that wearing such a gorgeous ring would be nice under different circumstances. Like a real engagement to someone she loved, and thinking about this deception had her feeling nervous and uncomfortable all over again. Was it wrong of her—and of Mateo—to be deceiving his parents this way?

Butterflies flapped around in Miranda's belly, even though she knew it didn't make sense, since she'd known all along why she was on this trip in the first place. And she'd already met Mateo's parents, right? Or sort of met them. While wearing Mateo's robe. With him naked in the other room.

Heat flooded her cheeks to join her nervous jitters. It seemed only a few hours ago she'd been so happy she'd agreed to come to Spain with Mateo. Now? Now she knew that *crazy* was exactly that—what had she been thinking?

"Are you ready?"

"I'm… Honestly, I don't know." She looked around the amazing old house, with its stone walls, fine carpets, and gorgeous furniture. Decorated even more lavishly for Christmas than the guest house, and she felt more out of place than when she'd first moved in with the Davenports as a teen. "I feel uncomfortable. I'm not sure I'll be able to act like we're engaged, to convince your parents that we really are."

"Then I'll be sure to do something to make you feel more convincing, hmm?"

She stared up into his dark eyes, filled with an impish teasing that had banished his frown. What that "something" might be had her worrying even more as he led her into a beautifully appointed room. A stunning Christmas tree so tall it touched the high ceiling was loaded with small white lights, gorgeous and unusual ornaments, and silver tinsel. Several surfaces in the room featured golden angels and heavy candles set in loops of evergreen that smelled wonderful.

The long, wide room they entered, filled with two settees and comfortable-looking chairs, was empty of humans, which had Miranda drawing a deep breath of relief. Maybe his parents weren't coming after all. The second that hope came to mind, she chided herself for the ridiculous thought. Getting together with them and making their big announcement was the whole point of the evening, and the entire trip, wasn't it?

"How about a drink? A cocktail or a glass of wine?"

"Wine, please. White." With any luck, maybe a little alcohol would calm her nerves, because right now they were jangling so much she thought Mateo might actually hear them.

He didn't let go of her hand until they'd walked to a well-stocked bar made of what looked like carved mahogany. After pouring wine into two crystal glasses, his dark gaze lifted to hers, so intense she wondered what he might be seeing on her face.

Then, to her utter shock, his hands cupped her face and he kissed her. Not a chaste kiss either—it was a full onslaught of heat that stole her breath and ignited a flame deep inside her quivering belly. The light scent of his cologne filled her nose and a tingle swept from her head to her toes as they curled in her shoes. The surprise of it faded as quickly as the kiss had begun, his mouth moving on hers so slowly, so expertly her heart pounded hard as she leaned into him. Her hands lifted to his wide shoulders and her head tipped involuntarily to one side, wanting more of the hot, delicious taste of him.

Just as she was sinking so deeply into the kiss she felt dizzy from it, he lifted his head. Barely able to open her eyes, she met his heated gaze, dark and alive, only to see it slide right past her one second later.

"Ah, Madre. Padre. I'm sorry, I didn't see you come in," Mateo said smoothly, not seeming at all embarrassed.

Dazed, Miranda spun to see his parents standing just inside the room, and horror froze her veins. First they'd seen her fresh from the shower, then kissing Mateo like she wanted to devour him whole. She was positive that's what it had looked like, because that's exactly how she'd felt. Good Lord, they probably thought she was a sex addict or something.

For a wild second, she wondered if that might be true, considering her embarrassing reaction to Mateo's kiss.

His parents both stood motionless, staring. Then with deep frowns they slowly moved toward the two settees set across from one another. A coffee table was placed between the couches, and Paula was currently putting plates on it, piled high with several kinds of food.

"You told us you were bringing a guest. We thought it was one of your old friends from here." And it was more than obvious that his mother was not at all pleased that it wasn't.

"Why would you assume that?"

"Because of our new situation. Your obligations."

Mateo didn't respond to that comment, but she could see him working to seem relaxed. Miranda tried hard to shore up indifference, remind herself she was here to help Mateo and not win a popularity contest, but couldn't help but feel that familiar hollow in her gut. The one she'd felt when she'd first shown up at the Davenport home to face Vanessa Davenport's hostility. That she felt every time she was at a family event she was supposed to pretend to be a part of, despite Vanessa's dislike.

"I don't see what our…difficulties have to do with Miranda. And I wanted it to be a surprise." He cupped Miranda's waist as he turned to her with an adoring smile on his face so convincing it was startling. The man should receive an acting award. "I was horribly amiss in not introducing you the last time you met. Miranda, I'd like you to meet my parents, Rafael and Ana. Mother and Father, I'd like you to meet my fiancée, Dr. Miranda Davenport."

"Fiancée?" Ana sank into the sofa, her face blanching so much that Miranda worried she might faint. "What?"

"I know this comes as a shock." Mateo tugged her closer. She wondered if he'd sensed that her legs felt a little wobbly, and she definitely needed the support. "Miranda and I met at a tunnel collapse, rescuing a man together. And it was love at first sight, wasn't it, *querida*?"

His smile was wide and coaxing, and she wanted to say, *Not exactly. I believe you yelled and cursed at me.* But she'd come here to help Mateo, though the way his mother was looking at her, like an unwelcome rodent that had found its way into their home, made her suddenly wish with all her heart that she'd never agreed to this.

"Yes, Mateo is a very special man." She choked out the words, though they should have been easy to say since she knew it was true. Giving him the adoring gaze he was giving her might be even harder, but she tried, forcing her lips to curve into a stiff smile. "He swept me off my feet. Literally."

Mateo chuckled and pressed his mouth to her temple, sliding it to her ear. "Nicely done," he whispered. "Thank you for letting me kiss you."

Her chest deflated a little, and she instantly berated herself for feeling disappointed at his words. Hadn't she realized almost immediately that he'd only kissed her because they had an audience? Why would it hurt her feelings to hear him confirm it?

"I can't believe you didn't discuss this with us first." His father focused his attention on Mateo as though Miranda wasn't even there. "If you had stayed here, where you belong, we wouldn't be so distant from one another. Why you had to move to New York is still a mystery to us. And to be an EMT when you could have chosen a dozen other careers here in Spain!"

"I chose to be an EMT because that's the path that called to me. As did New York City. I could be anyone there, not treated differently because of who I am. Surely you understand that."

"Yet you are part of this family, whether you like it or not. You must take on your responsibilities now that you are the heir." His father's voice quavered. "And marriage is a big decision. We would have liked to participate in that."

"I understand that." Miranda could see he was taking time to choose his words carefully. "I know Emilio was comfortable with you deciding who he should marry. But I'm a grown man who wants to decide on my own if, who, and when I'll marry."

"Camilla is a lovely girl, Mateo, and Emilio was very happy with her," Ana protested. "You would do well to have a bride as lovely a person as she is. You have a responsibility to marry someone who understands our culture. Who is one of us."

Miranda's gut clenched at their total dismissal of her. Even though their engagement was fake, she couldn't deny it felt horrible to be an interloper yet again. Someone utterly unwelcome to the matriarch of the house. Hadn't she spent years trying to come to terms with that? Being faced with it again, however temporarily, made her want to run from the room and never come back.

Maybe Mateo sensed she was about to flee because his grip on her tightened. His jaw ticked and he seemed to take a moment to draw breath before he spoke again. "I do have a bride who is not only a lovely person, she's a physician as well. I would appreciate it if you would welcome her— the first woman I have ever brought here."

"You should have warned us," Ana said sharply. "An American is not a suitable bride for you, as you well know."

"Perhaps in your view," Mateo said in a remarkably calm voice, considering the twitch Miranda could see in his jaw. "But I believe that the people who live here would welcome a beautiful, intelligent and accomplished woman as their duchess, don't you?"

Miranda stared up at him, wondering how he managed to sound so relaxed when his parents were attacking him. She also wondered about the glib compliments falling from his lips. Had she ever been called those things by anyone?

"The people who live here value our long heritage, Mateo. Something an outsider would not understand," Rafael said.

"You are being very selfish here, Mateo." Ana narrowed her eyes at him before sliding them toward Miranda. "An unwelcome shock like this is not good for your father's health. What is so hard about accepting your duties here? Your brother never hesitated to take on the role when asked. And yet you act like it's a burden to even come home briefly to visit."

"I'm fully aware of Father's health, and my duties. The pain we all feel over losing Emilio. I'm sorry to be such a grave disappointment to both of you."

"You are not a disappointment, Mateo." Frowning, his mother waved her hand. "It's just that…we are having a party here tomorrow to celebrate your coming home. I would prefer not to announce this…engagement yet. Give you some time to think more about it."

"There's nothing to think about." Mateo's voice had become hard now, and the look he was giving them would have had most people quaking in their shoes. "Miranda and I are engaged to be married, which I want announced to the world. In addition to that, I would appreciate some civility and manners toward her, which so far have been sorely lacking from you."

His parents glanced at one another, each huffing out a frustrated breath as they seemed to realize how unpleasant they'd been. "Our apologies, Dr. Davenport. This is…a very big surprise, but we certainly want all our guests to feel welcome here. Please sit down and have something to eat."

The thought of trying to swallow anything make Miranda choke. They wanted her to feel welcome? That wasn't going to happen because to say she was most definitely *not* welcome would be an understatement. And the way they spoke to Mateo? Anger on his behalf tightened her chest. She knew all too well how it felt to be talked to as though you're an outsider by someone who was supposedly family. If she didn't get out of there, she might say something she'd regret.

"Please call me Miranda," she said, drawing in a calming breath. "It's very nice to meet you. But I'm afraid I can't stay to eat at the moment. The…the busy day and traveling has left me feeling a little unwell. I'm sorry, but I'll have to visit with you a little later. Excuse me."

She pulled from Mateo's grasp and practically ran from the room. It wasn't a lie that she didn't feel well. Her stomach roiled as she hurried through the huge French doors at the back of the house that opened to a patio, and beyond to a garden that even in November was appealing.

The brisk air felt wonderful on her hot cheeks, and she gratefully gulped in large breaths of it. The moon hanging above the carefully trimmed hedges and shrubs lining the stone paths was barely larger than a sliver, but it cast enough light for her to see where she was going.

She'd wanted an adventure. Wanted to see more of Spain. Wanted to spend a little time with interesting and attractive Mateo Alves. But not anymore. Not when they'd said loud and clear how they felt about her being there.

Maybe she should just go home. Or somewhere else. Get on a train to Italy or France, or a plane to somewhere warm, before going back to cold and gray New York. Avoiding Thanksgiving with her family so she didn't have to feel like an outsider hadn't worked out so well, had it? She'd ended up feeling exactly the same way, worse even, in someone else's home.

Mateo could find some other solution to his problems with his family. She felt bad for him—she did. But she'd done what she'd promised, right? She'd posed as his fiancée, and now she could leave if she wanted to. Maybe he could still leverage that into the extra time he wanted to let his parents know he wasn't moving back permanently, and, wow, she sure understood now why he didn't want to.

A shiver racked her, and she wrapped her arms around herself, realizing she'd been in such a hurry to get away from the smothering situation in the house that she hadn't grabbed her coat. About to turn back, she felt warm wool drape over her shoulders and big hands holding it there. She didn't have to turn to know it was her own coat and Mateo's hands.

"I'm so sorry, Miranda." His fierce voice rumbled in her ear. "I knew they wouldn't be happy, but their behavior was worse than I expected. I apologize for the way they acted."

"It's okay."

"No, it's not okay. I'm trying to excuse them because they're frustrated with me that I moved away, now leaving our estate without anyone to manage it full-time. They're worried about my father's health problems, and I admit he looks more frail than I'd realized. And they're still struggling with the pain of my brother's death, their favorite son. I hope you understand that it's all a very heavy weight on them."

"Favorite son?" Miranda stared, then realized he was utterly serious. "Why would you say that? They want you to come back to your home. To take your brother's place."

"Only because he's gone. Believe me, there was no doubt they considered their elder son to be their best son. They insisted he serve only one year in the Spanish army because they needed him here. He was always a huge support to both of them. Whereas they were happy for me to serve four years, and I'm thankful for that. It helped me find my calling, which is one of the reasons I don't want to move back here permanently."

"Is your father too ill to take on the responsibilities of the estate again for at least a little while?"

"Unfortunately, yes." He sighed, and the deep pain in his eyes was obvious. "He was diagnosed with Parkinson's six years ago. You can see he speaks and moves slowly, and suffers from a tremor. He's diabetic as well. So it made sense for him to relinquish his responsibilities to Emilio. Except they insisted he marry as soon as possible, and chose his wife for him. As they've wanted to do for me, but I have no intention of ever getting married."

"No? You told me that on the plane, but I wasn't sure you meant it." Somehow, it didn't surprise her, though. Even when he was being charming and wonderful, there was a part of him that seemed closed off. That he didn't care to share. She wondered why, and even as she did so, that part of her brain that was self-protective started whispering again. Reminding her that she didn't really know him, that he didn't do long-term relationships, and that falling for him would be the worst idea ever. "Why not?"

"Even if it had ever crossed my mind, the way women always acted when they knew my lineage made it impossible to know if they liked me or my title. And if I ever did marry someday, it certainly wouldn't be someone of my parents' choosing. My brother's marriage definitely convinced me not to."

"It wasn't good? He didn't love her?"

"He actually cared for her very much." A bitter laugh came from his lips. "But Camilla cares only for herself, what she can buy with our family's money, and spending time with the wealthy Spaniards she's met through Emilio and my parents. She enjoys the company of men greatly, and hurt my brother deeply with her numerous affairs. I never told him that I was one of her targets before I moved to New York, but he knew about plenty of others."

"That's horrible! Why do your parents think she's so wonderful, then?"

"Emilio insisted that I not tell them, to let them continue to believe that the woman they'd chosen for their son was a paragon of virtue and a devoted wife. Which was probably a mistake on my part." He stared off toward the trees before heaving a sigh. "Anyway, I don't know how they've been able to turn a blind eye to her shallowness, though I suspect it's because they don't want to know."

The Alves family didn't have as many skeletons in the closet—or out of it—as the Davenports, but they certainly had their share. Maybe every family did.

"Listen, I get why you wanted me to come, with your parents putting pressure on you to marry someone they like, and come back here when you don't want to. But now that you've introduced me as your fiancée and they were obviously unhappy about it, I think I should leave. Maybe you can use that to play into your not coming back for a while or something. You'll have to figure that out, but I just… It's too uncomfortable for me to stay."

"Is that why you practically ran from the room? I hope

you know it has nothing to do with you—it's because of their grief, and their anger with me. Please don't take it personally."

Please don't take it personally. Isn't that what her father had always told her? It was hard not to take it personally, though, when you knew that, inside, someone greatly disliked you, even when they tried not to show it.

"I'm afraid that's impossible."

"Why? My parents don't even know the real you, so why would you care what they think?" The concerned brown eyes looking down at her seemed genuinely perplexed. Probably because self-confidence practically oozed from the man.

"I… Nothing." Sharing her sad, strange and shocking life history wasn't something she enjoyed doing. Lots of people in New York and elsewhere still remembered the scandal, but if they didn't, the last thing she wanted to do was talk about it.

"Miranda." His hands cupped her cheeks as they had before, reminding her of that searing kiss. "I'd like to know why you would let my parents' attitude mean anything to you."

She stared into his eyes, and the warmth and obvious caring there, so astonishingly sincere despite having known the man only a matter of days, somehow made her want to talk about it after all. Help him understand why she needed to leave, and not be angry with her about it.

"Everyone believed that the famous Davenport family was close-knit and perfect. And to some degree they are. My brothers and sister are all close to one another, and to…to Hugo and Vanessa. Until a huge scandal rocked the Davenports' world."

"What kind of scandal?"

"Me," she whispered. "I was the scandal."

"What do you mean?"

"I grew up in Chicago with a single mom. Well, I did meet Hugo a few times, then I guess he was worried that contact between us might hurt the rest of his family, and he couldn't allow that to happen. That it wouldn't be fair to his other children and wife if they knew about me, so we didn't have any more contact."

"That makes me think less of Hugo Davenport."

"I think he was in a difficult situation. He'd made a mistake having an affair with my mother, with me as the result. He had to put his wife and family first."

"And his reputation. I think you're giving him too much credit, Miranda."

Maybe. She'd chosen not to judge him, perhaps because her mother had always insisted she shouldn't. Had told her he was a good man, and that she was the one who insisted his responsibilities were to his other family.

"So what happened?"

"My mother died when I was sixteen, and I was all alone. I didn't know what I was going to do, but she'd always shown me where her important papers were, like her will, so of course I had to go through it, to see what was there."

Talking about it felt like she'd ripped open a scab from a painful wound that still hadn't fully healed. Even thirteen years later, the memories of how horrible all that had been brought tears to her eyes. Memories of feeling so lost and alone, missing her sweet, wonderful mother, and having no idea what her future might bring other than foster homes and poverty. Filled with hopelessness and a feeling of despair, wondering if she should even make the effort to endure it.

"Ah, Miranda." His hands moved from her cheeks to her back beneath her open coat, tugging her closer against the warmth of his hard body. "What a terrible thing for you to have to go through."

She nodded, letting her forehead rest against his chest, lingering there. It felt nice, and she realized it had been a long time since she'd allowed herself to really lean on someone else.

"In her papers, I found a letter she'd written to me, telling me that if anything ever happened to her, I should contact Hugo Davenport, and she gave me his phone number and address." She lifted her gaze back to his warm one. "At first, he was shocked to hear from me. Then even more shocked when we both found out money he'd instructed his accountant give to us every month for my support had been embezzled by the guy. My mother had had no idea he'd been sending money. So I had almost no financial resources."

"What? That's unbelievable!" He stared and shook his head. "So he finally stepped up? Acknowledged you?"

"He did. I became Hugo Davenport's daughter, and a member of the Davenport family. But not before someone leaked the news, much to the media's delight and my shame."

"Your shame? Your father's shame, not yours."

"I suppose, though it didn't feel that way. The whole family was not only shocked and humiliated that their father had had an affair that was now very publicly out in the open, but that a child had been conceived as a result. I give my father credit, though. He could have just financially supported me, but instead he insisted I live with all of them. It was a little rocky at first, as you can imagine." And was that an understatement, or what? An emotional and physical upheaval for everyone in the house. "No one was sure how to deal with the person responsible for all the turmoil and embarrassment in their lives at that moment.

A sister they'd never known about, a new-found daughter, a girl who was the result of your husband's infidelity."

"Dios mio," Mateo murmured. "I can't imagine. Were they unkind to you?"

"Not exactly. Distant, at first. You can guess that it felt beyond awkward, living there with all these people I didn't even know. I… I missed my mom so much." She swallowed down the tears that threatened even after all these years. "From the beginning, Charles was very kind to me. Eventually, as we spent time together, my brothers and sister accepted me, and I'm so grateful that we're close now. Especially Penny and me. Hugo went out of his way to be nice and supportive, I suppose to make up for all the years he wasn't there."

"As well he should have."

His tone was so dark and grim it made her smile a little. "I know the way he dealt with it before wasn't perfect. But his taking me in, his caring, was like a miracle. There were some dark days after my mom died, and I thought I'd be alone forever. I thought my life was over. But him wanting me to know my siblings and for them to know me was a wonderful gift. I'm coming to believe that, in spite of what I know about Hugo and Vanessa's relationship and his infidelity, good marriages do exist. That someday I might be able to find a man who loves me. A husband who will always be there for me and a family that is truly and completely my own."

"I'm surprised that you still believe that's possible, after all you've been through."

"There are a lot of times I'm not sure who I am or what I'm worth, but I'm learning as I go along."

"Now, that is something I completely understand." His gaze searched hers before he slowly nodded. "Learning things as we go along seems to be part of life, doesn't it?"

"Yeah, it does."

Thankfully, he left it at that. The insecurities she still carried around were private, and not something she liked to talk about.

Seconds ticked by before he spoke again. "You don't go into any detail about your stepmother. How did she feel about you moving in?"

"I'm sure you can guess the answer." Her lips twisted, and her stomach did, too, because even now her resentment toward Miranda was very clear. "Vanessa hated that my father insisted I come there to live. And I get that, you know? Probably every time she looked at me, it was like a slap in her face. A reminder that her husband had cheated on her."

"Again, though, it wasn't your fault."

"She tried, I think. And I tried. I tried so hard to be a model house guest. Which is how I felt for a long time, you know? To feel like a real member of the family was impossible. No matter what I did, I was the trespasser who wasn't truly welcomed by everyone in the house. Who wasn't quite a real Davenport." She forced a smile, figuring she should just stop talking now. Knowing she had to be boring Mateo with her sad story. "Anyway. I'm sorry, but I don't want to be that unwelcome person here, too, even if it's just for a short time. Maybe that's childish of me. But I think it's best if I just go somewhere else for the rest of my vacation, and not make your parents miserable."

CHAPTER SEVEN

THE VULNERABILITY, THE little-girl-lost look he'd glimpsed back in the tunnel and again on the funicular was clear in Miranda's eyes. It tugged at Mateo's heart the way it had then, and at the same time guilt tightened inside him. It seemed like he had an awful lot to feel guilty about these days, and he had to wonder if maybe that said something about the way he'd been living his life. If maybe he should figure out what changes he needed to make to fix it.

No one seeing her work at the hospital, the picture of calm confidence, would guess at the insecurity that lay behind her professional mask. And that her mask had slipped because of the situation he'd placed her in here, reminding her of her difficult adolescence, made him feel angry and remorseful and determined to make it up to her.

"Miranda, I wish my parents had behaved differently. That you weren't feeling the way you are now. All I can say is that I think you're absolutely perfect, and anyone who doesn't see you for who you are, appreciate you for who you are, is a fool."

"Thank you. That's… That's a very sweet thing for you to say. And in case you don't know it, that's true for you, too."

Her words and expression loosened the band of guilt in his chest. Even in the darkness, he could see that the eyes looking up at him looked less forlorn. Shining with the amazing blue that startled him nearly every time he looked into them, and he found himself reaching for her before he'd even thought about it. Pulling her close, and as he did so, her lips parted. He wasn't sure what his intention had been, but seeing the look on her face gave him a very clear idea of exactly what he wanted to do now.

"It's not sweet. It's just true." And he lowered his head to kiss her.

"Your parents aren't out here now," she whispered, her breath feathering against his lips before his mouth connected with hers. "There's no need to kiss me."

"Believe me, I do need to kiss you. I've been thinking of little else since I kissed you before. From the moment I saw you standing here in the moonlight."

And because it was true, he did, wanting to taste again the soft lips he'd barely been able to pull back from when his parents had come into the room. For a long moment she stood there motionless, a little stiff, seeming to absorb what was happening between them, until he could feel her finally melt against him. A gasp left her mouth and swirled into his and she wrapped her arms around his neck and kissed him back. It was so good, so intoxicating, he found himself crushing her close, loving the feel of her lush, full breasts against his chest, the chemistry between them practically igniting the air as he deepened the kiss. Her body fit perfectly with his, and vague thoughts of secretly slipping to one of their rooms and making love with her short-circuited the back of his brain.

No. The thought both aroused and disturbed him. He'd asked her to come here as a friend, to help him. Not to push himself on her while she was feeling vulnerable, stuck at his parents' home with only him for company in the midst of their disapproving attitudes that had disturbed her so much.

He forced himself to pull back and look into the blue of her eyes which, even in the night air, he could tell were focused on him with the same turmoil and uncertainty he felt. Not sure exactly what to say, to explain what had just happened, he dropped his arms.

He couldn't do this. Miranda was doing a favor for him by coming here with him. A bigger favor than he'd even realized, not knowing the lack of belonging and welcome she'd felt in the Davenport home, and now being subject to the same thing here.

Only a special woman who deeply cared about helping others would have agreed to this ruse, knowing his parents would probably be unhappy about their "engagement." What kind of rat would take advantage of her, kissing her and maybe even eventually making love with her, when, as far as he was concerned, their relationship would end as soon as they returned to the States in a week?

She'd admitted she'd like to have a family of her own someday, hadn't she? A husband who would be faithful and a home with children who loved their parents and one another. She hadn't had that growing up with a single mother, and while she now had a taste of that with her Davenport half-siblings, it was clear that having it all, belonging to a family that truly was all hers, was important to her.

And he was a man who could never give her that.

"I'm sorry. I hope you don't think I invited you here to be inappropriate with you. I'm not sure where that came from, but it won't happen again."

Confusion clouded her eyes, and he thrashed himself for being so weak as to kiss her when he shouldn't have. Had he hurt her feelings in the process? Reaching to hold her cold hand, he led the way back inside, not sure what exactly to do when they got there.

"Mateo."

"Yes?" He risked a glance down at her, relieved to see her expression was more normal now and, in fact, held some of the same determination he'd seen on the funicular earlier.

"I'd like to talk with your parents again. Have something to eat with them. It was silly of me to react the way I did. Part of the plan was to be engaged to a woman they wouldn't approve of, right? I'm fine with being that person. Really."

"Are you sure?" He studied her, wondering if keeping her here a few more days would be completely unfair. "I can't promise that my parents will magically be nice to you. In fact, I can guarantee that, right now, they're trying to figure out how to scare you off or change my mind. Stick me with some Catalonian girl who fits their criteria."

"Like I said, I can handle it. I survived moving into the Davenport mansion that was vibrating with disapproval when I was only sixteen, didn't I? If I could do that, I'm sure I can let your parents' dislike roll off my back."

"It didn't roll off twenty minutes ago."

"And I feel embarrassed about that. I'm a grown woman, not a child whose feelings get hurt at the least thing. I was being absurd, and I'm over it."

He looked at her closely, trying to decide the right and fair thing to do that wouldn't upset her any more. "It might still work for you to be angry with me and ditch me. I could play up having a broken heart to keep my parents' matchmaking at bay. Act wild and go out with a different woman every night, mortifying my parents so much they'd be happy to see the back of me returning to the States for a while."

"Would that work?" Her lips quirked. "I have to wonder if that's always been your MO, and everyone's used to it already."

He'd only been partly joking about seeing other women, since that strategy might actually work. But looking at the curve of her lips, the cute way she shook her head at him, he knew Miranda was the woman he wanted to spend time with here. There was something about the way she'd faced her fear on the ride up the mountainside, the way her intelligent mind worked, the way she smiled and laughed, that made the thought of spending time with anyone else seem utterly unappealing.

"Not exactly my MO. My wildness only comes out on occasions that warrant it." And there it came again. That shimmer of awareness, the chemistry that had zinged between them from practically the moment they'd met, was crackling all around them, and he knew he had to cool it before he did something he'd regret.

Like drag her to his room and make love with her all night, forgetting all about the reason they'd come here in the first place.

Mateo breathed deeply and picked up the pace to the house, forcing his mind away from thoughts of hot sex that kept interrupting his good intentions to keep it strictly friendly between them. "So, what's it to be?" he asked, somehow managing to make his voice sound calmly conversational. "I can have the Alves jet ready to fly later tonight or tomorrow morning. Or we can go back and talk to my parents more, setting the tone for this trip and my life. Giving them hints that they shouldn't expect me to move back permanently, at the same time reassuring them that I'm planning to take on at least some of the responsibility they're worried about."

"I'm in," Miranda said firmly. "I just realized with certainty that I'm not done adventuring here and trying to be at least a little crazy. I can do this. My sister Penny would be proud that I'm not bailing out."

"*Gracias*. I'm proud of you, too." He brought her cold hand to his lips and, after a long moment, forced himself to let go. "Tonight, we'll deal with my parents together. Steel ourselves for the party they'd already planned with a number of friends tomorrow night, which now will be a vehicle to announce our engagement. To try to take our minds off how awful that's going to be, we'll spend tomorrow adventuring again, okay? I think you'll enjoy what I have planned."

"You said that about Montserrat, completely leaving out details of the funicular flying through outer space up the mountain."

"Do you trust me, Miranda?"

Her eyes met his for a long time before she smiled, then said softly, "Yes, Mateo Alves. Yes, I think I do. I do."

"*Bueno.*" His chest felt lighter at her answer, and he couldn't help but drop a soft kiss to her lips one more time. "I promise not to let you down."

Miranda wasn't sure what all the emotions were that swirled around in her chest and belly. Excitement? Yes. Who wouldn't be, getting to spend another glorious afternoon with Mateo in amazing Spain?

But discomfort squiggled its way in there, too. Last night had been so strange, meeting his parents, Mateo upset with them, kissing her breathless, then backing off, clearly regretting that he had, even as he'd asked her to spend today with him.

Which made her regret the kiss, too. The last thing she wanted was to be worryingly attracted to a man who wanted to be "just friends." Except the way her heart fluttered as she combed her hair into the neat bob she kept it in told her that maybe it was too late. But she was no slave to her hormones, right? She could be friends with Mateo, and not want anything else. Couldn't she? A fierce little inner voice told her there was no question about it. The man was way out of her league, and falling for him would just set her up for heartache.

Mateo had refused to tell her what he'd planned for them to do this morning, just advising her to dress warmly and to bring extra layers, which was intriguing. Obviously, they were going to do something outdoors. Hopefully it wasn't anything more daring than hiking this time. She'd loved seeing Montserrat, but thinking about that funicular ride still gave her palpitations, as did anticipating what he had in mind, and whether or not it might include more kissing. Which, of course, it wouldn't, and why was she even thinking about it?

He'd been sure to keep his distance from her the rest of last night, even in front of his parents. No more kissing or touching, just that *I'm so in love with you* look he kept giving her that was impressively convincing. Maybe that look was what kept stirring her all up, even when she'd scolded herself to stop. She knew what this game was about, and deluding herself it could be anything else was just stupid.

Dinner with the Alveses had been awkward at best, but at least they'd been civil toward her. Less civil toward Mateo, which was hard to understand, and made Miranda glad she'd come to support him, no matter how odd and uncomfortable it felt to play this charade. How could they seem to disapprove of him so much? He'd served in the military, helping save lives. Then had honed those and other skills in the U.S., helping more people. And he'd come back as they'd asked, trying to find a balance between how he wanted to live his life and his obligations to family and their role here.

Yet, by the way they spoke to him, you'd think he was living his life as a frivolous playboy, off spending his family's wealth.

The part of her that saw such innate strength in the man told her that seemed impossible. But he'd fully admitted he didn't want to come home, and they'd always been able to rely on Emilio. Was part of the reason for that because he himself believed he didn't measure up to his brother?

She shook her head. It was true she didn't really know him, except that she knew he was good at his job. And it wouldn't be surprising if "playboy" fit into his lifestyle somewhere, since she was positive most women would fall into his arms at the least invitation. Hadn't she been one of them?

To her shock, she had, and the memories of that brought hot color to her face. Thinking bad thoughts at his apartment, then falling into his kisses so deeply she'd nearly forgotten how to breathe. Which was beyond embarrassing, since the first time he'd kissed her, he'd done it for his parents' benefit. And the second time? Who knew what that had been about, but the way he'd instantly backed off had told her loud and clear that it hadn't been because he felt the same pull she did. Maybe it was that playboy thing, and he always kissed any woman he was close to in a dark garden lit by a fingernail moon. And hadn't she learned that playboy types, or men wanting to date her for her Davenport connections, weren't to be trusted? Not with her heart, at least.

This whole thing is a charade, remember, Miranda? she scolded herself. *Not. Real.*

She huffed out a sigh and stepped down the beautifully decorated stairs to find Mateo waiting for her by the front door, as he'd promised, giving her a warm smile. Paula was standing patiently next to him, holding a pair of leather boots and beaming. Her expression helped Miranda relax and smile, too. At least one person in this house seemed to like her, and was happy for Mateo. Too bad her happiness would be dashed in the very near future when they broke off their "engagement."

"We're lucky to have a beautiful day," Mateo said. "Ready to get some fresh air and see more of the beauty of northern Spain?"

"I'm ready. Though I know there's skiing in the Pyrenees, and I'm hoping that you telling me to wear warm layers isn't because you're planning on us doing that, because I don't know how."

"Not today. Though I'm happy to teach you to ski tomorrow, if you like."

"No, thanks. I'm beginning to see that my desire to be adventurous is battling with the wimpy side of me I didn't realize was there." Embarrassingly true. Which was one more reason she was glad she'd agreed to come, despite everything. Definitely past time to push herself out of her cocoon a little more. "Tell me what you have planned, so I can stop worrying. Or start worrying, depending on what it is."

Paula looked up at a chuckling Mateo. "You are taking Dr. Davenport paragliding, yes? Show her the beautiful scenery of the area of my birth? I know that has always been a favorite pastime of yours. She will love it."

"No, Paula. My fiancée is not fond of heights." Mateo's smile flat-lined and he took the boots from the housekeeper's hands. "We'll just be hiking. Thank you for bringing her some boots."

"I am sorry, Mr. Mateo. I… I should have realized,"

Paula said, now looking upset and worried, her smile gone. "I know that it hasn't been very long, and—"

"It's fine, Paula. Are you ready, Miranda?"

He helped her with her coat before leading her to his car, and as they drove in silence she had to wonder about his exchange with Paula. The way he'd interrupted, then dismissed the woman's words seemed very unlike him. Coupled with the expression on his face, which could only be described as grim, and Paula's obvious distress, it was clear something was bothering him.

"We'll be driving through parts of the Parque Nacional de Ordesa y Monte Perdido—our national park. Then hiking some of the beautiful trails. Don't worry." His teeth flashed in a smile, banishing some of the grimness as they drove down the winding road from his parents' estate. "We'll stay in the lower elevations and off the cliffs. It's too late in the season to go on the high roads, which are likely covered in snow. But you'll enjoy the panoramic views and communing with nature, I promise."

"Sounds wonderful. This trip is helping me see that I spend way too much time in the city, and shut inside the busy hospital. Breathing fresh air and having nature all around me sounds like the perfect getaway." Especially with Mateo Alves to look at along with the mountains and valleys. She'd admire him the same way, with a detached appreciation for beauty. She could do that. If she tried hard enough.

"*Bueno*. Paula has packed us a picnic lunch. Hopefully it's warm enough to enjoy it outdoors, but if it's too cold, we'll make it a car picnic, if that's all right with you?"

"So long as we're not hanging up in the sky from a funicular, hang-glider, or ski lift, anything and everything is all right with me."

"I'll put that in my reference notes. Everything is fine

with you except hanging from the sky—does that al-most sound like a song lyric to you? I think I'll compose that, and title it 'Miranda in the Sky with Diamonds'." He grinned and reached across the console to tap the ring he'd given her to wear as part of their ruse.

"I think that song's sort of taken. And the diamond isn't really mine."

"All right, how about 'Miranda's eyes are like diamonds the color of the sky.' How's that for romantic?"

"Save it for when your parents are around to hear it. And who knew you had mad skills like song-writing to add to your résumé?" She kept her voice light, fighting down the silly flutter in her tummy when he talked about romance. And why was he? He'd made it clear last night he didn't think of her in that way. Or, at least, didn't want to. Flirting probably just came as naturally to the man as breathing, which she would do well to remember, and not read any meaning into it.

He gave her that grin that made her stomach flutter an-noyingly even more, then sent the car through mountain passes at speeds that would have thrilled Penny, but had Miranda clutching her seat and holding her breath. She knew if she asked, he'd slow down, but hadn't she de-cided that it was past time to live her life a little more on the edge? This trip was certainly accomplishing that in more ways than one.

Mateo told her about the old and charming towns, as well as educating her on the geographic elements they passed. She gazed in wonder, thinking how incredible it would be to live here. She knew Mateo's reasons for mov-ing to New York, but had to admit that the longer she was here, the harder it was for her to imagine he'd planned to leave all this behind forever, until the tragedy of his broth-er's death was forcing him to modify that plan.

"The hiking trail along the river is the easiest, but still beautiful," Mateo said as the road ended in a parking area. "I figured you weren't up for a long trek up the steepest trails, though the views are incredible from there."

"I appreciate that. I'd probably be sucking wind on a steep trail."

"You definitely need to get out of the hospital more. I see you practically every time I'm there."

"Maybe." It was true, she probably did work too much, but taking extra shifts was one more way to try to prove she was worthy of the Davenport name. Not to mention that dating wasn't high on her list of things to do. She'd learned the hard way that they either didn't like the work hours she kept, or they figured that she was the key to a fortune, and didn't really care for her personally at all. Not trusting a man's attention or words of love to be real was something she'd eventually taken to heart.

Mateo got their gear out of the trunk of the car and set everything on metal benches next to the parking area. Shoving her feet into the hiking boots was a bit of a challenge, but after she got them laced, she stole a look at the man sitting next to her. At his strong jaw, thick black hair, and sensual lips that brought back memories of their searing kisses.

Aside from his obvious sex appeal, she had to wonder if his status as the heir to a dukedom was one of the reasons she found herself so drawn to him? He had family money of his own, and wouldn't be interested in hers. Plus he'd said loud and clear that he wasn't looking for a long-term commitment with any woman. Which made him safe to spend a little time with, right? She didn't have to worry about impressing him in hope of something more.

The thought made her frown. Safe. Impressing others. Was her whole life focused on those two things? Keeping herself safe from heartache and pain? Safe from criticism by accomplishing things people expected of a Davenport? Safe from the hazards of the world, to the point where she wrapped herself in cotton wool to insulate herself?

"You're scowling." He leaned closer, his fingertip smoothing across her forehead. "Are you not wanting to hike? We can just have our picnic here, if you like, then drive some more and see the various views from the road."

"No." Miranda looked into Mateo's eyes, then noticed him shoving the backpack that presumably held their lunch to the end of the bench. Her heart warmed at his consideration—when was the last time she'd spent time with such a sweet and thoughtful man, who seemed to really want to do whatever made her happy and comfortable? "I'm just thinking about the way I've been living my life. Maybe this trip was meant to help me take a look at that in a way I haven't been doing."

"And how have you been living your life, other than working too much?"

"I guess I've been worried too much about trying to impress people. Prove I might be worthy of the Davenport name. Not put myself in situations that might be scary or potentially hurtful. I… Maybe I've been living my life as a coward."

"A coward? Now, there's a word no one would ever use about you, Miranda. Aren't you the woman who braved going into a collapsing tunnel? Who went up the funicular, even though it scared you? Who came on this trip with me after barely knowing me and having no idea how it would go?"

"I guess." His words, along with the admiring smile in his eyes, had her smiling back, even though she tried not to put too much trust into all he was saying. But a warm little glow filled her chest anyway. "Maybe it's being around you that makes me feel more brave than usual, putting myself in situations I normally wouldn't. So thank you for that."

He smiled and gently flicked his warm finger beneath her chin. "So I don't need to feel so guilty about dragging you here to terrify you on the funicular and have to deal with my parents?"

"Like I told you last night, I'm here by choice, and you know what? I'm ready to hit the trail."

"Bueno." He shrugged on the backpack, enfolded her hand in his, and they set off.

The farther they walked, the more Miranda was amazed at the beauty surrounding them. Tall beech trees, maples with a few gold and red leaves left, the beauty of the rocky cliffs and the valley, with trout clearly visible in the glassy river as they trekked beside it.

"This is incredible! I didn't know what to expect, but this is beyond anything I'd imagined. Living in big cities for my whole life, I guess I've forgotten how wonderful it is to enjoy nature and open spaces like this. I feel... I feel at peace here, you know?"

"Do you?" He paused, seeming struck by the comment. "I guess I always did too. Whenever I felt buried by schoolwork, or my family was driving me crazy, I'd come out here."

"How did your family drive you crazy back then? Did you and Emilio have sibling squabbles?"

"Of course." A smile twisted his lips. "But Emilio and I were close, and did a lot of things together. I only got a little jealous when my parents favored him so much, but it wasn't his fault. And honestly? He deserved most of the admiration they gave him."

"How did they favor him?"

"In lots of ways. Hey, look!" He pointed to the sky. "See

the eagles? If you pay attention you might see vultures, too, all looking for their lunch."

It seemed clear he didn't want to keep talking about his brother and the Alves family dynamics. "Wow, that's incredible. I've never seen an eagle before. The way they fly and glide is magnificent, isn't it?"

"There are ways humans can fly here, too, Miranda. Base jumping, hang-gliding, parasailing."

"Um, thanks, but you already know I'll leave the hanging in the sky to the birds. Parasailing and all that looks too dangerous, as far as wimpy me is concerned,"

To her surprise, he suddenly looked somber, instead of amused, at their banter. What had she said to make him look like that?

"This looks like a good place for our lunch break," Mateo said as they walked on in sudden silence. He stopped to gesture at a large, flat rock jutting from the hillside by the path. "Are you hungry?"

"Famished. I can't remember being this hungry before."

The dark eyes staring into hers held an odd expression. Miranda wasn't sure what it was, she only knew that her breathless feeling came back in spades and her heart beat a little faster.

"I can't either, *mi belleza*."

His gaze lingered on hers, and just as she felt she was drowning in it, he turned away to drop the backpack onto the rock. Miranda couldn't believe the containers of foods and sandwiches he pulled out, making her mouth water— or was it Mateo that had done that? Thoughts of kissing his beautiful mouth, tasting him again, suddenly seemed even more appealing than lunch, fool that she was.

With the food laid out, his gaze met hers again before dropping to her mouth. Mesmerized, she felt her lips part in anticipation. His face slowly lowered and his mouth met hers, soft and sweet and delicious.

The sound of voices coming from down the trail jerked Miranda back to reality as their lips parted, and she quickly looked down, pretending to decide on a sandwich. Wow, she needed to get her thoughts back on track. If he wanted a quick affair with her, he'd already be pursuing that, wouldn't he? Instead, he'd backed off each time they'd kissed, or come close to kissing.

Surely she had enough pride not to want a man who didn't particularly want her, didn't she? And she was well aware that a simple kiss on a rock in the middle of nature didn't mean a thing. So why did she keep trying to make it mean something it didn't?

The family passed by, two parents with three children, the youngest looking only three or so years old. They smiled and spoke in Spanish to Mateo, and he answered back.

"I really need to study Spanish," Miranda said as she picked up a sandwich. "It would be helpful when treating Hispanic patients in the hospital."

"It is very helpful. Some of the EMTs even call me to translate if I'm not on a run with them."

"So, was that family envious of all this food?" she asked, trying to bring back the pleasant normalcy they'd been enjoying before, squashing the heat she'd felt vibrating between them. Vibrating from her end at least. But she just couldn't seem to help it.

"They said they'd just enjoyed theirs, so I thankfully didn't feel a need to offer them some."

"Looks like Paula packed enough for them and us, too."

He smiled. "She always fussed over Emilio and me when we were kids. Almost like a second mother to us, you know?"

"How long has she been with your family?"

"As long as I can remember. Raised her own brood, and us, too. All of her adult children now work somewhere on the estate."

"That's really wonderful, having a connection like that."

"I guess it is." He looked at her as though he hadn't thought about that before. "I took it for granted, growing up with it. It's like having a huge, extended family, I suppose. I need to meet with some of them before we go back to New York, talk about the most pressing things that need to be dealt with now that Emilio's gone."

"Are you going to try to address some of it while you're here?"

"I don't know. First, I have to find out if things are in good shape or not so good. So, how's the food?"

Again, a change of subject. Miranda wondered if he didn't want to think about the weight of his family's expectations in running the estate, or the loss of his brother, or both. She was coming to realize even more how many really tough things he had to deal with right now, and she was glad all over again that she'd come, if her being here helped even a little.

"Speaking of family, I haven't told you. I got a message that Charles is engaged."

"Your brother? Is this good news, or bad?"

Trust a man who never wanted to marry to ask that question. "It's wonderful news. He's been very alone since his wife died, spending all his spare time taking care of his twin boys. And he's marrying Grace Forbes, another ER doc you probably know. I'm really happy for both of them."

"Well, if you're happy, I guess that's good."

His expression showed he couldn't really imagine an engagement—a real one—being good.

They ate in silence for a while, listening to the sound

of the river gently swirling by and the birds chattering in the trees. Even though he'd changed the subject several times, would it help Mateo if he talked a little more about his brother? Maybe offering him her ear was what a friend should do.

"Your brother," she said quietly. "How did he die?"

"Doing something we both loved to do. That we spent a lot of time doing together."

"How does that make you feel?"

"The way he died was the result of being very reckless. And I have to wonder if I'd been more in touch with him, talked with him about the problems in his life, that might have helped him feel more at peace. I don't know, but I do know that being here makes it feel more real than when I was in New York. It seems impossible that he's not here any more, where everywhere I turn, there are memories of him."

"Oh, Mateo." She wrapped her arms around him and gathered him close. "I'm so sorry that you lost him."

He pulled her close and pressed his cheek to hers. The long, silent connection made her realize it was the first time he'd really talked about it to her. Had accepted comfort from her. And that made anything his parents had to say to her much less important.

Slowly, he eased away. "So am I. For a lot of reasons. But being sorry won't bring him back." He gathered up the remnants of their lunch and stuck them in the backpack. "Ready to move on? There's a waterfall not too much farther on that I know you'll like to see."

Clearly, the subject was again closed. But at least he'd opened up a little, and that was a start.

"A waterfall sounds wonderful." The bleakness, the pain she could see in the depths of his eyes had her reaching to cup his cheek in her palm. "Just remember that I know well how much it hurts to lose someone you loved dearly. That it's the kind of pain that takes years to heal. The pain of losing my mother is still with me, and I have a feeling I'll miss her, miss getting to share important things in my life with her, forever."

He nodded, turning his head to press his mouth against her palm. "Talking with you is making me realize I can't keep just shoving it down and pretending it isn't there, when being home just brings it to the surface anyway. It's time to start dealing with it, I guess. I'm just not sure how."

He tugged her close against him and she lifted her mouth to his, intending the kiss to be comforting, to show she cared and was here for him, a chaste kiss before she pulled back. But his palms came up to her face and he kissed her slowly, sweetly, until one hand slipped into her hair and tilted her head back, deepening the kiss. Making her feel weak in the knees and way too hot in all her clothing layers, and she clutched the heavy coat covering his wide shoulders to keep from melting to the ground.

A piercing shriek, then alarmed shouts came from quite a distance away, sending their lips popping apart and both their heads swiveling toward the sound. There was no sign of anyone on the path, but as the shrieking grew even louder, Mateo took off running. Miranda, her heart pounding and already out of breath from that kiss and from trying to catch up with him, focused on getting to whoever needed help without breaking her neck on the stones and tree roots trying to trip up her feet as she ran.

CHAPTER EIGHT

THE SHRIEKS WERE eerily similar to the way Emily had sounded after falling from her father's shoulders, and Mateo knew it must be one of the children that had passed by earlier, or possibly a different family coming from the opposite direction. He knew not to panic, but also knew it could be something serious, and the only way to find out what they might be dealing with was to get there fast.

Miranda followed him, but he couldn't hear the sound of her steps anymore. Whatever had happened, he and Miranda could deal with a medical emergency. And if it was more than that, if there was some kind of rescue needed, he always came prepared.

Rounding a curve in the path, he saw the woman they'd seen before clutching two of the children close to her sides as she stared down the steep embankment toward the river, crying out to whoever was below. Mateo ran up next to her, looking down to see that the man who had passed them earlier was picking his way down, sliding at times as he went.

"Hang on!" the man yelled, obviously panicked. "I'm coming to get you. Don't let go!"

Mateo's chest tightened when he saw the gravity of the situation. The tiniest child was hanging on with only one arm to a scrubby, leafless bush growing straight from the side of the embankment, his feet and other arm dangling and swaying over the river. The water wasn't running fast enough to take the child downstream very quickly, but if he fell? He definitely could suffer a serious injury on the rocks below.

"I've got a rope." Mateo pulled the deceptively thin line from his pocket and moved toward the embankment, working as fast as he could to wrap and secure one end around a sturdy tree.

"Oh, my God, will that hold both of you?" The woman stared up him with wide, terrified eyes.

"Don't worry, it's stronger than it looks." One last wrap, and it was ready. "I'll get the child. Stay where you are," he yelled to the man below, "because you're as likely to fall as he is." He knew too well how true that was. He couldn't count how many times a second person, or more, had lost their footing trying to help someone else.

"Oh, my God, please help them," the mother cried as he unrolled the line and began to rappel down to the boy.

"I'm almost there. I can get him and hand him up to you," the man said, grabbing a root to stop from sliding before staring up at Mateo with wild eyes.

It was never good to have the rescuer as freaked out as the one in danger. "Let me. I'm a search and rescue specialist, and an EMT. You can trust me to get him, I promise. Stay right there."

Doubtless because Mateo had already moved past the man, he stayed there, gripping the root. When he got parallel to the boy, Mateo braced his leg against the rocky embankment, grasped the rope tightly with one hand, then curled his free arm around the child, holding him close to his body.

"I've got you, okay? Don't be scared, and don't look down. Are those your parents up there?"

The boy kept crying, but nodded through his tears, clutching at Mateo's coat.

"Look at them, okay? Wrap your arms around my neck and hold tight. All set? Up we go now."

Mateo wanted to make sure the child didn't look down at the river and get so scared he tried to loosen himself from Mateo's grip. That seemed counterintuitive, but he'd had more than one soldier or patient do exactly that, making it very hard to hold onto them, but at least this little guy probably weighed only thirty or so pounds.

"You stay there," Mateo commanded the father as he pulled himself and the boy up the rope, passing him. He'd learned that sounding firm and authoritative was important in this kind of situation, when people were panicking and not thinking straight. "I'll send it down for you after he's safe. Don't move."

The man nodded, stilling hanging onto the root, and Mateo prayed it would keep holding him for a few more minutes. He looked up to see if the mother was ready to take the boy, or if he'd need to bring him all the way over the ledge. Miranda was standing there, her arms open, reaching instead as the mother kept her other two safely away from the edge.

"Ready for me to hand him over?" Mateo asked as, with one more hard pull, his head rose above the ledge. "Don't try to take him straight from my arms. Let me get his bottom safely sitting before you take over."

"Got it."

Mateo reached to sit the kid on the ledge, and the moment he seemed secure there, Miranda had her arms around the child. She dragged him away from the edge until he was a good four feet from it, and Mateo was surprised to hear him start to cry even harder when the mother rushed over to him and Miranda and pulled him into her arms.

Mateo hauled himself up and over the ledge to stand by the tree. Barely glancing at the howling child, he turned to look down at the father, knowing Miranda was more than capable of handling whatever the problem was with the boy.

"Ready to catch the rope? When you do, pull yourself up with a hand-over-hand movement. On the count of three—one, two three." Relieved that his first attempt at tossing the rope went straight to his hands, he and the man worked together. The guy slowly heaved himself up, jamming his feet into the rocks for leverage, and at the same time Mateo helped by pulling on the rope as he climbed. In a matter of minutes he was scrambling over the ledge and Mateo grabbed him by the armpits to help him get to safety. Obviously shaken, he stood and pumped Mateo's hand.

"Thank you. Thank you so much," he gasped.

"You okay?"

The man nodded, catching his breath, then frowned when he saw their little boy was still extremely upset. "Is he hurt?" he asked, looking first at Mateo then at his wife. "Or is he just still scared?"

Mateo turned to see Miranda, who'd moved far away from the ledge and was carefully checking the boy. She was now every inch the calm, medical professional who would make any worried parent feel better, and not the sexy, vibrant woman he'd been unable to resist kissing not long ago. Then he realized she had no idea what the parents were saying and needed to connect them all.

"This is Dr. Davenport, she's an emergency room doctor in the States. She doesn't speak Spanish, but I'll interpret as soon as she finishes her exam. Miranda," he said, switching to English, "can you tell what's going on? Find anything?"

"One more minute." Miranda carefully wrapped her

fingers around the child's arm, and received a scream in response. She glanced up at him, then smiled at the parents. "See the way he's holding his arm close to his tummy? Tell them I'm almost positive this is nursemaid's elbow, which isn't serious. Can you ask if one of them yanked on his arm as he was falling off the path?"

Mateo did as she asked, and, sure enough, they confirmed that the dad had grabbed the boy's arm, trying to pull him up, but he'd slipped from his grasp.

"All right," Miranda said. "Please ask one of the parents to hold him in their lap. I'm going to check it again, then, assuming that's it, I'll pop the radius back into place. You have anything to distract him while I do that?"

If the boy had been a grown man, he'd say that Miranda and her calm, friendly demeanor, gorgeous blue eyes and disheveled hair, which he realized he liked as much as her carefully combed bob, were plenty of distraction on their own. "I have a whistle in my pocket. Let's see if he wants to blow it."

Her smile widened, and he loved the twinkle in her eyes. "That's perfect. Wish I could use a whistle at the hospital, but probably other patients wouldn't appreciate it. Is mom or dad ready?"

Mateo spoke with the parents, and the dad took over the two older ones as the mother held the child close in her arms. Now that he was looking, he could see the boy's arm was hanging limply at his side.

"Now I see why he was holding onto that bush with only one arm. Which was nerve-racking, let me tell you. I thought he might lose his grip and fall before I got there. But don't tell his parents."

"They already know you're a hero, so why keep that a secret?"

"Because heroes are never scared, don't you know that?"

She shook her head and grinned at him before turning to carefully palpate the boy's entire arm, with shrieks that made his parents cringe following each movement.

"Yep, that's definitely it," Miranda said. "Whistle time. Tell the parents to expect a loud scream, then he'll be feeling fine, just a little bruised."

Mateo translated again, and the boy was, thankfully, fascinated by the whistle. As he was blasting everyone's ears, Mateo watched Miranda gently tug on his arm, and even through the whistling he could hear the bone pop back into place. As expected, the boy screamed, the parents exclaimed in distress, then visibly relaxed when the boy's misery quieted to mere sniffles.

"You're good with that whistle, young man," Mateo said, trying to distract all of them now that the worst was over. "You want to keep it?"

He nodded, and when he began to blow it again, his parents laughed, obviously relieved. They thanked both he and Miranda over and over again, the mother giving her a hard hug as Mateo re-rolled his rigging and placed it back in his pocket.

"I bet they're going to hang on to all three of them all the way back to wherever they're parked," Miranda said with a smile as she watched them move down the path. "How scary to see their little one fall over the embankment like that. I wonder what happened?"

"Kids can move fast. One second they're walking on a sidewalk, or in this case a path in the woods, the next they've darted into the street or off the edge. I see it all the time."

"I know. I regularly see the results of kids' impulsiveness in the ER. I guess there's no way to keep everyone safe all the time, is there?"

"No." His chest got that heavy feeling again, as her

words sent him back to their earlier conversation. Some accidents—fatal accidents—were incomprehensible. Seemingly impossible. But when they happened, everyone else had to live through the tragedy, wondering what they might have done to prevent it.

"I guess we'd better go back and gather up the picnic stuff before it attracts bears and we have another problem on our hands," Miranda said. "And as I say that, I hope you're going to tell me there aren't really any bears here."

The way her eyes had gone from grinning to questioning and slightly worried brought him out of the dark place he'd gone. "*Ursus arctos*—brown bears—definitely live here. And I'm thankful for that, as there are very few left, and they're an important part of our great wilderness."

"I'm all for brown bears being part of your wilderness, but not if they show up when I'm hiking."

"I can't disagree with that. Let's gather up our stuff and go. I think I've had enough excitement for one day. You?"

"Definitely yes. And by the way, you were amazing. When I saw how fast you rappelled down that embankment, and how calmly you got the boy and brought him back up, I couldn't believe it. You really are an expert at rescuing people, aren't you? They were so lucky to have you close by."

"To have ER doc extraordinaire Miranda Davenport here, too. Diagnosing his injury and fixing it also made them very lucky."

"Anyone at any hospital could have fixed his arm, including you. Not too many could have rescued him the way you did."

The blue eyes looking up at him were utterly serious now, and something about the way she was looking at him gave him an odd sensation. A little uncomfortable at accolades he didn't need to hear—he did what he did because it was his calling. A little bit proud, too, despite not needing that kind of praise. And a little confused at the first thing that came to mind when she'd said all that was that they worked remarkably well together. Both when it came to taking care of patients and when it came to enjoying time together in a way he couldn't quite remember enjoying so much with anyone before.

"We make a good team." He hadn't meant to say it out loud, but there it was, hanging between them. Words that felt bigger and more significant than a simple statement about working together.

"Yeah, we do."

Mateo stared down to see the same confusion in her eyes that swirled through his mind and body. Let his gaze travel to her lush lips, down to the pulse he could see beating in her throat just above her coat collar, and couldn't believe he felt so aroused when he wasn't even touching her and both of them wore heavy clothes covering nearly every inch of their skin.

After each kiss they'd shared, he'd promised himself it would be the last. And yet, at this moment, he wanted to do nothing more than lie down on the hard rock slab they'd picnicked on and kiss her breathless.

Damn. How had this gotten so complicated and confusing? He'd dreaded coming back home, but being with Miranda had made it so much better than he'd imagined it would be. Seeing his home through her eyes, as well as parts of Catalonia he hadn't visited for years, made him feel completely different than he'd expected. Filled him with pleasure and happy memories, and not just the painful ones he'd known he'd have to deal with. It had brought a smile and joy to his heart to spend time with a woman who enjoyed simple pleasures like hiking and picnicking. Kissing and holding each other close.

Much as he knew he shouldn't be doing that kissing and holding, there was something irresistible about Miranda. Maybe it was the combination of sweetness and smarts, of vulnerability and bravery, of caring and giving that was a soul-deep part of her.

Whatever it was, he knew he didn't want the day with her to end with their hike. The enjoyment to be over before they had to deal with going to the party, where he'd have to answer questions he didn't want to answer. Where there'd be hushed conversations about Emilio being gone, and about Mateo not being the kind of man his brother had been. About what would happen now.

He didn't want to think about all that quite yet, and looked down into Miranda's beautiful face. "It's early still. How do you feel about a little tour of part of the estate as I talk to a few managers before we have to get ready for the party? There's probably more to do than I realize, and I should get started scheduling meetings with them now, and not wait."

"I'd love that. It's all so beautiful to see from the guest house. Looking at it up close, learning about all you raise and grow there, about the horses and all the different livestock, would be really interesting."

"*Bueno*. We'll take an hour or so to do a quick tour while I set up times to meet with everyone before we have to get ready for tonight."

"Well, this makes me happy." He could tell from her shining eyes and wide smile that she really meant it, and somehow her excitement had him looking forward to it, too. "I admit I wanted to see more of the place, but didn't know if I'd just be in the way."

"You could never be in the way. Having you with me will make a difficult task easier." *In the way?* That she'd actually say that bothered him. How could such a special woman still carry around those kinds of worries that must stem from her early years at the Davenports?

He reached for her hand and drew her closer. "You'll have to keep your boots on, as trudging through fields will be part of it. And climbing olive trees. And walking across barn beams."

Her chuckle and laughing eyes reached inside him, making him feel grateful all over again that she was here. Knew that having her with him for at least a little of this necessary task would help him get through it. He was sure the various estate managers could handle taking over all the things Emilio wasn't here to do anymore. In fact, they'd probably all prefer to do it themselves, instead of working with him if he tried to fill his brother's shoes.

No way could he come close to doing all the things his brother had accomplished here. And he was sure they all knew he couldn't either, despite what his parents claimed to believe.

"Look at all the olives on these trees! How many acres... er...hectares of olive groves do you have?" Miranda asked as they walked between the rows of trees, now more gnarled-looking than Mateo remembered, on their way to the horse barns.

"Not sure exactly what we have anymore." He'd talked earlier to several of the livestock managers, but hadn't yet spoken to those who took care of the various crops. "But in the past, not a huge number. The olives we grow here have mostly been eaten by everyone living on the estate, with about two thirds of the crop pressed into oil."

"How do you press it?"

"There's a local press that all the nearby orchards use. The harvest is taken to be processed pretty much the same way it's been done for hundreds of years."

"When is it harvested? And how? There's no way you could pick all these tiny olives off the trees—it would take forever."

He chuckled at the way she stared at the trees, reaching to touch the silvery gray leaves and not yet ripe olives before running her hand over the rough bark. "You're such a city girl, with an inquisitive mind. The harvest will be soon. Probably in the next month or two, depending on the weather. They're raked off the tree onto nets."

"What? You rake them off?"

"Yes, and I know from personal experience how hard it is. By the end of the day your shoulders and back muscles are groaning big time." He smiled at the memories of Emilio and himself complaining like mad, even though they both secretly liked the labor of pulling the olives from the trees. "Our parents insisted that Emilio and I do some of the raking, even though most of our friends on neighboring estates never had to. They felt we needed that personal connection with the land, and our home. Be a real part of it all."

Miranda turned to look at him, and he could practically read her mind, because his words struck him exactly the same way.

A personal connection. A real part of it all. Walking across the land of his ancestors, he couldn't deny that, for the past couple days, he'd been filled with powerful memories of his childhood. Happy memories of how much this place had always meant to him, until he'd realized he had to forge his own path away from here. Even the memories of Emilio and himself doing things together brought a smile to his lips, along with the ache of loss.

"And your personal connection to the horses? You told me you and your brother spent a lot of time here."

They'd arrived at the paddock, with a few of their horses

inside. One whinnied at them, and as he reached to rub the animal's nose, Mateo's chest filled with some kind of emotion he couldn't quite identify. It had been a long time since he'd ridden a horse, and he suddenly knew he wanted to make that happen before he went back to New York.

"We did. Again, my parents made us do some of the mucking out and feeding. Said we couldn't have just the fun of riding, we had to do some of the work, too."

Miranda moved close to him, pressing her shoulder to his arm. "You love this place, don't you? Admit it."

He could feel her looking at him, and finally turned to meet her serious gaze. How she could see that so clearly, when he hadn't, had refused to, was a mystery.

But she was right.

"I guess I do. I grew up here. It's in my blood, I suppose. But loving the land and the animals and the beauty doesn't mean I belong here any more. My job in New York helps me make a difference in other people's lives."

"Have you thought about how this place makes a difference in people's lives?"

"What do you mean?"

"All the people who work here. Who live here. You said they were like family, didn't you? Without this place, their lives would change completely. They'd all have to find work on other horse farms, other olive farms, other places that raise the livestock you do."

He stared out across the fields. Miranda was right, and yet it didn't really change anything. "Emilio worked to make sure this whole place ran like a well-oiled machine. Nothing will change with him gone."

Except everything had changed. This place would never be the same without him, and the thought of living here in his brother's big shadow, facing grief and guilt every day, felt unbearable.

"Mateo." She grasped his hands, and just that touch made him feel a little steadier. "Perhaps you need to take a little more time to think about everything. That's what our pretend engagement's really all about anyway, right? To give your parents time to adjust to their new situation without demanding you do exactly what they want. To give yourself time to figure out how you want to handle it."

"I don't need more time to know that I can't take Emilio's place. And, deep inside, I have to believe my parents know that, too."

"Being yourself will always be enough. Remember that."

Her words squeezed his heart, and he folded her in his arms. "You seem to have trouble believing that about yourself, Miranda."

"Yeah, maybe I do," she whispered as she wrapped her arms around his back and held him close. "Maybe that's something we can both work on, hmm?"

"Yeah." He pressed his lips to her warm cheek, calling upon all his strength not to move on to her sweet lips. "And tonight's party will be a good place for us to start."

CHAPTER NINE

"I HOPE THE dresses fit, Miss Miranda," Paula said, showing her to a guest room in the main house for her to change in. "Mr. Mateo wanted you to have several to choose from. He asked me to tell you to wear whichever you like best."

"I admit the dress I brought isn't quite this fancy, but it's adequate, I think."

"Mr. Mateo wanted you to feel comfortable at the party, not worrying about your clothes. He made a special effort to get them for you. Miss Camilla never liked the dresses her husband chose for her, and I know it made him sad."

She looked at the woman in surprise, wondering why she'd mentioned Emilio's widow. "It bothered him?"

A shadow crossed Paula's face. "Yes. But he tried very hard to make Miss Camilla happy."

Miranda felt a flash of anger at the self-centered woman who'd hurt Mateo's brother, and who was part of the reason Mateo had kept such a distance between himself and his family for so long. From the place he'd admitted today that he loved very much. "Were Emilio and Mateo close?"

"Oh, yes. Very close. When they were both home, they did everything together. Rode the horses, skied, sailed boats, and—"

She abruptly stopped talking, and Miranda prodded, "And?"

"And many other things." Paula moved to the dresses and smoothed the skirts. "So, please, choose whichever dress you like. Just ring if you need me to help you find the one that fits best."

"Thank you, Paula. I'm sure at least one will fit me perfectly. I'll be pleased to wear one, especially since Mateo picked them out."

"I'm so happy that Mr. Mateo has found a wonderful woman he wants to marry," she said, smiling again. "We all wondered if he ever would, and if he'd return home. It's…it's a very happy Christmas celebration here at Castillo de Adelaide Fernanda."

Did she really think so? Surely Paula knew Mateo's parents didn't approve of their engagement. But maybe she figured they'd get over it if Mateo came back to live here. The thought made her feel a little sad that everyone in this beautiful house was going to be disappointed that Mateo—the man they'd seen grow up and who was their new heir—wasn't planning to return to his home full-time at all. Unless he thought more about that decision. After walking around the estate with him today, seeing how he felt about the place, she hoped he would.

"Well, thank you again. I'll see you downstairs."

Paula beamed and nodded, leaving Miranda alone, still battling the melancholy she'd felt after her hours with Mateo that afternoon.

Why were family situations often so difficult? Even though he hadn't said much about it, she knew the loss of Mateo's brother had been hard on him. Add to that the stress of his father's health, his parents' demands, and all the people depending on the estate for their livelihoods, and indirectly depending on Mateo, well, she had a feeling he hadn't fully shared the weight he must be carrying around from it all.

No time to dwell on that now. She took a deep breath as she looked at the beautiful dresses neatly hanging in the closet. Ever since she'd become a Davenport, she'd been blessed to be given glamorous clothing like she'd never seen in her life before that. Wearing them to attend various charitable events and symphonies and Broadway shows never got old, she had to admit. But despite having done that now for thirteen years, having these dresses brought here for her to choose from made her feeling absurdly Cinderella-like.

She wished Vanessa was here to see her as the guest and fiancée of a Spanish duke, and couldn't help but enjoy the vision of how her mouth would fall open. Wished Penny was here to see her doing this crazy thing, too, and couldn't wait to tell her about it. Though that reminded her that the adventure would be over and she'd be back to regular old Miranda, living her boring life and working all the time, very soon.

As she flicked through each dress, she couldn't help but imagine which one Mateo would like best. Which one would be the most flattering. Which one would make Mateo look at her the way she caught him doing sometimes. As though he liked what he saw.

The same way she caught herself looking at him.

She drew another deep breath, wishing she could feel totally confident, without worrying which dress would suit her best. But how could she not feel nervous about it, knowing all the guests would be staring at her even before they announced their fake engagement? Feeling curious about the two of them together? Knowing Mateo would be seeing her in a beautiful dress for the very first time, instead of her usual scrubs, or the jeans she'd worn on their excursions?

With her stomach all jittery, she debated the choices in

front of her. Should she go with classic black? The shimmery one in pale gold was made of her favorite fabric, a crepe that hung in beautiful folds. Or would the blue one bring out the color of her eyes, which she knew were her best feature? It was probably the one she liked best, so long as it wasn't so low cut that her full figure didn't threaten to fall out of the bodice.

Turning this way and that in front of the full-length mirror, she smiled at the way the cobwebs of blue and aqua threads shimmered as she moved. She eyed the neckline, and decided that, even though her breasts were slightly on display, it wasn't so overt as to be in poor taste, or a reason for people to talk.

The light caught the diamond on her hand, and as she looked at it, melancholy poked at her again. Such a beautiful ring from a beautiful man. Would she ever have someone like him for real?

With a sigh, she grabbed an exquisitely beaded evening bag that had also been provided by her fairy godmother—or in this case, Mateo—and went down the stairs. Nervous butterflies danced in her belly as she wondered how the evening would go; at the same time anticipation welled in her chest at what Mateo would think of how she looked. And what would he look like dressed in his finery? Drool-worthy, without a doubt.

Paula appeared at the base of the stairs, and showed her to the large ballroom where at least three dozen people were already gathered. As she stood in the doorway, her gaze went straight to the most gorgeous man in the room, and her breath caught in her throat.

A perfectly cut tuxedo that had doubtless been tailor made for him enhanced his broad shoulders and regal bearing. One hand held a glass of champagne, the other was tucked in his trouser pocket, elegance and power simply exuding from the man. It struck Miranda that his fellow EMTs would be astounded that the hard-working man usually wearing a uniform and sometimes heavy gear could also look like he'd stepped straight out of a James Bond movie. Calm, capable, and, yes, very, very drool-worthy.

Feeling unable to move, Miranda just stared. She saw him smile and nod to whoever he'd been talking to, then move toward another guest. Maybe he sensed her gawking at him, because he turned and, as their eyes met, she saw him stop dead.

His gaze slowly traveled from her hair to her sparkly shoes, then back up to linger on her breasts before meeting her eyes again. Something about that leisurely perusal made her pulse leap, then flutter even faster as he moved toward her in a relaxed gait that somehow enhanced his graceful sophistication.

When he stopped only inches from her, his hand reached for hers, thumbing the blue diamond ring circling her finger. "You look incredible."

She managed to unstick her tongue from the roof of her mouth. "Thank you. Did you get the dresses because you feared I might wear something to embarrass you?"

"Nothing you could do or wear would ever embarrass me. Even if you wore your hospital scrubs. Though I admit you look even more stunning than you do at work." He smiled, leaning forward to brush his lips against her cheek before speaking softly in her ear. "I know this thing isn't something you've looked forward to. So thank you again for coming. There's not a soul here who won't be dazzled by you."

"You...you look pretty dazzling yourself."

The intimate smile that curved his lips made it hard to breathe, which was further complicated when he closed the small gap between them, pressing his mouth to hers.

So softly and sweetly, she closed her eyes and soaked in the sensation, drowned in it, even as the niggle at the back of her mind reminded her he was kissing her to make everyone in the room believe they were in love.

When he drew back, his lips stayed parted, his breath feathering across her moist mouth as their eyes met again. He reached to slide a strand of her hair between his fingers before tucking it behind one ear. "I like your earrings, but I may have to get you blue stones for your ears, too. Of course, your amazing eyes bring the sky into any room you enter."

"There's that romantic, poetic side of you coming out. Who would have guessed?" Her voice was breathy, she knew, but it was the best she could do. The current swirling around them felt like an electrified tornado, holding her close to him.

"Not me. I never knew I had a romantic bent until I met you." He dropped another soft kiss to her mouth. "And speaking of never guessing, who would suspect that Dr. Miranda Davenport was hiding such an incredible body beneath the scrubs she always wears?"

She felt a blush heat her cheeks. "You've seen me out of scrubs."

"Wearing winter street or hiking clothes covering you from neck to toe. Or a thick robe." His voice went lower. "And now I think we should stop talking about seeing you out of scrubs before something happens and I embarrass myself." The crooked grin he gave her somehow managed to be both amused and sexy at the same time, and she forced herself to look away from it, knowing there had to be a number of people here watching them.

"So, now what? We talk with your parents? Mingle?"

"Both. Then, when we can't take it any more, we dance, so I have an excuse to hold you close."

Miranda swallowed hard, and tried to concentrate on the various people Mateo introduced her to. But it all felt so surreal. Standing beside a handsome, elegant man, wearing a beautiful dress and spectacular engagement ring, with him touching her and looking at her like she meant everything to him. The whole fairy tale come to life.

Except it wasn't. None of it was real, not the flirtatious things he'd said, not the kisses and not the engagement. He was playing the part of loving fiancé for his parents and their guests, and that reality made her throat ache and her chest feel a little hollow.

Stupid. She'd known exactly how this would be, hadn't she? Except she hadn't, not really. All the pretending, knowing Mateo didn't really feel that way about her, made her feel a little empty. Made her ask herself if she'd ever have a man in her life who really did love her.

Somehow she managed to keep her end of the bargain. So many introductions and chit-chat for what seemed like forever left Miranda's cheeks aching. Her smile felt frozen on, especially when talking with Mateo's parents, aunts and uncles.

She'd assumed that Rafael and Ana would at least pretend to be happy about their son's engagement, but it seemed like every time Ana looked her way, she scowled instead of smiled. They hadn't even officially announced it yet, and now it seemed that they really might not, probably to give Mateo more time to think about it, as they'd said yesterday. Though it was obvious people had figured it out, as she'd seen and heard the whispers about Mateo's future wife.

Miranda knew she shouldn't be bothered by his parents' attitude. She should try to understand that they were hurting horribly over their son's death, and because of that weren't able to think in a normal way right now. Except

Mateo had told her they'd always favored his brother and, watching their distant and cool treatment of him, it was sadly easy to believe.

"Mateo! My handsome brother-in-law. It's been far too long since you've come home."

Miranda knew it was wrong to instantly judge the small blonde with an obviously saccharine smile as she hugged Mateo, giving him the European two-cheek kiss as she did so. Except how could she not? She'd been prejudiced by what Mateo, and Paula, too, had told her about the woman who was obviously his brother Emilio's widow.

"Hello, Camilla." Mateo quickly extricated himself from her grasp and turned to Miranda. She couldn't help but feel impressed at his impassive expression. She knew how he felt about Emilio's wife, but no one would know it. For the first time that night, he introduced her as his fiancée, despite his parents not having made any announcement, and Miranda wondered if it was to keep the woman from making a play for him, as he'd said she'd done in the past.

"Well, well. The woman who finally reined in Mateo Alves. I didn't think I'd ever see the day. It's so very good to meet you." Camilla smiled brightly, but her eyes were even colder than Mateo's mother's, and held something else besides disapproval.

Disdain? Jealousy? Miranda had no idea, but she did know that she disliked the woman instantly.

"Nice to meet you, too." If only to see that Mateo wasn't making things up about the woman. The way she looked at Mateo, then Miranda, showed loud and clear how she felt about him belonging to someone else. Was she the kind of woman who wanted any man she could claim, or did she have a real thing for her late husband's brother?

"When is the big, happy day?"

"We're still finalizing our plans. But don't worry, I'm sure my mother will apprise you of it as soon as we decide." Mateo's arm tightened around Miranda's waist, but his cordial expression didn't change.

"I'm glad to see you're finally stepping up to your duty to your parents. Emilio felt so frustrated, hurt really, that you never came to help."

Miranda cringed at the woman's nasty barb, knowing that had to score a painful, direct hit on Mateo. She glanced up at him, and the tic in his jaw and tightness of his lips showed she was right.

"I don't think I'm the one who hurt him. But do I wish I'd been here for him when things got rough? Yeah. I regret that more than you'll ever know."

He swung away with Miranda still held in the crook of his arm and strode toward the dance floor. She thought about saying something about his exchange with Camilla, but his hard, fierce expression told her that keeping quiet was a better choice.

A headache began to form in both temples, and just as she was considering telling Mateo she'd like to excuse herself for a while he led her onto the dance floor. His arm stayed closed around her as he grasped her hand, but he didn't pull her close. Probably, he was as exhausted by the charade as she was.

"How are you holding up?"

"I was about to ask you the same thing."

"Don't worry about me." The tension around his eyes and in his jaw had her wanting to reach up to somehow smooth it away. "I'm used to people whispering and talking about me. About why I moved away. About why I don't come home often. Bringing you here has greased the gossip wheel, doubtless making everyone's day as they wonder what's going on."

No mention of Camilla and her words. "It doesn't bother you that your parents obviously aren't going to announce our...our engagement?"

He shrugged as he swept her into a turn. "My goal with our engagement was to buy some time. Give my parents a reason to understand why I'm not coming back full-time. We've accomplished that goal, so I don't care about the rest."

She wished she could say the same. Stupid as it was, there was still that tiny part of her that felt a little like she had as a teenager showing up at the Davenport home, barely tolerated by the matriarch.

Another turn took them to the edge of the room, and to her surprise Mateo swept them out the French doors onto a wide stone loggia dimly lit by the lights from the ballroom. The cool air felt good against her cheeks, and it felt wonderful to be away from the crowded room.

They came to a stop next to a wide pillar, and Mateo tipped her chin up, their eyes meeting.

"You didn't answer my earlier question."

"What question?"

"About how you were holding up. Is it bothering you that people are talking about you? That my parents have virtually ignored you?"

She nearly denied it, not wanting him to worry about something so silly when they weren't really a couple. But the brown eyes looking into hers seemed to already see what she was feeling. "It shouldn't, I know. But I can't help feeling a little...uncomfortable about it, you know?"

"I know. After what you told me about your lack of welcome by Vanessa Davenport, I've been worried. I wouldn't have asked you to do this if I'd known. I'm sorry."

"No need to be sorry. Honestly." He looked so concerned, she tried to reassure him. "It's just baggage that I shouldn't still be carrying around with me."

"There's no 'should' or 'shouldn't' when it comes to feelings, Miranda," he said quietly. "We feel how we feel."

She stared up at him, seeing that was true for both of them. And it struck her that observing the way Mateo was dealing with tough issues and feelings of grief and loss had made her think about her own life and how she'd been living it. While all the flirting and kissing didn't mean anything, his confidence in her did. And maybe that meant it was long past the time she should learn to have more confidence in herself.

"I know. But maybe what we're feeling isn't based on reality. Vanessa didn't want me around, but it didn't take long for everyone else to accept me. Maybe it's time I accept myself."

"What about yourself haven't you accepted?"

"That I don't have to keep pushing myself to try to live up to the Davenport name. Maybe I've accomplished that."

"No maybe about it." He tugged her closer. "You're a very special woman in a beautiful, tempting package."

The warm rumble of his voice, the way he was looking at her, sent her thoughts away from her past and her lack of confidence. They made her think about him, and that he was right. That how she felt wasn't something she could control, which was a deep attraction and connection to this man. Could he have been thinking that, too, when he'd talked about feeling what they felt? Was there any way his kisses and touches were more than a show of make-believe?

"I guess that's true," she whispered. She licked her lips, wanting more than anything to kiss him, to explore those feelings squeezing her chest and heating her body even in the crisp November air. But what if that's not what he'd meant at all? What if she embarrassed him, and herself, which would just complicate an already odd situation? What if putting herself at risk like that would be a huge mistake?

Wearing her high heels, his mouth was at her eye level, and she found herself fixated on the shape of it, thinking of how it felt to kiss him, and her own lips involuntarily parted. Heat curled in her belly, and that swirling electricity seemed to charge the air around them all over again. She managed to lift her gaze to his, and the eyes that met hers held a hot flicker of awareness that sent her pulse racing.

His hands tightened on her arms, bringing her close. The slight tic showed in his jaw again, and his eyes slid to her mouth, but he didn't move to kiss her.

She pressed her palms against his hard chest. Feeling the heavy beat of his heart, she suddenly decided to go for it. To use her new-found confidence. To find out exactly what he might be feeling—hadn't doing crazy things been part of her reason to come here?

"So what are you feeling right now?" she asked. Before he had a chance to answer, she shocked herself, finding she couldn't wait to hear his response, sliding her hands up around his neck to kiss him. For a split second his mouth stayed soft until, with a soft groan, he kissed her back. Taking it deeper, hotter, sliding one hand up her back to tangle his fingers in her hair.

Her body melted against his, the kiss spreading fire across her skin and weakening her knees. When his lips separated an inch from hers, she looked up into hungry eyes gone black, both of them breathless.

"What I'm feeling is obvious, isn't it?" he said in a low rumble. "I think you know that I want you, Miranda. That I'm attracted to you in a way I don't remember feeling before. But I can't offer you what you want and need in your life. And it wouldn't be fair to take advantage of you after I've brought you nearly captive into this ruse."

"I'm not captive. And I'm not asking for anything other than for you to kiss me. Unless even that's more than you're willing to offer."

A slow smile curved his lips, even as he looked at her like getting her naked was suddenly all he wanted. "As you've already noticed, kissing you any time, any place, has always been high on my list of offerings, *mi belleza*."

His lips caressed her jaw, moved to the sensitive spot beneath her ear, sending a delicious shiver down her spine. Slowly traveling down her neck, his hot mouth kept going until they rested on the mounds exposed there, his tongue leisurely licking along her neckline making her gasp.

"Your breasts tantalize me, Miranda." His breath whispered across the dampness of her skin. "So beautiful, so soft."

She clutched the back of his head, loving the way he nuzzled the cleft between her breasts, nearly hyperventilating with the sensation of it as his hands moved to her hips and over her buttocks.

"Mateo! Mateo, where are you?"

The distant voice permeated the sexual fog clogging her brain. Miranda opened her eyes as he lifted his head, his eyes glittering into hers. "Shh." He pressed his lips to hers. "My mother. Probably someone important in her world has arrived and she wants me to talk to them. If we're lucky, she won't look out here."

"She'll think even less of me if I'm keeping you away from her guests."

"And you care because?"

Just as they were smiling at one another, his mother's voice calling him got louder, frantic sounding, and Mateo straightened to his full height, a frown dipping between his brows as his arms fell to his sides. "I'd better go and see what's wrong. I'll be back."

"I'll come with you."

In her heels, Miranda couldn't keep up with him as he strode through the ballroom, all the guests moving to make way for him. Across the room, she could see his mother leaning over a large, wingback chair and in it sat Mateo's father, slumped to one side, looking extremely ill.

CHAPTER TEN

"MOVE BACK, PLEASE. Mother, give us some room." Fear tightened Mateo's chest, but he ignored it as best he could, relying on his medical training to address the problem, without letting emotion cloud his perspective. This wouldn't be the first time his father's Parkinson's disease had left the poor man feeling weak and out of it, but it was always alarming, no matter how much they'd all become somewhat used to it.

Mateo crouched next to his father's chair, concentrating on getting his pulse. Trying hard to ignore the way his head was lolled back and the gibberish and strange sentences he was stringing together in a slurred voice that constricted Mateo's gut even more.

"When did he start to feel this way?"

"I'm not sure." His mother stood to the side, clutching her hands together. "I was talking with guests, and haven't been with him for a while. But he was having a bad day to begin with. Felt extra-shaky this morning and couldn't sit very straight. He was feeling anxious about that, with our guests coming tonight."

"What's his pulse?"

Miranda asked the question in a quiet voice as she crouched beside him. He glanced up to see that piercing blue carefully studying his father. "Bradycardia—about fifty. Some arrhythmia."

Sweat prickled his body as he turned back to his father, feeling uneasy about the way he was staring at him, barely blinking. "I think we should get him to bed and give him a dose of his medications. Usually when he's having a bad day, that helps."

"The horses!" Rafael suddenly exclaimed, shakily waving his hand. "There! Don't let them in the house!"

God, he hated that this terrible disease was slowly whittling away at the strong man his father had always been. No matter how many times he experienced it, his father suffering hallucinations because of his disease deeply disturbed Mateo, and his mother, too, and he sucked in a breath, forcing himself to respond in a matter-of-fact tone.

"No horses here, Padre. They're all safe in the stable. Let's get you to bed so you can rest, okay?"

"No! Not leaving." His father was shouting now, looking a little wild-eyed and mulish. "We're waiting for Emilio to get here."

Emilio. Mateo's chest squeezed, wishing with all his heart that could be true. "Emilio's not coming, Father, so you don't need to wait. Let's go so you can get a little rest now." He pinned his gaze on his mother with a message he hoped she read loud and clear. "Get the staff to clear the room. You know he wouldn't want this kind of audience."

She stared at him before jerkily nodding. Instantly, she instructed the staff to move the food to another room, and asked the guests to follow.

"Didn't you say he's diabetic, too?" Miranda asked, a frown dipping deep between her brows. "We should check his blood sugar before you take him to his room. Where is his glucose meter?"

Mateo glanced at her, surprised. "It's not uncommon

for his Parkinson's symptoms to flare up sometimes. A decreased blink rate and hallucinations are all part of that."

"I understand. But shakiness, delirium, and belligerence are all symptoms of hypoglycemia, too, which you know."

Well, damn. Because his father's Parkinson's was such a big concern, both he and his mother had assumed he was just having a bad day. But could Miranda be right? "Paula, can you please get Father's glucose monitor?"

"You think this might be his diabetes?" His mother looked anxiously at Mateo, then her gaze slid to Miranda.

"Not sure. Do you know what he's eaten today?"

"I don't know. We were all busy with the party, and I didn't pay attention like I usually do. Perhaps he didn't…" She stopped talking and turned, obviously distraught, to one of the staff who'd been tending the buffet. "Please bring some food right away."

"Not yet," Miranda said gently, reaching for her hand to try to calm her down. "If it's hypoglycemia, he could easily choke, trying to eat."

His mother stared at Miranda, then nodded as she gripped her hand. "Then what…?"

"We need some regular, granulated sugar, please," Miranda said. "As soon as possible."

"Yes. Do as the doctor says. Right away."

The staff member rushed off, and Miranda wrapped her arm around Ana's shoulders to give her a reassuring hug. The respect in her eyes as she looked at Miranda was beyond good to see. Much as Mateo hated seeing his father feeling so ill and unsteady, maybe the silver lining would be new respect for his pretend bride-to-be.

Paula rushed in with the glucose monitor, and he quickly pricked his father's finger to draw the drop of blood they needed, his father now practically bellowing in protest, yanking his hand back, making it harder to get the test strip in place. In moments, though, the test showed exactly what Miranda had obviously expected.

An extremely low reading practically screamed from the monitor. Miranda's gaze lifted from the test at the same time his did. Their eyes met, and he gave her a smile and a nodding salute.

"Miranda was right. His blood sugar is very low, Mother."

"Oh, dear. This is terrible." She wrung her hands, looking nearly ready to cry. "This is my fault for not attending to him."

"It's not your fault." Mateo reached for her tense hands again, giving them a reassuring squeeze. "We need to set up a system where others in the house are also paying attention to his meals from now on. It isn't fair to you to feel you have to hover over him every time he's supposed to eat, and be the only one checking his blood sugar."

"Thank God you were here to help. To find what was wrong."

His gut clenched at the tears that sprang into his mother's eyes. That she was right made his chest ache. Made him wonder if he could let himself make the same mistake with his parents that he'd made with Emilio. In not being here for him when his brother had needed him most.

He rubbed his hand across his forehead and looked away from his mother's distress. What was he going to do about this complicated problem?

He drew a deep breath before turning back to his mother, explaining what needed to happen now. At the same time, Miranda went to work. He knew it definitely wasn't the way she'd normally take care of hypoglycemia in the hospital. But had he really said in the tunnel that she didn't know anything about field medicine? Her simple but efficient treatment showed he'd been wrong about that as he watched her stick her finger straight into the sugar bowl she'd been given and wipe it directly onto his father's tongue.

She talked soothingly as she slathered on another tea-spoon-sized dollop of sugar, his father no longer protesting but making little smacking sounds as he swallowed. His eyes began to focus and blink more when he stared up at Miranda and Mateo, obviously slowly becoming more alert, though at the same time he clearly was confused by what was going on.

"Feeling a little better?" Miranda asked with a smile.

"What…? I don't… Why?"

"It's all right, Father." Mateo reached for his father's thin hand. "You can't have eaten much today, and got into a little trouble because of that. But your blood sugar is coming up now. You're going to be okay."

His father nodded, obviously feeling a little wiped out, which was hardly a surprise. Mateo stood, helping Miranda up to stand next to him. He kept his arm around her waist as he spoke to his mother, then ordered some food brought to his father. His mother insisted on sitting next to him, poking food into his mouth, and Mateo knew it was because she didn't trust anyone else to do it, feeling guilty that he'd gotten into trouble to begin with.

With everything settled, he finally could turn to look at Miranda's beautiful smile, and he knew it wasn't just gratitude that filled his chest with an overwhelming emotion. The chatter and dishes clanking around them faded as he looked into her warm blue eyes, felt how perfectly her body fit in his arm, and it seemed as though the world was turning on its axis. His breath backed up in his lungs as the truth smacked him square in the solar plexus. As he realized that what he was feeling for Miranda was something he'd never experienced before.

He was teetering dangerously close to loving this amazing woman. He wanted to pull her close and kiss her, but wasn't sure if he should let himself do that. Though he had a feeling there was no way he could resist, since he sure as hell hadn't managed to keep his distance so far. Except she deserved so much more than a man like him, and he battled back the urge to tell her exactly how he was feeling.

The quizzical expression on her face as she looked at him had him wondering what his face looked like, and he swallowed hard, still reeling from his revelation.

"Are you okay?"

He nodded, having no idea if he was okay or not, then somehow managed to speak. "Thank you. You just might have saved my father's life tonight."

Her face went pink. "You would have figured it out."

"Maybe not in time to prevent him from going into a coma. Having experienced my father's Parkinson's symptoms so many times, I was being tunnel-visioned, assuming that was what was happening."

"Easy to do when you're as close to it as you are. I had the advantage of being an impartial observer."

"And an excellent doctor."

"Like you said before, we make a good team."

"Yeah, we really do." The truth of that shocked him. When was the last time he'd felt that way? Once he'd left the army, he'd mostly isolated himself, except when he'd worked on patients with other EMTs. But the more time he spent with Miranda, the more he realized what a truly special woman she was, in so many ways. A woman he was falling way too hard for.

He leaned down to give her a soft kiss, wishing they could go back to what they'd been doing before, which had involved having his lips and tongue kissing her and caressing her beautiful breasts. "I'm going to help my father to his room and keep an eye on him for a little while. I'll find you later?"

"I'll be here."

She'd be there. His chest filled again with a mix of emotions at her words. He knew it was true. Knew that she'd be there for him because that was the kind of woman she was, and he'd never needed her more than at this moment. And yet it was also a reminder that he hadn't done the same for his brother, which was a terrible regret he somehow had to learn to live with.

"Gracias," he said, his voice rough. "I'll see you as soon as I can. And, *mi belleza*? Please plan for us to take up right where we left off."

Each time she walked along the stone paths meandering through the back gardens of the Alves estate, Miranda found it a little more peaceful. The fingernail moon still hung within a thin mist of clouds, surrounded by the kind of twinkling stars she rarely got to see back in the city. The night sky of New York City was lit by millions of city lights, not nature and the universe, and this sight made her heart feel a calmness and serenity she hadn't felt since... well, she couldn't remember ever feeling quite this way.

Mateo had told her the gardens had been there for hundreds of years, carefully tended and refurbished as necessary, full of gorgeous blooms of all kinds during the spring and summer months. She found herself wishing she could see it during other seasons, instead of dormant as it was in November. Found herself wishing she could spend more time with Mateo, too.

Neither of those was going to happen. Yes, he'd said he wanted to take up where they'd left off an hour or so ago, and just the thought made her feel flushed and breathless. He might have kissed her because he'd wanted to, because he'd wanted *her*, as he'd so excitingly told her, and not because he was trying to convince everyone that their fake engagement was real. But kissing her now, wanting her tonight and for as long as they were here together was a far cry from wanting a relationship once they were back in the city.

He'd stated very clearly that he wasn't interested in a long-term relationship with any woman. And she wanted the loving husband her mother had never had, wanted to be blessed with children. A close-knit family that was all her own, that no one could ever take away from her. But did that rule out a simple but doubtless glorious fling with Mateo?

A deep sigh left her lungs. Feeling confused and unsettled by the question, she looked up at the stars for guidance. "Star light, star bright, what do you think I should wish for tonight?" she asked aloud.

"If you don't already know, why are you here with my son?"

Startled, Miranda's hand flew to her chest as she swung toward the voice to see Ana walking toward her. "I'm sorry, I didn't know you were out here."

"I'm glad we have this time to talk privately. First, I wish to thank you for your help with my husband tonight."

Relaxing a little, Miranda smiled. "I became an ER doctor to help others, so I'm glad I could be of assistance."

Ana inclined her head, and as she moved closer, Miranda's smile faded. The woman might have slightly thawed with her thanks, and her expression might not be cold any more, but it was weary rather than warm.

"I appreciate it more than I can express. But, despite that, you must know that neither my husband nor I will ever give our blessing to a wedding between you and our son."

And there it was all over again. It shouldn't feel like she'd been stabbed in the chest with a sharp instrument, since it wasn't exactly news that the Alveses didn't approve of her, but it felt like that anyway. "Why not?"

"I have tried to help you and Mateo understand, but neither of you seem to be listening. With the death of our special Emilio…" Her voice hitched for a moment before she continued, "Mateo must take over his role as the heir to the dukedom. And you cannot fill the role of his wife."

"Why not?" Miranda repeated, somewhat stupidly. Why was she even asking, when their engagement wasn't real anyway? Did she want all the reasons she didn't fit in spelled out in capital letters to make her feel inadequate, like a lesser human being, just like she had thirteen years ago?

"Because you are American, and have an important job there. We are so very afraid that if he marries you, he'll never come back." She reached to clutch Miranda's hands. "We need him to marry a Spaniard, someone who will be content, happy to live here at the Castillo de Adelaide Fernanda. Surely seeing how ill my husband was tonight shows you how much Mateo is needed here, especially since…since Emilio left us. I can't bear to lose both my sons."

Miranda's heart squeezed at the pain and fear in Ana's eyes. "Mateo does understand." Miranda chose her words carefully, not wanting to speak for Mateo but wanting to pass on basically what he'd told her. "Our being together does mean he'll be living in New York part of the time, but he expects to come here several times a year."

"That's not enough. We need him here, which is why you must let him go." She reached to touch Miranda's arm, an imploring expression on her tired face. "You met my Emilio's wife tonight. You saw what a wonderful woman she is. A woman who adored her husband. My son." She lifted her wrist, encircled with a glittering gold bracelet studded with pearls. "Emilio gave this to me when he first took over running the estate, on my birthday. A gift to show me his commitment to me and our family and his responsibilities. Camilla helped him choose it, I know. She's a woman full of grace and style, loving and giving and from a good family with deep roots here. She has told me she will help find a suitable wife for Mateo."

Astonishment, anger, and hurt burned in Miranda's chest. Even if Mateo hadn't told her the truth about his sister-in-law, she'd have been upset at Ana's utterly rude dismissal of *her* as being worthy in any way of her second son. "What makes you think I don't adore your other son the way you believe Camilla adored Emilio? And why would he want to marry someone who doesn't love him? Perhaps your attitude is why Mateo doesn't want to come back here to live and work full-time."

"What do you mean? I love my son more than anything in the world. A wild boy as a child, we knew the army would bring him focus, and his many medals prove that it did. He's a fine man now, and I have to believe he will step up to his duties as the heir."

"Have you tried to talk to him about all this? About his plans? Maybe his answers would surprise you."

"The only surprise has been his engagement to you, which is the one thing that would keep him away. I would guess that once you found out Mateo wasn't like other emergency medical professionals in the U.S., but, in fact, a wealthy man from a family whose dukedom goes back hundreds of years, you set your net out to snag him as quickly as possible. It's what too many women do."

Miranda gasped in disbelief, anger surging so fast into her skull it made her brain scorch. "I can't believe you would actually say such a thing when you don't know me at all." She wanted to talk about her own family's wealth, her personal hardships, her hard work to prove herself to everyone, but decided she wouldn't stoop to the other woman's arrogant and judgmental depths. But she couldn't keep from telling her, at least when it came to the money, how wrong she was.

"For your information, it's been my experience that fortune hunters impressed by pedigree and money are often represented by the male sex, disguised as appreciative suitors. I've been targeted by fortune hunters interested in everything but me personally since I was in high school. Believe me, the absolutely last reason I'm attracted to Mateo is his money and position here, and the expectations you carry for him as the next Duke. In fact, that's the only thing I can think of that would make me walk away."

She spun away, the woman's words clawing at her gut, her own words disturbing her in a different way.

The only thing that would make her walk away was his parents' attitude?

As she nearly ran back to the house, her breathing went haywire at the realization that, deep inside, she'd meant it. And what did that mean, when all this had begun as a charade? A planned strategy by Mateo, with some pleasant vacation time in the midst of it?

She clutched her coat close to her throat, a stark and scary reality slamming into her, making it hard to breathe.

What had started out as pretence had become horrifyingly real for her. Somehow she'd let herself fall hard for Mateo Alves. A man who had no interest in a real and lasting relationship with any woman.

She dropped onto one of the outdoor chairs on the loggia and clutched her cold hands together. Mateo had wanted a simple excuse to bide his time taking on his family duties, and have them eventually accept that he wouldn't live here full-time. She'd wanted to help him with that, not fully understanding the difficult dynamics of his family situation after his brother's death.

Now she did. His parents' pain over losing their son was still raw. And even though he hadn't said much about it, she knew Mateo's was, too. No one thought clearly during times of grief. If she was truly a friend to Mateo, she'd help him see that all of them needed more time to process it, to figure out what needed to happen next.

Maybe Mateo really should move back here for a while. Ease his parents' fears. Studying psychology was part of medical school, and she had to assume that the reason Ana had lashed out at her with such harsh words was because, deep inside, she felt scared to death. Her husband was ill, and would slowly get worse with time. She'd lost her beloved son who'd been there to support her. She didn't realize that she'd driven her other son away once, and was doing it again.

As she thought it through, trying hard to see it from Ana's perspective, Miranda's heart felt heavy, hurting for Mateo and for all of them. Because to make one of them happy, the other would be unhappy. So where did that leave them?

She didn't know, but what she did know? She'd lived that quandary herself. Being able to leave behind poverty and an uncertain future to become part of the Davenport family, eventually becoming close to her half-siblings, meant Vanessa had had to endure seeing the physical reminder of her husband's infidelity every single day. Vanessa being happy instead would have left Miranda in a very dark and hopeless place.

A shadowy figure emerged from the garden, and she looked up to see Ana moving up the ancient stone steps to stand next to her, her face now filled with worry instead of hostility.

"I am sorry to have insulted you by assuming you are after money and prestige. Maybe you genuinely care for Mateo. But you must see why we need him here, where he belongs, while you have your work and your own family back where you belong. Do you understand?"

"I believe I do." She rose and let herself really see the pain and anxiety in the woman's eyes. Seeing it there forced her to really look at what a tough situation the Alves family was in. And because she wasn't a part of it, not for real, she suddenly knew it was time for her to go. To let Mateo and his parents work out this problem for themselves, without her being there to muddy everything up with a relationship and engagement that wasn't even real. Her being here, participating in this charade, was just making things worse. Making it impossible for Mateo to stay longer, to deal with the pain of Emilio's death together with his parents. To mend the fences between them.

"I'll be going now," she said quietly. "I'll ask Mateo to cut our trip short so I can go back to New York. Let him decide if he's coming back with me now or staying longer as you...talk more about everything."

A tremulous smile formed on Ana's lips. "Thank you. With you breaking off your engagement, I know Mateo will—"

"Breaking off our engagement?"

Both women swung toward the French doors to see a frowning Mateo striding toward them.

CHAPTER ELEVEN

"WHAT'S GOING ON out here?" Mateo asked. "I was trying to find you, to tell you that Father is feeling much better, only to hear my fiancée is leaving me?" He folded his arms across his chest, giving his mother a sharp look. "What are you talking about? What have you said to her?"

"Merely what you already know, and that she now understands." His mother lifted her chin defiantly. "You must think about your family and why we need you here, without an engagement complicating your thoughts and decisions."

"My decisions are exactly that—mine! Why do you refuse to accept that?"

"Because you know there's more at stake here than selfishly pandering to your own desires! What has happened to you? You spent four years in the army, defending our country and our way of life, always living up to your responsibilities. How has that changed now that you're needed here more than ever?"

"I like my life in New York. I still see no reason why I can't take care of the responsibilities you speak of while living here only part of the year."

"Your brother worked hard here, many hours a week, managing all the business interests of the estate. That's not something that can be done part-time, or from across the ocean." His mother stepped close to him and glared. "You know that Camilla was the perfect wife for Emilio. Glamorous and conscientious, the perfect hostess. You can't choose a mate who has significant work, like being a doctor. A career that would make those other important obligations impossible to meet. Surely you see that!"

"What I see is a woman who refuses to open her eyes to the truth." Mateo's voice vibrated with anger. "Camilla made Emilio miserable! And that's the kind of woman you would choose again for your other son? Camilla hurt my brother over and over again with her infidelity, having numerous affairs with all kinds of men, from politicians to horse trainers to men with trust funds who care only for their jet-setting lifestyle."

Ana gasped. "That is not true!"

"It is true. Why do you think he got so reckless? Began base jumping from places he shouldn't, and went paragliding on a day he *knew* was dangerously windy, only to be killed because of it!"

"It…it was just a terrible accident!"

"Yes, but he knew that mountain like the back of his hand, and I'm as sure as I am of my own name that it was one of Camilla's hurtful affairs that filled him with the desperate need to go out paragliding on a day he knew he shouldn't. He needed the escape from pain that paragliding always gave both of us. You pushed Emilio into a terrible marriage, just as you're trying to push me to be who you want me to be. But I won't accept that. I want the freedom to choose the life I want with the woman I love, and that woman is Miranda!" He moved away from his mother, tugging Miranda up from her seat to hold her close against his side. "We will be leaving tomorrow morning. I'll be in touch from New York."

And with that he marched back into the house, taking

Miranda with him. Her heart pounded hard in her chest from the tense exchange and confusion from his words.

Of course he'd just been angry and upset. He didn't mean what he'd said about her being the woman he loved. She knew that. And yet there'd been something about the way he'd said it—something about the timbre of his voice and the look in his eyes when he'd wrapped his arm around her that seemed to say he had meant it.

Could that be possible? Could he really have come to care for her the way she had for him, even though they'd spent mere days together? Surely that was just wishful thinking on her part.

"I'm so sorry, Miranda," he said through gritted teeth as he led her through the house. "I would never have brought you here if I'd known how bad it would be for you. And even after you diagnosed my father's hypoglycemia and took care of him! My mother should be ashamed."

"She's suffering, Mateo." Miranda wrapped her arm around his waist and gave it a squeeze as they walked side by side toward the stairs leading to the room where she'd changed into her gown. "I've been thinking about how hard all this must be for her, how scary to feel somewhat alone now. Your father is sick and you all know the prognosis for his future is grim. She's lost a son that she loved."

"And I lost a brother that I loved. That's not an excuse to act horribly to someone."

"People do and say things in times of deep stress that they might not otherwise," she said quietly.

He came to a stop. "You amaze me." He grasped her shoulders and pulled her hard against him, his eyes still angry but looking at her searchingly, too. "Another example of how sweet and special and wonderful you are. Trying to understand and forgive someone who's treated you badly, instead of feeling angry and resentful. You did it with Vanessa, too, and your father. It's just one more reason why I've come to love you."

Her heart felt like it stopped beating completely. She stared up at him, trying to see if he truly meant the words that seemed impossible. Impossibly wonderful. Had he said it just because he was feeling emotional? Upset with his mother and with the situation he faced?

"Love me?"

"Yes, love you." He kissed her long and hard, and through it she could feel a passion that made her legs wobble, tightly interwoven with clear anger and distress. "I want our engagement to be real, Miranda. I want to make a life with you in New York, far away from here and my parents."

"Mateo, you...you don't mean that." Miranda's chest constricted so hard she couldn't breathe. "You're just feeling frustrated with everything, and will feel different tomorrow when you've got a little distance from your mother to understand her better."

"I do mean it. And there's something that *you* don't understand." His hands gripped her shoulders. "I told you that my parents never thought highly of me, the way they did Emilio. But now that I'm all they've got, suddenly they want me to come home. If I come back here for good, I'll be surrounded by the knowledge, every day, that I'm not good enough to take his place. I'm just not. I never have been."

"Of course you are," she protested, finding it unimaginable that he seemed to truly believe it. "Why do you say that?"

"Because I've never been the son to them that Emilio was. I wasn't here for my brother when he needed me most." He pressed his mouth to hers for another hard kiss.

"I know I don't deserve you, but for the first time in my life I want to share it with someone. Share it with you. Forever."

Oh, God. She wanted to believe it. So much. She searched his eyes, trying to figure out what was really happening here. To see if tomorrow he'd regret his declaration of love, his claim that he wanted a forever-after with her. What she saw in their dark, smoldering depths sent cautious joy surging to her heart.

Heat. Shimmering desire. And the same glow of love that had slowly, insistently crept into every pore, every inch of her being over the past few days.

"I don't know what to think," she whispered. "I don't know what to say."

"Then let me show you how I'm feeling. Let me take you back to the guest house and convince you I mean every word."

He moved toward a side door that led into the dark night, heading quickly toward the small house as the stars twinkled above them.

Gulping in the crisp air, excitement surged through Miranda's veins, and her stomach flipped inside out. "Show" her how he was feeling? That could only mean one thing, couldn't it?

He pushed open the front door and, seeming like he was in a hurry, backed her into the bedroom and kicked the door closed behind them. "I don't expect Paula or anyone to show up, but just in case, hmm?"

The hard edge of anger had left his voice. The low rumble that replaced it was so full of seduction and promise, Miranda trembled in anticipation. He shoved off the coat she hadn't even noticed she was still wearing and tossed it on a chair before turning her around. His warm fingers swept her hair from the back of her neck and she felt his lips follow, pressing tiny kisses to her nape as he unzipped the beautiful dress.

"Mateo…" She had no idea what to say after his name, but even if she had, all ability to speak disappeared as cool air slipped across her bare back inch by inch, his fingers following in a shivery path across her skin. Finally fully unzipped, his hands gently shoved the dress to the floor with a swish. His lips moved to her bare shoulders as he turned her to face him again, his dark eyes glittering as he slowly, excruciatingly ran his finger along the lacy top of her bra.

Part of her wanted him to just keep going, but she didn't want to be the only one standing there in her underwear. She reached for his bow-tie and gave it a tug, sliding it from his collar to drop on the floor before reaching for his shirt. Struggling with the small buttons, she couldn't help making a frustrated noise, and with a heated smile he swept her hands aside.

"Let me."

"All right," she breathed. "That leaves me free to work on the rest of your clothes."

Another chuckle morphed abruptly into a moan as she quickly loosened his belt, undid his pants, pushed them to his ankles, then pressed the palm of her hand to feel the hard erection tenting his underwear.

"*Dio mio.* Slow down." He kicked his pants legs off at the same time he yanked off his shirt. "We have all night."

"I'm feeling in a hurry." And, wow, was that ever true. All worries about how he truly felt about her were forgotten as, with the sexiest smile she'd ever seen, he drew her close and kissed her. First on her mouth then her cheeks and throat then back to her mouth, speaking melodic Spanish words between each one, until she was gasping and clutching his bare shoulders to keep from slithering to the floor.

His hands had tantalizingly stroked and caressed her skin as they'd kissed, exploring her shoulder blades, her hips, her ribs, until one finally moved to unhook her bra, and he drew it off to toss it somewhere. His hands lifted to cup her breasts, his thumbs sliding softly across her nipples.

He lifted his fathomless dark gaze to hers. "You have the most beautiful breasts I've ever seen," he whispered. "Ever touched. Ever kissed." He lowered his hot mouth and slowly ran his tongue over each mound and Miranda held him close, resting her cheek against his soft hair, amazed at the intense connection she felt with this man after mere days spent together.

In a sudden, swift scoop he lifted her against his chest, her breasts being teased this time by the soft rasp of his chest hair as he pressed her against him. He moved to the bed, pulled back the quilt and laid her on the cool sheets, quickly following to lie on her, kiss her and touch her. The heavy weight of him felt so good, so right, and when he slid his fingers down to caress her she gasped into his mouth. He responded with sweet-sounding Spanish words, repeating them over and over as he pushed her thighs farther apart, touching, teasing, until she couldn't bear it any longer.

"I need you inside me now," she gasped.

"I'm here to give you whatever you want, my beautiful one," he whispered. "Always." He rose up to slowly fill her, and her legs wrapped around his back to pull him as close as two people could possibly be.

"Mateo. Mateo. I feel so… It's so…" She found she couldn't say anything more, just moaned at the bliss building inside her as he moved, deep and slow and unbearably delicious.

"I know, *querida*," he said, his gaze locked passionately with hers. "For me, too."

They moved together in a perfect rhythm that built, grew faster and faster until she couldn't hold back the intense pleasure any longer. She cried out as she came, feeling Mateo follow her with a deep groan of his own, until they lay gasping against one another, unable to move.

Long minutes later Mateo lifted his head. The dark eyes staring into hers seemed to hold a deep seriousness, but at the same time a small smile curved his lips. "Miranda Davenport, I love you."

"I love you too," she whispered.

"Finally!" His smile widened. "Hearing you say it back shows me you finally believe I love you. Took you long enough."

Her heart squeezed with an overflowing bubble of happiness. Until something sharply stabbed to deflate that joy.

Disquiet.

Did she believe him? She wanted to. So much. Yet a niggling doubt told her again that it seemed sudden. Too sudden. Right on the heels of the stress of the whole visit, of time spent in the orchards and seeing the horses, of his dad getting ill, of arguing with his mother. Of coping with his brother's death. Of dealing with his obviously deep-rooted feelings of inadequacy when it came to his place in the family.

Spending time together in Catalonia and on the estate had been a pleasant distraction from the weight of all that. Great sex was the perfect way to ease pain, she knew. Was he confusing all those feelings with love?

God, she just didn't know. The chemistry between them from the very beginning, the feelings they'd seemed to share at the dance, wasn't necessarily love on his part. Maybe it was simple chemistry. Lust.

Except surely a man like Mateo knew the difference between lust and love. Much as she wanted to believe with all her heart that he really did love her, she had to question it. Had to wonder.

Did he truly believe it himself?

Mateo held tight to Miranda's gloved hand as they navigated the crowded sidewalks on their way to his apartment. They'd enjoyed another dinner together, talking and laughing and learning about one another, and every hour he spent with her, the more he appreciated her. Her pretty face and beautiful smile, her inquisitive mind, her insight into so many things he didn't usually bother to spend much time thinking about.

He hated that they both had to go back to work the next day, since their vacation time had been far less than satisfying. Had hardly counted as a vacation at all, with all the stress of faking their engagement and dealing with his parents.

She'd protested that he should think about it longer, but he was more than glad they'd left early the next morning. Once they'd arrived back home, they'd spent their last days off going to a few museums he hadn't taken the time to go to recently, to a show, even ice skating at the Rockefeller Center. Laughing as they both fell a few times, enjoying the beauty and magic of Christmastime in New York City.

And making love. Making love with Miranda was like nothing he'd experienced before, probably because he'd never really loved a woman before. How incredible that this woman he'd planned to spend only one week with had sneaked into his heart so completely. Turning upside down his conviction that he never wanted to be committed to one woman, because he knew without a doubt that he wanted to spend his life with her.

He smiled down at her, tugging her away from a gaggle of laughing teenagers dancing along the sidewalk. New York City was always busier this time of year as tourists came to do Christmas shopping or stay for the week to watch the Rockefeller Center Christmas tree be erected, then lit, in all its spectacular glory.

"Oh, my gosh, I haven't told you yet!" Miranda exclaimed, as she hung onto his arm. "Grace wants me to be a bridesmaid at her and Charles's wedding. I guess we'll be going dress shopping soon."

"I'm sure you'll enjoy that. Is there a woman alive who doesn't like shopping?"

"Probably one or two, but I'm not one of them." She grinned up at him. "Do you have any Christmas shopping you want to do while you're still on vacation? It's still early—we have time to look in a few stores."

He looked down at her rosy cheeks and the cute knit hat she had pulled over her soft hair, and realized that Christmas shopping had been off his to-do list for so long, he hadn't even thought about it. He definitely needed to come up with something to give this special woman to show how much she'd brought to his life.

"The only Christmas shopping I need to do is for you, and since I can't do that with you peeking, the answer is no."

"You don't have to get anything for me. I'm still wearing the amazing ring I was supposed to give back to you at the end of this week."

"Except that's changed now. An engagement ring given to my beautiful bride before Christmas can't qualify as a Christmas gift, too."

The eyes lifting to his looked like maybe they were

smiling and worried at the same time. "I... Don't you ever buy gifts for your parents?"

His gut tightened, not wanting to think about his parents and their disappointment in him and their nastiness to Miranda. Glad to be far away from that disaster. "Not unless I'm there with them at Christmas, which hasn't happened in a long time. They don't expect me to ship anything from here."

"Do they send you gifts?"

"Usually a basket of fruits and candies that I take to the hospital for the nursing staff or share with other medics. I've told them not to bother, but I guess parents never stop thinking about what their offspring are eating. Or they feel required to make the gesture." He looked down at her again, wondering why she was frowning. "Why?"

"Because I can't help but feel bothered by this...situation. I mean, we're engaged for real now, but you don't seem to want them involved in any way. You haven't called once since we've been back. And now you tell me you don't bother with Christmas gifts. I'm betting not even a card."

"All true. And your point?"

"It's not good. I mean, for better or worse, they're your parents and they love you. I know deep inside you love them too. You can't just shut them out."

"Watch me." He shoved down the uneasy feeling in his chest, the tiny nagging voice that told him Miranda was right. That he shouldn't completely shut out the two people who'd given him life, especially now, when their lives had become so difficult. But both had made unreasonable demands on him. Refused to accept beautiful and special Miranda as his future wife, and if he had to choose her over his parents, he absolutely would.

Miranda opened her mouth then shut it again, obviously deciding not to pursue it. Which he was more than happy about. Talking wasn't going to change a thing, other than to make his stomach hurt and make Miranda worry about it. He'd made his decision about his future, and was more than happy with that.

"Come in here." Miranda took an abrupt left toward a shop doorway, dragging Mateo with her.

He looked around and saw they'd entered a jewelry store. "You have some jewelry you'd like to show me that I can choose from for you for Christmas? A bit of a surprise, but not completely a surprise?" He dropped a kiss to her temple, let it linger there. "I like that idea."

"Not for me. For your mother."

"My mother?" What was she talking about? "First, I haven't given my mother jewelry since I bought her some gaudy fake gold and diamond pin when I was about nine years old. And didn't I just tell you I don't buy her gifts at all? Especially now, considering how upset she is with me."

"All the more reason to buy her something, as a peace offering. A…a really nice bracelet that she could wear and think of you every time she does."

"Miranda." He held her face in his hands, trying to understand why she was so concerned about his relationship with his parents when he wasn't. After all, he'd been more or less estranged from them for years, and this was nothing new. "You need to stop worrying about this. I don't think she needs or wants anything to remind her of me. Especially when every time she thinks of me she concentrates on all the ways I disappoint them. Let's forget all that and enjoy our last night together before work gets hectic again, hmm?"

He read the hesitation in her eyes, then sighed in relief when she finally smiled and took his hand. "All right. I have to be at the hospital early, so what should we do that won't keep us out late? Enjoy a sweet dessert somewhere?"

"There's one thing I can think of that I'd like to do that won't keep us out late but might keep us up late, and would taste very, very sweet," he said in her ear, glad to be moving to a conversation that involved being alone and kissing and making love. "How about we go to my apartment, and I'll show you what I have?"

"I can't imagine what that would be," she said in faux, wide-eyed innocence. "Did you bake a cake? Buy ice cream?"

He had to laugh, tugging her close and dropping a kiss on her luscious mouth. How had he gotten so lucky as to have the fates throw him and Miranda together in such a surprising way? To meet a woman who was smart and sweet and fun as well, making him feel things, want things he'd never known were missing from his life?

"I think you already know what my very favorite sweet dessert is, and I can't wait to enjoy it all night long."

Miranda grabbed her phone to silence the alarm so as to not awaken the man whose warm, masculine and delicious-feeling body was half-draped over hers. Very gently, she moved his heavy arm from her waist and twisted to look at him. At his chiseled jaw and sensually shaped mouth that had kissed every inch of her body last night. At the dark lashes fanning his cheeks, looking almost boyish in a relaxed sleep. Far different from the fire and passion he'd shown her throughout the night as they'd made love in a way she'd never dreamed possible. In a way that had scorched her body at the same time it reached deeply and tenderly all the way inside her soul.

It was beyond wonderful at the same time it felt awful. She just couldn't feel truly good about it. Good in a way that told her without a doubt that she was doing the right thing by holding him close and marrying him. Distancing him, both physically and emotionally, from his family. Without their engagement, he might well have stayed in Spain longer. Probably would have. He'd have been there for his father, and maybe even have had honest conversations with his mother that would have brought them closer.

All of them were still grieving Emilio's death, and she knew well that people didn't always think rationally during times of extreme stress and pain and worry. Nearly going off the deep end after her mother had died had shown her that first-hand, but at the time she hadn't even realized she couldn't think straight for a long time.

She reached to tenderly stroke her fingertip across his strong cheekbone, and a sad smile touched her lips as his face twitched in response. Marrying him after such a short time, in the midst of a true-life crisis for him and for his parents, would be wrong. She'd been responsible for ripping a hole in the fabric of the Davenports' lives thirteen years ago, and couldn't allow herself to do that to another family.

Stepping away was the only fair and right thing to do, no matter how much she loved him. Losing his brother and facing responsibilities he wasn't sure he wanted meant that Mateo wasn't in a good place emotionally to make a big, life-changing decision.

No, she had to let Mateo think longer about what he should do. Allowing his family to work together to heal wouldn't happen if she was permanently bound to the man. He'd been so convinced for so long that he never wanted to get married, it seemed impossible that he'd completely changed his mind in one week, much as she'd wanted to believe he could.

If it was meant to be, perhaps someday in the future they'd be together again. But for now, leaving him to figure out what he really wanted, when grief and anger and feelings of inadequacy were clouding his judgement, was her only choice. To know for certain if he really loved her, or if being with her had simply been temporary pain relief.

A lump formed in her throat as she oh-so-gently touched her lips to his forehead. Why did love have to hurt so much? The effort it took to somehow force herself to slip from the bed felt nearly impossible. To dress for work and leave a note for Mateo, explaining why it had to be over between them, at least for now, hoping he'd understand. Hoping he'd be able to look inside his heart and mind more clearly with her gone.

Clicking the door quietly behind her, she crept away with dawn rising between the tall buildings of New York City. The wind that bit her skin and whipped her hair felt colder than it had yesterday. Her chest felt like someone had kicked all the air out of it, knowing that Mateo's arm wouldn't be holding her close, to make her feel safe, to make her feel appreciated, to make her feel loved.

Head down against the wind fighting her progress, she made herself keep going. Hoping that letting him go would truly help him find his way.

CHAPTER TWELVE

FOR AT LEAST the tenth time, Mateo read the note Miranda had left him, and it didn't make any more sense now than it had the first time he'd read it.

Miranda was the most giving, loving, astute woman he'd ever met. A woman anyone could rely on to be honest and trustworthy. A woman who would always be there to help anyone who needed it.

Which meant this staggering news, her breaking off their engagement, breaking off any kind of relationship with him, was clearly all his fault, not hers.

And yet he couldn't figure out how she could be so sure that he only thought he loved her because of the stress he'd been under. That it was all a reaction to his brother dying, to his life changing in ways he wasn't comfortable with. That she was a passing thing to him.

Hadn't he shown her in so many ways how much he loved her? Couldn't she see it in his eyes, feel it in his touch, sense it when they made love?

He crumpled the note in his hand and set it next to the ring she'd left on the table. Yeah, maybe he did have to deal with his grief and guilt, his parents' pain and the situation back home before he could begin to think about another big life change. But they could have stayed together, without setting a date for a wedding yet, right? Spent time learning about one another, loving one another?

But instead she was gone. And he was left trying to cope with the ache in his chest she'd left behind.

He dragged his hand through his hair, forcing himself to face the truth. His insistence that they make their engagement real had come too fast. He saw that now. He'd exposed her to the stress and upheaval back at home and given her a glimpse of the same upheaval he felt in his heart and mind and gut. So, of course, she couldn't believe he really loved her. Wanted her in his life forever. Hadn't he spent half their time together telling her why he never wanted to get married?

Damn it.

He wanted to run after her, somehow convince her that his love for her was real, and not a reaction to everything else going on in his life. But maybe the truth was that Miranda deserved better than him, which he'd thought all along. A man who had the kind of stable family life she craved, that she wanted for herself, that she'd never fully had. God knew, he wasn't that man, the way he'd let his brother down. With his relationship with his parents a complete wreck.

Maybe his attitude about his parents, his avoiding the grief and guilt he felt from Emilio being gone, really was selfish. Maybe he'd been being selfish with Miranda, too.

Not going after her to try to convince her they should be together made his heart feel like a huge hunk of it was being chopped off. She made him feel whole in a way he'd never felt in his life. But would that be what was best for her?

It was time to face the hard truth that it damn well wasn't.

Hadn't she been learning to be the kind of person she

wanted to be? A person who knew her self-worth wasn't tied to her past or her relationship with Vanessa Davenport? She was teaching him that he needed to fix himself first, just like she was doing.

He couldn't give her damaged goods, which was what he was right now. He had to let her go.

He sat quietly, his heart aching as he absorbed the pain of that reality. He'd thought having to live at the Castillo de Adelaide Fernanda would have changed his life in a bad way. After having Miranda in his life for just the briefest time, he knew with certainty his life really had completely changed. Without her in it, he'd have a hole in his world that only she could fill.

The end of a twelve-hour shift always left Miranda exhausted, but today she felt more jittery than tired. All week she'd worked extra hours, trying to keep busy so she had less time to think about Mateo. To wonder what he was doing. If he'd talked with his parents. If he'd thought more about her suggestion to go back home for a while to think things through.

If he missed her as much as she missed him.

Every time an ambulance brought a patient to the ER, she found herself looking to see who the EMT was. Not once all week had it been Mateo, and she'd cautiously hoped he might have gone to Spain. But when she casually asked one of his co-workers, she was shocked to learn he'd asked to be moved to a different precinct.

Guilt clawed at her chest. He hadn't gone home. Her breaking up with him had just pushed him to move on to a different job. He'd talked about how much he enjoyed working as a team with the other EMTs, and now he had to learn to work with new people all over again.

Miranda grabbed her coat from her locker and slowly

headed to the hospital's back door, wondering if she'd made a mistake. Had she abandoned him right when he'd needed her most? Should she have stayed to be there for him, gently encouraging him to talk with his parents? Nudging him to go home again to try to mend the fences that had yawned even wider apart after she'd agreed to fake an engagement?

Feeling too unsettled to think about going to her apartment, she decided she should stop being such a hermit and mingle with the New Yorkers and visitors who were enjoying the Rockefeller Center Christmas tree that had gone up the day before. It would remind her of skating with Mateo on the plaza, but it wasn't as though he wasn't on her mind anyway.

Maybe one good thing could come of this pain and emptiness she felt. Maybe she'd change the way she lived in New York, get out and explore and have adventures like Mateo had encouraged her to. Be bolder and braver. Or would that just make her miss him even more, wishing so much he was there to share it all with her?

Standing in front of the huge pine tree, she hardly noticed the cold wind stinging her cheeks. Dozens of people were there, but somehow she felt more alone than she could remember ever feeling in her life. She took a breath, forcing herself to participate in the cheers as thousands of colorful lights came on and brightened all of Rockefeller Center.

Couples and families stood smiling, holding hands and hugging, and Miranda swallowed back the tears that threatened to spill over. Wishing so much that Mateo was standing there with her, holding her hand, smiling at her. That his mother, who loved Christmas and holiday decorations, could be there too, bringing Ana some happiness in the midst of such a difficult time in her life.

As she stared at the sparkling tree, bringing happiness

to so many people, an idea seeped into Miranda's mind, then grew.

She'd been the one to bring chaos and stress to the Davenports' home thirteen years ago. Had made things worse between Mateo and his parents, widening the divide between them. What if it was time for her to be the one to fix things instead? To mend a rift and bring people closer together instead of pulling them apart?

A small smile started to form, banishing her tears. Optimism slowly filled her heart, followed by a conviction that it was the absolute right thing to do. Christmas was about miracles, wasn't it? Maybe, just maybe, she could make a miracle of her own.

Mateo trudged up the stairs to his apartment, wondering when the days might start feeling different from one another. When Saturdays and Mondays and Thursdays wouldn't all blur together into a week of just going through the motions. Taking care of patients, then running errands, then heading back to his apartment, alone. Seeing happy couples hand in hand and kissing, which made him physically ache. Seeing mothers and fathers and children laughing and window-shopping and obviously enjoying the kind of close family bond only parents and siblings were blessed to have.

How had his family gotten it so wrong? How much of it was his fault? The more he thought about what Miranda had said in her note, the more he wondered if he'd blamed his parents when, truthfully, they'd all had a hand in the way their family had fractured over the years.

He'd been more than happy to stay extra time in the army when Emilio had been released early. He was the one who'd left the country and rarely returned for visits. For the first time, he tried to see it from his parents' perspective, and he could understand why they'd been angry—hurt, really—at the distance he'd put between them, both physically and emotionally.

He fingered the box in his pocket that he'd planned to mail home, and suddenly realized that wasn't good enough. That Miranda, as usual, had been right. That he needed to go to Spain and deliver it himself. He had to quit hiding from the guilt and pain about Emilio. Now that Miranda was gone from his life, protecting himself from that pain by living in New York wasn't working anymore.

He'd go home and spend time with his parents. Really spend time with them, and let them know that, despite being gone for so many years, he loved them. Talk about how much he'd loved Emilio, confess the guilt he felt over not being there for him during tough times. Deal with that pain. And once he had, once his family was more together than it was now, he'd come back and find Miranda. Maybe if he had his life together, she'd finally see that he truly loved her.

Yeah, that's what had to happen, and the sooner it happened, the sooner he could come back and see Miranda again. He hurried to his apartment to make a plane reservation to Spain, pronto. He unlocked his door then came to a dead stop. Stunned, because there were three people sitting in his living room.

The three people who meant the most in the world to him.

"Hello, Mateo," Miranda said, her voice sounding a little thin as she stood. "I thought you should have an early Christmas gift. A visit from your parents, so you can talk things through."

"Miranda. Madre. Padre. I can't…believe you're all here."

His mother stood and walked to him, her face anxious and strained and full of something else. Remorse?

"Mateo, I'm so sorry we have been such fools, only expressing anger and disappointment instead of telling you how much we love you."

To his shock, her eyes filled with tears, and he closed the gap between them to take her hands. "Mother, it's all right. I've made mistakes too. Things have been hard for all of us."

"Miranda tells me that you believe we loved Emilio more. That's just not true." She squeezed his hands tightly. "We loved you every bit as much, and were heartbroken when you left."

"I didn't think you needed me there, with Emilio taking care of everything."

"We always needed you, if only to have you close." A tremulous smile touched her lips. "Emilio missed you, too, and I understand now how you tried to protect him. The two of you always had such a special bond, and I know you were a good brother to him."

His throat closed, knowing that wasn't true. And now was the time to confess that. "I let him down. I should have been there for him when things with Camilla got worse. I might have kept him from paragliding that day."

"No." His mother shook her head sadly. "It wasn't your job to ensure that Emilio made good decisions. If anyone must feel guilt, it's your father and me for insisting they marry. For being so blind."

That statement struck Mateo like a hard blow. He realized they all shared the same pain, feelings of guilt they had to let go of to move on.

Mateo's gaze moved to Miranda. Their eyes met, and just seeing that beautiful blue from across the room made his chest ache. Made him want to grab her into his arms and never let her go, no matter if she tried to leave him again or not.

And wouldn't that make him the same, pushy man he'd been last time?

No, what he needed to do was romance her, give her the time he hadn't given her before. Prove to her how much he loved her. How much he needed her. How much he wanted the forever-after with her he'd never thought he'd want with anyone.

"I need to talk to you, Miranda."

"Talking with your parents is more important." She looked down, then away, apparently wanting to look anywhere but at him, which scared the hell out of him. But he had to force himself to breathe and be patient. "I think they have other things they want to say."

"Yes, we do," his mother said.

It was all he could do to turn his attention from the woman he loved to focus on his mother as she continued. "We're very sorry for trying to make you move back home. We'll stop trying to make you step into Emilio's shoes, if only you'll do what you already promised. Which I don't think you'll mind, *si*? That you'll come visit sometimes, and bring Miranda with you. That's all we want."

"Bring Miranda with me?" His heart thumped in his chest as he swung his attention back to her, wondering if for some reason she'd told them they were still engaged. Then again, he hadn't told them they weren't, so who knew what they thought? "I would love to do that, but Miranda broke off our engagement, even though I'm crazy in love with her."

"What?" His mother swung toward Miranda, her eyes wide. "You didn't tell me this! How could you leave my Mateo? He is the best man you could possibly want."

That his mother was saying those words about him were unbelievable enough, and her next words astonished him even more.

"You must convince Miranda to marry you, Mateo," she said in the commanding voice he was used to. Hearing it this time would have made him smile if the stakes weren't so high. "She is wonderful, coming to us and insisting we all get past our frustrations with one another. Talk about Emilio and how much we miss him. If you come to Spain for an extended visit, she could even take over the old doctor's office and see patients there. Locals, and your father and I, would be most grateful not to have to always go to Barcelona to get medical advice and treatment."

"Yes. We need a doctor, and Miranda has already shown how good she is," his father chimed in.

"A very interesting idea, Madre and Padre." He reached for his mother and gave her a hug, wanting to end this particular visit fast so he could get on with the next important reconnection—with his ex-fiancée. "I have to talk with Miranda about all that, but first I do have a gift for you."

"A gift?"

The surprise on his mother's face would have made him feel guilty enough, but when tears swam in her eyes again he thrashed himself for neglecting her for so long. But those days were over.

"Miranda's suggestion. I hope you like it."

He held out the wrapped box, and his mother opened it, then gasped as the tears overflowed. "A bracelet, to go with the one Emilio gave me." She lifted her watery gaze to his. "Does this mean you're coming home for good?"

He glanced at Miranda, and his heart stumbled because, instead of looking like she wanted to run into his arms, she was biting her lip and looking worried, the same way she had before she'd left him. "That has a lot to do with Miranda. Will you leave us alone to talk about it? I'll come to your hotel for breakfast to work out some details."

"Fine. Good." She gave his father the "look", which

meant she wanted to give them the privacy he'd asked for. "Here's our hotel information. Let us know what time. Come, Rafael."

Mateo hugged them both, and already the heavy weight that had hung on his shoulders the past six months felt lighter. Except there was another, even bigger weight crushing his chest until he could barely breathe.

Closing the door behind them, he moved toward Miranda, not sure whether he should fold her in his arms and kiss her, or give her space, which he hadn't done enough of before. He pulled in a breath and forged forward with the most critical conversation he'd had in his life.

"Thank you for reaching out to them and bringing them here. You're incredible. The most special woman I've ever known. And now my parents finally realize it, too."

Miranda's heart stuttered at his words before she reminded herself that him saying she was a special woman wasn't a big deal, under the circumstances. "Your situation helped me see things about my own life I hadn't fully realized. That I'd carried the weight of Vanessa's dislike for all these years to the point where I'd let it dictate who I believed I was. That I was the cause of the rift in my family. But I know now that I can't change that situation, that all I have control over is how I react to it. It struck me that you were doing the same thing, and I felt bad about making your family situation worse. So I brought them here to help you all put that baggage behind you. Move toward a better relationship that will make you all happy."

"Miranda." He wrapped his arms around her, bringing her close to the warm body she'd missed so much. "It's terrible that you've believed your family issues were your fault when in truth the problems were caused by your father."

"Hey, I'm not the only one. You were sure your parents thought Emilio was better than you, and you believed it, too. But of course it's not true at all."

"Maybe the reason we fell in love so fast is because we're more alike than we knew. That we were meant to help each other let go of those things. To have wonderful adventures together, bring out the best in each other."

"I don't think you really love me, Mateo," she whispered, wanting so much to be wrong. "It was just the difficulties in your life that made you believe you did."

"Is that why I think about you all day, every day? Why I close my eyes and remember how you looked with the breeze blowing your hair on the funicular? Why I remember how tough you were in the tunnel, and all the ways you're a great doctor? Why I can taste you and feel your soft skin against mine even when I'm sleeping? Why I've been completely miserable without you for the past week? I guess you're right. I guess that's not love."

Her chest expanded with emotion, but she was so afraid to believe it. So afraid he'd regret marrying when he'd never wanted that in his life. She looked up at him, tears stinging the backs of her eyes. "I don't know what to say. What to think."

"Up at Montserrat, you told me you'd had a miracle in your life once, and I said I didn't believe in miracles. But I was wrong." He cupped her face in his hands, and the tender look in his eyes stopped her breath. "You made me believe in miracles, Miranda, and my miracle is you. You've made me see how I shut myself off from being hurt. By my parents, by the guilt I felt over not being there for my brother, by any woman after seeing how much he was hurt by his wife. You've done that, too. Not believed in yourself enough. What do you say we spend our lives believing in each other? Loving each other? Please say yes."

"Yes." She flung her arms around his neck and sniffed back the tears. "I love you so much. I've missed you so much."

He lowered his mouth and kissed her, long and sweet and wonderful. When he pulled back, she felt dazed, even as a happiness bloomed in her chest unlike anything she'd experienced in her life. Then she frowned when his warm body moved away from hers and he went to his bedroom.

"Um, am I supposed to follow you in there?"

"Not quite yet. Soon." He emerged again, smiling, his eyes dark and alive, looking at her with such clear, real love she felt weak all over again. "First, this. Will you marry me, Dr. Davenport? For real, and forever?"

She looked down at the beautiful blue stone winking at her, and held out her hand. "Yes, Mr. Mateo. For real and forever and as soon as possible."

He laughed, sliding the ring on her finger before kissing her senseless.

"So," he said as they came up for breath, "how do you feel about moving to Spain? You can become the region's doctor. But only if you like the idea. We can stay here, and just go a few times a year if you prefer. I'll be happy any place in the world, so long as you're there with me."

"I fell in love with your home almost as fast as I fell in love with you." It was true, and the idea of living in that beautiful place made her chest nearly overflow with the joy of all he was offering her. "Miranda Alves, wife of the future Duke of Pinero, has a nice sound to it, don't you think?"

"Yes." He kissed her again before pressing his forehead to hers. "Almost as wonderful a sound as both of us saying 'I do'."

* * * * *

THE MÉLENDEZ FORGOTTEN MARRIAGE

MELANIE MILBURNE

To Gaile Donoghue,
a loyal and trusted friend for more years
than I can count.
Thank you for your love and support.

Also, special thanks to Rebecca Fleming
and her grandmother, who were so helpful with
translating some words for me into Spanish.
Thanks!

CHAPTER ONE

EVEN before Emelia opened her eyes she knew she was in hospital. At the blurred edges of her consciousness she vaguely registered the sound of shoes squeaking on polished linoleum and the swish of curtains and voices, both male and female, speaking in low hushed tones.

She half-opened her eyes. The light was bright, making her pupils shrink painfully. She squeezed her eyes shut and, after a moment or two, blinked again and, narrowing her still flinching gaze, looked at the nurse who was standing at the end of the bed with a chart in her hands.

'W-what happened?' Emelia asked, trying to lift herself upright in the bed. 'What am I doing here? What's going on?'

The nurse clipped the folder on the end of the bed before coming to lay a gentle hand on Emelia's shoulder to ease her back down. 'Mrs Mélendez, please don't upset yourself. You're in hospital. You had a car accident a week ago. You've been in a coma.'

Emelia felt her heart give a jerky beat in her chest like a kick. She frowned and then wished she hadn't as it made her head ache unbearably. She put a hand up to her forehead, her fingers encountering a thickly wadded bandage positioned there.

Hospital? Accident? Coma?

The words were foreign to her, but the most foreign of all was how the nurse had addressed her. 'W-what did you call me?' she asked, staring at the nurse with her heart still thudding out of time.

The nurse glanced over her shoulder as if looking for backup. 'Erm…I think I'd better get the doctor to explain,' she said and quickly bustled away.

Emelia felt as if she were trying to find her way through a thick fog while blindfolded. *Accident? What accident?* She looked down at her sheet and hospital blanket-covered body. Although she ached all over, she seemed to be in all one piece. No plaster casts were on any of her limbs so she obviously hadn't broken any bones. The worst pain was from her head, although she felt horrendously nauseous, but she assumed that was from the pain medication she had been given. She could see the drip leading from a vein in the back of her left hand where it was lying on the top of the bed. She quickly looked away as her stomach gave a rolling turn.

What had the nurse called her again… Mrs Mel… something or other? Her heart gave another little stutter. *Married?* Of course she wasn't married! There must be some mistake, a mix-up in the paperwork or something. They'd obviously got her name wrong. Her name was Emelia Louise Shelverton. She had moved abroad from Australia a couple of months ago. She lived in London, in Notting Hill. She worked part-time as a singer in The Silver Room at one of the top hotels a couple of blocks from Mayfair while she looked for a more permanent position as a music teacher.

Married? What a laugh. She wasn't even dating anyone.

'Ah, so you are finally awake.' A man who was clearly one of the senior doctors swished the curtains around Emelia's bed closed. 'That is very good news indeed. We've been quite worried about you, young lady.'

Emelia glanced at his name tag through eyes that were still slightly blurry. 'Dr…um…Pratchett? What am I doing in hospital? I don't know what's going on. I think there's been some sort of mistake. The nurse called me Mrs something or other but I'm not married.'

The doctor gave her a formal trust-me-I'm-a-doctor smile. 'You have suffered a head injury, Emelia,' he said. 'This has obviously caused you to have some memory loss. We don't know how extensive it is until we conduct further tests. I will have the staff psychologist assess you presently. We may also need to rescan you under MRI.'

Emelia put her hand to her head again, her brows coming together in a tight frown. 'I…I have amnesia?'

The doctor nodded. 'It seems so. Do you know what day it is?'

Emelia thought for a moment but knew she was only guessing when she offered, 'Friday?'

'It is Monday,' Dr Pratchett said. 'September tenth.'

Emelia drew in an uneven breath. 'What year is it?' she asked in a frightened whisper.

The doctor told her and she blinked at him in horror. 'That can't be right,' she said. 'I can't have forgotten two years of my life. That's ridiculous!'

Dr Pratchett placed his hand over hers where it was lying on the bed clutching the sheet in her fingers. 'Try to keep calm, Emelia,' he said soothingly. 'This is, of course, a very frightening and confusing time for you. You have been in a coma for several days so things will seem a little strange at first. But in time you may well remember everything. It just takes a little time. You need to take things very slowly at first. Baby steps, my dear. Baby steps.'

Emelia pulled her hand out from beneath the doctor's, holding it up like an exhibit at an investigation. 'Look,' she said, pushing her chin up. 'No rings. I told you—there's been some sort of mix-up. I'm not married.'

'You are very definitely Mrs Emelia Louise Mélendez,' the doctor assured her with authority. 'That is the name the police found on your driver's licence. Your husband is waiting outside to see you. He flew over from Spain as soon as he was informed of your accident. He has positively identified you as his wife. He has barely left your bedside the whole time you have been unconscious. He just stepped out a moment ago to take a phone call.'

Emelia's mouth fell open so wide she felt her chin drop almost to her chest. She felt her heart boom like a cannon exploding in her chest.

Her husband?

Her *Spanish* husband?

She didn't even know his Christian name. How could it be possible for her to forget something as important as that? Where had they met? When had they got married? Had they? How many times…?

Her stomach gave a funny little quiver… It wasn't possible…*was it*? How could she have lived with and loved a man and not remember him? Her skin broke out in a sweat, her palms hot and moist with uncertainty and fear. Was she dreaming? Surely she must be dreaming.

Think. Think. Think.

What was the last thing she had been doing? She scrunched her eyes closed and forced herself to concentrate but her head pounded sickeningly as she tried to recall the last few days. It was all a blur, a foggy indistinct blur that made little, if any, sense.

When Emelia opened her eyes the doctor had already moved through a gap in the curtains and a short time later they twitched aside again, the rattle of the rings holding the curtain on the rail sounding too loud inside her head.

She felt her breath stall in her throat.

A tall raven-haired stranger with coal-black deep set eyes stood at the end of the bed. There was nothing that was even vaguely familiar about him. She studied his face for endless seconds, her bruised brain struggling to place him. She didn't recognise any one of his dark, classically handsome features. Not his tanned, intelligent-looking forehead or his dark thick brows over amazingly bottomless eyes or that not short, not long raven-black hair that looked as if it had last been groomed with his fingers. She didn't recognise that prominent blade of a nose, and neither did she recognise that heavily shadowed jaw that looked as if it had an uncompromising set to it, and nor that mouth… Her belly gave another involuntary movement, like a mouse trying to scuttle over a highly polished floor. His mouth was sculptured; the top lip would have been described as slightly cruel if it hadn't been for the sensual fullness of his lower one. That was a mouth that knew how to kiss and to kiss to conquer, she thought, as her belly gave another little jiggle. She sent the tip of her tongue out to the sand dune of her lips. Had *she* been conquered by that mouth? If so, why couldn't she remember it?

'Emelia.'

Emelia felt her spine prickle at the way he said her name. His Spanish accent gave the four syllables an exotic allure, making every part of her acutely aware of him, even if she didn't know who the hell he was.

'Um… Hi…' What else was she supposed to say? *Hello, darling, how nice to see you again?*

She cleared her throat, her fingers beginning to pluck at the hem of the sheet pulled across her middle. 'Sorry…I'm a little confused right now…'

'It's quite all right.' He came to the side of her bed in a couple of strides, his tall presence all the more looming as he stood within touching distance, looking down at her with those inscrutable black eyes.

Emelia caught a whiff of his aftershave. It wasn't strong, but then he looked as if he hadn't shaved for a couple of days. There was a masculine urgency about the black stubble peppering his jaw, making her think of the potent male hormones surging through his body. She shakily breathed in another waft of his aftershave. The light fragrance had citrus undertones that smelt vaguely familiar. Her forehead creased as she tried to concentrate… Lemons…sun-warmed lemons…a hint of lime or was it lemon grass?

'The doctor said I can take you home as soon as you are well enough to travel,' the man said.

Emelia felt the skin on her back tingle all over again at the sound of his voice. It had such a sexy timbre, deep and low and unmistakably sensual. She could imagine him speaking in his native tongue; the musical cadences of Spanish had always delighted her. But there was something about his demeanour that alerted her to an undercurrent of tension. There was something about the unreachable depths of his eyes. There was something about the way he hadn't yet touched her. Not that she wanted him to…or did she?

She glanced at his long fingered tanned hands. They were hanging loosely by his sides—or was that a tight clench of his fingers he had just surreptitiously released?

Her eyes slowly moved up to meet his. Her chest tightened and her breathing halted. Was that anger she could see in that tiny flicker of a nerve pulsing by the side of his mouth?

No, of course it couldn't be anger. He was upset, that was what it was. He was obviously shocked to see her like this. What husband wouldn't be, especially if his own wife didn't even know who he was?

She moistened her lips again, trying to find a way out of the confusing labyrinthine maze of her mind. 'I'm sorry…you must think I'm terrible…but I don't even know…I mean…I…I…I don't remember your name…'

His top lip lifted in a movement that should have been a wry smile but somehow Emelia suspected it wasn't. 'I do not think you are terrible, Emelia,' he said. 'You have amnesia, *sí*? There is much you do not remember, but in time hopefully it will all come back to you. The doctor seems to think your memory loss will not be permanent.'

Emelia swallowed. What if it was? She had read a story a couple of years ago about a young woman who had lost her memory after a horrific attack. Her whole life had changed as a result. She hadn't even recognised her parents. Her brother and two sisters were total strangers to her.

'Perhaps I should introduce myself,' the man said, breaking through her tortured reverie. 'My name is Javier Mélendez. I am your husband. We have been married for almost two years.'

Emelia felt the cacophonous boom of her heart again. It felt as if her chest wall was going to blow open with the sheer force of it. She struggled to contain her composure, her fingers now clutching at the sheet of the bed either side of her body as if to anchor herself. 'M-married?' she choked. 'Truly? This is not a joke or something? We are legally married?'

He gave a single nod. 'It is our anniversary at the end of next month.'

Emelia had no hope of disguising her shock. She opened and closed her mouth, trying to get her voice to work. Her brain was flying off in all directions, confused, frightened, lost. How could this be? How could this man be her husband? How could her mind let her down in such a way? How could she forget her own wedding day? What cruel stroke of fate had erased it from her memory? She let out a breath that rattled through her lungs. 'Um…where did we meet?' she asked.

'We met at The Silver Room in London,' he said. 'You were playing one of my favourite songs as I walked in.'

Emelia ran her tongue over her lips again as part of the fog cleared in her head. 'I…I remember The Silver Room…' She put her hand to her aching eyes. 'I can picture it. The chandeliers…the piano…'

'Do you remember your employer?' Javier asked.

Emelia looked up at him again but his eyes were like glittering diamonds: hard and impenetrable.

'Peter Marshall…' she said after a moment, her spirits instantly lifting as the memories flooded back. At least she hadn't lost too much of her past, she thought in cautious relief. 'He manages the hotel. He's from Australia like me. I've known him since childhood. We went to neighbouring private schools. He gave me the job in the piano bar. He's been helping me find work as a private music teacher…'

Something flickered in his gaze, a quick lightning flash of something she couldn't quite identify. 'Do you remember why you came to London in the first place?' he asked in a voice that was toneless, showing no hint of emotion.

Emelia looked down at her hands for a moment. 'Yes…yes I do…' she said, returning her gaze to his. 'My father and I had a falling out. A big one. We have a rather difficult relationship, or at least we have had since my mother died. He married within a couple of months of her death. His new wife…the latest one? We didn't get on. Actually, I haven't got on with any of his wives. There have been four so far…' She lowered her gaze and sighed. 'It's complicated…'

'Yes,' he said. 'It always is.'

She brought her gaze back to his, searching his features for a moment. 'I guess if we're married I must have told you about it many times. How stubborn my father is.'

'Yes, you have,' he said, 'many times.'

Emelia pressed her fingers to the corners of her eyes, her frown still tight. 'Why can't I remember you?' she asked. 'I *should* be able to remember you.' *I need to be able to remember you, otherwise I will be living with a total stranger,* she thought in rising alarm.

His dark eyes gave nothing away. 'The doctor said you should not rush things, *querida*,' he said. 'You will remember when the time is right. It might take a few days or maybe even a few weeks.'

Emelia swallowed a tight knot of panic. 'But what if I don't?' she asked in a broken whisper. 'What if I never remember the last two years of my life?'

One of his broad shoulders rose and fell in a dismissive shrug that Emelia somehow felt wasn't quite representative of how he felt. 'Do not concern yourself with things that are out of your control,' he said. 'Perhaps when you are back at home at my villa in Seville you will remember bits and pieces.'

He waited a beat before continuing. 'You loved the villa. You said when I first took you there it was the most beautiful place you had ever seen.'

Emelia tried to picture it but her mind continued to be a blank. 'What was I doing in London?' she asked as soon as the thought popped into her head. 'You weren't with me in the car, were you?'

That lightning-quick movement came and went in his gaze again; it was like the hand of an illusionist making something disappear before the audience could see how it was done. 'No, I was not,' he said. 'You were with your—' he paused for a moment '—with Peter Marshall.'

Emelia felt a hand grab at her insides and twist them cruelly. 'Peter was with me?' Her heart gave a lurch against her breastbone. 'Was he injured? Is he all right? Can I see him? Where is he? How is he?'

The ensuing silence after her rapid fire of panicked questions seemed to contain a deep and low back beat, a slow steady rhythm that seemed to be building and building, leading Emelia inexorably to a disharmonious chord she didn't want to hear.

'I am sorry to be the one to inform you of this, but Marshall did not survive the accident,' Javier said again without any trace of emotion in his voice.

Emelia blinked at him in stunned shock. *Peter was dead?* Her mind couldn't process the information. It kept shrinking back from it, like a battered dog cowering out of reach of the next anticipated blow. *'No...'* The word came out hoarsely in a voice she didn't recognise as her own. 'No, that can't be. He can't be dead. He *can't* be... We had such plans...'

Javier's expression didn't change. Not even a flicker of a muscle in his jaw revealed an iota of what he was feeling. It was as if he were reading from a script for a role he had no intention of playing. His words were wooden, cool. 'He is dead, Emelia. The doctors couldn't save him.'

Emelia felt tears burst from her eyes, hot scalding tears that ran unchecked down her cheeks. 'But I loved him so much...' Her voice was barely audible. 'We've known each other for years. We grew up in the same suburb. He was such a supportive friend to me...' A thought hit her like a glancing blow and her eyes widened in horror. 'Oh, God...' she gulped. 'Who was driving? Did I kill him? Oh, God, God, God—'

He touched her then. His hand came down over hers on the bed just like the doctor's had done earlier, but his touch felt nothing like the cool, smooth professional hand of the *medico*'s. Javier's touch was like a scorching brand, a blistering heat that scored her flesh to the fragile bones of her hand as he pinned it beneath the strength of his. 'No, you did not kill him,' he said flatly. 'You were not driving. He was. He was speeding.'

Her relief was a minute consolation given the loss of a dear friend. *Peter was dead?* The three words whirled around and around in her head but she wouldn't allow them to settle. Maybe she was dreaming. Maybe this was nothing but a horrible nightmare. Maybe she would wake up any second and find herself lying in her sunny shoebox flat in Notting Hill, looking forward to meeting up with Peter later to discuss the programme for that night's performance, just as she did every night before taking her place at the grand piano.

Emelia looked down at her hand beneath the tanned weight of Javier Mélendez's. There was something about his touch that triggered something deep inside her body. Her blood recognised him even if her mind did not. She felt the flicker of it as it began to race in her veins, the rapid escalation of her pulse making her heart pound at the thought of him touching her elsewhere. *Had* he touched her elsewhere? Well, of course he must have if they were married…

She gave her head a little shake but it felt as if a jar of marbles had spilled inside. She groaned and put her free hand to her temple, confusion, despair, grief and disbelief all jostling for position.

Javier squeezed her hand with the gentlest of pressure but even so she felt the latent strength leashed there. 'I realise all this must be a terrible shock. There was no easy way of telling you.'

Emelia blinked away her tears, her throat feeling so dry she could barely swallow the fist-sized wad of sadness there. As if he had read her mind, he released her hand and pulled the bed table closer, before pouring her a glass of water and handing it to her.

'Here,' he said, holding the glass for her as if she were a small child. 'Drink this. It will make you feel better.'

Emelia was convinced nothing was ever going to make her feel better. How was a sip of water going to bring back her oldest friend? She frowned as she pushed the glass away once she had taken a token sip. 'I don't understand…' She raised her eyes to Javier's ink-black gaze. 'Why was I in London if I am supposedly married and living with you in…in Seville, did you say?'

His eyes moved away from hers as he set the water glass back on the table. 'Seville, yes,' he said. 'A few kilometres out. That is where I…where we live.'

Emelia heard the way he corrected himself and wondered if that was some sort of clue. She looked at his left hand and saw the gold band of a wedding ring nestled amongst the sprinkling of dark hairs of his long tanned finger. She felt another roller coaster dip inside her stomach and doing her best to ignore it, looked back up at him. 'If we are married as you say, then where are my rings?' she asked.

He reached inside his trouser pocket and took out two rings. She held her breath as he picked up her hand, slipping each of the rings on with ease. She looked at the brilliance of the princess cut diamond engagement ring and the matching wedding band with its glittering array of sparkling diamonds set right around the band. Surely something so beautiful, so incredibly expensive would trigger some sort of memory in her brain?

Nothing.

Nada.

Emelia raised her eyes back to his. 'So...I was in London...alone?'

His eyes were like shuttered windows. 'I was away on business in Moscow,' he said. 'I travel there a lot. You had travelled to London to...to shop.'

There it was again, she thought. A slight pause before he chose his words. 'Why didn't I go to Moscow with you?' she asked, frowning.

It was a moment before he answered. Emelia couldn't help feeling he was holding something back from her, something important.

'You did not always travel with me on my trips, particularly the foreign ones,' he finally answered. 'You preferred to spend time at home or in London. The shops were more familiar and you didn't have to worry about the language.'

Emelia bit her lip, her fingers plucking again at the sheet covering her. 'That's strange...I hate shopping. I can never find the right size and I don't like being pressured by the sales assistants.'

He didn't answer. He just stood there looking down at her with that expressionless face, making Emelia feel as if she had stepped into someone else's life, not her own. If she was deeply in love with him she would have gone with him, surely? What sort of wife was she to go off shopping—an activity she normally loathed—in another country instead of being by his side? It certainly didn't sound very devoted of her. More disturbing, it sounded a little bit like something her mother would have done while she was still alive.

After a long moment she forced herself to meet his gaze once more. 'Um...I know this might seem a strange question but—' she quickly licked her lips for courage before she continued '—were we…happily married?'

The question seemed to hang suspended in the air for a very long time.

Emelia's head began to ache unbearably as she tried to read his expression, to see if any slight movement of his lips, eyes or forehead would provide some clue to the state of the relationship they apparently shared.

Finally his lips stretched into a brief on-off smile that didn't involve his eyes. 'But of course, *cariño*,' he said. 'Why would we not be happy? We were only married for not quite two years, *sí*? That is not long enough to become bored or tired of each other.'

Emelia was so confused, so very bewildered. It was totally surreal to be lying here without any knowledge of her relationship with him. Surely this was the stuff of movies and fiction. Did this really happen to ordinary people like her? She began to fidget with the sheet again, desperate to be alone so she could think. 'I'm sorry but I'm very tired…'

He stepped back from the bed. 'It's all right,' he said. 'I have business to see to, in any case. I will leave you to rest.'

He was almost through the curtains when she found her voice again. 'Um…Javier?'

His long back seemed to stiffen momentarily before he turned to look at her. 'Yes, Emelia?'

Emelia searched his features once more, desperate to find some hook on which to hang her new, totally unfamiliar life. 'I'm sorry…so very sorry for not recognising you…' She bit her lip again, releasing it to add, 'If it was me in your place, I know I would be devastatingly hurt.'

His dark eyes seared hers for a beat or two before they fell away as he turned to leave. 'Forget about it, *querida*,' he said.

It was only after the curtains had whispered against each other as they closed did Emelia realise the irony of his parting words.

CHAPTER TWO

'WELL, today's the big day,' the cheery nurse on duty said brightly as she swished back the curtains of the private room windows where Emelia had spent the last few days after being moved out of the High Dependency Unit. 'You're finally going home with that gorgeous husband of yours. I tell you, my girl, I wouldn't mind changes places with you, that I wouldn't,' she added with a grin as she plucked the pillows off the bed in preparation for a linen change. 'If his looks weren't enough compensation, just think—I wouldn't have to work again, married to all that money.'

Emelia gave the nurse a tight smile as she tried to ignore the way her stomach nosedived at the mention of the tall, dark, brooding stranger who had faithfully visited her each day, saying little, smiling even less, touching her only if necessary, as if somehow sensing she wasn't ready for a return to their previous intimacy. To limit her interaction with him, she had mostly feigned sleep, but she knew once she went home with him she would have to face the reality of their relationship.

She had seen how the nurses practically swooned

when he came onto the ward each day. And this one called Bridget was not the only one to gently tease her about not recognising him. Everyone seemed reasonably confident her memory loss would be temporary, but Emelia couldn't help worrying about the missing pieces and how they would impact on her once she left the relative sanctuary of the hospital.

She had spoken to the staff psychologist about her misgivings and what she perceived was Javier's tension around her. Dr Carey had described how some partners found it hard to accept they were not recognised by the one they loved and that it would take a lot of time and patience on both sides to restore the relationship to what it had been before the accident. There could be anger and resentment and a host of other feelings that would have to be dealt with in time.

The psychologist had advised Emelia to take time to get to know her husband all over again. 'Things will be more natural between you once you are in familiar surroundings,' Dr Carey had assured her. 'Busy hospitals are not the most conducive environment to re-establish intimacy.'

Emelia thought about her future as she waited for Javier to collect her. She sat on the edge of the bed, trying not to think about the possibility of never remembering the last two years of her life. She had no memory of her first meeting with Javier, no memory of their first kiss, let alone their wedding day and what had followed. He had said she loved his villa but she couldn't even imagine what it looked like. She was being taken to live in a foreign country with a man who was a stranger to her in every way.

She ran her hands down her tanned and toned thighs.

She couldn't help noticing how slim she was now. Surely she hadn't lost that much weight during her coma? She had only been unconscious a week. She had struggled on and off with her weight for most of her life and yet now she was almost reed-thin. Her legs and arms were toned and her stomach had lost its annoying little pouch. It was flat and ridged with muscle she hadn't known she possessed.

Was this how Javier liked her to look? Had she adopted a gym bunny lifestyle to keep him attracted to her? How soon had she succumbed to his attentions? Had she made him wait or had she capitulated as soon as he had shown his interest in her? What had he seen in her? She knew she was blessed with reasonable looks but somehow, with his arrestingly handsome features and aristocratic bearing, he seemed the type who would prefer supermodel glamour and sophistication.

The police had come in earlier and interviewed her but she had not been able to tell them anything at all about the accident. It too was all a blank, a black hole in her memory that no attempt on her part could fill.

One of the constables had brought Emelia her handbag, retrieved from the accident, but even searching through it she felt as if it belonged to someone else. There was the usual collection of lip gloss and pens and tissues and gum, a frighteningly expensive atomizer of perfume and a sophisticated mobile phone that hadn't survived the impact. The screen was cracked and it refused to turn on.

She took out a packet of contraceptive pills and stared at the name on the box: *Emelia Mélendez*. There were only a couple of pills left in the press out card. She fingered the foil rectangle for a minute and then, without another thought, tossed it along with the packet in the rubbish bag taped to the edge of her bedside table.

Emelia placed her hand on her chest near her heart, trying to ease the pain of never seeing Peter again. That was a part of her life that was finished. She hadn't even been given the chance to say goodbye.

Javier schooled his features into blankness as he entered the private suite. '*Cariño*,' he said, 'I see you are all packed and ready to leave.'

He saw the flicker of uncertainty in her grey-blue gaze before she lowered it. 'There wasn't much to pack,' she said, slipping off the bed to stand upright.

He put out a hand to steady her but she moved out of his reach, as if his touch repelled her. He set his jaw, fighting back his fury. She didn't used to flinch from his touch. She used to be hungry for it. He thought of all the times he had taken her, quickly, passionately, slowly, sensually. She hadn't recoiled from his love-making until Marshall had come back on the scene. Javier's gut roiled with the thought of what she had got up to while his back was turned. How convenient for her to forget her perfidy now when the stakes had changed. The way she had received the news of Marshall's death confirmed her depth of feeling for him. She hadn't forgotten her lover and yet she had forgotten him—her legal husband.

Javier clenched his fingers around the handle of the small bag containing Emelia's belongings. A tiny flick knife of guilt nicked at him deep inside. He had to admit there were some things he hoped she wouldn't remember about their last heated argument. He had lost control in a way that deeply ashamed him. Had his actions during that ugly scene driven her into her lover's arms? Or had she been planning to run away with Marshall in any case?

What if she *never* remembered him?

No. He was not going to think about that possibility, in spite of what the doctors and the psychologist had said. He lived for the day when she would look at him with full recognition in her grey-blue eyes. For the day she would smile at him and offer her soft, full bee-stung mouth for him to kiss; she would give him her body to pleasure and be pleasured until every last memory of her dead lover was obliterated.

And then and only then he would have his revenge.

'My car is waiting outside,' Javier said. 'I have a private jet waiting for our departure.'

She gave him one of her bewildered looks. 'You... you have a private jet?'

'*Sí,*' he answered. 'You are married to a very rich man, *mi amor*, or have you forgotten that too?'

She bit into her bottom lip, her gaze falling away from his as she continued walking by his side. 'Dr Carey, the psychologist, told me some husbands find it very hard to accept their wives don't remember them,' she said. 'I know this must be hard for you. I know you must feel angry and upset.'

You have no idea how angry, Javier thought as he led the way out of the hospital. Anger was like a turbulent flood inside him. His blood was surging with it, bulging in his veins like red-hot lava until he felt he was going to explode with it. How could he conceal the hatred he felt for her at her betrayal? The papers were full of it again this morning, as they had been for the past week.

Every headline seemed to say the same: the speculation about her affair with Marshall, their clandestine dirty little affair that had ended in tragedy. Javier knew he would have to work harder at controlling his emotions. This was not the time to avenge the past. What was the point? Emelia apparently had no recollection of it.

He cupped her elbow with the palm of his hand as he guided her into the waiting limousine. 'I am sorry, *querida*,' he said. 'I am still getting over the shock of almost losing you. Forgive me. I will try and be more considerate.'

She looked at him once he took the seat beside her, her eyes like luminescent pools. 'It's OK,' she said in a whisper-soft voice. 'I'm finding it hard too. I feel like I am living in someone else's body, living someone else's life.'

'It is your life,' Javier said. 'It is the one you chose for yourself.'

She frowned as she absently stroked her fingers over the butter-soft leather of the seat between them. 'How long did we date before we got married?'

'Not long.'

She turned her head to look at him. 'How long?'

'Six weeks.'

Her eyes went wide, like pond water spreading after a flood. 'I can't believe I got married so quickly,' she said, as if talking to herself. She shook her head but then winced as if it had hurt her. She lowered her gaze and tucked a strand of her honey-blonde hair back behind her ear, her tongue sweeping out over her lips, the action igniting a fire in his groin despite all of his attempts to ignore her physical allure. Sitting this close, he could smell the sweet vanilla fragrance of her skin. If he closed his eyes he could picture her writhing beneath him as he pounded into her, his body rocking with hers until they both exploded. He clenched his jaw and turned to look out of the window at the rain lashing down outside.

'Was it a white wedding?' she asked after a little silence.

Javier turned and looked at her. 'Yes, it was. There were over four hundred people there. It was called the wedding of the year. Perhaps if you see the photographs it will trigger something in your memory.'

'Perhaps…' She looked away and began chewing on her bottom lip, her brow furrowing once more.

Javier watched her in silence, mulling over what to tell her and what to leave well alone. The doctor had advised against pressuring her to remember. She was disoriented and still suffering from the blow of losing her lover. Apart from that first show of grief, she hadn't mentioned Peter Marshall again, but every now and then he saw the way her eyes would tear up and a stake would go through his heart all over again.

She suddenly turned and met his gaze. 'Do you have family?' she asked. 'Brothers or sisters and parents?'

'My mother died when I was very young,' he said. 'My father remarried after some years. I have a half-sister called Izabella.' He paused before adding, 'My father left Izabella's mother and after the divorce remarried once again. As predicted by just about everyone who knew him, it didn't work out and he was in the process of divorcing his third wife when he died.'

'I'm sorry for your loss,' she said quietly. 'Did I ever meet him?'

Javier stretched his lips into an embittered smile.

'No. My father and I were estranged at the time. I hadn't spoken to him for ten years.'

Her expression was empathetic. 'How very sad. How did the estrangement come about?'

He drew in a breath and released it slowly. 'My father was a stubborn man. He was hard in business and even harder in his personal life. It's why each of his marriages turned into war zones. He liked control. It irked him that I wanted to take charge of my own life. We exchanged a few heated words and that was it. We never spoke to each other again.'

Emelia studied his stony expression, wondering how far the apple had fallen from the tree. 'Were you alike in looks?' she asked.

His eyes met hers, so dark and mysterious, making her stomach give a little unexpected flutter. 'We shared the same colouring but had little else in common,' he said. 'I was closer to my mother.'

'How old were you when she died?' Emelia asked.

His eyes moved away from hers, his voice when he spoke flat and emotionless. 'I was four, almost five years old.'

Emelia felt her insides clench at the thought of him as a dark-haired, dark-eyed little boy losing his mother so young. She knew the devastation so well. She had been in her early teens when her mother had died, but still it had hit hard. Her adolescence, from fourteen years old, had been so lonely. While not particularly close to either of her high-flying parents, there had been so many times over the years when Emelia had wished she could have had just one more day with her mother. 'Are you close to your half-sister?' she asked.

His lips moved in a brief, indulgent-looking smile

which immediately softened his features, bringing warmth into his eyes. 'Yes, strangely enough. She's a lot younger, of course. She's only just out of her teens but, since my father died, I've taken a more active role in her life. She lives in Paris with her mother but she comes to stay quite regularly.'

'So…I've met her, then?' Emelia asked, trying to ignore the way her stomach shifted in response to his warmer expression.

His eyes came back to hers, studying her for a pulsing moment. 'Yes,' he said. 'You've met her numerous times.'

Emelia moistened her lips, something she seemed to do a lot around him. 'Do we…get on?' she asked, choosing her words carefully.

His unreadable gaze bored into hers. 'Unfortunately, you were not the best of friends. I think it was perhaps because Izabella was used to having my undivided attention. She saw you as a threat, as competition.'

She frowned as she thought about what he had said about his sister. The girl sounded like a spoilt brat, too used to having her own way. No wonder they hadn't got on. 'You said Izabella was used to having you to herself. But surely you'd had women in your life before…before me?'

'But of course.'

Emelia felt a quick dart of jealousy spike her at the arrogant confidence of his statement. Just how many women *had* there been? Not counting him, for she could not recall sleeping with him, she had only had one lover. She had been far too young and had only gone out with the man to annoy her father during one of her teenage fits of rebellion. It was not a period of her life she was particularly proud of and the loss of self-esteem she had experienced during that difficult time had made it hard for her to date with any confidence subsequently.

Her belly gave another little quiver as she thought about what Javier might have taught her in the last two years. Had he tutored her in the carnal delights he seemed to have enjoyed so freely?

His dark eyes began to glint as if he could read her mind. 'We were good together, Emelia,' he said. 'Very, very good.'

She swallowed tightly. 'Um…I…it's…I don't think I'm ready to rush into…you know…picking up where we left off, so to speak.'

He elevated one of his dark brows. 'No?'

Emelia pressed her trembling thighs together, the heat that had pooled between them both surprising and shocking her. 'The doctor said not to rush things. He said I should take things very slowly.'

The little gleam in his eyes was still there as he held her gaze. 'It would not do to go against doctor's orders, now, would it?'

She couldn't stop herself from looking at his mouth. The sensual curve of his lips made her heart start to race. How many times had that mouth sealed hers? Was he a hard kisser or soft? Fast and furious with passion or slow and bone-meltingly commanding? The base of her spine gave a shivery tremor, the sensation moving all the way up to nestle in the fine hairs on the back of her neck.

Her thoughts went racing off again.

Had he kissed her *there*? Had he stroked his long tanned fingers over the nape of her neck? Had he dipped his tongue into the shell of her ear?

Her heart rammed against her ribcage.

Had he gone lower to the secret heart of her? Had he explored her in intimate detail, making her flesh quiver and spasm in delight? What positions had they made love in? Which was their favourite? Had she taken him in her mouth; had she…? Oh, God, *had* she…?

She sneaked a quick glance at him, her face flaming when she encountered his unknowable eyes.

He lifted his hand and with a barely there touch tracked the tip of one of his fingers over the curve of her warm cheek. 'You don't remember anything, do you, *querida*?' he asked in a husky tone.

Emelia pressed her lips together in an effort to stop them from prickling with sensation, with an aching burning need. 'No…no… I'm sorry…'

He gave her a crooked smile that didn't quite make the full distance to his eyes. 'It is no matter. We can take our time and do it all again, step by step. It will be like the first time again, *sí*?'

Emelia felt her heart start to flap as if it had suddenly grown wings. 'I wasn't very experienced…I remember that. I'd only had one lover.'

'You were a fast learner.' His eyes dipped to her mouth, lingering there for a moment before coming back to her eyes. 'Very, very fast.'

She swallowed again to clear the tightness of her throat. 'You must find this rather…unsettling to be married to someone who doesn't even remember how you kiss.'

His fingers went to her chin, propping her face up so she had to lock gazes with him. 'You know, I could clear up that little mystery for you right here and now.'

She tried to pull back but he must have anticipated

it as his fingers subtly tightened. 'I…I wasn't suggesting…' she began.

'No, but I was.'

Emelia felt her skin pop up in goosebumps as he angled his head and slowly brought his mouth within touching distance of hers. She felt the warm breeze of his breath waft over her lips, a feather-light caress that made her mouth tingle with anticipation for more. She waited, her eyes half closed, her heart thudding in expectation as each second passed, throbbing with tension.

His fingers left her chin to splay across her cheeks, his thumbs moving back and forth in a mesmerising motion, his eyes heavy-lidded as they focused on her mouth. She sent her tongue out to moisten her lips, her heart giving another tripping beat as his mouth came just that little bit closer…

'It might complicate things for you if I kiss you right now,' he said in a rumbling deep tone. 'It wouldn't do to compromise your recovery, now would it, *cariño*?'

'Um…I…I…It's probably not a good idea right now…'

He gave a low deep chuckle and released her, sitting back in his seat with indolent grace. 'No,' he said. 'I thought not. But it can wait. For a while.'

Emelia sat in silence, trying to imagine what it was like for him. Of course he would find this situation unbearably frustrating. He was a full-blooded healthy male in the prime of his life. And for the last two years he had been used to having her as his willing wife. Now she was like a stranger to him and him to her. Would her reticence propel him into another woman's arms? The thought was strangely disturbing. Why would the thought of him seeking pleasure in another woman's arms make her feel so on edge and irritable? It wasn't as if she had any memory of their time together.

Emelia looked down at the rings on her finger. It was strange but the weight of them was not as unfamiliar as the man who had placed them there. She turned them around; they were loose on her but she had lost even more weight from being in hospital. She hadn't noticed it earlier but she had a slight tan mark where the rings had been, which put to rest any lingering doubts about the veracity of their marriage. She glanced at him and found him watching her with a brooding set to his features. 'Is everything all right?' she asked.

'Of course,' he said. 'I just hope the flight will not be too tiring for you.'

He leaned forward to say something to the driver. Emelia felt the brush of his thigh against hers and her heart stopped and started at the thought of how many times those long strong legs had been entwined with hers in passion. He had held off from kissing her but how long before he decided to resume their physical relationship in full? She squeezed her thighs together again, wondering if she could feel where he had been; might it have been only just over a week ago?

They boarded the private jet after going through customs. She couldn't remember flying on a private Gulfstream jet before. She couldn't recall even seeing one other than in a magazine. Even her father, as wealthy as he was, always used a commercial plane, albeit business or first class. Had travelling in such opulent luxury and wearing diamonds that were priceless become commonplace to her in the last two years?

Even though Emelia could see her married name on

her passport, it still seemed as if someone had stolen her identity. The stamps on her passport made no sense to her. She had been to Paris, Rome, Prague, Monte Carlo and Zurich and London numerous times yet she remembered nothing of those trips.

The jet was luxuriously appointed, showcasing the wealth Javier had alluded to earlier. He was clearly a man who had made his way in the world in a big way. The staff members were all very respectful and, unlike some of the wealthy men Emelia had met amongst her father's set, Javier treated them with equal respect. He addressed each of them by name and asked after their partners and family as if they were as important to him as his own.

'Would you like today's papers?' one of the flight attendants asked once they were settled in their seats.

'Not today, thank you, Anya,' Javier said with a ghost of a rueful smile.

Emelia suppressed a little frown of annoyance. She would have liked to have read up on the news. After all, it was a different world she lived in now. She had two years' worth of news and gossip to catch up on. And then another thought came to her. Maybe there was something about the accident in the papers, some clue as to what had caused it. Peter, as the manager of a trendy hotel, well frequented by the jet-setting crowd of London, had been a popular public figure. Surely she had a right to know what had led up to the tragic accident that had taken her friend from her.

'Don't pout, *querida*,' Javier said when he caught the tail end of her look. 'I am trying to protect you.'

Emelia frowned at him. 'From what?' she asked.

He gave her one of his unreadable looks. 'I think you

should know there has been some speculation about your accident,' he said.

Her frown deepened. 'What sort of speculation?'

'The usual gossip and innuendo the press like to stir up from time to time,' he said. 'You are the wife of a high profile businessman, Emelia. You might not remember it, but you were regularly hounded by the press for any hint of a scandal. It's what sells papers and magazines, even if the stuff they print isn't always true.'

Emelia chewed on the end of one of her neatly mani-cured nails. *She* was the focus of the press? How could that be possible? She lived a fairly boring life, or at least she thought she had until after she had woken up from her coma. She had long ago given up her dreams of being a concert pianist and was now concentrating on a career in teaching. But the sort of fame or infamy Javier was talking about had definitely not been a part of her plan.

She dropped her finger from her mouth. 'What are the papers saying about the accident?' she asked.

His dark eyes hardened as they held hers. 'They are saying you were running away with Peter Marshall.'

Emelia opened her eyes wide. 'Running away? As in…as in leaving you?'

'It is just gossip, Emelia,' he said. 'Such things have been said before and no doubt they will be said again. I have to defend myself against similar claims all the time.'

She pressed her lips together. 'I might not be able to remember the last two years of my life but I can assure you I'm not the sort of person to run away with another man whilst married to another,' she said. 'Surely you don't believe any of that stuff?'

He gave her a slight movement of his lips, not exactly a smile, more of a grimace of resignation. 'It is the life we live, *querida*. All high profile people and celebrities are exposed to it. It's the tall poppy syndrome. I did warn you when we met how it would be. I have had to live with it for many years—lies, conjecture, gossip, innuendo. It is the price one pays for being successful.'

Emelia gnawed on her fingernail again as the jet took off from the runway. She didn't like the thought of people deliberately besmirching her name and reputation. She wasn't a cheater. She believed in absolute faithfulness. She had seen first-hand the damage wrought when a partner strayed, as her father had played around on each of his wives, causing so much hurt and distress and the betrayal of trust.

'Do not trouble yourself about it for now,' Javier said into the silence. 'I wouldn't have mentioned the press except they might be waiting for us when we arrive in Spain. I have made arrangements with my security team to provide a decoy but, just in case, do not respond to any of the press's questions, even if they are blatantly untrue or deliberately provocative. Do you understand?'

Emelia felt another frown tug at her brow. 'If they are as intrusive and persistent as you say, I can't evade the press for ever, though, can I?' she asked.

His eyes were determined as they tethered hers. 'For the time being, Emelia, you will do as I say. I am your husband. Please try to remember that, if nothing else.'

Emelia felt a tiny worm of anger spiral its way up her spine. She squared her shoulders, sending him a defiant glare. 'I don't know what you expected in a wife when you married me, but I am not a doormat and I don't intend to be one, with or without the possession of my memory.'

A muscle clenched like a fist in his jaw, and his eyes became so dark she couldn't make out where his pupils began and ended. 'Do not pick fights you have no hope of winning, Emelia,' he said in a clipped tone. 'You are vulnerable and weak from your injury. I don't want you to be put under any more pressure than is necessary. I am merely following the doctor's orders. It would help if you would do so too.'

She folded her arms tightly beneath her breasts. 'Do not speak to me as if I am a child. I know I am a little lost at present, but it doesn't mean I've completely lost my mind or my will.'

Something about his expression told Emelia he was fighting down his temper with an effort. His mouth was flat and white-tipped and his hands resting on his thighs were digging into the fabric of his trousers until his knuckles became white through his tan.

It seemed a decade until he spoke.

'I am sorry, *cariño*,' he said in a low, deep tone. 'Forgive me. I am forgetting what an ordeal you have been through. This is not the time to be arguing like an old married couple.'

Emelia shifted her lips from side to side for a moment, finally blowing out her cheeks on a sigh. 'I'm sorry too,' she said. 'I guess I'm just not myself right now.'

'No,' he said with an attempt at a smile. 'You are certainly not.'

She closed her eyes and, even though she had intended to feign sleep, in the end she must have dozed off as when she opened her eyes Javier was bringing his airbed seat upright and suggested she do the same, offering her his assistance as she did so.

Within a short time they were ushered through customs and into a waiting vehicle with luckily no sign of the press Javier had warned her about.

The Spanish driver exchanged a few words with Javier which Emelia listened to with a little jolt of surprise. She could speak and understand Spanish? She hadn't spoken it before coming to London. Had she learned in the last couple of years? Why, if she could remember his language, could she not remember the man who had taught it to her? She listened to the brief exchange and, for some reason she couldn't quite explain, she didn't let on that she understood what was being said.

'*Ella se acuerda algo?*' the driver asked. *Does she remember anything?*

'*No, ninguno,*' Javier responded heavily. Not a thing.

During the drive to the villa Emelia looked out at the passing scenery, hoping for a trigger for her memory, but it was like looking at a place for the first time. She felt Javier's gaze resting on her from time to time, as if he too was hoping for a breakthrough. The pressure to remember was all the more burdensome with the undercurrent of tension she could feel running beneath the surface of their tentative relationship. She kept reassuring herself it was as the doctors had said: that Javier would find it difficult to accept she couldn't remember him, but somehow she felt there was more to it than that. Even the driver's occasional glances at her made her feel as if she were under a microscope. Was it always going to be like this? How would she bear it?

When the car purred through a set of huge wrought iron gates, Emelia felt her breath hitch in her throat. The villa that came into view as they traversed the tree-lined driveway was nothing if not breathtaking. Built on four levels with expansive gardens all around, it truly was everything a rich man's castle should be: private, imposing, luxurious and no expense spared on keeping it that way. Even from the car, Emelia could see a team of gardeners at work in the grounds and, as soon as the driver opened the car door for her and Javier, the massive front doors of the villa opened and a woman dressed in a black and white uniform waited at the top of the steps to greet them.

'*Bienvenido a casa, señor.*' The woman turned and gave Emelia a haughty look, acknowledging her through tight lips. '*Señora. Bienvenido a casa.*'

'Thank you,' Emelia said with a strained smile. 'It is nice to be…er…home.'

'*Querida.*' Javier put his hand in the small of Emelia's back. 'This is Aldana,' he said. 'She keeps the villa running smoothly for us. Don't worry. I have explained to all of the staff that you will not remember any of them.'

'I'm so sorry,' Emelia said to Aldana. 'I hope you are not offended.'

Aldana folded her arms across her generous bosom, her dark sparrow-like eyes assessing Emelia in one sweeping up and down look. 'It is no matter,' she said.

'I will take Emelia upstairs, Aldana,' Javier said and, switching to Spanish, asked, 'Did you do as I asked when I phoned?'

Aldana gave a nod. '*Sí, señor.* All is back where you wanted it.'

Emelia continued to pretend she hadn't understood what was being said but she couldn't help wondering what exactly Javier had asked the housekeeper to do.

Her lower back was still burning where his hand was resting. She could feel each and every long finger against her flesh; even the barrier of her lightweight clothes was unable to dull the electric sensation of his touch. Her body tingled from head to foot every time she thought of those hands moving over her, stroking her, caressing her, touching her as any normal loving husband touched a wife he loved and desired.

When he led her towards the sweeping grand staircase she felt the wings of panic start to flap inside her with each step that took her upwards with him.

Even though he was nothing but a stranger to her would he expect her to share his bedroom?

His bathroom?

Or, even more terrifying…his bed?

CHAPTER THREE

'TRY not to be too upset by Aldana's coldness,' Javier said as they came to the first landing. 'It means nothing. She will get over it in a day or so. She was like that the first time I brought you home with me after we were married. She thought I was making the biggest mistake of my life, not just by marrying a foreigner, but by marrying within weeks of meeting you.'

Emelia suppressed a frown as she continued with him up the stairs. She had seen undiluted hatred in the housekeeper's eyes. How long had that been going on? Surely not for the whole time they had been married? How had she coped with such hostility? It surely wouldn't have made for a very happy home with a household of staff sending dagger looks at every opportunity.

She put her hand on the banister to steady herself after the climb. Her legs felt weak and her chest tight, as if she had run a marathon at high altitude.

'Are you all right?' he asked, taking her free hand in his.

She gave him a weak smile. 'Just a little light-headed… It'll pass in a moment.'

Emelia felt his fingers tighten momentarily on hers, the itchy little tingles his touch evoked making her feel even more dazed than the effort of climbing the staircase. His eyes were locked on hers, penetrating, searing, all-seeing, but showing nothing in return. 'Did your housekeeper eventually come to approve of your choice of wife?' she asked.

He released her hand, his eyes moving away from hers. 'I do not need the approval of my housekeeper, Emelia,' he said. 'We are married and that is that. It is no one's business but our own.'

Emelia's teeth sank into her bottom lip as she trudged up the rest of the stairs. She looked for signs of her previous life in the villa but there was nothing to show her she had lived here for close to two years. The walls were hung with priceless works of art; as far as she could see, there were no photographs of their life together. The décor was formal, not relaxed and welcoming. It spoke of wealth and prestige, not family life and friendliness. She could see nothing of herself in the villa, no expression of her personality and taste, and wondered why.

Javier opened a door further along the hall that led into a master bedroom of massive proportions. 'This was our room,' he said.

Emelia wasn't sure if he spoke in the past tense to communicate he would no longer be sharing it with her and she was too embarrassed to ask him to clarify. 'It's very big…'

'Do you recognise anything?' he asked as he followed her into the suite.

Emelia looked at the huge bed and tried to imagine herself lying there with Javier's long strong body beside her. Her stomach did a little flip-flop movement and she shifted her gaze to the bedside tables instead. On one side there was a wedding photograph and she walked over and slowly picked it up, holding her breath as she looked at the picture of herself smiling with Javier standing by her side.

She wrinkled her brow in concentration. Surely there was somewhere in her mind where she could locate that memory. The dress she was wearing was a dream of a wedding gown, voluminous and delicately se-quinned all over with crystals. She could only imagine how much it must have cost. The veil was at least five metres long and had a tiara headpiece, making her look like a princess. The bouquet of orange blossom she carried and the perfection of her hair and make-up spoke of a wedding day that had been meticulously planned. It looked like some of the society weddings she had been forced to attend back at home with her father. All show and fuss to impress others, crowds of people who in a year or so would not even remember the bride's and groom's names. She loathed that sort of scene and had always sworn she would not be a part of it when or if she married. But, as far as she could tell from the photograph in her hands, she had gone for shallow and showy after all.

She shifted her concentration to Javier's image. He was dressed in a dark suit and a white shirt and silver and black striped tie that highlighted his colouring and his tall commanding air. His smile was not as wide as Emelia's; it seemed a little forced, in fact. She wondered if she had noticed it on the day and been worried about it or whether she had been too caught up in being the centre of attention.

Emelia looked up from the photograph she was holding to see Javier's watchful gaze centred on her. 'I'm sorry…' She placed it back on the bedside table with a hand that was not quite steady. 'I can't remember anything. It's as if it happened to someone else.'

His dark gaze dropped to the image of them in their wedding finery. 'Sometimes when I look at that photograph, I think the very same thing,' he said, the slant of his mouth cryptic.

Emelia studied him for a moment in silence. Was he implying he had come to regret their hasty marriage? What had led him to offer her marriage in the first place? So many men these days shied away from the formal tie of matrimony, choosing the less binding arrangement of living together or, even more casually, moving between two separate abodes, thus maintaining a higher level of independence.

Had those first two years of marriage taken the shine off the passion that had apparently brought them together? Relationships required a lot of hard work; she knew that from watching her father ruin one relationship after another with no attempt on his part to learn from his previous mistakes. Had Javier fallen out of love with her? He certainly didn't look like a man in love. She had seen desire in his eyes, but as for the warmth of lifelong love…well, would she recognise it even if she saw it?

Javier caught her staring at him and raised one brow. 'Is something wrong, Emelia?'

She moistened her lips, trying not to be put off by the dark intensity of his gaze as it held hers. 'Um…I was wondering why you wanted to get married so quickly. Most of the men I know would have taken years to propose marriage. Why did you decide we should get married so quickly?'

There was a movement deep within his eyes, like a rapid-fire shuffle of a deck of cards. 'Why do you think?' he said evenly. 'Do you think you were not in the least agreeable to being married to me? I can assure you I did not have to resort to force. You accepted my proposal quite willingly.'

Emelia gave a little shrug, trying not to be put off by the black marble of his gaze as it held hers. 'I don't know…I guess it's just that I don't remember being on the hunt for a husband or anything. I'm only twenty-five—'

'Twenty-seven,' he corrected her.

Emelia chewed at her lip. 'Ri-ght…twenty-seven…' She lowered her gaze and frowned.

He tipped up her face with one finger beneath her chin. 'I wanted you from the moment I saw you sitting at that piano,' he said. 'It was an instant attraction. You felt it too. There seemed no point in delaying what we both wanted.'

Emelia looked into the blackness of his eyes and felt the tug of attraction deep and low in her body. Was this how it had been? The magnetic pull of desire, an unstoppable force that consumed every bit of common sense she possessed? She felt the burn of his touch; the nerve endings beneath her skin were jumping and dancing where his fingertip rested. 'How soon did we—' she swallowed tightly '—sleep together?'

He brushed the pad of his thumb across her bottom lip. 'How soon do you think?' he asked in a low, smoky tone.

Emelia felt the deep thud of her heart as his strong

thighs brushed against hers. 'I…I'm not the type to jump into bed with someone on the first date.'

His dark eyes glinted. 'You sound rather certain about that.'

Her eyes widened in shock. 'Surely I didn't…?'

He dropped his hand from her face. 'No, you didn't,' he said. 'I was impressed by your standards, actually. You were the first woman I had ever dated who said no.'

Emelia gave herself a mental pat on the back. He would be a hard one to say no to, she imagined. 'Did that make me a challenge you wanted to conquer?' she asked.

He gave her an enigmatic smile. 'Not for the reasons you think.'

Her gaze went to the wedding photograph again. 'I don't suppose we waited until the wedding night.'

'No.'

Emelia wondered how one short word could have such a powerful effect on her. Her skin lifted all over at the thought of him possessing her. Her breasts prickled with sensation, her belly flapped like washing on a line in a hurricane and her heart raced. But all she had was her imagination. Her mind was empty, a total blank. She felt cheated. She felt lost and afraid she might never be able to reclaim what should have been some of the most memorable days of her life. She gave a little sigh and faced him again. 'The funny thing is there are some people—like my father, for instance—who would give anything to forget their wedding days. But I can't recall a thing…n-not a thing…' Her voice cracked and she placed her head in her hands, embarrassed at losing control of her emotions in front of him.

He placed a gentle hand on her shoulder. 'Don't cry, *querida*,' he said.

His low soothing tone was her undoing. She choked on another sob and stumbled forward into the rock-hard wall of his chest. Her arms automatically wound around his lean waist, her face pressing into his shirt front, breathing in his warm male scent. Her body seemed to fit against him as if fashioned exactly to his specifications. She felt the strong cradle of his pelvis supporting hers, his muscled thighs holding her trembling ones steady. Her body tingled with awareness as she felt the swelling of his groin against her. How many times had he held her like this? She felt the flutter of her pulse in response, the tight ache between her thighs that felt both strange and familiar.

One of his hands went to the back of her head and began stroking her in a gentle, rhythmic motion, his voice when he spoke reverberating against her ear, reminding her of the deep bass of organ pipes being softly played in a cavernous cathedral. 'Shh, *mi amor*. Do not upset yourself. Do not cry. It can't change anything.'

Emelia tried to control her trembling bottom lip as she eased back to look up at him. 'I want to remember. I want to remember everything. What girl can't remember her wedding day? How can I live my life with whole chunks of it missing?'

Javier brushed her hair back from her face, his dark steady eyes holding her tear-washed ones. 'There are no doubt other things you have forgotten that are worth forgetting. What about that, eh? That is a positive, *sí*?'

He took out a handkerchief and used a folded corner of it to mop up the tears that had trailed down her cheeks. Emelia found it a tender gesture that seemed at odds with his earlier aloofness. Was he finally coming to terms with her inability to remember him?

'What things would I want to forget?' she asked with a puzzled frown.

His eyes shifted away from hers. He refolded the handkerchief and put it in his trouser pocket. 'No marriage is perfect,' he said, 'especially a relatively new one. We had the occasional argument, some of them rather heated at times. Perhaps it is a good thing you can't remember them.'

Emelia tried to read his expression but, apart from a small rueful grimace about his mouth, there was little she could go on. 'What sort of things did we argue about?' she asked.

He gave a one shoulder shrug. 'The usual things. Most of the time little things that got blown all out of proportion.'

She angled her head at him questioningly. 'Who was the first to say sorry?'

There was a slight pause before he answered. 'I am not good at admitting it when I am in the wrong. I guess I take after my father more than I would like in that regard.'

'We all have our pride,' Emelia conceded.

'Yes.' He gave her another brief rueful twist of his mouth. 'Indeed.'

He moved over to a large walk-in wardrobe and opened the sliding doors. 'Your things are in here. You might feel more at home once you are surrounded by your own possessions. The travelling bag you had with you in London was destroyed in the accident.'

Emelia looked at the rows and rows of elegant clothes and shelves of shoes and matching bags. Again, it was like looking into someone else's life. Did *she* wear all these close-fitting designer dresses and sky-high heels? Her eyes went to the other side of the wardrobe where the racks and shelves were empty. She turned and looked at Javier. 'Where are your things?' she asked.

His eyes became shuttered. 'I had Aldana move them into one of the spare rooms for the time being.'

Emelia felt a confusing mixture of relief and disappointment. The relief she could easily explain. The disappointment was a complete mystery to her. 'So—' she quickly ran her tongue over her lips '—so you're not expecting me to…to sleep with you…um…like right away?'

He hooked one dark brow upwards. 'I thought you said you don't usually sleep with perfect strangers?'

She frowned at his tone, not sure if he was teasing her. 'Technically, you're not a stranger, though, are you?' she said. 'I might not remember you, but there's enough evidence around to confirm we are married.'

A glint appeared in his dark-as-night gaze as it held hers. 'Are you inviting me to sleep with you, Emelia?'

Emelia felt her belly fold over itself. 'Er…no…not yet…I mean…no. No. It wouldn't be right for me or even fair to you.'

He came up close, lifting a portion of her hair, slowly twirling it around his finger until she felt the subtle tension on her scalp as he tethered her to him. 'We could do it to see if it unlocks your memory,' he said in a voice that sounded rough and sexy. 'How about it, *querida*? Who knows? Perhaps it is just your mind that has forgotten me. Maybe your body will remember everything.'

Emelia could barely breathe. His chest was brushing against her breasts; she could feel the friction of his shirt through her clothes. Her nipples had sprung to attention, aching and tight, looking for more erotic stimulation. A warm sensation was pooling between her thighs, a pulsing feeling that was part ache, part pleasure, making her want to move forwards to press herself against the hardness she knew instinctively would be there. Her mouth was dry and she sent the point of her tongue out to moisten it, her heart slipping sideways when she saw the way his eyes dropped to follow its passage across her lips.

The pad of his thumb pressed against her bottom lip, setting off livewires of feeling beneath her sensitive skin. 'Such a beautiful mouth,' he said in that low sexy baritone. 'How many times have I kissed it, hmm? How many times has it kissed me?' He pressed himself just that little bit closer, pelvis to pelvis, the swell of his maleness heating her like a hot probe. 'What a pity you can't remember all the delicious things that soft full mouth of yours has done to me in the past.'

Emelia swallowed tightly, the sensation between her thighs turning red hot. She could imagine what she had done; she could see it in his eyes. The erotic pleasure he had experienced with her seemed to be gleaming there to taunt her into recalling every shockingly intimate moment.

His thumb caressed her bottom lip again, pushing against it, watching as it bounced back to fullness as it refilled with blood.

Emelia couldn't take her eyes off his mouth; the enigmatic tilt of it fascinated her. The way he half-smiled, as if he was enjoying the edge he had over her in knowing every sensual pleasure they had shared while she remained in ignorance. Her spine loosened with each stroke of his thumb, the tingling sensation travelling from her lips to every secret place.

'Do you want me to tell you some of the things you did with me, Emelia?' he asked in a gravel-rough tone that made the hairs on the back of her neck lift one by one.

She stood silently staring up at him, like a small nocturnal animal caught in the high beam of headlights: exposed, vulnerable, blinded by feelings she wasn't sure belonged to her. 'I…I'm not sure it would be a good idea to force me to…to remember…' she faltered.

He smiled a lazy smile that made her spine loosen even further. His palm cupped her cheek, holding it gently, each long finger imprinted on her flesh. 'You were shy to begin with, *cariño*,' he said. 'But then perhaps you were shy with your other lovers, *sí*?'

Emelia frowned. 'But I have only had one lover. I must have told you about it, surely? It happened when I was singing in a band in Melbourne. I was too young and didn't realise what I was getting into with someone so much older and experienced. I should have known better, but I was in that rebellious stage a lot of teenagers go through.'

His hand moved from her cheek to rest on her shoulder, his eyes still holding hers like a searchlight. 'You told me some things about it, yes,' he said. 'But then perhaps there are other things you didn't tell me. Things you preferred to keep a secret from me even during our marriage.'

Her frown deepened across her forehead. 'Like what?'

He gave her an inscrutable look and dropped his hand from her shoulder. 'Who knows?' he said. 'You can't remember, or so you say.'

The ensuing silence seemed to ring with the suspicion of his statement.

Emelia sat on the bed in case her legs gave way. 'You think I'm *pretending*?' she asked in an incredulous choked whisper. 'Is that what you think? That I'm making my memory loss up?'

His eyes bored into hers, his mouth pulled tight until his lips were almost flattened. 'You remember nothing of me and yet you grieve like a heartbroken widow over the loss of Marshall.'

She pushed herself upright with her arms. 'Have I not got the right to grieve the loss of a beloved friend?'

His jaw tightened as he held her stare for stare. 'I am your husband, Emelia,' he bit out. 'Your life is with me, not with a dead man.'

She glared back at him furiously. 'You can't force me to stay with you. I might never remember you. What will you do then?'

'Oh, you will remember, Emelia,' he said through clenched teeth, each bitten out word highlighting his accent. 'Make no mistake. You will remember everything.'

Emelia felt a rumble of fear deep and low in her belly. 'I don't know you. I don't even know myself, or at least that's what it feels like it,' she said. 'I don't know who I've become over the past two years. Do you have any idea what it's like for me to step back into the life that was supposedly mine when I don't recognise a thing about it or me?'

He let out a harsh breath. 'Leave it. This is not the time to discuss it.'

'No I can't leave it,' she said. 'You don't seem to trust me. What sort of marriage did we have?'

His eyes were fathomless black pools as they held hers. 'I said I don't wish to discuss this,' he said. 'You need to rest. You are pale and look as if a breath of wind would knock you down.'

'What would you care?' she asked with a churlish look.

'I am not going to continue with this conversation,' he said with an implacable set to his mouth. 'I will leave you to rest. Dinner will be served at eight-thirty. I would suggest you stay close to the villa until you become more familiar with your surroundings. You could easily get lost.'

Emelia sank back down on the mattress once the door had closed on his exit. She put a shaky hand up to her temple, wishing she could unlock the vault of memories that held the secrets of the past two years. What sort of wife was she that her husband didn't seem to trust her? And why did he look at her as if he was torn between pulling her into his arms and showing her the door?

After changing into riding gear, Javier strode down to the stables and, politely declining the offer from his stable-hand, Pedro, quickly saddled his Andalusian stallion, Gitano, and rode out of the villa courtyard. The horse's hooves rattled against the cobblestones but, once the stallion was on the grass of the fields leading to the woods, Javier let him have his head. The feel of the powerful muscles of his horse beneath him was just the shot of adrenalin he needed to distract himself from being with Emelia again.

Holding her in his arms when she had cried had been like torture. He couldn't remember a time when she had shown such emotion before. She was usually so cool and in control of herself. It had stirred things in him to fever pitch to have her so close. Her body had felt so warm and soft against his, so achingly familiar. He could so easily have pushed her down on the bed and reclaimed her as his. His body had throbbed to possess her. It disgusted him that he was so weak. Had he learned nothing? Women were not to be trusted, especially women like his runaway wife.

He had noted every nuance of her face on the journey home to Spain. If she truly had forgotten how wealthy he was, she was in no doubt of it now. Even if she did recall what a sham their marriage had become, she was unlikely to admit it now. Why would she? He could give her everything money could buy. Her lover was dead. She had no one else to turn to, nowhere else to go. She was back in his life due to a quirk of fate. There was no way now that he could toss her out as he had sworn he would do when he'd found out about her affair. The public would not look upon him kindly for divorcing his amnesiac wife. But there could be benefits in keeping her close to his side, he conceded. He still wanted her. That much had not changed, even though it annoyed him that he could not dismiss his attraction for her as easily as he wanted to. It had been there right from the beginning; the electric pulse of wanting that fizzled between them whenever they were within touching distance. She might not recognise him mentally but he felt sure her body was responding to him the way it always had. It would not take him long to have her writhing and twisting beneath him; all memory of her lover would be replaced with new memories of him and him alone.

He would cut her from his life when he was sure she was back on her feet. Their marriage would have fulfilled its purpose by then, in any case. Their divorce would be swift and final. All contact with her would cease from that point. He had no intention of keeping her with him indefinitely, not after the scandal she had caused him. The public would forget in time as new scandals were uncovered, but he could not.

He *would* not.

The horse's hooves thundered over the fields, the wind rushing through Javier's hair as he rode at breakneck speed. He pulled the stallion to a halt at the top of the hill, surveying the expanse of his estate below. The grey-green of the olive groves and the fertile fields of citrus and almonds reminded him of all he had worked so hard and long for. For all the sacrifices he had made to keep this property within his hands. His father's gambling and risky business deals had cost Javier dearly. He'd had to compromise himself in ways he had never dreamed possible. But what was done was done and it could not be undone. It eased his conscience only slightly that he hadn't done it for himself. Izabella had a right to her inheritance, and he had made sure it was not going to be whittled away by his father's home-wrecking widow.

The stallion tossed his head and snorted, his hooves drumming in the dust with impatience. Javier stroked the stallion's silky powerful neck, speaking low and soothingly in Spanish. The horse rose on his hindquarters, his front hooves pawing at the air. Javier laughed as he thought of his wayward wife and how fate had handed her back to him to do with her as he wished. He turned the horse and galloped him back down through the forest to the plains below, the thrill of the ride nothing to what waited for him at the end of it.

Emelia ignored the comfort of the big bed and, after a refreshing shower and change of clothes, went on a solitary tour of the villa in the hope of triggering something in her brain. Most of the rooms were too formal for her taste. They were almost austere, with their priceless works of art and uncomfortable-looking antiquated furniture. She couldn't help wondering why she hadn't gone about redecorating the place. Money was certainly no object, but perhaps she'd felt intimidated by the age and history of the villa. It was certainly very old. Every wall of the place seemed to have a portrait of an ancestor on it, each pair of eyes following her in what she felt to be an accusatory silence. She found it hard to imagine a small child feeling at home here. Was this the place where Javier had grown up? There was so much she didn't know about him, or at least no longer knew.

She breathed out a sigh as she opened yet another door. This one led into a library-cum-study. Three walls of floor to ceiling bookshelves and a leather-topped desk dominated the space, but she could see a collection of photo frames beside the laptop computer on the desk, which drew her like a magnet. The floorboards creaked beneath the old rugs as she walked to the desk, the hairs on the back of her neck lifting like antennae.

'Don't be stupid,' she scolded herself. 'There's no such thing as ghosts.' But, even so, when she looked at the photographs she felt as if she were encountering something supernatural—the ghost of who she had been for the past two years.

She picked up the first frame and studied it for a

moment. It was a photo of her lying on a blanket in an olive grove, the sun coming down at an angle, highlighting her honey-blonde hair and grey-blue eyes. She was smiling coquettishly at the camera, flirting with whoever was behind the camera lens.

She put the frame down and picked up the next one, her heart giving a little skip when she saw Javier with his arms wrapped around her from behind, his tall frame slightly stooped as his chin rested on the top of her head, his smile wide and proud as he faced the camera. She could almost feel his hard body pressing into her back, the swell of his arousal, the pulse and thrum of his blood…

The door of the study suddenly opened and Emelia dropped the frame, the glass shattering on the floor at her feet. She stood frozen for a moment as Javier stepped into the room, closing the door with a click that sounded like a prison cell being locked.

'Don't touch it,' he commanded when she began to bend at the knees. 'You might cut yourself.'

'I'm sorry…' Emelia said, glancing down at the floor before meeting his gaze. 'You frightened me.'

His black eyes didn't waver as they held hers. 'I can assure you that was not my intention.'

Emelia swallowed as he approached the desk. He was wearing a white casual polo shirt and beige jodhpurs and long black leather riding boots, looking every inch the brooding hero of a Regency novel. He smelt of the outdoors with a hint of horse and hay and something that was essentially male, essentially *him*. He filled her nostrils with it, making her feel as if she was being cast under an intoxicating spell. His tall authoritarian presence, that aura of command he wore like an extra layer of skin, that air of arrogance and assuredness that was so at odds with her insecurities and doubts and memory blanks. 'I...I was trying to see if anything in here jogged my memory,' she tried her best to explain.

He hooked a brow upwards. 'And did it?'

She bit her lower lip, glancing at the shattered glass on the floor, which seemed to sever them as a couple. Was it symbolic in some way? A shard of glass was lying across their smiling faces, almost cutting them in two. She brought her gaze back to his. 'No...' She let out a sigh. 'I don't remember when that photo was taken or where.'

He bent down and carefully removed the remaining pieces of glass from the photo frame before placing it back on the desk. 'It was taken a few days after we got home from our honeymoon. I took you for a picnic to one of the olive groves on the estate. The other photo with us together was taken in Rome.'

Emelia ran her tongue over her dry lips before asking, 'Where did we go for our honeymoon?'

He was standing close, too close. She felt the alarm bells of her senses start to ring when he stepped even closer. The wall of bookshelves was at her back, each ancient tome threatening to come down and smother her. His dark eyes meshed with hers, holding them entranced. She felt her heart give a knock against her breastbone in anticipation of that sensuous mouth coming down to hers. She suddenly realised how much she wanted that mouth to soften against hers, to kiss her tenderly, lingeringly, to explore every corner of her mouth in intimate detail.

He placed his hand under the curtain of her hair, his

fingers warm and dry against the sensitive skin of her neck. 'Where do you think we went?' he asked.

Emelia's teeth sank into her bottom lip, her brain working overtime. 'Um…Paris?'

His hand stilled and one of his dark brows lifted. 'Was that a guess or do you remember something?' he asked.

'I've always dreamed of honeymooning in Paris,' she said. 'It's supposed to be the most romantic city in the world. And I saw the stamp on my passport so I suppose it wasn't such a wild guess.'

He continued to hold her gaze for endless moments, his fingers moving in a rhythmic motion at her nape. 'Your dream came true, Emelia,' he said. 'I gave you a honeymoon to surpass all honeymoons.'

She sucked half of her bottom lip into her mouth, releasing it to say, 'I'm sorry. You must be thinking what a shocking waste of money it was now that I can't even recall a second of it.'

He gave a couldn't-care-less shrug. 'We can have a second honeymoon, *sí*? One that you will never forget.'

Emelia's eyes went to his mouth of their own volition. He was smiling that sexy half-smile again, the one that made her blood race through her veins. What was it about this man that made her so breathless with excitement? It was as if he only had to look at her and she was a trembling mass of needs and wants. She felt the tingling of her skin as he touched her with those long fingers. The fingers that had clearly touched her in places she wasn't sure she wanted to think about. He knew her so well and yet he was still a stranger to her.

A second honeymoon?

Her belly turned over itself. How could she sleep

with a man she didn't know? It would be nothing but physical attraction, an animal instinct, an impulse she had never felt compelled to respond to before.

Or had she?

How did she know what their history was? She could only go on what he had told her. She hadn't thought herself the type to fall in love so rapidly, to marry someone within weeks of meeting them. But then maybe she hadn't fallen in love with him. Maybe she had fallen in lust. She shied away from the thought but it kept creeping back to taunt her. He was so dangerously attractive. She could feel the pull of his magnetism even now, the thrill of him touching her, the stroke of his fingers so drugging she could feel herself capitulating second by second. His eyes were dark pools of mystery, luring her in, making her drown in their enigmatic depths. She felt her eyelids come down to half mast, her breathing becoming choppy as his hand stilled at the back of her neck, pressing her forwards with a gentle but determined action as his mouth came within a breath of hers.

'D-don't…' Her voice came out hoarse, uncertain and not at all convincing.

His hand still cupped the nape of her neck, warm and strong, supportive and yet determined. 'Don't what?' he asked in a low deep burr.

She swallowed. 'You know what…'

'Is it not right for a husband to kiss his wife?' he asked.

'But I…I don't feel like your wife,' Emelia said breathlessly.

There was a three beat pause as his dark eyes locked on hers.

'Then it is about time you did,' he said and, swooping down, covered her mouth with his.

CHAPTER FOUR

EMELIA's heart almost stopped when his mouth touched down on hers. The raw male scent of him was intoxicating, dangerous, and that alone would have had her senses spinning, but the pressure of his lips upon hers drew from her a response she wasn't entirely sure she should be giving. He cradled her head in his hands, giving her no room to pull away even if she had the wherewithal to do so. The contact of his mouth on hers was explorative at first, light, tentative almost, but then, with just one very masculine stroke of his tongue, everything changed.

Her lips opened to him as if of their own volition, instinctively, welcoming him inside the moist cave of her mouth. Her tongue met his briefly, flirting around it, dancing with it until finally mating with it at its command. He subdued her with the power of each stroke and thrust of his tongue, teasing her into submission, relishing the victory by crushing his mouth to hers with increasing pressure. Emelia felt the surge of his body against her, his arousal so thick and hard it made her realise how much history existed between them, a history she had yet to discover. Her body, however, seemed familiar with it. It was reacting with fervour to every movement of his mouth on hers, her arms automatically going around his neck, holding him to her as if she had done it many times before, her pelvis seeking the hardened throb of his, her inner core melting with longing. Her breasts bloomed with pleasure against the contact with his hard chest, her nipples tightening to buds, aching to feel the slippery warmth of his mouth and tongue.

His mouth moved from hers on a searing pathway down the side of her neck, slowly, sensuously bringing every nerve to gasping, startled life. Goosebumps rose all over her skin as he discovered the delicate scaffold of her collarbone, his tongue dipping into the tiny dish of her tender flesh. His lips feathered against her skin as he spoke in a low sexy tone. 'You taste of vanilla.'

Emelia felt electric jolts shoot up and down her legs at the thought of where that mouth and tongue had been on her body. She could almost feel its pathway now, the way her secret feminine flesh was pulsing, as if in anticipation of him claiming it. She clutched at his head with her fingers, feeling the thick strands of his dark hair move like silk beneath her fingertips.

'I want you.' He mouthed the words against her neck, making her nerves leap and dance again. 'God, but I want you.'

'W-we can't...' Emelia gasped as his mouth showered kisses all over her face: over her eyelids, over her cheeks, her nose and so temptingly close to her tingling, swollen lips.

'What's to stop us?' he said in a husky tone as he pressed a hot moist kiss to her trembling mouth. 'We are married, are we not?'

Emelia was too drunk on his kiss to answer. His tongue went in search of hers again, mating with it in an erotic tango that left her gasping with need. His kiss was hungry, demanding, leaving her in no doubt of where it was leading. It was a pre-sex kiss, blatant in its intent, shockingly intimate as his hands moved from cradling her head, sliding down her bare arms to encircle her wrists. The latent strength of him sent a shiver of reaction through her. He was so strong; she was so weak, but not just in physical strength. Her will-power seemed to have totally evaporated. She was molten wax in his arms, fitting to his hard form as if she had known no other place.

He released her hands and moved his up under her top, sliding his warm palms over her belly and her ribcage. Her heart gave a lurching movement as his fingers splayed over her possessively. Emelia thought she would die if he didn't touch her breasts and she moved against him, silently pleading for him to pleasure her.

His hand cupped her and she let out a tiny whimper of pleasure, for even through the fine lace of her bra she could feel the tantalising heat of his touch. 'You want more, *querida*?' he asked softly, seductively.

Emelia gasped as he pushed aside the cobweb of lace, his fingers skating over her burgeoning flesh. His thumb lingered over her engorged nipple, moving back and forth, hot little rubs that lifted every hair on her scalp.

'You want this, *sí*?' he said and bent his mouth to her breast and suckled softly at first and then harder.

Emelia's fingers clutched at his hair, trying to anchor herself as delicious sensations washed through her. 'Oh… Oh, God…' she whimpered.

'You like this too,' he said and swept his tongue down the outer curve of her breast, licking like a jungle cat, the sexy rasp of his tongue melting every vertebrae of her spine into trembling submission.

'And this,' he added, pressing her back against the desk, his thighs parting hers with shockingly primal intention.

Emelia's passion-glazed eyes flew open and her hands thrust against his chest. 'N-no…' she said but it came out so hoarsely she had to repeat it. 'No…no, I can't.'

One of his dark brows hooked upwards, his body still poised against hers. 'No?'

She shook her head, her teeth sinking into her lower lip as her eyes momentarily fell away from his.

He let out a theatrical sigh and straightened, pulling her upright against him, his hands settling on her waist, his powerful body, hot, aroused and hard, just a breath's distance away. 'That wasn't what you used to say,' he said with a taunting gleam in his dark eyes. 'This was one of your favourite places for a quick—'

Emelia pushed two of her fingertips against his mouth, blocking off the coarse word she was almost certain he intended to use. 'Please…don't…' she said hollowly.

He peeled her fingers away from his mouth, kissing the tips one by one, his bottomless eyes holding hers. 'Don't you want to be reminded of how sensually adventurous you were, Emelia?' he asked.

Her throat rose and fell over a tight swallow. 'No… no, I don't.'

He pressed a soft kiss to the middle of her palm and then dipped his tongue right into the middle of it, hotly, moistly, his eyes still locked with hers. 'I taught you everything you know,' he went on. 'You were so eager to learn. A straight A student, in fact.'

She closed her eyes tight. 'Stop it. Stop doing this.'

'Open your eyes, Emelia,' he commanded.

She scrunched them even tighter. 'No.'

His hands went to her waist, holding her against his rock-hard arousal. 'This is what you do to me, *querida*,' he said in a sexy growl.

Emelia wrenched out of his hold with a strength she had no conscious knowledge of possessing. Her chest heaved with the effort as she stood, trembling and shaken, a few feet away. She folded her arms across her chest, fighting for breath, fighting for control, fighting for some self-respect, which seemed to have gone AWOL some minutes ago.

Javier gave her an indolent smile. 'What are you frightened of, *mi amor*?' he asked.

'I don't know you,' Emelia said.

'But you want me, all the same.'

'I'm not myself right now.' She tightened her arms beneath her breasts. 'I don't know what I want.'

'Your body remembers me, Emelia. It wants me. You can't deny it.'

Emelia moved even further away because she had a sneaking suspicion what he said was true. Every sense was alive to him, to his presence and to his touch. She could still taste him in her mouth, the musky male heat of him lingering there like a fine wine on her palate. Was he an addiction she had developed over the last two years? How could any woman resist such incredible potency? He oozed sensual heat through the pores of his skin. She felt the waves of attraction tighten the air she breathed in. Every part of her body he had touched was still tingling with the need for more. His incendiary suggestion was still ringing in her ears, making her mind race with erotic scenarios: of her spread before him like a feast; her legs open to his powerful thrusting body, her senses in a vortex of sensation, her back arching in pleasure, her mouth falling open in sharp, high cries of ecstasy.

He came to where she was standing, her back pressed against the bookshelves, his eyes smouldering so darkly they seemed to strip her bare. 'Maybe it was a mistake for me to move out of our room,' he said. 'Perhaps I should insist on you sleeping with me, even though you can't remember me.'

Emelia's back felt as if it was being bitten into by the shelves. 'You c-can't mean that,' she said croakily.

He tipped up her chin, holding her frightened gaze with the powerful beam of his. 'Making love with me might trigger something in your brain. It might be the part of the missing puzzle, *sí*?'

His disturbing presence was triggering all sorts of things in her body, let alone her brain, Emelia thought in rising panic. She placed her hands on his chest with the intention of pushing him away again, but the feel of his hard muscles under her palms sent off a little flashbulb in her head. It was a tiny spark of memory, a pinpoint of light in the darkness. She splayed her fingers experimentally and, as if of their own accord, her fingertips began moving over his hard flat nipples, over his perfectly sculptured pectoral muscles and up to his neck, where she could see a pulse beating like a hammer beneath his skin. She moved her fingertips to the raspy skin of his lean jaw, the prickle of his stubble sending tantalising little tingles right up her arms.

'What is it?' he asked, holding her hand against his face with the broad span of his. 'Have you remembered something?'

She frowned as she fought to retrieve the fleeting image. It was like the shadow of a ghost, barely visible, but she could sense its presence. 'I don't know…' She bit down on her lip, pulling her hand out from under his. 'I thought for a minute…but I just don't know…'

He picked up her hand again and held it against his mouth, his lips feathering against her curled up fingers as he spoke. 'Touch me again, *cariño*,' he commanded softly. 'Touch is an important part of memory. Taste and smell, too.'

Emelia uncurled her fingers and carefully traced the outline of his lips, her fingertip grazing against his stubble again. She felt transfixed by the shape of his mouth, the way his top lip was carved almost harshly and yet his lower one was so generous and sensual. He drew her fingertip into his mouth and sucked on it. It was such an intimate thing to do, flagrantly sexual, especially when his eyes captured hers and glinted at her meaningfully. She pulled out of his hold once more, gathering herself with an effort. 'I'm sorry,' she said crisply. 'I don't remember anything.'

His expression gave little away but Emelia sensed a thread of anger stringing his words together as he spoke. 'I will leave you to rest before dinner. Leave this.' He indicated the broken glass on the floor. 'I will get Aldana to clean it up later. If you need anything just press nine on the telephone by the bed upstairs. It is a direct line to Aldana's quarters. She will bring you some tea or coffee or a cool drink if you should require it.'

She watched as he strode out of the library, the squeak of the expensive leather of his riding boots the only sound in the silence.

Emelia woke from a nap feeling totally disoriented, her heart beating like the wings of a frightened bird as she sat upright on the big bed. She put a hand to her throat, trying to control her breathing to bring down her panic to a manageable level. She dragged herself off the bed and stumbled into the en suite bathroom. Seeing her reflection was like looking at another version of herself, a more sophisticated and yet unhappier version. She put a fingertip to each of her sharp cheekbones. Her mouth was pulled down at the corners as if smiling had become a chore. Her eyes looked tired but also a little haunted, as if they were keeping secrets they didn't really want to keep.

She washed her face with cold water and then turned and looked longingly at the huge spa bath next to the double shower cubicle. She had at least an hour before dinner and the thought of sinking into a huge bath tub full of fragrant bubbles was too much for her to resist.

The water lapped at her aching limbs as she lowered herself into the bath, the scent of honeysuckle filling the air, reminding her of the hot summers and long lazy days of her childhood back in Australia. She closed her eyes and laid her head back, her body relaxing for the first time since she had woken from the coma.

Even in her languid repose, it was hard not to think of Peter. The thought of him lying in a cold dark grave was surreal when it seemed only a few days ago they were having coffee together at the end of her session at The Silver Room. The police had told her it had been a high speed accident but the knowledge hadn't sat well with her. Peter had lost a close mate in a car accident when he was a teenager. His intractable stance on reckless and dangerous driving was one of the things she had admired about him—one of the many things. During their youth, he had hinted more than once that he wanted more than a platonic friendship from her but she had let him down as gently as she could. While they had been close friends and had many interests in common, she had never envisaged him as an intimate partner. She had always looked on him as a brother. There was no chemistry, or at least not from her point of view. She knew it was different for men, and Peter had not been an exception. She had seen his head turned by many beautiful women who came into his hotel bar. She knew men's desires were more often than not fuelled by their vision. Sex was a physical drive that could just as easily be performed with a perfect stranger.

Emelia felt her belly give a distinct wobble when she thought of the stranger who was her husband. She saw raw unbridled desire in Javier's eyes; it smouldered there like hot coals every time he looked at her. He had openly declared how much he wanted her. She had heard the erotic promise in the words. It was not a matter of *if* but *when*.

He knew it.

She knew it.

Emelia looked down at her breasts, her rosy nipples just peeping out of the water amidst the bubbles, a riot of sensations rippling through her as she thought of how he had caressed her earlier. He had touched her with such possessive familiarity. Was that why she had responded so instinctively? She felt her insides give another fluttery movement as she thought about him possessing her totally. Would she remember him in the throes of making love as he suggested? She reared back from her thoughts like a horse shying at a jump. It was too soon to be taking that step. She couldn't possibly give herself to a man she didn't know.

But you're married to him, a little voice reminded her.

And you're attracted to him, another voice piped up.

Emelia slipped under the water to escape her traitorous thoughts, holding her breath for as long as she dared…

Javier tapped on the bathroom door but there was no answer. It was quiet. Too quiet. There was not even the sound of running or splashing water.

He opened the door and when he saw Emelia's slim body lying submerged in the bath he felt a hand clutch at his insides.

'Emelia!' He rushed to the tub and grabbed her under the armpits, hauling her upright as water splashed everywhere.

She gave a gasping cry of shock, her wet hair like seaweed all over her face. 'What do you think you're doing?' she spluttered.

Javier waited until his heart had returned to his chest from where it had leapt into his throat. 'I thought you were unconscious,' he explained in a voice that sounded as ragged as he felt. 'I thought you might have hit your head again or something.'

She flashed him a livid glare as she hastily crossed

her arms over her breasts. 'You could have knocked before you came barging in.'

'I did knock.' He stepped out of the puddle of water he was standing in, glancing ruefully at his sodden trousers and shoes. 'You didn't answer.'

Her knees bent upwards, shielding her chest even further. 'You had no right to come in without my permission,' she said.

He sent one of his brows up in a mocking slant. 'That little knock on the head has turned you into a prude, eh, Emelia? I remember a time not so long ago when you made room for me in there.' He bent down and scooped up a handful of bubbles, holding them just above her bent knees. 'Do you want to know what we got up to?'

She stiffened as if the water had turned to ice around her. 'Get out,' she said in a clipped voice.

Javier let the bubbles fall from his hand, his eyes unwavering on hers. He felt her tension, the way she gave a tiny, almost imperceptible flinch as each cluster of bubbles slid down from her kneecaps and down her thighs to slowly dissipate as they landed on the surface of the water. As each throbbing second passed he could hear the soft popping sound of the lather gradually losing its vigour. Within minutes the soapy shield she was hiding behind would be gone.

In spite of her betrayal, he felt his body surge with excitement. Hot rushing blood filled his groin, the ache for release so quick, so urgent it made him realise how hard it was going to be to keep his distance from her. But then wanting her had always been his problem, his one true vulnerability.

From that first moment he had heard her clever little fingers playing those lilting cadences when he'd walked into The Silver Room, he had felt something deep inside shift into place. She had looked up from the piano, her fingers stumbling over a note as their eyes had locked. He had smiled at her with his eyes—that was all it had taken—and she had been his.

He looked down at her now, wondering if she had any idea of the war going on inside him. She was cautious around him, understandable given she no longer recognised him, but he felt the sexual undertow of her gaze every time it meshed with his. It would not take him long to have her back in his bed and threshing in his arms as she used to do. But would that finally dissolve the anger and hatred he felt whenever he thought of her with the man she had run away to be with?

'It is not the behaviour of a devoted wife to order her husband out of his own bathroom,' Javier said, breaking the taut silence.

'I…I don't care,' she said, her teeth chattering slightly.

He plucked a bath sheet off the warming rail and held it just out of her reach. 'You'd better get out. You're starting to get cold.'

Her grey-blue eyes battled with his. 'I'm not getting out until you leave.'

He settled his tall frame into a trenchant stance. 'I am not leaving until you get out.'

She clenched her teeth, her voice coming out as a hiss, reminding him of a snarling cat. 'Why are you doing this? Why are you being such a beast?'

'What is all the fuss about, *querida*?' he asked evenly. 'I have seen you naked countless times.'

Her throat rose and fell. 'It's different now… You know that…'

He came closer with the towel, unfolding it for her to step into. 'Come on, Emelia. You are shivering.'

She flattened her mouth and, giving him another livid glare, stood and grasped for the towel, covering herself haphazardly, but not before he feasted his eyes on her slim feminine form. There were catwalk models who had less going for them, Javier thought. With her coltish long legs and beautifully toned arms and those small high breasts with their delectable rosy nipples, it was all he could do not to pull her out of the slippery tub and crush his body to hers. How many times had he tasted the sweet honey of her feminine body? How many times had he plunged into her, his cataclysmic release unlike any he had ever experienced with anyone else? As much as it felt like a dagger in his gut, he wondered how it had been with her lover. Had she gone down on him with the same fervour? Had she whispered words of love to him in the afterglow of lovemaking? Javier felt his top lip curl as he watched her try to cover herself more effectively. 'You are wasting your time, Emelia,' he said. 'I know every inch of your body and you know every inch of mine.'

Her eyes shifted away from his, her throat doing that nervous up and down thing again. 'I would like some privacy,' she said, wiping her brow with the back of her hand. 'I…I'm not feeling well.'

Javier's brows shot together. 'Why didn't you tell me?' he asked. 'What is wrong? A headache? The doctor said headaches are common after—'

'It's not a bad one, just an ache behind one eye.' She brushed at her damp brow once more, this time with a corner of the towel. 'It's making me feel a little nauseous. Perhaps it's the change of climate. It's a lot hotter here than in England.'

'You were only in London a week,' he pointed out. 'Hardly time to be reacclimatising, don't you think?'

Her gaze returned to his, two small frown lines sectioning her forehead. 'Oh…yes…yes, of course…I forgot.' She pressed her lips together and looked away.

Javier saw the shadow of grief pass through her eyes before she averted her gaze. He fought down his anger, reminding himself she was with him now. His rival was dead. It was just Emelia and him now, to get on with their lives as best they could. 'Dinner is not long away,' he said. 'I will need to get changed. Do you want me to escort you downstairs or do you think you will find your way?'

She clutched at the towel as she looked at him with her guarded gaze. 'I'll find my own way…thank you.'

He gave a brisk nod and left the bathroom.

Emelia opened the wardrobe and, searching through the array of clothes, selected a simple black dress and heels to match. As she dressed she couldn't quite suppress the feeling that she was dressing in someone else's clothes. The dress was made by a French designer and must have cost a fortune; the shoes, too, were a brand celebrities and Hollywood stars regularly wore. She used the cosmetics in the drawer in the en suite bathroom, but only lightly and, after drying her hair with a blow-dryer, she left it lying about her shoulders.

As she came down the grand staircase she heard Javier's voice from the study. He was speaking in Spanish and sounded angry. Emelia knew it was probably beneath her to eavesdrop but, even so, she couldn't resist pausing outside the closed study door. Of course hearing only one side of a conversation was not all that revealing and, although she understood very

basic Spanish, he spoke so rapidly she found it hard to
follow everything he said. One or two sentences did
stand out, however.

'There is not going to be a divorce.'

Emelia's eyes widened as she listened even harder,
wincing as one or two expletives were uttered before his
next statement.

'The money is not yours and never has been and, as
long as I live, it never will be.'

The phone slammed down and, before Emelia could
move even a couple of paces down the hall, Javier came
storming out of the study. He pulled up short as if
someone had jerked him back by the back of his jacket
when he saw her standing there with guilt written all
over her face.

'How long have you been standing out here?' He
almost barked the words at her.

Emelia took a layer of her lip gloss off with the
nervous dart of her tongue. 'I...I was just walking past.
I heard you raise your voice.'

His expression was thunderous but Emelia had a
feeling the anger was not directed at her. He raked a hand
through his hair and released a heavy sigh, as if deliberately trying to suppress his fury. 'Just as well you
don't remember any Spanish,' he said. 'I don't usually
swear in the presence of women, but my father's third
wife is nothing but a gold-digging, trouble-making
tramp.'

Emelia wondered if she should tell him she could
speak and understand a little of his language, but in that
nanosecond of hesitation she decided against it.
Wouldn't it seem strange that she couldn't remember
him and yet she could remember every word of Spanish

she had learned over the past two years? After all, he had already implied she might be pretending. Why he would think that was beyond her, although, given the conversation she had just overheard, it made her wonder if their marriage had been as happy as he had intimated. She had just heard him say there was not going to be a divorce. Did that mean there had been recent speculation about their marriage ending? Javier had mentioned how the press had made some scurrilous comments about her relationship with Peter Marshall. There would be few men who would cope well with their private life being splashed all over the papers and gossip magazines, but Javier struck her as a particularly proud and intensely private man. There was so much she didn't know and she didn't feel comfortable asking in case the answers he gave were not the ones she wanted to hear.

'It must be very difficult for you, under the circumstances,' she offered.

He gave her a long look and sighed again, taking her elbow to lead the way to the dining room. 'My father was a fool leaving Izabella's mother for Claudine Marsden. That woman is a home wrecker. Why he couldn't see it is beyond me.'

'Some men are like that,' she said. 'My father is the same.'

He glanced down at her as they came to the dining room door. 'Did your father contact you while you were in hospital?' he asked.

Emelia's mouth tightened. 'No, why should he? As far as he is concerned, I am as good as dead to him. He told me he never wanted to see me again. I have no reason to suspect he didn't mean it.'

Javier pressed his lips together, a frown creasing his

forehead as he led her to the table. 'People say all sorts of things in the heat of the moment.' He paused before adding, 'I should have phoned him. I didn't think of it, I'm afraid. There was so much going on at the time. He should have been notified about the accident.'

'Did I at some point give you his contact details?' Emelia asked.

'No, but it wouldn't have been all that hard to track him down,' he said. 'Would you like me to make contact now, just to let him know you are all right?'

Emelia thought about her father with his new wife, who was only three years older than her. After their last insult-throwing argument, she couldn't see him flying all the way to Spain with flowers and a get well card in hand. He was probably sunning himself at his luxurious Sunshine Coast mansion with his child bride waiting on him hand and foot. 'No, don't bother,' she said, trying to remove the bitterness from her tone. 'He's probably got much more important things to see to.'

Javier gave her a thoughtful look as he drew out her chair.

Emelia took the seat, waiting until he sat down opposite to say, 'Our backgrounds—apart from the level of wealth—are very similar, aren't they? Your father was estranged from you and mine from me. Is that something that drew us together when we first met?'

His dark eyes held hers for a moment before he answered. 'It was one of many things.'

'What were some of the other things?' she asked.

He poured wine for each of them, his mouth tilting slightly. 'Lust, lust and more lust,' he said.

Emelia pursed her lips, hating that she was blushing,

hating him for watching with such mocking amusement. 'I can assure you I would never fall in lust with someone,' she said. 'I would only ever love someone I admired as a man, for his qualities as a person, not his possessions or social standing. And I most certainly wouldn't marry a man on physical attraction alone.'

His mocking smile was still in place. 'So you must have loved me, eh, Emelia?' He flicked his napkin across his lap, his eyes still tethering hers. 'The thing is, will you remember to love me again?'

CHAPTER FIVE

EMELIA placed her own napkin over her lap, all the time avoiding those black-as-pitch eyes. The hairs on the back of her neck were tingling and her stomach was rolling like a ball going down a very steep hill. Had she felt like this during their marriage? Had her skin felt prickly and sensitive just with his gaze on her, let alone his touch? She desperately wanted to remember everything about him, everything about them—their relationship, the love they supposedly had shared.

Or had they?

The thought slipped into her mind, unfurling like a curl of smoke beneath a closed door. Did he love her the way she had evidently loved him? It was so difficult to know what he felt; he kept himself to himself most of the time. She understood his reluctance to reveal his feelings, given her loss of memory. He might resent looking a fool if she never regained her memory of him. In any case, the doctors had warned him not to pressure her. Was that why he was acting like the perfect stranger, polite but aloof, with just occasional glimpses of his personality? There was so much she didn't know about him, things she would need to know in order to navigate her way through the complex labyrinth her mind had become. With an effort she raised her eyes back to his. 'I feel such a fool for not asking you this earlier, but what is it you do for a living?'

'I buy and sell businesses,' he said. 'I own and head an international company. We do work all over the world. That was why I have been in Moscow a lot lately. I have a big deal I am working on. It requires a lot of intense negotiation.'

Emelia sat quietly absorbing that information, hoping it would trigger something in her brain. She looked at his hands as they poured wine into both of their glasses. She could imagine him being a formidable opponent in business, his quick mind and sharp intelligence setting him apart from his rivals. 'What sort of businesses do you buy?' she asked.

'Ailing ones,' he said. 'I buy them and reinvent them and sell them for a profit.' He hitched one shoulder indifferently. 'It's a living.'

Emelia picked up her crystal wine glass. 'Apparently quite a good one.' She took a tentative sip and put the glass back down. 'Was your father in the same field of work?'

'No, he was in retail,' he said. 'Electrical, mostly. He had several outlets in Spain. He expected me to go into the business with him but I never wanted that for myself. Selling refrigerators and televisions and toasters never appealed to me. I wanted more of a challenge.'

'Is that what caused the rift between you?'

'That and other things,' he said, frowning slightly as he returned his glass to the table.

Aldana came in with their starters and, while she was serving them, Emelia thought about Javier's background. There was no shortage of wealth; the private jet, the villa and grounds and the staff to maintain it must cost a fortune. Had he inherited it from his father or accumulated it himself? He must be very good at what he did. No one could buy a company without a huge amount of money behind them. And if he was buying and selling more than one and all over the world, he must be far more successful than she had thought. She decided to check out his profile on the Internet later, to see a little more into the man she was married to.

'*Gracias*, Aldana,' Javier said as the housekeeper left with a sour look in Emelia's direction, which she was sure he didn't see. Emelia wondered if she should comment on it but then decided against it. Maybe Javier would think she was making trouble. Aldana seemed very much a part of the woodwork of the villa. But it worried Emelia that the housekeeper had not warmed to her over the last two years. She was not used to people disliking her on sight. It made her feel as if she didn't know herself any more. Who was she now? Why had the housekeeper taken such an active dislike to her?

A moment or two of silence passed.

'Is the wine not to your liking?' Javier asked. 'It used to be one of your favourites.'

Emelia wrinkled her nose. 'Sorry, I guess my palate has changed or something. I'll stick to water. I need the fluids, in any case.'

'Would you like me to call a doctor?' he asked. 'You might have picked up a bug in the hospital.'

'No, I'm fine.' She twisted her mouth wryly. 'To tell you the truth, I'm a little sick of doctors. I just want to get well again.'

He gave her a tight smile. 'Of course.'

Emelia picked at her main course after Aldana had brought it in, but with little appetite. The tight band of tension around her forehead she had been trying so hard to ignore was making her feel ill again. All she could think of was retreating to the sanctuary of bed.

'You're really not feeling well, are you?' Javier asked once the housekeeper had cleared the plates.

Emelia gave him an apologetic grimace. 'I'm sorry. My headache's been getting worse all evening.'

He rose from the table and gently helped her out of her chair. 'Come on,' he said. 'I'll take you upstairs and help you get settled. Are you sure about the doctor? What if I just make a call to ask his opinion?'

'No, please don't bother. Dr Pratchett told me head-aches are common sometimes up to weeks after a head injury. I just need a painkiller and sleep.'

Javier left the bedroom while Emelia changed into nightwear and after a few minutes he came back in with a glass of water and a couple of painkillers. Once she had taken them, he took the glass and set it down on the bedside table. 'I have to fly back to Moscow tomorrow,' he said, sitting on the edge of the bed next to her. 'I just got a phone call while I was downstairs. I am sorry about the short notice but, with the accident and every-thing, I had to cut short my business there.'

'I'm sorry to have been such a bother—'

He placed a hand over hers, silencing her. 'I have given Aldana and the others instructions to keep a watch over you. I will only be away two days, three at the most.'

'I'm perfectly able to look after myself.' She pulled her hand out from under his and crossed her arms over her chest. 'I don't need to be watched over like a small child.'

'Emelia, there are journalists lurking about looking for a story,' he said. 'If you set foot outside the villa grounds you will be under siege. You are not well enough to fend off their intrusive questions. You will end up even more confused and disoriented.'

Her grey-blue eyes narrowed slightly. 'Are these precautions for me or for you?'

He squared his shoulders. 'What exactly are you implying?'

She bit down on her bottom lip so hard it went white. 'I don't know what's going on,' she said. 'I don't know what's what any more. You say we were happily married, but you don't seem to like me, let alone love me.'

Javier placed his hand on the curve of her cheek, turning her head to face him. 'This is not the time to be talking about my feelings,' he said. 'This is the time for you to concentrate on getting well again. That's why I want you to stay within the confines of the villa grounds.'

'What did I used to do to occupy myself when you went away on business?' she asked.

Javier would have dearly liked to ask her the same thing. How long had her affair gone on, for instance? How many times had she met her lover while he was abroad on business? How many of her 'shopping trips' to London been a cover for other activities? 'You used the gym in the building near the pool and you occasionally practised the piano.'

She frowned as she looked down at her manicured hands with their elegant French-polished nails. When had she stopped biting her nails? And how on earth did she play the piano with them so long? She looked up at him after a moment. 'So I wasn't teaching?'

'No. You said you were no longer interested in teaching children,' he said. 'You said it didn't suit your lifestyle any more.'

She was still frowning. '*I* said that?'

Javier studied her for a moment. 'You said a lot of things, Emelia.'

'What other things did I say?' she asked.

'You didn't want children, for one thing,' he said. 'You were adamant about it.'

Her eyes widened. 'Not want children?'

He nodded. 'You didn't want to be tied down.'

She put a hand to her head, as if to check it was still there. 'I can't believe I didn't want kids. That seems so…so selfish.' She looked at him again. 'Did *you* want children?'

'No, absolutely not,' he said. 'Children need a lot of attention. They can be a strain on a strong marriage, let alone one that is suffering some teething problems.'

Her forehead creased again. 'So we were having some problems?'

Javier carefully considered how to answer. 'Very few relationships don't go through some sort of adjustment period. It was hard for both of us initially. I travel a great deal and you were new to my country and my language. In any case, it wasn't always convenient to take you with me because I like to concentrate on business when I am away. On the few occasions you did come with me, you were bored sitting around waiting for me. Some meetings go on and on until things are sorted out to everyone's satisfaction.'

'So I decided to stay at home and play the corporate wife role…' She chewed her lip again, as if the concept was totally foreign to her.

'Emelia.' He took her hand in his again, stroking the back of it with his thumb. 'It was the way things were between us. It was what we both wanted. You seemed happy with the arrangement when I asked you to marry me. You understood the rules. You were happy to play the game. You slipped into the role as if you were born to it.'

She looked at their joined hands, a sigh escaping from her lips. 'When I was a little girl I used to wish I could see into the future.' She looked back up into his gaze. 'But now I wish I could see into the past.'

He let her hand go and stood up from the bed. 'Sometimes the past is better left alone,' he said. 'It can't be changed.'

She pulled the sheet up to her chest, her forehead still creased in a frown. 'Will I see you before you leave tomorrow?' she asked.

He shook his head. 'I am leaving first thing.' He bent down and brushed his mouth against hers. *'Buenas noches.'*

'Buenas noches.' Her voice was a soft whisper that feathered its way down his spine as he left the room.

Aldana was in the kitchen when Emelia came downstairs the next morning. The atmosphere was distinctly chilly but she decided to ignore it. Ignore the bad, praise the good seemed the best way to handle a difficult person, she thought.

'Good morning, Aldana,' she said with a bright smile that she hoped didn't look too forced. 'It's a beautiful day, isn't it?'

The housekeeper sent her a reproachful look. 'I suppose as usual you will turn your nose up at the food I have set out for you?'

Emelia's smile fell away. 'Um…actually, I am quite hungry this morning,' she said. 'But you shouldn't have gone to any trouble.'

Aldana made a snorting noise and turned her attention to the bread she was making. 'I am paid to go to trouble,' she said. 'But it is a waste of my time and good food when people refuse to eat it.'

'I'm sorry if I've offended you in the past,' Emelia said after a tense silence. 'Would it help if I sat down with you and planned the week's menus? It would save you a lot of trouble and there would be less waste.'

Aldana dusted her hands on her apron in a dismissive fashion. 'You are not the right wife for Señor Mélendez,' she said. 'You do not love him as he deserves to be loved. You just love what he can give you.'

Emelia tried to disguise her shock at the housekeeper's blunt assessment by keeping her voice cool and controlled. 'You are entitled to your opinion but my relationship with my husband is no one's business but my own.'

Aldana gave another snort and turned her back to open the oven, signalling the end of the conversation.

Emelia decided to carry on as if things were normal, even though it troubled her deeply that the housekeeper thought her so unsuitable a wife for Javier. She had always imagined she would make a wonderful wife. After all, she had learned what not to do by watching first her parents' disastrous and volatile marriage, and then her father's subsequent ones after her mother had died. She had determined from a young age to marry for love and love only. Money and prestige would hold no sway with her. But now she wondered how closely she had clung to her ideals.

She ate a healthy breakfast of fruit and yogurt and toast and carried a cup of tea out to a sun-drenched terrace overlooking the villa's gardens.

The scenery was breathtaking and the fresh smell of recently cut grass teased her nostrils. Neatly trimmed box hedges created the more formal aspect of the garden, but beyond she could see colourful herbaceous borders and interesting pathways that led to various fountains or statues.

After she carried her cup back into the kitchen, Emelia went on a tour of the garden. The sun was warm but not overly so and a light breeze carried the delicate scent of late blooming roses to her. She stopped and picked one and, breathing in its fragrance, wondered how many times she had done exactly this. She poked the stem of the rose behind her ear and carried on, stopping at one of the fountains to watch the birds splashing and ruffling their feathers in the water.

The sound of a horse whinnying turned her head. In the distance Emelia could see a youth leading a magnificent looking stallion to what appeared to be a riding arena near the stables a little way from the villa. She walked back through the garden and made her way to where the youth was now lunging the horse on a lead rope. He was a powerful-looking animal with a proud head and flaring nostrils, his tail arched in defiance as his hooves pounded through the sand of the arena.

Emelia stood on the second rail of the fence so she could see over, watching as the stallion went through his paces. Without thinking, she spoke in Spanish to the youth. 'He's very temperamental, isn't he?'

'*Sí, señora,*' the youth answered. 'Your mare is much better mannered.'

Emelia looked at him blankly. 'I have a horse of my own?'

The youth looked at her as if she was *loca* but then he must have recalled what he had been told about her accident. *'Sí, señora,'* he said with a white toothed smile. 'She is in the stable. I exercised her earlier this morning.'

'Could I ride her, please?' Emelia asked.

He gave her a surprised look. 'You want to *ride* her?'

She nodded. 'Of course I do.'

'But you have never wanted to ride her before,' he said with a puzzled frown. 'You refused to even look at her.'

Emelia laughed off the suggestion. 'That's crazy. I love to ride. I had my own horse when my mother was alive. I used to spend every weekend and holidays at Pony Club or on riding camps.'

Pedro shrugged his shoulders as if he wasn't sure what to make of her as he made his way to the stables.

Emelia jumped down from the railing and followed him. 'I'm sorry but I've forgotten your name,' she said.

'Pedro,' he said. 'I look after the horses for Señor Mélendez. I have been working for him for two years now. The same time you have been married, *sí*?'

Emelia gave him a small smile, not sure how much he knew of her situation. The stallion snorted and pawed the ground and she stepped up to him and stroked his proud forehead. 'You are being a great big show-off, do you know that?' she crooned softly.

The stallion snorted again but then began to rub his head against her chest, almost pushing her over.

Pedro's look was still quizzical. 'He likes you, Señora Mélendez. But you used to be frightened of him. He is big and proud and has a mind of his own. He is…how you say…a softie inside.'

Emelia wondered if Pedro was talking about the horse or her husband. Probably both, she imagined. She breathed in the sweet smell of horse and hay and felt a flicker of something in her memory. She put a hand to her head, frowning as she tried to retrieve it before it disappeared.

'*Señora?*' Pedro's voice was concerned as he pulled the horse back from her. 'Are you all right? Did Gitano hurt you?'

'No, of course not,' Emelia said. 'I was just trying to remember something but it's gone now.'

Pedro led the stallion back to his stall and a short time later led out a pretty little mare. She had the same proud bearing as Gitano but her temperament was clearly very different. She whinnied when she caught sight of Emelia and her big soft round eyes shone with delight.

Emelia put her arms around the horse's neck, breathing in her sweet scent, closing her eyes as she searched her memory. A scene filtered through the fog in her head. It was a similar day to today, sunny with a light breeze. She was being led blindfolded down to the stables; she could even feel the nerves she had felt buzzing in the pit of her stomach. She could feel warm strong hands guiding her, a tall lean body brushing her from behind, the sharp citrus of his aftershave striking another chord of memory in her brain…

'*Señora Mélendez?*' Pedro's voice slammed the door on her memory. 'Are you all right?'

Emelia opened her eyes and, disguising her frustration, sent him a crooked smile. 'I'm fine,' she said.

'Callida looks very well. You must be doing a wonderful job of looking after her.'

'Señora,' Pedro said with rounded eyes, 'you remember her name, *sí*? Callida. Señor Mélendez bought her for you as a surprise for your birthday last month.'

Emelia stared at the youth for a moment, her brain whirling. 'I...I don't know how I remembered her name. It was just there in my head,' she said.

Pedro smiled a wide smile. 'It is good you are home. You will remember everything in time, *sí*?'

Emelia returned his smile but a little more cautiously. If only she had his confidence. But it did seem strange that Callida's name had been there on her tongue without her thinking about it; strange too that her Spanish had come to her equally as automatically. What else was lying inside her head, just waiting for the right trigger to unlock it?

Callida nudged against her, blowing at her through her velvet nostrils. Emelia tickled the horse's forelock. 'Can you saddle her for me?' she asked Pedro.

The lad's smile was quickly exchanged for a grave look. 'Señor Mélendez...I am not sure he would want you to ride. You have a head injury, *sí*? Not good to ride so soon.'

Emelia felt her neck and shoulders straighten in rebellion. 'I am perfectly well,' she said. 'And I would like to take Callida out to see if it helps me remember anything else. I need some exercise, in any case. I can't sit around all day doing nothing until my...hus...until Señor Mélendez returns.'

Pedro shifted his weight from foot to foot, his hands on Callida's leading rein fidgeting with agitation. 'I have been given instructions. I could lose my job.'

Emelia took the leading rein from him. 'I will explain to Señor Mélendez that I insisted. Don't worry. I won't let him fire you.'

The lad looked uncertain but Emelia had already made up her mind and led the mare to the stables. Pedro followed and, wordlessly and with tight lips, saddled the horse, handing Emelia a riding helmet once he had finished.

Emelia put it on and, giving him a smile, swung up into the saddle and rode out of the stable courtyard, relishing the sense of freedom it afforded her. She rode through the fields to the woods beyond, at a gentle walk at first and then, as her confidence grew, she squeezed Callida's sides to get her to trot. It wasn't long before she urged the horse into a canter, the rhythm so easy to ride to she felt as if she had been riding her for ever. How strange that Pedro had said she had refused to ride the horse Javier had bought for her. The horse was well bred and would have cost a mint. Why had she rejected such a beautiful precious gift?

After a while Emelia came to an olive grove and another flicker of memory was triggered in her brain. She slipped out of the saddle and led the horse to the spot where she thought the photograph she had seen in Javier's study was taken. Callida nudged against her and Emelia absently stroked the mare's neck as she looked at the soft green grass where she had lain with Javier. Had they made love under the shade of the olive trees? she wondered. Her skin tingled, the hairs on the back of her neck rising as she pictured them there, limbs entangled intimately, Javier's leanly muscled body pinning hers beneath the potent power of his.

She thought back to their conversation about the

terms of their marriage. The rules she had accepted supposedly without question. No children to tie either of them down. When had she decided she didn't want children? Had she said it just to keep Javier happy? He struck her as a man who valued and enjoyed his freedom. In many ways he seemed to still live the life of a playboy: regular international travel on private jets, a disposable income, no ties or responsibilities other than a relatively new wife who apparently didn't travel with him with any regularity. Children would definitely require a commitment from him he might not feel ready to agree to at this stage of his life.

Emelia, on the other hand, had always loved children; it was one of the reasons she had wanted to teach instead of perform. She loved their innocence and their wonder at the world and had always dreamed of having a family of her own some day. Growing up as an only child with numerous stepmothers entering and exiting her life had made her determined to marry a man who would be a wonderful husband and father, a man who was faithful and steadfast, nothing at all like her restless father. Why then had she married a man who didn't want the same things she did? Surely she hadn't slept with him for any other reason than love. She had vowed ever since her disastrous affair of the past that she would never make that mistake again. But, thinking about the current of electricity that had flared between her and Javier from the first moment he had stepped up to her bedside in the hospital, Emelia had to wonder if she had fallen victim to the power of sexual attraction after all. If only Peter was still alive so she could ask him to fill in the gaps for her.

She had made a couple of girlfriends at the hotel but

none of them were particularly close. Besides, they had been on temporary visas and would have moved on by now. It seemed the only way to find out her past was piece by piece, like putting a complicated jigsaw puzzle back together without the original picture as a guide.

Emelia rode back to the villa and handed Callida over to Pedro, who had very obviously been hovering about, waiting for her return. He took the mare with visible relief and reluctantly agreed on having the horse ready for another ride at the same time tomorrow.

When Emelia came downstairs after a shower she was informed by Aldana she had a visitor.

'She is waiting in *la sala*,' the housekeeper said with a frosty look.

'*Gracias*, Aldana,' Emelia said. 'But who is it? Someone I should know?'

Aldana pursed her lips but, before she could respond, female footsteps click-clacked from behind Emelia and a young voice called out, 'So you are back.'

Emelia turned to see a young female version of Javier stalking haughtily towards her. The young woman's dark-as-night eyes were flashing, her mouth was a thin line of disapproval and her long raven hair practically bristled with anger. 'Izabella?'

The young woman's eyes narrowed to paper-thin slits. 'So you remember me, do you? How very interesting.'

Emelia took a steadying breath. 'It was a guess, but apparently a very good one.'

Izabella planted her hands on her boyishly slim hips, sending Emelia another wish-you-were-dead glare. 'You shouldn't be here. You have no right to be here after what you did.'

Emelia marshalled her defences, keeping her tone civil but determined. 'I'm not sure what I am supposedly guilty of doing. Perhaps you could enlighten me.'

Izabella tossed her glossy dark head. 'Don't play the innocent with me. It might have worked with my brother but it won't work with me. I know what you are up to.'

Emelia was conscious of the housekeeper listening to every word. 'Would you like to come into *la sala* and discuss this further?' she asked.

Izabella gave another flash of her midnight eyes. 'I don't care who hears what I have to say.'

'Does your brother know you are here?' Emelia asked after a tense pause.

The young woman's haughty stance slipped a notch. 'He is not my keeper,' she said, making a moue of her mouth.

'That's not what he told me,' Emelia returned.

Izabella gave her head another toss as she folded her arms across her chest. 'He wouldn't have taken you back, you know. He only did it because he had no choice. The press would have crucified him if he'd divorced you so soon after the accident.'

Emelia felt as if a heavy weight had landed on her chest. She felt faint and had to struggle to remain steady on her feet. She would have excused herself but her desire to know more about her forgotten marriage overruled any concern for her well-being. 'Wh-what are you saying?'

'He was going to divorce you,' Izabella said with an aristocratic hoist of her chin. 'He had already contacted his lawyer.'

Emelia moistened her lips. 'On…on what grounds?'

Izabella's gaze was pure venom. 'Adultery.' She almost spat the word at Emelia. 'You ran away to be with your lover.'

Emelia stood in a frozen silence as she mentally replayed every conversation she'd had with Javier since she had woken in the hospital. While he hadn't accused her of anything openly, he had alluded to what the press had made of her relationship with Peter. He had also expressed his bitterness at her remembering Peter while not remembering him, which she had thought was a reasonable reaction under the circumstances. But if Javier truly believed her to have been unfaithful, what was he waiting for? Why not divorce her and be done with it? Did he really care what the press would make of it? What did he hope to gain by taking her back as if nothing had happened? It didn't make sense, not unless he loved her and was prepared to leave the past in the past, but somehow she didn't think that was the case. He desired her. She was acutely aware of the heat of his gaze every time it rested on her, indeed as aware of her own response to him. She was not immune to him, in spite of her memory loss. One kiss had shown how vulnerable she was to him.

'But it's not true,' she said after a moment. 'I didn't commit adultery.'

Izabella rolled her eyes. 'Of course you would say that. Your lover is dead, so what else could you do? You had to come back to Javier. He is rich and you had nowhere else to go. Even your own father would not take you back. You are nothing but a gold-digger.'

Emelia felt ill but worked hard to hold her composure. 'Look, Izabella, I realise you must be upset if you have heard rumours such as the outrageous one you just relayed to me, but I can assure you I have never been unfaithful to your brother. It's just not something I would do. I know it in my heart.'

Izabella gave her a challenging glare. 'How would you know? You say you don't remember anything from the past two years. How do you know *what* you did?'

It was a very good point, Emelia had to admit. But, deep down, she knew she would never have betrayed her marriage vows. How she was going to prove it was something she had yet to work out. Her reputation had been ruined by scandalous reports in the media. Who would believe her, even if she could remember what had happened that fateful day?

'Did you ever love my brother?' Izabella asked.

The question momentarily knocked Emelia off course. She looked at the young woman blankly, knowing as each pulsing second passed another layer of blame was being shovelled on top of her. 'I...I don't feel it is anyone's business but Javier's and mine,' she said.

Izabella gave a scathing snort. 'You never loved him. What you love is what he can give you—the lifestyle, the clothes, the jewellery. It's all you have ever wanted from him.'

'That is not true.' *Please don't let it be true*, Emelia thought.

'He is not going to remain faithful to you, you know. Why should he when you played up behind his back?'

Emelia felt a stake go through her middle. It surprised her how much Izabella's coolly delivered statement hurt her. Her mind filled with images of Javier with other women, his body locked with theirs, giving and receiving pleasure. Perhaps even now he was entertaining himself with some gorgeous creature in

Moscow. She shook her head, trying to get the torturous images to disappear. 'No,' she said in a rasping whisper. 'No…'

'He should never have married you,' Izabella said. 'Everyone told him it would end in disaster.'

Emelia lifted her aching head to meet Izabella's gaze. 'Why did he marry me, then?'

'Because he needed to be married to gain access to our father's estate,' Izabella said.

Emelia felt her heart give another sickening lurch. 'He married me to…to get *money*?'

'You surely don't think he loved you, do you?' Izabella threw her a disdainful look. 'He wanted you and what he wants he usually gets. You were a convenient wife. A trophy he wanted by his side. But that is all you are to him. He does not love you.'

'Did I *know* this?' Emelia asked in a hoarse whisper.

Izabella's expression lost some of its hauteur. 'I am not sure…' She bit down on her bottom lip in a way that seemed to strip years off her. 'Perhaps not. Maybe I shouldn't have said anything…'

Emelia reached for something to hold onto to steady herself. 'I can't believe I agreed to such an emotionless arrangement…' She looked at the young girl with an anguished expression on her face. 'I always wanted to marry for love. Are you sure I was not in love with Javier?'

Izabella looked troubled. 'If you were, you never said anything to me. You kept your feelings to yourself, although it was pretty obvious you were attracted to him. But then he's attractive to a lot of women.'

Emelia didn't want to think about that. It was just too painful. 'I'm sorry if I've given you the wrong impression,' she said after a moment. 'Javier told me you and I haven't had the easiest of relationships. I hope I haven't done anything to upset you. I have never had a sister before. I've always wanted one, especially after my mother died. It would have been nice to have someone to talk to about girl stuff.'

Izabella's dark brown eyes softened a fraction. 'Javier is the best brother a girl could have but there are times when I would rather share what is going on in my life with another woman. My mother is OK but she just worries if I talk to her about boys. She always thinks I am going to get pregnant or something.'

Emelia smiled. 'I guess it's what mothers do best—worry.'

Izabella's mouth tilted in a wary smile. 'You seem so different,' she said. 'Almost like a completely different person.'

'To tell you the truth, Izabella, I feel like a completely different person from the one everyone expects me to be,' Emelia confessed. 'I look at the clothes in my wardrobe and I can't believe I have ever worn them. They seem so…so…I don't know…not me. And when I was down at the stables Pedro told me I had refused to ride the horse Javier bought me last month for my birthday. I don't understand it. Why would I not ride that beautiful horse?'

'Ever since your birthday you seemed a little unsettled,' Izabella said. 'When you had the accident we all assumed it was because you were in love with another man. Now, I wonder if it wasn't because you were becoming a little tired of your life here. There is only so much time you can spend in the shops or the gym.'

Emelia felt her face heat up with colour. 'Yes, well,

that's another thing I don't get. I *hate* the gym. I can think of nothing worse than an elliptical trainer or a stationary bike and weight machines.'

'You worked out religiously,' Izabella said. 'You lost pounds and pounds within weeks of meeting Javier. And you are always dieting whenever Javier's away.'

Emelia thought back to her hearty breakfast that morning. 'No wonder I've been such a pain to be around,' she said with a wry grimace. 'I'm hopeless at diets. I have no self control. I get bitchy when I deprive myself.'

Izabella grinned. 'I do too.'

There was a little pause.

'You won't tell Javier I was so horrible to you, will you?' Izabella said with a worried look. 'He will be angry with me for upsetting you. I should have thought… You have just had a terrible accident. I am sorry about your friend. You must be very sad.'

'I am coping with it,' Emelia said. 'But I wish I knew what really happened that day.'

Izabella bit her lip again. 'Maybe you were leaving Javier because you didn't want to continue with the marriage as it was. The press would have latched on to it pretty quickly and made it out to be something it wasn't. Javier was furious. He was determined to divorce you but then he got news of the accident.' Her slim throat rose and fell. 'He was devastated when he heard you might not make it. He tried to hide it but I could tell he was terrified you would die.'

Emelia frowned as she tried to make sense of it all. If Javier didn't want her in his life permanently, why suffer her presence just because of her memory loss? Given what he believed of her, what hope did she have of restoring his trust in her? Had he known her so little that he had readily believed the specious rumours of the press? What sort of marriage had they had that it would crumble so quickly? Surely over the almost two years they had been together a level of trust had been established? She felt sure she would not have settled for anything else. It was so frustrating to have no way of finding out the truth. Her mind was like the missing black box of a crashed aircraft. Within it were all the clues to what had happened and until it was found she would have to try and piece together what she could to make sense of it all. Her head ached from the pressure of trying to remember. Her eyes felt as if they had been stabbed with roofing nails, pain pulsed from her temples like hammer blows.

Izabella touched Emelia on the arm. 'You are very pale,' she said. 'Is there anything I can ask Aldana to get for you?'

'I don't think Aldana will appreciate having to act as nursemaid to me,' Emelia said, putting a hand to her throbbing temple. 'She doesn't seem to like me very much.'

'She has never liked you but it's probably not your fault,' Izabella said. 'Her daughter once had a fling with Javier. It wasn't serious but, ever since, Aldana has been convinced no one but her daughter was good enough for Javier. I think you tried hard at first to get along but after a while you gave up.'

It explained a lot, Emelia thought. She couldn't imagine being deliberately rude to the household staff under any circumstances. But perhaps she had lost patience with Aldana, as Izabella had suggested, and consequently acted like the spoilt, overly indulged trophy wife everyone assumed her to be. 'I am so glad you came here today,' she said. 'I hope we can be friends.'

'I would like that very much,' Izabella said and, looking sheepish, added, 'I haven't always treated you very well. You were so beautiful and accomplished, so talented at playing the piano. I was such a cow to you, I guess because I was jealous. I probably contributed to your unhappiness with Javier.'

'I am sure you had no part to play in that at all,' Emelia said. 'I should have been more mature and understanding.'

'Please, you must promise not to tell Javier I was rude to you before,' Izabella said. 'I am so ashamed of myself.'

'You have no need to be,' Emelia said. 'Anyway, you were only acting out of your concern for him.'

Izabella's gaze melted. 'Yes, he's a wonderful brother. He would do anything for me. I am very lucky to have him.'

'He's lucky to have you,' Emelia said, thinking of all of her years alone, without anyone to stand up for her. It seemed nothing had changed: this recent scandal demonstrated how truly alone she was. No one had challenged the rumours. No one had defended her.

Izabella suddenly cocked her head. 'Your memory must be coming back, Emelia,' she said with an engaging grin.

Emelia shook her head. 'No, I've tried and tried but I can't remember much at all.'

'Except Spanish.'

Emelia felt her heart knock against her ribcage. She

hadn't realised until that point that every word she had exchanged with Izabella had been in Spanish.

Every single word.

CHAPTER SIX

IZABELLA had arranged to join some friends in Valencia the following day before she flew back to Paris so Emelia was left to her own devices. After a shower and breakfast, she wandered out into the gardens, stopping every now and again to pick a rose until, after half an hour, her arms were nearly full. She went back to the villa and laid them down on one of the large kitchen benches, breathing in the delicate fragrance as she searched for some vases.

Aldana appeared just as Emelia was carrying a vase full of blooms into *la sala*. 'What are you doing?' she asked, frowning formidably.

'I picked some roses,' Emelia said. 'I thought they would look nice in some of the rooms to brighten them up a bit. I hope you don't mind.'

Aldana took the vase out of Emelia's grasp. 'Señor Mélendez does not like roses in the house,' she said in a clipped tone.

Emelia felt her shoulders slump. 'Oh…sorry, I didn't realise…'

The housekeeper shot her another hateful glare as she carried the roses out of the room. The look seemed to suggest that, in Aldana's opinion, Emelia had never known her husband's likes and dislikes like a proper loving wife should do.

Emelia let out a sigh once she was alone. There was a baby grand piano at one end of *la sala*, positioned out of the direct sunlight from the windows. She went over to it and sat down and after a moment she opened the lid and ran her fingers over the keys, trying to remember what song she had played the night she had met Javier, but it was like trying to play a new piece without the musical score. She played several pieces, hoping that one would unlock her mind, but none did. She closed the lid in frustration and left the room to make her way down to the stables.

Pedro had Callida saddled for her when she arrived but he looked disgruntled. 'Señor Mélendez will not be happy about this,' he said. 'He told all the staff to watch out for you, to make sure you do not come to any harm while he is away.'

'Señor Mélendez is several thousand kilometres away,' Emelia said as she swung up into the saddle. 'While the cat's away this little mouse is going to do what she wants.'

Pedro stepped back from the horse with a disapproving frown. 'He sometimes comes back early from his trips abroad,' he said. 'He expects his staff to act the same whether he is here or not. He trusts us.'

But not me, Emelia thought resentfully as she rode off. No doubt he had only put his staff on watch over her to see that she didn't stray too far from the boundaries of the villa. His solicitous care had nothing to do with any deep feelings on his part. He wanted to keep her a virtual prisoner until the press interest died down. After that, who knew what he planned to do? All she knew was his plans would probably not include her being in his life for the long term.

As enjoyable as the ride was, it didn't unearth any clues to her past. She came back to the stables an hour and a half later, fighting off a weighty despondency. The olive grove today had simply been an olive grove. No further memories surfaced. Nothing struck a chord of familiarity.

Disappointment and frustration continued to sour her mood as she walked back to the villa through the gardens. She felt hot and sticky so when she came across a secluded section of the garden where an infinity pool was situated, she decided to take advantage of the sparkling blue water and the warmth of the afternoon.

Rummaging through the walk-in wardrobe in search of swimwear was another revelation to her. Naturally modest, she found it hard to believe she wore any of the skimpy bikinis she found in one of the drawers. There were pink ones and red ones and yellow ones and ones with polka dots, a black one with silver diamantés and a white one with gold circles in between the triangles of fabric that would barely cover her breasts, let alone her lower body. In the end she chose the red one as it was the least revealing, although once she had it on and checked her appearance in the full length mirrors she was glad Javier was not expected home. She might as well have been naked.

The water was warmed by the sun but still refreshing enough to make Emelia swim length after length without exhaustion. She wondered how many times she had done this, stroking her way through the water, perhaps with Javier swimming alongside her, or his long legs tangling with hers as he kissed or caressed her. In spite of the warmth of the pool and the sun, Emelia felt her skin lift in little goosebumps the more she let her mind wander about what had occurred in the past.

As she surfaced at the end of the pool she saw a long pair of trouser-clad legs, the large male feet encased in expensive-looking leather shoes. Her heart gave a stop-start as her eyes moved upwards to meet the coal-black gaze of Javier.

'I thought I might find you here,' he said.

Emelia pushed her hair out of her face, conscious of her barely clad breasts just at the water's level. 'I didn't realise you would be back. I thought you were coming home tomorrow.'

He tugged at his tie as his gaze held hers. 'I managed to get through the work and flew back ahead of schedule.'

Emelia swallowed as she saw him toss his tie to one of the sun loungers. His fingers began undoing the buttons of his business shirt, one by one, each opening revealing a little more of his muscular chest. 'Um… what are you doing?' she said.

'I thought I might join you,' he said, shrugging himself out of his shirt, tossing it in the same direction as his tie, his dark eyes still tethering hers.

She watched in a spellbound stasis as his hands went to his belt, slipping it through the waistband of his trousers, casting it on top of his shirt and tie. The sound of his zip going down jolted her out of her trance. 'Y-you're surely not going to swim without bathers…are you?'

A corner of his mouth lifted. 'Do you have any objection, *querida*?' he asked.

Emelia could think of several but she couldn't seem to get her voice to work. She stood in the water as he heeled himself out of his shoes and purposefully pulled off his socks. Her heart started thumping irregularly as he stepped out of his trousers, leaving him in close-fitting black briefs that left almost nothing to her imagination. She felt a stirring deep and low in her belly. He was so potently male, so powerfully built, lean but muscular at the same time, hair in all the right places, marking him as different from her as could be. His skin was a deep olive, tanned by the sun, each rippling ridge of his abdomen like coils of steel. Her fingertips suddenly itched to explore every hard contour of him, to feel the satin quality of his skin and unleash the latent power of his body. She wondered if her attraction was a new thing or an old thing. Was her body remembering what her mind could or would not? How else could she explain this unbelievable tension she felt when he was near her? She had never felt like this with anyone before. It was as if he awakened everything that was female in her body, making her long to discover the power of the passion his glittering dark gaze promised.

Being at the shallower end, he didn't dive into the water; instead, he slipped in with an agility that made Emelia aware of every plane of his body as the water his entry displaced washed against her. It was as if he had touched her; the water felt just like an intimate caress: smooth, gentle, cajoling, tempting. Her eyes were still locked with his; she couldn't seem to move out of the magnetic range of his dark-as-night eyes. They burned, they seared and they smouldered as he closed the distance between their bodies, stopping just in front of her, not quite touching but close enough for her to feel the pull of his body through the weight of the water.

'Why so shy?' he asked.

Emelia licked a droplet of water off her lips. 'Um…I know this is probably something you…I mean we have done lots of times but I…I…feel too exposed.'

His lips slanted in a smile. 'You got rid of your timidity a long time ago, Emelia. We skinny-dipped together all the time.'

She felt the pit of her stomach tilt. 'But surely someone could have seen us?'

He gave a little couldn't-care-less shrug. 'The pool area is private. In any case, what would it matter if someone had seen us? We are married and this is private property. It is not as if we were doing anything wrong.'

Emelia chewed at her lip, wishing she could download all her memories so she wasn't feeling so lost and uncertain. While she had been dressing in the bikini earlier she had seen from her lightly tanned skin that she had been in the sun and not always with all her clothes on. She had not been the type to sunbathe topless in the past, but then two whole years of her life were missing. Who knew what she had grown comfortable with over that time? It made her feel all the more on edge around Javier. He knew far more about her than she knew about him. And yet she could sense in her body a growing recognition that flickered a little more each time they were together.

'Aldana told me you had a visitor while I was away,' Javier said.

Emelia kept her expression masked. 'Yes. Izabella called in. She's gone to stay with friends in Valencia before she goes back to Paris.'

'Did you recognise her?'

She shook her head. 'No, but I soon figured out who she was. She is very like you. It is obvious you are related. You have the same hair and eyes.'

'I hope you refrained from getting into an argument with her,' he said, still holding her gaze. 'I would not want either of you upset.'

'No, we didn't argue,' Emelia said. 'I found her to be friendly and pleasant and not in the least hostile. She's a very beautiful and poised young woman. You must be very proud of her.'

He frowned as he studied her through narrowed eyes. 'What did you talk about?'

'The usual girl stuff,' she said. 'We have a lot in common, actually.'

'She is a little headstrong at times,' he admitted. 'But then she is still young.'

Emelia went to move to the steps leading out of the pool but he placed a hand on her arm, stopping her from moving away from him. 'Where are you going?' he asked.

'I'm getting cold,' she said. 'I want to have a shower.'

He cupped both of her shoulders with his hands. 'No kiss for my return?'

Emelia felt her eyes widen and her stomach did another flip turn. 'It's not as if things are the same...as before,' she said. 'I need more time.'

Something moved at the back of his eyes. 'I think the sooner we slip back into our previous routine the better,' he said. 'I am convinced it will help you remember.'

'You're assuming I will remember,' she said. 'I had no such assurance from any of the doctors or therapists at the hospital.'

His hands tightened as soon as he felt her try to escape again. 'It doesn't matter if you remember or not. It doesn't change the fact that we are married.'

Emelia straightened her spine in defiance but, by doing so, it brought her pelvis into direct contact with his. The hot hard heat of him was like being zapped with a thousand volts of electricity. She felt the tingles shoot through her from head to foot. His eyes dropped to the startled *'O'* of her mouth and then, as if in slow motion, gradually lowered his head until his lips sealed hers.

It was a slow burn of a kiss, heating her to her core as each pulsing second passed. His tongue probed the seam of her mouth for entry and she gave it on a whimper of pleasure. The rasp of his tongue as it mated with hers sent a cascading shiver down the backs of her legs and up again, right to the back of her neck. She felt her toes curl on the tiled floor of the pool as his kiss deepened. His arms had gone from the tops of her shoulders down the slim length of her arms to settle about her waist, holding her against his pelvis, leaving her acutely aware of his rock-hard arousal. Her body responded automatically, the ache between her thighs becoming more insistent the firmer he held her against him. She moved against him, a slight nudge at first and then a blatant rub to feel the pleasure his body offered.

He slowly but surely walked her backwards, his thighs brushing hers with each step, his mouth still locked on her mouth, his body jammed tight against her. His hands moved up from her waist to deftly untie the strings of her bikini. It fell away, leaving her breasts free for his touch. She drew in a sharp breath as his hands cupped her, his thumb gently stroking over each nipple, making her flesh cry out for more. His mouth left hers and went on a leisurely mission, exploring every dip and curve on the way down to her breasts: the sensitive pleasure spots behind each of her earlobes, the hollows above her collarbone and the super-reactive skin of her neck. She tilted her head to one side as he nibbled and nipped in turn, her belly turning over in delight as he finally made his way to her breasts. He left her nipples alone this time and concentrated instead on the sensitive under curves of each breast, first with his fingers and then with the heat and fire of his mouth. She arched up against him, wanting more, wanting it all, wanting to feel whatever he had made her feel in the past.

His mouth came back to her searching, hungry one, his hands going to the strings holding her bikini bottom in place. Emelia's hands moved from around his neck to the small of his back, delighting in the way he groaned deeply as he surged against her. Casting inhibition aside, she peeled away his briefs, freeing him into her hands. She felt a hitch in her breath as she shaped his steely length, the throb of his blood pounding against her fingers. He was so thick with desire it made her own blood race at the thought of him moving inside her.

He tore his mouth off hers, looking down at her with eyes glittering with desire. 'You have certainly not forgotten how to drive me wild with wanting you,' he said. 'How about it, *querida*? Shall we finish this here and now, or wait for later?'

Emelia felt the cold slap of shock bring her back to reality. What was she doing allowing him such liberties and outside where anyone could see if they put their mind to it? And what was she doing touching him as if she wanted him to finish what he had started? What was wrong with her? Surely she had not become such a slave of the flesh? She had always abhorred such irresponsible behaviour amongst her peers; the casual approach to sex was something she had never gone in for. She put up her chin, working hard to maintain her composure when she was stark naked. 'What makes you so sure I would give my consent, here or anywhere?'

His smile was on the edge of mocking. 'Because I know you, Emelia. I know how you respond to me. A couple of minutes more and you would have been begging for it.'

There was nothing figurative about the slap Emelia landed on the side of Javier's face. It jerked his head back, made his nostrils flare and his mouth tighten to a flat line of tension. 'You know, you really shouldn't have done that,' he said with a coolness she was sure he was nowhere near feeling.

Emelia refused to wilt under his hard black gaze. 'You insulted me. You practically called me a wanton tramp.'

One of his hands rubbed at the red hand-sized mark on his jaw. 'So if someone allegedly insults you it's OK to use violence?' he asked.

She bit the inside of her mouth, suddenly ashamed of how she had reacted, but there was no way she was going to apologise to him. She turned and searched for her bikini, struggling to put it back on while still in the water. She was conscious of Javier's eyes following her every movement and her resentment and anger hardened like a golf ball-sized lump in the middle of her chest. Once she was covered, she stomped up the pool steps, snatching up her towel on the way past the sun lounger where she had left it.

* * *

The moment Emelia came out of the en suite bathroom after a lengthy shower she knew something was amiss. Her eyes went to the bed where a black leather brief-case was lying at the foot of it. She heard the sound of someone moving about in the walk-in wardrobe and, clutching her bathrobe a little tighter, spun around to find Aldana coming out with some spare coat hangers.

'What's going on?' Emelia asked in Spanish.

The housekeeper gave her a pursed-lipped look. 'Señor Mélendez instructed me to hang his clothes.'

Emelia's eyes widened in alarm. 'What? In…in *here*?'

Aldana gave a shrug as she walked past. 'It is none of my business what he wants or why. I just do as I am told. He wanted me to bring his things back in here where they belong.'

The housekeeper left before Emelia could respond and within seconds Javier strode in. She turned on him, her eyes flashing with fury. *'Qué diablos está pasando?'* she asked. 'What the hell is going on?'

He stood very still for a moment before responding in Spanish. 'I could ask you the very same thing. What the hell *is* going on? Especially as it seems at least some part of your memory has returned without you telling me.'

Emelia felt her cheeks fill with colour. 'I…I was going to tell you…'

'When did it happen?' he asked.

She could barely hold his gaze as she confessed. 'I found myself understanding it and speaking it from the start. I don't know why. It was just…there.'

'How convenient.'

Emelia's hands tightened where they clutched the

neckline of her bathrobe. 'I know what you're thinking but it's not true. I don't remember anything else. I swear to you.'

He gave her a cynical smile that contained no trace of amusement. 'I met Pedro the stable boy on my way in earlier,' he said. 'He was full of excitement over how you remembered your mare's name without any prompting from him.'

Emelia pressed her lips together. 'I forgot I remembered…' It sounded as stupid as she felt and she lowered her gaze from the hard probe of his, hating herself for blushing.

'He also told me you have finally ridden your horse,' he said.

'I can't explain why I never rode Callida before.' She looked up at him again. 'You must have been very annoyed with me after spending so much money on such a beautiful animal.'

He held her gaze for a long moment. 'It wasn't the first present you rejected of late,' he said. 'It seemed over the last few weeks nothing I did for you or bought for you could please you.'

Emelia wondered if she had been hankering after more from him than what money could buy. It seemed much more in line with her true character. She had been given expensive gifts for most of her life but they hadn't made her feel any more secure.

Javier used two fingers to lift her chin, searing her gaze with his. 'I want you to tell me the moment you remember anything else, do you understand? I don't care what time of day it is or if I am away or here. Just tell me.'

She let out an uneven breath as she stepped out from

under his hold. 'You can't force me to remember you, Javier. It doesn't happen like that. I read up about it. Sometimes the memories are blocked because of trauma, either physical or emotional or maybe even both.'

A muscle worked in his jaw, the silence stretching and stretching like a threadbare piece of elastic.

'So what you are saying is you might be subconsciously blocking all memory of our life together?' he finally said.

Emelia released her bottom lip from the savaging of her teeth. 'I'm not sure if that's what has happened or not,' she said. 'Was there something that happened that might have caused me to do that? Something deeply upsetting, I mean.'

The silence stretched again, even further this time.

'I was away the day you left for London,' Javier said heavily. He waited a beat before continuing. 'I had only just come back from Moscow when we had an argument. I flew straight back afterwards.'

Emelia felt a frown tugging at her forehead. 'What did we argue about?'

His eyes met hers briefly before moving away to focus on a point beyond her left shoulder. 'The papers had printed some rubbish about me being involved with someone in Russia, a nightclub singer.'

Emelia felt a fist wrap itself around her heart. 'Was it…was it true?'

His dark eyes flashed with irritation as they came back to hers. 'Of course it wasn't true. I have to deal with those rumours all the time. I thought you were OK about it. We'd talked about it early in our marriage. We used to laugh about some of the stuff that was printed.

I warned you what it would be like, that there would be constant rumours, often set off by business rivals.'

He stopped to scrape a hand through his hair. 'But this time for some reason you refused to accept my explanation. You got it in your head that I was playing up behind your back. It seemed nothing I said would change your mind.'

'So we had an argument…'

'Yes,' he said. 'I'm afraid it was a bit of an ugly scene.'

Emelia raised her brows questioningly. 'How ugly?'

He let out a long tense breath. 'There was a lot of shouting and name calling. We were both angry and upset. I should have cut the argument short but I was annoyed because you seemed determined to want our marriage to be something it was never intended to be.'

Emelia sent him a let's-see-if-you-can-deny-this look. 'So apparently I wasn't too happy you had married me to gain access to your father's estate, right?'

His dark gaze turned flinty. 'That was one of the things we argued about, yes. While I was away, my father's mistress had rung you and filled your head with that and other such nonsense to get back at me. But the truth is my reasons for marrying you had very little to do with my father's will.'

She rolled her eyes in disbelief. 'Oh, come now, Javier. You talk of our marriage as some sort of business proposal, rules and regulations and me suddenly stepping outside of them. What the hell was the point of being married if not because we loved each other?'

'Love was not part of the deal,' he said, shocking Emelia into silence. 'I wanted a wife. Some of the business people I deal with are old-fashioned and conservative in their views. They feel more comfortable dealing with a man in a seemingly stable relationship. I know it sounds a little cold-blooded but you were quite happy to take on the corporate wife role. We were ideally matched physically. It was all I wanted from you and you from me.'

She stood looking at him with her emotions reeling. How could she have agreed to such a marriage? A relationship based on sex and nothing else? Had she turned into a clone of her father's set, in spite of her determination not to? She had become a trophy wife, an exotic bird in a gilded cage. Indulged and pampered until her mind went numb.

Javier let out another breath and sent his hand through his hair again. 'Emelia…' He hesitated for a moment before he continued. 'You might not remember it but we made love during that last argument.'

Emelia felt her brows lift again but remained silent.

His gaze remained steady on hers. 'In hindsight, it was perhaps not the best way to leave things between us. There was so much left unresolved. I have had cause to wonder if that is why you rushed off to London the way you did.'

Emelia searched her mind for some trace of that scene but nothing came to her. 'Did I explain why I left? In a note or something?'

'Yes,' he said.

Hope flickered in her chest. 'Can I see it?'

'I tore it into shreds,' he said, his mouth tightening at the memory. 'I got home from Moscow two days after you left. That is another thing I am not particularly proud of. I should have come straight to London as soon as I knew you were there. I was packing a bag when I got the call about the accident.'

'What did I say in the note?' Emelia asked.

He looked at her silently for several moments. 'You said you were leaving me, that you no longer wanted to continue with our marriage. You wanted out.'

Emelia rubbed at her forehead, as if that would unlock the memories stored inside her head. OK, so she had been leaving him. That much was pretty certain. Was it because she had become tired of their shallow relationship, as Izabella had suggested? Emelia knew she must have been very unhappy to have come to that decision. Unhappy or desperate. 'The rumours…' she said. 'You mentioned a few days ago there was some speculation about my relationship with Peter Marshall. Did you afford me the same level of trust you expected of me, in similar if not the same circumstances?'

He visibly tensed; all of his muscles seemed to contract as if sprayed with fast setting glue. 'I am the first to admit that I was jealous of your relationship with him,' he said, biting each word out from between his clenched teeth. 'He seemed at great pains whenever I was around to show me just how close you were. He was always touching you, slinging an arm around your waist or shoulders. It made me want to lash out.'

Emelia frowned at his vehement confession. 'Peter was a touchy-feely sort of person. It was just his way. I am sure I would have told you that right from the start.'

His eyes flashed with heat. 'You did, but it still annoyed the hell out of me.'

He was jealous. He hated admitting it, Emelia was sure, but he was positively vibrating with it. She could see it in the way he held himself, his hands clenching and unclenching as if he wanted to hit something.

He paced the room a couple of times before he came back to stand in front of her. 'If I was wrong about your relationship with Marshall then I am sorry,' he said. 'All the evidence pointed to you being guilty of an affair, but in hindsight there are probably numerous explanations for why you were in that car with him.'

Emelia felt a weight come off her shoulders. 'You truly believe I wasn't unfaithful?'

He held her look for endless seconds. 'Let's just let it go,' he said on a long breath. 'I don't want to be reminded of the mistakes I have made in the past. We have to concentrate on the here and now. I want to see you get well again. I feel it is my fault you were almost killed. I cannot forgive myself for driving you away in such an emotionally charged state. I should have insisted we sit down and sort things out like two rational adults. Instead, I let business take precedence, hoping things would settle down by the time I got back.'

Emelia stood looking at him in silence. His gruff admission of guilt stirred her deep inside. She could tell it was unfamiliar territory for him. He didn't seem the type to readily admit when he was in the wrong.

She breathed in the clean male scent of him as he stood so broodingly before her. He had showered and changed into a polo shirt and casual trousers. His hair was still damp, ink-black and curling at the ends where it needed a trim. She wanted to run her hands through it the way she used to do... She jolted as if he had struck her, staring up at him, her heart beating like a hyperactive hammer.

'What's wrong?' he asked, taking her by the shoulders.

She looked up into his face, frowning as she tried to focus on the sliver of memory that had made its way through. As if by their own volition, her hands went to his hair, her fingers playing with the silky strands in slow, measured strokes. She saw his throat move up and down and, glancing at his mouth, she felt another tiny flicker of recognition. Her right hand went to his lips, her fingers tracing over the tense line, again and again until it finally softened, the slight rasp of his evening shadow as she stroked the leanness of his jaw, the only sound, apart from their breathing, in the silence.

'Emelia—' his voice was low and deep and scratchy '—what have you remembered?'

She looked into his dark eyes. 'Your hair…I remembered running my fingers through it…lots and lots of times… It's longer now, isn't it?'

'Yes, I've been too busy to get it cut.' His grip on her shoulders tightened and his eyes were intense as they held hers. 'Can you remember anything else?' he asked.

'I'm not sure…' Emelia tried to focus again. 'It was just a fleeting thing. Like a flashback or something.'

His hands slipped down from her shoulders to encircle her wrists, his thumbs absently stroking her. 'Don't force it. It will come when it wants to. We have to be patient.' He let out a rough sounding sigh and added ruefully, '*I* have to be patient.'

Emelia felt the drugging warmth of his touch on the undersides of her wrists. Her blood leapt in her veins and she wondered if he could feel the way he affected her. Her belly was turning into a warm pool of longing, her legs unsteady as his eyes came to hers, holding them for a pulsing moment.

Time seemed to slow and then stand impossibly still.

Without a word, he lifted one of his hands to the curve of her cheek, cupping her face gently, his thumb moving back and forth in a mesmerising touch that seemed to stroke away every single reason why she should ease back out of his embrace. Instead, she found herself stepping closer, her body touching his from chest to thigh, feeling the stirring of his body against her, the hot hard heat of him lighting a fire that she now realised had smouldered within her from the moment she had woken up in the hospital and encountered his dark unreadable gaze.

'Emelia.'

The way he said her name was her undoing. Low and deep, an urgency in the uttering of the syllables, a need that she could feel resonating in her own body, like a tuning fork being struck too hard, humming, vibrating and quivering with want.

She lifted her mouth to the slow descent of his, her arms snaking around his middle, her breasts pressed up against his hard chest, a feeling, as his lips sealed hers and his hands cradled her head, that she had finally come home...

CHAPTER SEVEN

EMELIA sighed with pleasure as Javier's mouth urged hers into a heated response. Desire was like a punch, hitting her hard as his tongue deftly searched for hers. He found it, toyed with it, stroking and stabbing, calling it into a dance that mimicked what was to come. Her body felt as if spot fires had been set all through it, the blood raced and thundered in her veins as his kiss grew all the more insistent, all the more hotly sensual. The delicate network of nerves in her core twanged with need, her breasts tightened and tingled where they were pressed against him, and her mouth was slippery and wet and hot with greedy want as it fed off his.

His hands moved from cupping her face to pressing against the small of her back, bringing her hard against him. Emelia felt the outline of his erection; it stirred something deep and primal in her. Her thighs trembled as she felt the slickness of need anointing her. She sent her hands on their own journey of discovery: the hard planes of his back and shoulders, the taut trimness of his waist, the leanness of his hips and the heat and throbbing of his blood rising so proud and insistent from between his legs.

He groaned against her mouth, something unintelligible, a mixture of Spanish, English and desperation as her fingers freed him from his clothing. He stepped out of the pool of his trousers, his shoes thudding to the floor as he succumbed to her touch. She felt another punch of lust in her belly. She wondered if this was how it had been from the start of their relationship. Physical attraction that was unstoppable, not underpinned with feelings other than primal lust.

Javier shrugged himself out of his shirt, tossing it aside before he started to work on hers. He pulled her top away from one of her shoulders, his hot mouth caressing the smooth flesh he had uncovered. Emelia gave herself up to the heady feel of his lips and teeth, her legs quivering with expectation as he continued the sensual journey, removing her clothes and replacing them with his mouth until she was standing in nothing but her lacy knickers.

His eyes were almost completely black as he stood looking at her, his hands on her hips, his touch sending livewires of need to her core.

Emelia's fingers splayed over his chest, the hard smooth muscles delighting her, the thunder of his heartbeat against her palm. She pressed a hot wet kiss to his throat, moving down, through the rough dark hair that narrowed from his chest to his groin. She went to her knees in front of him and he sprang up against her, hard, hot and swollen. She breathed over him, the air from her mouth making him tense all over. She touched him with the tip of her tongue, a light experimental taste that had him gripping her by the shoulders, his fingers digging in almost painfully as he anchored himself. She stroked her tongue along the satin length of him, feeling each pulsing ridge of his flesh, delighting in the way his breathing intervals shortened, the way the muscles of his abdomen clenched and his fingers dug even deeper into the flesh of her shoulders.

Before she could complete her sensual mission he hauled her back up to her feet, his eyes almost feverish with desire as they locked on hers. 'Enough of that for now,' he said. 'I won't last.'

Emelia could feel the pressure building inside him and wanted to feel it inside her, to feel him stretching her, filling her, possessing her totally, irrevocably.

His mouth came back to hers, hungrily, feeding off her with a new desperation as his body pulsed with urgency against hers. His hand cupped her feminine mound, a possessive touch that made every hair on her scalp lift in anticipation. The lacy barrier of her knickers only intensified the scalding heat of his touch. She arched up against him, an unspoken need crying out from every pore of her flesh.

He moved her to the bed, guiding her, pushing her, urging her with his mouth still seared to hers, his tongue enslaving hers.

Emelia gasped as he peeled her knickers away, the brush of lace against her thighs nothing to what it felt like to have his mouth do the same. His hot breath whispered down her thighs and up again and then against her feminine folds, his fingers gently separating her, his tongue tasting her like an exotic elixir. She whimpered as the sensations rippled through her, everything in her fizzled and sparked with feeling. She writhed under his erotic touch, panting against the building crescendo. Her fingers dug into the cover on the bed, her heart racing as he continued his shockingly intimate caress until she finally exploded. It was a hundred sensations at once: a cataclysmic eruption, a tidal wave, a landslide, every nerve twitching in the aftermath, her chest rising and falling as her breathing fought to return to normal. She felt limbless, floating on a cloud of release, wondering how many times he had done this to her. How could she have forgotten such rapture?

But it was not over.

Javier moved up over her, his strong thighs gently nudging hers apart, his erection brushing against her swollen flesh. His expression was contorted with concentration, a fierce determination to keep control. She felt it in the way he held himself as if he was worried he would hurt her in his own quest for release. She reassured him by stroking his back, urging him to complete the union, positioning her body to receive him, aching to feel that musky male thickness inside her.

He groaned as he surged into her slick warmth, the skin of his back lifting under her fingertips. She felt him check himself but she was having none of it. She urged him on again, lifting her hips to meet the downward thrust of his, the pumping action of his body sending waves of shivering delight through her. His breathing quickened, his body rocking with increasing speed, carrying her along with him on the racing breakneck tide. She felt the stabbing heat of him, the primal rush of her senses pulling her into another vortex. She arched some more, the tight ache beginning all over again as he thrust all the harder and faster. She panted beneath the sweat-slicked heat of him, the hairs on his chest tickling her breasts, her molten core tingling for that final trigger that would send her to paradise once more.

He slid one of his hands down between their rocking

bodies, his fingers finding the swollen-with-need pearl of her body, the stroking motion tipping her over the edge into oblivion.

As she was swirling back from the abyss of pleasure she felt him work himself to orgasm, the way he thrust on, his breathing ragged and heavy, his primal-sounding grunts as he finally let go making her shiver all over in response.

The silence was heavy and scented with sex.

Emelia opened her eyes after timeless minutes to see Javier propped up on his elbows, looking down at her with those unreadable black eyes. She felt shy all of a sudden. She had not thought her body capable of such feeling, of such powerful mind-blowing responses. He had stirred her so deeply, and not just physically. It was more than that, so much more. She felt a feather brush over her heart. She felt a fluttering feeling in her stomach, like the wings of a small bird. She tried to hold on to the image that had appeared like a ghost inside her mind, but it vaporised into nothingness before she could make sense of it.

Javier brushed a damp strand of her hair back from her face. 'You have a faraway look on your face,' he said.

Emelia blinked herself back to the present. 'I thought I remembered something else but it's gone.'

As if sensing her frustration, he bent his head and kissed her forehead softly. 'As long as you don't forget this,' he said, kissing both of her eyebrows in turn. 'And this.' He kissed the end of her nose. 'And this.' He kissed the corner of her mouth and she turned her head so her lips met his.

The heat leapt from his mouth to hers, the lightning

flash of his tongue meeting hers causing an instant con-
flagration of the senses. Emelia felt the stiffening of his
body where it was still encased in hers, the rapid rise
of her pulse in time with his as he started moving within
her. She ran her fingers through his hair, down over his
shoulders, his back and then grasped the firm flesh of
his buttocks, relishing the tension she could feel
building in his body.

'It is always this way between us,' he growled against
her mouth. 'Once is never enough. I want you like I
want no other woman. This need, it never goes away.'

Emelia felt a spurt of feminine pride that she had
captivated his desire in such a way. 'I want you too,' she
said, giving herself up to his passionately determined
kiss.

He left her mouth to suckle on her breasts, a light
teasing movement of his lips that left her breathless for
more. He kissed the sensitive underside of each breast
before coming back to her mouth, crushing it beneath
his as his need for release built.

This time his lovemaking was fast and furious, as if
all the frustration at her not remembering could only be
expressed through the passionate connection of their
bodies. He rolled her over until she was on top, his
hands cupping her breasts as his dark eyes held hers.
'You like it like this, *querida*,' he said in a deep gravelly
voice. 'Make yourself come against me. Let me watch
you.'

Shyness gripped her but the sensual challenge was
too tempting to ignore. She could feel him against her
most sensitive point when she shifted slightly. It was
like a match to a flame to feel him hard and thick against
her, the friction so delicious she was gasping out loud

as she rode him unashamedly. She came apart within seconds, her cries of ecstasy ringing in the silence, her breathing choppy and her heart rate uneven.

He used her last few contractions to bring himself to completion, his eyes now screwed shut, his face contorted with the exquisite pleasure he was feeling. Emelia felt him empty himself, each rocking pulse of his body triggering aftershocks in hers.

She slumped down over him, more out of shyness than exhaustion, although her limbs felt leaden after so much pleasure. She felt his fingers absently stroking over each knob of her spine, lingering over her lower vertebrae, his touch still lighting fires beneath her skin.

When he spoke his voice reverberated against her chest. 'Did that trigger anything in your memory?'

Emelia opened her eyes and, raising her head, looked down at him. Her heart squeezed in her chest as if a hand were closing into a fist around it. His dark eyes were like liquid, melted by passion, warm and softer than she had ever seen them. A feeling rushed up from deep inside her, an overwhelming sense of rightness. It was like a door creaking open in her head. Memories started filing through, like soldiers called to action. It was blurry at first, but then it cleared as she put the pieces together in her mind.

She remembered their first meeting. She remembered the way he had met her gaze across the room and how her fingers had stumbled on the piece she was playing. She had quickly looked away, embarrassed, feeling gauche and unsophisticated as she continued playing through her repertoire. She had never before reacted like that to any man who had come in. It had been an almost visceral thing. His presence seemed to reach out across the space that divided them and touch her.

She remembered how he had come over to the piano when she was packing up and asked her to join him for a drink. An hour later he had offered to drive her home, an offer she politely declined. He came the next night and the next, sitting listening to her play, slowly sipping at his drink, watching her until she finished. And each night he would offer to drive her home. By the third night she agreed. She remembered how she fell in love with him after their first kiss. She remembered how it felt to feel his arms go around her and draw her close to his body, the way her body felt in response, the way her heart beat until it felt as if it was going to work its way out of her chest.

She remembered the first time they made love. It was a month after they had met. He had been so gentle and patient, schooling her into the delights of her own body and the heat and potency of his. She could feel herself blushing just thinking about where they had gone from there. How eager she had been to learn, how willing she had been to be everything he wanted in a partner and then as his wife.

In spite of her initial reservations, she had moulded herself into the role, trying so hard to fit into his life-style, fashioning herself into the sort of trophy wife she assumed he wanted: a rail-thin clothes horse, a glamour girl always with a glass of champagne in one hand and a brilliant smile pasted on her perfectly made-up face. She had ignored the doubts that kept lurking in the shadows of her mind. Doubts about the way he refused to discuss his feelings, doubts about his adamantine stance about not having children, doubts about having signed the prenuptial document he'd insisted she sign, doubts about the intimidation she felt when alone at the villa with just his staff for company when he was away on business, which he seemed to be so often.

She had begun to feel she didn't really belong in his life and that the fiery attraction that had brought them together initially was not going to be enough to sustain them in the long term. She had always known he desired her; it was the one thing she could count on. He never seemed to tire of making love with her. It had thrilled her at first but after a while she had begun to crave more from him than sex. She had fooled herself she would be able to change him, to teach him how to love her the way she loved him.

And then, in spite of what she had told him, she had begun to dream of having a baby. She silently craved to build a family with him, to put down the roots that had been denied her throughout her childhood. But she had never been brave enough to bring up the subject. She had obediently taken her contraceptive pills and done her best to ignore the screeching clamour of her biological clock until that fateful day when she had finally had enough. Finding out about his father's will, on top of the press photo of him with the Russian singer, had tipped her over the edge. She had left him in the hope he would come after her and beg her to return. She had hoped he would insist on changing the rules of their marriage so they could have a proper fulfilling life together.

But of course he hadn't. A man as proud as Javier would not beg anyone to come back to him. Look at what had happened between him and his father. A decade had gone past and he hadn't budged.

'Emelia?' Javier's deep voice broke through her thoughts. 'What's going on?'

She met his concerned gaze. 'I remember…'

He sat upright, tumbling her onto her back, his fingers grasping her by both arms. 'What? Everything?' he asked.

She shook her head. 'Bits and pieces. Like when and how we met. Some of our time together. Most of our time together.'

One of his hands moved in a slow stroking motion up and down her arm. 'So I was right,' he said. 'Your body recognised me from the first. Your mind just had to catch up.'

She touched his lips with her fingers, tracing over their contours. 'How could I have forgotten you? I can't believe I didn't remember you. Were you very angry about that?'

Javier captured one of her fingers with his mouth, sucking on it erotically, all the while holding her gaze. He released her finger and said, 'I have to admit I was angry, especially when you hadn't forgotten Marshall.'

Her eyes dropped from his, a frown pulling at her forehead. 'I can't explain that. I'm sorry.'

'It is not important now,' he said. 'We have to move on.'

'Javier?' Her soft voice was like a feather brushing along his lower spine.

Javier looked down at her tussled hair and slim naked body. His groin tightened as he thought of having her back in his life permanently. His plans to divorce her seemed so ridiculous now. He had acted stupidly, blindly and in anger. His pride had taken a hit from what had been reported in the press about her and Marshall and he had let it block out his reason. He wanted her too much to let her go. He didn't like admitting it. He would rather die than admit it. She was the one woman who had brought him to his knees. He had nearly gone out of his head when he found she had left him. He had not realised how much he wanted and needed her until she had gone.

A part of him blamed himself. He had been so pre-occupied with the Moscow takeover. It was the deal of a lifetime. The negotiations had been tricky from the get-go but he had always believed he could pull it off. His goal had been to add that Russian bank to his empire and he had done it. It was the ultimate prize, the bench-mark business deal. But he just hadn't realised it would come at such a personal cost.

He brushed some damp tendrils of hair back off her face. 'Tired, *cariño*?'

She shook her head, her grey-blue eyes like shimmering pools. 'Not at all.' She stretched her slim body against him just like a sinuous cat and smiled. 'Not one little bit.'

His blood rocketed through his veins and he pressed her back down and covered her mouth with his, kissing her hungrily, delighting in the way she responded just as greedily. His tongue played with hers, stroking and sweeping until she succumbed with a whimpering sigh of pleasure. His hands moved over her breasts, the already erect nipples a dark cherry-red. He closed his mouth over each of them, flicking them with the point of his tongue, before sucking deeply. Her fingers scored through his hair, her body bucking under him as she opened for him.

He knew he was rushing things but he was aching

and heavy with longing. She was already slick with his seed from before, hot, wet and wanting him just as much as he wanted her. It sounded prehistoric but he wanted to stake his claim again and again, to mark his territory in the most primal way of all. Her body wrapped around him tightly as he thrust into her, the walls of her inner core rippling against him. He had to fight to stay in control, each thrusting movement sending gushing waves of need right through him. She squirmed beneath him, searching for that extra friction to send her to paradise. He made her wait; he wanted to make her beg. It seemed fitting since he had suffered so much because of her leaving him, for putting him through such a tormented hell.

'I want…' she panted beneath him. 'I want you to… Oh, please, Javier…'

He smiled over her mouth as he took it in another scorching kiss, his hands sliding between her thighs, teasing her with almost-there caresses.

She whimpered again and grasped at his hand, pushing it against her pearly need. 'Please,' she begged him passionately.

Javier flicked his fingers against her, just the way she liked. He knew her body like a maestro knew his instrument. She felt so silky and feminine, the scent of her driving him mad with the need to let go. He waited until she had started to orgasm, the spasms of her body gripping him until he had no choice but to explode. He pumped into her harder and harder, forcing the images of her alleged affair that had tortured him out of his head. He felt her flinch, he even felt her fingers grasping at his shoulders but he carried on relentlessly, until finally he spilled himself with a shout of triumph.

He rolled onto his back, his chest rising and falling as he tried to steady his breathing. He turned his head as he felt the mattress shift. Emelia had rolled away with her back to him, huddled into a ball. He reached out and stroked a finger down her spine. 'Emelia?'

She flinched and moved further away from him, mumbling something he didn't quite catch.

Javier sat upright and, taking her nearest shoulder, turned her onto her back. 'What's wrong?' he asked.

Her eyes flashed at him like lightning. 'I think you know what's wrong.'

'I'm not a mind reader, Emelia. If you have something to say, then, for God's sake, say it.'

She continued to glare at him but then her eyes began to swim with tears. 'Don't ever make love to me as if I was your mistress,' she said, her voice cracking over the words. 'I am your wife.'

Javier felt a knife of guilt go between his ribs. 'I got carried away,' he said. 'I'm sorry. You said you liked it like that in the past.'

She gave him a cutting look. 'Did you ever think I might have been saying that just to please you?'

He sent his fingers through his hair before he reluctantly faced her. 'I am not sure of what you want any more, Emelia,' he said. 'It's like I have a different wife from the one I had only a month or so ago. It's going to take some time to adjust.'

She looked at him through watery eyes. 'Was our relationship about anything but sex?' she asked.

He got off the bed as if she had pushed him. 'Now that some of your memory has returned you should know how much I detest these sorts of discussions,' he said with a harsh note of annoyance. 'I laid out the terms of our marriage and you agreed to them. Now you want to change things.'

She pulled the bedcovers over her. 'Why don't you just answer the question? Did you ever feel anything for me other than desire? Did you love me, even just a little?'

Javier tried to stare her down but she held firm. He let out a savage breath. 'My father told me he loved me but it didn't mean a thing. It was conditional, if anything. He wanted me to be a puppet. As soon as I wanted to choose my own path, his love was cut off.'

'That was wrong of him,' she said. 'Parents should never withhold their love, not for any reason.'

He made a scoffing sound in his throat. 'My father loved his wives, all four of them, and they apparently loved him back, but look where that ended—an early death and two, almost three, very expensive divorces.'

Her brow wrinkled with a frown. 'So what you're saying is you don't believe love can ever last?'

'It's not a reliable emotion, Emelia. It changes all the time.'

'I'm not sure what you're saying in relation to us…'

'The things that make a relationship work are common ground and chemistry,' Javier said. 'A bit of mutual respect doesn't go amiss either.'

Her expression was crestfallen and he felt every kind of heel as a result. Was he incapable of loving or just resistant to being that vulnerable to another person? He couldn't answer with any certainty.

'Don't push me on this, Emelia,' he said into the silence. 'Our relationship has been through so much of late. This is not the time to be saying things neither of us are certain is true.'

'But I know I love you,' she said. 'I know it with absolute certainty. I loved you from the first moment I met you. I didn't tell you because I knew you didn't want to hear it. But I need to tell you now. I can't hold it in any longer.'

He pinned her with his gaze. 'You speak of loving me and yet you were leaving me, Emelia, or have you not remembered that part? You had given up on our relationship. You wouldn't be here now if you hadn't been injured and lost your memory. You would be back in Australia. You were in that car with Marshall because he was driving you to the airport.'

Her teeth sank into her bottom lip until it went white.

'Why don't we wait until all the pieces are in place before you start planning the future?' he said when she didn't speak. 'Unless we deal with the past, we might not even have a future.'

'You…you want a divorce?' Her voice sounded like a wounded child's.

'I don't believe we should stay shackled together if one or both of us is unhappy,' he said. 'We'll give it a month or two and reassess. It is early days. You've only just come out of hospital after a near-fatal accident. You're damned lucky to be alive.'

Her mouth went into a pout. 'No doubt it would have been much better for you if I had been killed.'

Javier ground his teeth as he thought about that moment when Aldana had informed him there was a call from the police in London. His heart had nearly stopped until he had been assured she hadn't been fatally wounded. 'My mother died when she was three years younger than you are,' he said. 'She didn't see my first day at school. She didn't hear the first words I learned to read. I didn't get the chance to tell her how much I loved her or if I did I was too young to remember doing it. Don't you dare tell me I would rather have you dead and buried. No one deserves to have their life cut short through the stupidity of other's actions.'

She sent him a defiant glare. 'Maybe it suits you to have me alive so you can pay me back for daring to leave you. I bet I'm the first woman who ever has.'

Javier drew in a sharp breath. 'You're the one who moved the goalposts, not me.'

'I can't be the sort of wife you want,' she said, her eyes shining with tears. 'I can't do it any more. I'm not that sort of person, Javier. I want more from life than money and sex and endless hours in the gym or the beauty salon. I want to be loved for who I am, not for what I look like.'

He snatched up his trousers and zipped himself into them. 'I care about you, Emelia. Believe me, you would not be here now if I didn't.'

'Is that supposed to make me feel better?' she asked. 'You *care* about me. For God's sake, Javier, you make me sound like some sort of pet.'

He sent her a frustrated look as he grasped the door handle. 'We will talk about this later,' he said. 'You are not yourself right now.'

'You're damn right I'm not,' she said. 'But that's the heart of the problem. I have never been myself the whole time we've been married. I am a fake wife, Javier, a complete and utter fraud. How long do you expect such a marriage to last?'

He set his mouth. 'It will last until I say it's over.' And then he opened the door and strode out, snapping the door shut behind him.

CHAPTER EIGHT

EMELIA went to bed totally wrung out after her conversation with Javier. She lay awake for hours, hoping he might come in and join her but he apparently wanted to keep his distance. She spent a restless night, agonising over everything, ruminating over all the stupid decisions she had made, all the crazy choices to be with him in spite of how little he was capable of giving her emotionally. No wonder she had grown tired of their arrangement. She was amazed it had lasted as long as it had. She had compromised herself in every way possible. With the wisdom of hindsight, she knew that if she'd had better self-esteem she would never have agreed to such a marriage. But, plagued with insecurities stemming from childhood, she had been knocked off her feet with his passionate attention. His ruthless determination to have her in his bed had curdled her common sense. She had acted on impulse, not sensibly.

When she woke the next morning after snatches of troubled sleep she felt the beginnings of a vicious headache. The light spilling in from the gap in the curtains was like steel skewers driving through her skull. She groaned and buried her head under the pillow, nausea rolling in her stomach like an out of control boulder.

The sound of the door opening set a shockwave of pain through her head and she groaned again, but this time it came out more like a whimper.

'*Mi amor?*' Javier strode quickly towards the bed. 'Are you unwell?'

Emelia slowly turned her head to face him, her eyes half-open. 'I have the most awful headache…'

He placed a cool dry hand on her forehead, making her want to cry like a small child at the tender gesture. 'You're hot but I don't think you're feverish,' he said. 'I'll check your temperature and then call for the doctor.'

Right at that moment Emelia didn't care if he called for the undertaker. She was consumed with the relentless, torturous pain. The nausea intensified and, before he could come back with a thermometer, she stumbled into the en suite bathroom and dispensed with the meagre contents of her stomach in wretched heaves that burned her throat.

Javier came in behind her. 'Ah, *querida*,' he said soothingly. 'Poor baby. You really are sick.' He dampened a face cloth and gently lifted her hair off the back of her neck and pressed the coolness of the cloth there.

Emelia brushed her teeth once the nausea had abated. She slowly turned, embarrassed at her loss of dignity. She felt so weak and being in Javier's strong, commanding presence only seemed to intensify her feelings of feeble vulnerability. She could not remember a time when she had been sick in front of him before. He was always so robustly healthy and energetic, which had made her feel as if he would be revolted by any sign of weakness or fragility. In the past she had hidden any of her various and mostly minor ailments, putting on a brave face and carrying on her role of the always perfect, always biddable wife.

'The doctor is on her way,' he said, supporting her by the elbow. 'Why don't you get back into bed and close your eyes for a bit?'

'I'm sorry about this...' she said once she was back in bed. 'I thought I was getting better.'

'I am sure you are but perhaps yesterday was too much for you,' he said. He brushed the hair back from her face, his expression more than a little rueful. 'I'm sorry for upsetting you. I keep forgetting you're not well enough to go head to head with me.'

'I am fine...really...'

He grimaced and added, 'I shouldn't have made love with you. Perhaps it was too soon.'

Emelia wasn't sure what to say so stayed silent. It seemed safer than admitting how much she had wanted him to make love to her.

There was the sound of someone arriving downstairs and Javier rose from the bed. 'That sounds like the doctor,' he said. 'I'll be right back.'

Within a couple of minutes a female doctor came in, who had clearly been briefed by Javier, and she briskly introduced herself and proceeded to examine Emelia, checking both of her pupils along with her blood pressure.

'Have you had migraines in the past?' Eva Garcia asked as she put the portable blood pressure machine back in her bag before taking out a painkiller vial and needle for injection.

'Not that I can remember,' Emelia said. 'But I've had a few headaches since I had the accident a couple of weeks ago.'

'Your husband tells me you've recovered a bit of your memory,' Eva said, preparing Emelia's arm for the injection. 'That was yesterday, correct?'

'Yes…'

'You need to take things more slowly,' Dr Garcia said. 'I'm going to take some bloods just to make sure there's nothing else going on.'

Emelia felt a hand of panic clutch at her throat, imagining an intracranial haemorrhage or the onset of a stroke from a clot breaking loose. 'What else could be going on?' she asked hollowly.

The doctor took out a tourniquet and syringe set. 'You could be low on iron or have some underlying issue to do with your head injury.' She expertly took the blood and pressed down on the puncture site, her eyes meeting Emelia's. 'What about your periods? Are they regular?'

Emelia was suddenly glad Javier had left the room as soon as he had brought the doctor in. 'Um…I really can't remember…'

'So you haven't had one since the accident?'

Emelia bit her lip. 'No…'

'Don't worry,' the doctor said. 'After the ordeal you've been through, your system is probably going to take some time to settle down. Stress, trauma, especially physical as in your case, would be enough to temporarily shut down the menstrual cycle. Are you taking any form of oral contraception?'

'My prescription has run out,' Emelia said. 'I wasn't sure whether to go back on it or not. I thought I should wait until…until I knew more about…things…'

'I'll write you one up, just in case.' The doctor took out her prescription pad and Emelia told her the brand name and dose.

Within another minute or two the doctor was being seen out and Javier came back in. 'How are you feeling now? Headache still bad?'

'The doctor gave me an injection,' she said. 'It's starting to work. I'm already feeling a bit sleepy.'

He stroked a hand over her forehead. 'I'll bring something for you to drink. Do you fancy anything to eat?'

Emelia winced at the thought of food. 'No. Please, no food.'

His hand lingered for a moment on her cheek before he left her, closing the door so softly Emelia hardly heard it as her eyelids fluttered down over her eyes…

When she woke it was well into the evening. She gingerly got out of bed and dragged herself into the shower. As she came out of the bathroom, wrapped in nothing but a towel, the bedroom door opened and Javier came in.

'Feeling better?' he asked.

'A lot.' Emelia tried to smile but it didn't quite work. 'Thank you.'

'Do you feel up to having some dinner?' he asked. 'Aldana's prepared something for us.'

'I'll just get dressed,' she said, feeling shy, as if she was on her first date with him.

She could see he was trying hard to put her at ease. He had been so gentle earlier, so concerned for her welfare she wondered if he loved her just a tiny bit after all. She chided herself for dreaming of what he couldn't or wouldn't give. As much as she loved him, she couldn't afford to waste any more of her life waiting for him to change. If he didn't want the same things in life she did, then she would have to have the courage to move on without him, for his sake as well as her own. She hated to think of never seeing his face again or, worse, imagining him with some other woman. How would she endure it?

'Take your time,' he said, gently flicking her cheek with the end of his finger. 'I have some business proposals to read through.'

She touched her face when he left, wishing for the moon that was so far out of reach it was heartbreaking.

Javier came back to find Emelia dressed in a simple black dress that skimmed her slim form, highlighting the gentle swell of her breasts and the long trim legs encased—unusually for her—in ballet flats. Her hair had been blow-dried but, rather than styling it, she had pulled it back into a simple ponytail. She had the barest minimum of make-up on, just a brush of mascara which intensified the grey-blue of her eyes, and a pink shade of lip gloss which drew attention to her soft full mouth with its rounded upper lip. He felt the heat of arousal surge into his groin as he remembered how that mouth felt around him. She was the most naturally sensual woman he had ever met and yet at times, especially right now, he seriously wondered if she was aware of it.

'You are looking very beautiful this evening, *querida*,' he said.

She smoothed her hands down over the flatness of her stomach as if she was conscious of the close-fitting nature of the dress. 'Thank you,' she murmured and shifted her gaze from his to pick up a light wrap she had laid on the end of the bed.

He escorted her down the stairs, holding her hand in his, noting how her fingers trembled slightly as they approached the formal dining room.

Aldana brought in the meal and Javier watched as Emelia kept her gaze down, as if she was frightened of saying or doing the wrong thing. He was the first to recognise that Aldana was a difficult person, but she was dependent on the income he gave her after her husband had gambled away everything they had owned. Javier didn't want to dispense with her services just because of a personality clash with his wife, but he could see Emelia was on edge and he had cause to wonder if things were worse when he wasn't around to keep an eye on things.

After watching Emelia pick at her food for several minutes, he dabbed his napkin at the edges of his mouth and laid it back over his lap. 'Emelia,' he said, 'I know, like many women, you are keen to keep slim, but I have never agreed with you starving yourself. In my opinion, you were perfectly fine the way you were when I first met you. There is no need to deny yourself what you want. Your health is much more important.'

She looked up at him with a sheepish expression. 'I haven't been to the gym once since I've been home. I can't believe I did it before. Izabella said I was obsessive about it. I normally have no self-discipline. I much prefer incidental exercise, like walking or swimming.'

'And sex?' he asked with a teasing smile.

Her face coloured and she lowered her gaze to her plate. 'Is that all you think about?' she asked in a tight little voice.

'It's what we both used to think about,' he said. 'You are the most sensually aware woman I have ever been with.'

Her grey-blue eyes flashed back to his. 'And I bet there have been hundreds.'

He took a moment to respond. 'You knew about my lifestyle when we met. I have made it no secret that I lived a fast-paced life.'

'Which is no doubt why you wanted a shallow smokescreen marriage to impress your business contacts,' she put in. 'I can't believe I agreed to it. I never wanted to turn out like my poor mother, preening herself constantly in case her wayward husband strayed to someone slimmer or better looking or better groomed or better dressed.'

Javier frowned at the sudden vehemence of her words. Her face was pinched and her mouth tight and her shoulders tense. Without her veneer of sophistication, she looked young and vulnerable, and yet she looked far more beautiful than he had ever seen her. 'I didn't realise you felt like that,' he said after a little pause. 'You always seemed so confident. I didn't know you felt so unsure of yourself.'

Her throat moved up and down, as if she regretted revealing her insecurities to him. 'I haven't been honest with you,' she said. 'I mean right from the start. I should have told you but I was frightened you would walk away, that I would appear too needy or something. I guess back then I wanted you on any terms. I was prepared to suspend everything I wanted in life to be with you.'

He reached out a hand and picked up one of hers, entwining his fingers with her soft trembling ones. 'I don't want to lose you, *querida*,' he said. 'But I can only give you what I can give you. It might not be enough.'

She pressed her lips together, he assumed to stop herself from crying, but even so her eyes moistened. 'I want to be loved, Javier,' she said softly. 'I want to be loved the way my mother craved to be loved but never got to be loved. I want to wake up each morning knowing the man I love is right there by my side, supporting me, loving me, cherishing me.' She drew in an uneven breath and added in an even softer voice, 'And I want a baby.'

Javier felt a shockwave go through his chest. He recalled his lonely childhood: the ache of sudden loss, the devastation of being cast aside by his father after his mother had died. He could not face the responsibility of being a parent. He would mess it up, for sure. Even people from secure backgrounds occasionally ran into trouble with their kids. What chance would *he* have? He would end up ruining a child's potential, crippling them emotionally, stunting their development or making them hate him as much as he had ended up hating his own father for his inadequacies.

He couldn't risk it.

He *would not* risk it.

'That is not negotiable,' he found himself saying in a cold hard voice that he could scarcely believe was coming from his throat. 'There is no way I want children. I told you that right from the start and you were in total agreement.'

She looked at him with anguished eyes that scored his soul. 'I only accepted those terms because I was blindsided by love. I still love you, Javier, more than ever, but I don't want to miss out on having children.'

Javier pushed out his chair and got to his feet. 'You can't spring this sort of stuff on me, Emelia,' he said. 'Less than a month ago everything was fine between us. It was fine for almost two years. You did your thing. I did mine.' He pointed his finger at her. 'You are the one who suddenly changed things.'

Emelia put up her chin. 'I'm tired of doing things your way. I'm tired of seeing your picture splashed over every international paper with yet another wannabe model or starlet. Surely you have more control over who you are seen with?'

He clamped down on his jaw. 'The person I should be seen with is my wife,' he said. 'But she is always too busy shopping in another country or having her hair or nails done.'

Emelia flinched at his stinging words. But perhaps the sliver of truth in them was what hurt the most. She had been caught up in the world of being his wife instead of being his companion and soulmate. There was a big difference and it was a shame it had taken this long for her to see it. 'I'm sorry,' she said. 'I thought I was doing what you wanted.'

There was a stiff silence.

'Forget I said that,' Javier said. 'I didn't exactly make it easy on you on the few occasions you came with me. I am perhaps too task-oriented. I tend to focus on the big picture and lose sight of the details.'

'We've both made mistakes,' she said. 'I guess we just have to try not to make them again.'

He pushed his hand through his hair. 'I want this to work, Emelia,' he said. 'I want us to be happy, like we were before.'

'Javier, you were happy but I wasn't, not really,' she

said. 'My accident has shown me what a lie I've been living. The woman you want in your life is not the one I am now. I have never been that person.'

He came over and took her hands in his, pulling her to his feet. 'You *were* happy, Emelia,' he said, squeezing her hands for effect. 'I gave you everything money could buy. You wanted for nothing. I made sure of it.'

Emelia tried to pull away but he held firm. 'You're not listening to me, Javier. We can't go back to what we were before. *I* can't go back.'

'Let's see about that, shall we?' he said and brought his mouth down hard on hers.

At first Emelia made a token resistance but her heart wasn't in it. She wanted him any way she could get him, even if it was in anger or to prove a point. At least he was showing some emotion, even if it was not the one she most wanted him to demonstrate. She kissed him back with the same heat and fire, her tongue tangling with his in a sensual battle of wills.

He pressed her back against the nearest wall, pulling down the zip at the back of her dress, letting it fall into a black puddle at her feet, his mouth still locked on hers. She clawed at his waistband, her fingers releasing his belt in a quest to uncover him.

He tore his mouth off hers. 'Not here,' he said. 'Aldana might come in to clear the table. Let's take this upstairs.'

Emelia had her chance then to call an end to this madness but still she let her heart rule her head. Later, she barely recalled how they got upstairs; she seemed to remember the journey was interspersed with hot drugging kisses that ramped up her need of him unbearably.

By the time they got to the bedroom she was almost delirious with desire. He came down heavily on top of her on the bed, his weight pinning her, his mouth crushing hers in a red-hot kiss that made her toes curl.

He removed her bra and cupped her breasts possessively, subjecting them to the fiery brand of his mouth. He went lower, over the plane of her belly, lingering over the dish of her belly button before he parted her thighs. She gulped in a breath as he stroked her with his tongue, the raw intimacy as he tasted her making her spine unhinge. She felt the tension building and building to snapping point, the waves of pleasure coming towards her from a distance and then suddenly they swamped her, tossing her around and around in a wild sea of sensual pleasure that superseded anything she had felt before.

Then he drove into her roughly at first and then checked himself, murmuring something that sounded like an apology before he continued in a rhythmic motion that triggered all of her senses into another climb to the summit of release. His thrusts came closer together, a little deeper each time, his breathing intervals shortening as he approached the ultimate moment.

Emelia felt her body preparing for another freefall into pleasure. She pushed her hips up to intensify the feeling his body provoked as it rubbed against her point of pleasure, her breathing becoming increasingly ragged as she felt the tremors begin. This time when her orgasm started she pushed against him as if trying to expel him from her body, the action triggering her G spot, sending her into an earth-shattering release that rippled through her for endless seconds.

Javier came with an explosive rush, his deep grunt

of ecstasy sending shivers of delight down Emelia's spine. This was the only time she felt he allowed himself to be vulnerable. She clung to him as he emptied himself, the shudders of his body as it pinned her to the bed reverberating through her. She kept her arms wrapped around him, hoping he wouldn't roll away and spoil the moment.

'Am I too heavy for you?' he asked against the soft skin of her neck.

'No,' she said as she ran her fingers up and down his back.

He lifted himself on his elbows, looking down at her for a lengthy moment. 'I didn't hurt you, did I?'

She shook her head. 'No.'

His eyes travelled to her mouth, watching as she moistened it with her tongue. 'Still unhappy?' he asked.

Emelia searched his features for any sign of mockery but she couldn't find anything to suggest he was taunting her. But then he was a master at inscrutability when he chose to be. Even his dark eyes gave nothing away. 'There are times when I am not sure what I feel,' she said, taking the middle ground.

His mouth tilted in a rueful smile. 'I suppose I deserve that.'

Emelia let a silence underline his almost apology.

After another moment or two he lifted himself off her, offering her a hand to get up. 'Want to have a shower with me?'

The invitation she could see in the dark glitter of his eyes stirred her senses into a heated frenzy. How could he do this to her so soon after such mind-blowing satiation? Just one look and he had her quivering with need all over again. Wordlessly, she took his hand, allowing him to lead her into the en suite bathroom, standing to one side as he turned on the shower lever that was set at a controlled temperature.

He stepped under the spray and pulled her in under it with him. The fine needles of hot water cascaded over them as he brought his mouth to hers. It was a softer kiss this time, a leisurely exploration of her mouth that lured her into a sensual whirlpool. His tongue swept over hers, stroking and gliding with growing urgency, his erection hot and heavy against her belly. She slid down the shower stall and took him in her hands, exploring him with sensuous movements that brought his breathing to a stumbling halt. 'Careful, *cariño*,' he said. 'I might not be able to hold back.'

'I don't care,' she said recklessly.

She gave him a sultry look from beneath her lashes before taking him in her mouth in one slick movement that provoked a rough expletive from him. She smiled around his throbbing heat, her tongue gliding wetly along his length. She tasted his essence, inciting her to draw more of him into her mouth. His hands shot out to the glass walls of the shower to anchor himself, his thighs set apart, his chest rising and falling as he struggled to control his breathing. 'You don't have to do this,' he said, but the subtext, she knew, was really: *please don't stop doing this*.

'I like doing this to you,' she said. 'You do it to me so it's only fair I get to do the same to you.'

He swallowed tightly, his jaw clenching as he watched her return to his swollen length. Emelia felt the tension in the satin-covered steel of his body. He was drawing closer and closer to the point of no return and it excited her to think she could have such a powerful hold over him.

He jerked and then shuddered into her mouth, spilling his hot life force, his flesh lifting in goose-bumps in spite of the warmth of the shower.

Emelia glided back up his body, rinsing her mouth under the shower spray before meeting his dark lustrous eyes. He didn't say anything. He just looked at her with dark intensity, his hands reaching for the soap and working up a lather. She quivered with anticipation as he started soaping her, firstly her neck and shoulders, and then her breasts, the length of her spine and then her belly. He used circular movements that set all her nerves into a frantic dance, his touch so smooth and sensual she felt every bone inside her frame melt.

His hand cupped her feminine mound, seeking the swollen nub of her desire. She felt her breathing come to a stumbling halt as he bent down before her as she had done to him. His tongue separated her, teasing her, a soft flicker at first and then increasing the pace until she was gasping her way through an orgasm that shook her like a rag doll.

She collapsed against him as he rose to hold her, his arms coming around her as she rested her head against his chest. His heart was drumming under her cheek, one of his hands coming up to stroke her wet hair. He rested his chin on the top of her head and for a moment she wondered if he was going to tell her he loved her after all, that he wanted the same things she wanted.

But of course he didn't. Instead, he turned off the water and silently reached for a bath towel, wrapping her in it as one would a small child.

Emelia stepped out of the shower cubicle and did her best to squash her disappointment. Was this intense physical attraction the only thing she could cling to in order to keep him by her side? How long would it last? What if he tired of her and went to someone else to fulfil his needs? The thought of it was like an arrow through her heart. She hated even thinking about all the partners he had had before her. He never spoke of them and she never asked, but she knew there had been many women who had come and gone from his bed.

Javier turned her face to look at him. 'What is that frown for?' he asked.

She gave him a half-smile. 'Nothing…I was just thinking.'

His hand moved to cradle her cheek. 'About what?'

She pressed her lips together momentarily. 'I don't know…just where this will lead, I guess.'

His hand dropped from her face. 'Life doesn't always fit into nice neat little boxes, Emelia,' he said. 'And it doesn't always give us everything we want.'

'What do you want from life?' she asked.

He paused in the process of drying himself to look at her. 'The same things most people want—success, a sense of purpose, fulfilment.'

'What about love?'

He tossed the damp towel on the bed. 'I don't delude myself that it's a given in life. Love comes and it goes. It's not something I have ever relied on.'

Emelia mentally kicked herself for setting herself up for more hurt. If he loved her, he would have told her by now. He'd had almost twenty-three months of marriage to do so, irrespective of what had occurred over the past couple of weeks.

'Come to bed, *querida*,' he said. 'You look like a child that has been kept up way past its bedtime.'

She crawled into bed, not for a moment thinking she

would be able to sleep after spending so much of the day in a drug-induced slumber, but somehow when Javier pulled her into his body she closed her eyes and, limb by limb, her body gradually relaxed until, with a soft sigh, she drifted off…

Javier lay with her in his arms, his fingers laced through the silky strands of her hair, breathing in its clean, newly washed fragrance. In sleep she looked so young and vulnerable. Her soft full mouth was slightly open and one of her hands was lying against his chest, right where his heart was beating.

He'd thought he had the future all mapped out but now he was not so sure. Things were changing almost daily. The more time he spent with her, the more he wanted to believe they could be in this for the long haul.

He tried to picture a child they might make together: a dark-haired little boy or perhaps a little girl with grey-blue eyes and hair just as silken and golden as her mother. But the image faded, as if there was no room in his head for it.

Perhaps it was fate. He wasn't meant to be a father. It wasn't that he didn't like children. One of his business colleagues had recently become a father and Javier had looked at the photos with a strange sense of loss. His lonely childhood had marked him for life. He couldn't imagine himself as a parent. He didn't think he would know what to do. He hated the thought of potentially damaging a child's self-esteem by saying or doing the wrong thing. Children seemed to him to be so vulnerable. *He* had been so vulnerable.

He had never forgotten the day his mother had died. She had been there one minute, soft and scented and nurturing, and the next her body was in a shiny black coffin covered with red roses. He still hated the sight of red roses, any roses, in fact. They made his stomach churn. Within a year he had been sent off to boarding school in England as his father couldn't handle his ongoing grief. Javier had taught himself not to love anything or anyone in case it was ripped away from him without warning.

The thing that worried him the most was that it might be too late to change.

CHAPTER NINE

EMELIA woke up in bed alone and when she came downstairs Aldana informed her that Javier had left to see to some business in Malaga and would be back later that evening. She handed her a note with pursed lips. Emelia thanked her politely and, taking a cup of tea with her, went out to the sunny terrace overlooking the gardens.

The note was simple and written in Javier's distinctive handwriting, the strong dark strokes reminding her of his aura of command and control. It read:

Didn't want to wake you. See you tonight. J.

Emelia felt disappointed she hadn't woken before he'd left. There was so much she still wanted to say to him. She felt he had sideswiped her yet again by enslaving her senses. It was always the way he dealt with conflict, by reminding her of how much she needed him. It made her less and less confident of him shifting to accommodate her needs. He still had control, as he had always done. Nothing had changed, except the depth to which she could be hurt all over again.

The phone rang a little later in the morning and Aldana came out to the pool where Emelia was doing some laps and handed her the cordless receiver. 'It is the doctor,' she said, leaving the receiver on the table next to the sun lounger.

Emelia got out of the pool and quickly dried her hands on her towel before she picked up the phone. 'Hello? This is Emelia Mélendez speaking.'

'Señora Mélendez, I have some results for you from the blood tests I took,' Eva Garcia said.

Emelia felt her stomach shuffle like the rapidly thumbed pages of a book. 'Y-yes?'

'You are pregnant.'

Emelia's fingers clenched the phone in her hand until her knuckles became white, her heart thumping like a swinging hammer against her breastbone. 'I…I am?'

'Yes,' Dr Garcia said. 'Of course I am not sure how far along. It can't be too many weeks, otherwise I am sure the doctors who examined you after your accident would have noticed. You had an abdominal CT scan at some stage, didn't you?'

'Yes,' she said, still reeling from the shock announcement. 'It was done to check for internal bleeding but it was all clear. But how can I be pregnant? I was taking the Pill, or at least I assume I was. I don't really remember that clearly.'

'Perhaps you missed a dose here and there,' Dr Garcia suggested. 'It is very easy to forget and with these low dose brands it can create a small window of fertility. If you can remember when your last menstrual period was, I can calculate how far along you might be.'

Emelia thought for a moment. 'I think it might have been about three or four weeks before the accident. I remember I got a stomach virus right after. I couldn't keep anything down for forty-eight hours.'

'That would have been enough to render the Pill ineffective,' Dr Garcia said. 'But if, as you say, your last period was well over a month ago, you had probably fallen pregnant before you went to London. It is still very early days, but that doesn't mean you are not having all the symptoms. Some women are more sensitive to the hormonal changes than others.'

Emelia wondered how much her headaches and nausea were the result of the accident or of the early stages of pregnancy. She wondered too if her decision to leave Javier had been an irrational one brought on by the surge of hormones in her body. She could recall being more emotional than usual, her frustration at his absence escalating to blowout point when he'd come back just as the newspaper article had appeared, showing him with the nightclub singer. She was almost thankful she couldn't remember that 'ugly scene' as he called it. She was almost certain she would have been as wanton and needy as ever. It would not have helped her cause, saying with one breath she wanted out and begging him to pleasure her with the next.

'Well, then,' the doctor continued in a businesslike manner, 'I'd like you to start some pregnancy vitamins and we can make an appointment now if you like so we can organise that ultrasound.'

Emelia ended the call a minute or two later, her head spinning so much she had to sit down on the sun lounger.

Pregnant.

She placed a hand on her smooth flat abdomen. It

seemed impossible to think a tiny life was growing inside there. What would Javier say? she wondered sickly. Would he think she had 'accidentally' fallen pregnant? He was so cynical, she couldn't see how else he would react. But she didn't for a moment believe she had done it on purpose. Yes, she had become increasingly unhappy about taking the Pill, but she would not have deliberately missed a dose. She had wanted Javier to commit to bringing a child into their relationship. Foisting one on him was not something she had thought fair. It was a joint decision that she had longed he would one day be ready to make, but now it seemed neither of them had made the decision—fate, chance or destiny had made it for them.

She spent the rest of the day in an emotional turmoil as she prepared herself for facing Javier. She would have to tell him. She couldn't possibly keep it from him. He had a right to know he was to become a father, even if it was the last thing he wanted to be.

She heard him arrive at eight in the evening. Each of his footfalls felt like hammer blows to her heart as he made his way into *la sala* where she was waiting. She stood as he came in, her hands in a tight knot in front of her stomach.

'Sorry I'm late,' he said, coming over to her. He brushed his knuckles down the curve of her cheek. 'You look pale, *querida*. You haven't been overdoing it, I hope.'

She gave him a nervous movement of her lips that sufficed for a smile. 'No, I spent most of the day by the pool. It was hot again today.'

He pressed a soft kiss to her bare shoulder. 'Mmm, you are a little pink here and there.' He met her eyes again. 'You shouldn't lie out there without protection. Did you put on sunscreen?'

Emelia lowered her gaze from his. 'I did have some on but it must have worn off while I was in the water.'

He tipped up her face, studying her with increasing intensity. 'Is something wrong?' he asked. 'You seem a little on edge.'

She took a breath but it caught on something in her chest. 'Javier...I have something to tell you...'

A frown pulled at his brow. 'You've remembered something else?'

She bit the inside of her mouth. 'No, it's not that. I...I got a call from the doctor.'

His eyes narrowed slightly and his voice sounded strangely hollow. 'There's nothing seriously wrong, is there?'

Emelia gave him a strained look. 'I guess it depends on how you look at it.'

'Whatever it is, we will deal with it,' he said. 'We'll get the best doctors and specialists. They can do just about anything these days with conditions that had no cure in the past.'

She couldn't quite remove the wryness from her tone. 'This isn't a condition you can exactly cure, or at least not for a few months.'

'Are you going to tell me or am I supposed to guess?' he asked after a slight pause.

Emelia could feel his suspicion growing. She could see it in his dark eyes, the way they had narrowed even further, his frown deepening. She took another uneven breath. 'Javier, I'm pregnant.'

The words fell into the silence like a grenade in a glasshouse.

She saw the flash of shock in his face. His eyes flared and he even seemed to jolt backwards as if the words had almost rocked him off his feet.

'Pregnant?' His voice came out hoarsely. 'How can you possibly be pregnant? You've been on the Pill for the whole time we've been together.' He cocked his head accusingly. 'Haven't you?'

Emelia wrung her hands, deciding there was no point in pretending she was invincible any longer. 'I was sick about a month or so ago. I didn't tell you. I had some sort of stomach upset. I think that would have been enough to cancel out the Pill.'

His rough expletive made Emelia flinch. He turned away from her and rubbed a hand over his face. Then he paced the floor a couple of times, back and forth like a caged lion, his jaw pushed all the way forward with tension.

'Don't dare to mention a termination,' she said. 'I won't agree to it and you can't force me.'

He stopped pacing to look at her. 'I do have some measure of humanity about me, Emelia. This is not the child's fault.'

She gave him an accusing glare. 'Are you saying it's *my* fault?'

He raked his hair with his fingers. 'You should have told me you weren't well. What were you thinking?'

'Being sick doesn't come with the job description of corporate trophy wife,' she threw back. 'I'm supposed to be glamorous and perfectly groomed and ready for you at the click of your fingers, remember?'

He stood staring at her, as if seeing her for the first time. 'You think that is what I always expected of you?'

'Wasn't it?' she asked with an embittered look.

He swallowed tightly and sent his hand back through his hair. 'You have it so wrong, Emelia.'

'I know you probably won't believe me, but this is not something I planned,' she said. 'Not like this. I wanted to have a baby but I wanted us to both want it.'

He was so silent she started to feel uncomfortable, wondering if his mind was taking him back to what the press had speciously claimed about her relationship with Peter Marshall.

'This baby is yours, Javier,' she said, holding his gaze. 'You have to believe me on this. There has been no one but you.'

'No one else is going to believe that,' he said, pacing again.

Emelia flattened her mouth. 'So that's what's important to you, is it? What other people think? You didn't seem to mind what people thought when that nightclub singer draped herself all over you.'

He frowned darkly as he turned back to face her. 'Emelia, this is not helping. We have to deal with this.'

'*You* have to deal with it,' she said. 'I have already dealt with it. I want this baby more than anything. It's a miracle to me that it's happened.'

'How many weeks are you?'

'I'm not sure,' she said. 'The doctor thinks only a month, if that.'

He gave a humourless laugh, shaking his head in disbelief. '*Dios mio*, what a mess.'

'This is a child we are talking about,' Emelia said, feeling a little too close to tears than she would have liked. 'I don't consider him or her to be a mess or a problem that has to be solved. I want this baby. I will love it, no matter how or why or when it was conceived.'

Javier saw the shimmering moisture in her eyes and felt a hand grab at his insides. Her hormones were no doubt all over the place and he wasn't helping things by reacting on impulse instead of thinking before he spoke. No wonder she had been so het up about his regular trips to Moscow, especially when that ridiculous article came out on his return. 'Emelia, we'll deal with it,' he said. 'I will support you. You have no need to worry about that. You and the baby will want for nothing.'

She looked at him with wariness in her grey-blue gaze. 'I'm not sure I want my child to grow up with a parental relationship that is not loving and secure.'

He came over and unpeeled her hands from around her body, holding them in the firm grasp of his. 'There are not many things you can bank on in life, Emelia. But I can guarantee you this—whatever happens between us will not affect our child. I won't allow it. We will have to put our issues aside. They can never have priority over the well-being of our child.'

Her expression was still guarded. 'You're not ruling out divorce at some stage, though, are you?'

He drew in a breath, holding it for a beat or two before releasing it. 'There is no reason why a divorce cannot be an amicable arrangement,' he said. 'If we feel the attraction that brought us together is over, I see no reason not to move on with our lives as long as it doesn't cause upset to our child.'

She pulled out of his hold and hugged herself again. 'We clearly don't share the same views on marriage,' she said. 'I've always believed it should be for life. I know things can go wrong but that's true of every relationship, not just a marital one. Surely two sensible adults who respect each other can work their way through a rough patch instead of bailing out in defeat.'

'I find it intriguing that you are suddenly an expert on marriage when you were the one to leave the marital home, not me,' Javier said. 'You pulled the plug, remember?'

Her mouth was pulled so tight it went white at the edges. 'That is so like you, to put the blame back on my shoulders, absolving yourself of any culpability. You drove me from you, Javier. You had no time for me. I was just a toy you picked up and put down at your leisure. I had no assurances from you. I didn't know from one day to the next whether you would be called away on business. Business always came first with you. I gave up everything to be with you, and yet you didn't give me anything in return.'

'I beg to differ, *cariño*,' he said. 'I spent a fortune on clothes and jewellery for you. Every trip I returned from, I gave you a present of some sort. I know many women who would give anything to be in your position.'

She glared at him hotly. 'You just don't get it, do you? I don't want expensive jewellery and designer clothes. I hate those clothes and ridiculous shoes upstairs. They make me feel like a tart. I've never wanted any of that from you.'

'Then, for God's sake, what do you want?' he asked, goaded into raising his voice.

She looked at him bleakly. 'I just want to be loved,' she said so softly he had to strain his ears to hear it. 'I have dreamed of it for so long. My father couldn't do it without conditions. I thought when I met you it would be different, but it wasn't. You want something I can't give you, Javier. I can't be a trophy wife. I can't be a shell of a person. I have to love with my whole being. I gave you my heart and soul and you've crushed it beneath the heel of your cynicism.'

Javier watched as she turned and left the room. She didn't slam the door, as many women would have done. She closed it with a soft little click that ricocheted through him like a gunshot.

CHAPTER TEN

ALMOST a week went past and Emelia saw very little of
Javier over that time. He hadn't even come to bed each
night until the early hours of the morning, which made
her wonder if he was avoiding talking to her. He seemed
to be throwing himself into his work until he fell into
bed exhausted. Even in sleep she could see the lines of
strain around his mouth, and on the rare occasions when
his eyes met hers during waking hours they had a
haunted shadowed look.

Aldana had come across Emelia being sick a couple
of mornings ago as she'd come into the master suite to
change the bedlinen. The housekeeper's dark gaze
seemed to put two and two together for she said, 'Is that
why you came back to Señor Mélendez—because you
need a father for your bastard child?'

Emelia straightened her shoulders and met the
housekeeper's derisive gaze head on. 'I have tried my
best to get on with you. I know you don't think I am
good enough for Javier. But if you wish to keep your
job, Aldana, I think you should in future keep your
opinions to yourself.'

Aldana mumbled something under her breath as she

bundled the rest of the linen in her arms on her way out of the bedroom.

Emelia had put the incident out of her mind but when Javier came home from a trip to Cadiz on Friday evening she could tell something was wrong. She came into the sitting room to see him with a glass of spirits in his hand and it apparently wasn't his first. His mouth was drawn and his eyes were even more shadowed than days before. She could see the tension in his body, his shoulders were slightly hunched and his tie was askew and his shirt crumpled.

'Did you have a hard day?' she asked.

'You could say that.' He took another deep swallow of his drink. 'How about you?'

She sat on the edge of one of the sofas. 'It was OK, I guess. I went for a long ride on Callida.'

'Is that wise?' he asked, frowning at her. 'What if you fell off?'

'I didn't fall off and I will only ride until the doctor says it's time to stop.'

There was a long silence.

'Is something wrong, Javier?' she asked.

He gave her a brooding look. 'Have you spoken to anyone about your pregnancy? I mean outside the villa. A friend or acquaintance or anyone?'

She frowned at him. 'No, of course not. Who would I speak to? I've been stuck here for days on end with nothing better to do than lounge about the pool or ride around in circles while you're off doing God knows what without telling me when you'll be back.'

He moved across to the coffee table and picked up a collection of newspapers. He spread them out before her, his expression dark with fury. 'Have a look at these,' he said. 'You don't need to read them all. Each one of them says the same. *Mélendez Reunion—Love-Child Scandal.*'

Emelia felt her heart slip sideways in her chest. She clutched at her throat as she looked down at the damning words. 'I don't...I don't understand...' She looked up at him in bewilderment. 'How would anyone find out I was pregnant? The doctor wouldn't have said anything. It would be a breach of patient confidentiality.'

In one sweep of his hand he shoved the papers off onto the floor. 'This is exactly what I wanted to avoid,' he said, scowling in anger.

Emelia moistened her bone-dry lips. 'I exchanged a few words with Aldana the other day,' she said. 'I was going to mention it to you but you were late getting back.'

His gaze cut to hers. 'What did you say?'

'It was more what she said to me,' she said. 'She was in our room changing the bed when she heard me being sick. When I came out she accused me of only coming back to you because...because I needed a father for my child.'

His brow was like a map of lines. 'What did you say to her in response?'

Emelia elevated her chin. 'I told her she should keep her opinions to herself if she wanted to continue working here.'

A dark cloud drifted over his features. 'I see.'

'She's never liked me, Javier,' she said. 'You know yourself she's never really accepted me as your wife. She won't let me do anything or touch anything or bring anything into this stupid over-decorated, too formal mausoleum. I've tried to be polite to her but I can't allow her to say such an insulting thing to me.'

'I understand completely,' he said. 'I will have a word with her.'

'You don't have to fire her on my account,' she said, looking down at her hands. 'It might not have been her, in any case…I mean, leaking the news of my pregnancy to the press.'

Javier came over to her and placed one of his hands on her shoulder. 'You are prepared to give her the benefit of the doubt when everything points to her being guilty?'

She looked up at him. 'But of course. She's never spoken to the press before. She loves working for you. It's her whole life, managing the villa. I don't think she would deliberately jeopardise that.'

He placed his fingers beneath her chin, his thumb moving over the fullness of her bottom lip. 'You are far too trusting, *querida*,' he said. 'People often have nefarious motives for what they do, even the people you care about.'

'That stuff in the paper…' She glanced down at the scattered mess on the floor. 'Is there nothing we can do?'

He pulled her gently to her feet, holding her about the waist. 'Don't worry about it,' he said. 'It will blow over eventually.'

She looked into his eyes. 'Javier… You really believe this baby is yours, don't you?'

Javier realised she was asking much more than that. She was asking for a commitment from him that he had never wanted to give before. He wasn't sure he wanted to give it even now. How could he be sure he wouldn't turn out like his father? But what he had begun to realise over the past few days was that being a father was not just a biological contribution. It was a contract of love and commitment with no conditions attached. His father had not been capable of going that step further. He had impregnated his mother but once she had died he had not fulfilled his responsibilities as a father. He had shunted Javier off to teachers and nannies while he'd got on with his life. This baby Emelia was carrying deserved to be loved and cherished and he was going to make sure it lacked for nothing. 'The baby is ours,' he said watching as her eyes shone with tears. 'I am proud to be its father.'

'I love you,' she said as she wrapped her arms around him tightly.

He rested his chin on the top of her head and held her close. 'I'm very glad that is one thing you remembered,' he said.

She looked up from his chest and smiled. 'I would have fallen in love with you all over again if I hadn't.'

'You think so?'

'I know so,' she said and reached up to meet his descending mouth.

Paris was enjoying an Indian summer and each day seemed brighter and warmer than the previous one. The first week they had spent wandering around the Louvre and Notre Dame, stopping for coffee in one of the numerous cafés. They had mostly been able to avoid the paparazzi, although one particularly determined journalist had followed them all the way up the Eiffel Tower steps for an impromptu interview. Javier had been extremely protective of Emelia, holding her close against his body as he'd curtly told the reporter to leave them alone. It had made Emelia glow inside to think of him standing up for her like that. It made her wonder if he was in love with her after all. She sometimes caught him looking at her with a thoughtful expression on his face, as if he was seeing her with new eyes.

The hotel Javier had booked them into was luxurious and private and close to all the sights. He even organised a private tour of the Palace of Versailles, outside of Paris, which meant she didn't have to be jostled by crowds of tourists.

They were walking past the fountain towards the woodland area when Emelia felt the first cramp. She had been feeling a little out of sorts since the night before but had put it down to the rich meal they had eaten in one of Paris's premier restaurants.

Javier noticed her slight stumble and put his arm around her waist. 'Steady there, *cariño*,' he said. 'You don't want to take a fall.'

She smiled weakly and settled against his hold, walking a few more paces when another pain gripped her like a large fish hook. She placed a hand against her abdomen, her skin breaking out in clamminess.

'Emelia?' Javier stopped and gripped her by both arms. 'What's wrong?'

She bit down on her lip as another cramp clawed at her. 'I think something's wrong…I'm having cramps. Oh, God…' Her legs began to fold but he caught her just in time.

He scooped her up in his arms and walked briskly to the nearest guide, who promptly called an ambulance.

Emelia remembered the pain and the ashen features of Javier as she was loaded into the back of the ambulance and then nothing…

* * *

When she woke the first thing Emelia saw was Javier sitting asleep in the chair beside her bed. He jolted awake as if he had sensed her looking at him. Relief flooded his features as he grasped her hand and entwined his fingers with hers. 'You gave me such a fright, *querida*. I thought I was going to lose you all over again. You have taken ten years off my life, I am sure.'

Emelia dreaded asking, but did so all the same. 'The baby?'

He shook his head. 'I'm sorry, *mi amor*. They couldn't prevent the miscarriage but you are safe, that is the main thing.'

Emelia felt her hopes plummet. The main thing was he was off the hook, surely? No more baby. No more commitment. No more pretending to be happy about being a father. 'How far along was I?' she asked in an expressionless tone.

'Not long, just a month, I think I heard one of the doctors say.'

Emelia studied his expression without saying anything.

He shifted in his seat, his eyes going to their joined hands. 'I know what you are thinking, Emelia,' he said gruffly. 'And I know I deserve it for how I reacted to the news of the pregnancy. I didn't exactly embrace the idea with any enthusiasm.'

'I'd like to be alone for a while,' she said.

He looked at her again. 'But we need to talk about the future.'

She pulled her hand away and stuffed it under the sheets. 'I don't want to talk right now.'

He slowly rose to his feet as if his bones ached like those of an old man. 'I'll be waiting outside.'

Emelia held off the tears until he had left but once

the door closed on the private room she let them fall. So he wanted to talk about the future, did he? What future was that? She had been lulled into thinking they could make a go of their marriage but he had not once told her he loved her. He always held something of himself back. She was never going to be able to penetrate the fortress of his heart. Not now, not without the baby she had longed for, the baby she had hoped would be the key to showing him the meaning of love. She had seen the flicker of relief in his eyes. No pregnancy meant he could continue with his life the way he always had—free and unfettered. Well, he was going to be much more free and unfettered than he bargained for, she decided.

'How is she?' Javier asked the doctor on duty when he came back from the bathroom.

'She doesn't want to see anyone right now,' the doctor said. 'She is still feeling rather low. It's quite normal, of course. The disruption of hormones takes its toll. She can go on some antidepressants if she doesn't improve.'

'When can I take her home?'

'She lost a lot of blood,' the doctor said. 'She's had a transfusion so we'd like her to stay in for a few days to build up her strength. She has been through rather a lot just lately, I see from the notes.'

'Yes,' Javier said, feeling guilt like a scratchy yoke about his shoulders. 'Yes, she has.'

'Just be patient,' the doctor advised. 'There's no reason why she can't conceive again. These things happen. Sometimes it's just nature's way of saying the time is not right.'

Javier sighed as the doctor moved on down the

corridor. He had never thought there would be a right time, and yet the right time had come and gone and he had not even realised it.

The nurse handed Emelia her discharge form with a disapproving frown. 'The doctor is not happy about you wanting to leave so soon, especially without your husband with you. Can't you wait until he gets here? He's probably stuck in traffic. There was an accident in one of the tunnels this morning.'

Emelia straightened her shoulders. 'I have been here for four days as it is. I am sick of being fussed over. I am sick of hospitals. I want to get on with my life.'

'But your husband—'

'Will understand completely when he hears I have left,' Emelia said with a jut of her chin as she picked up her bag. 'You can tell him goodbye for me.'

Emelia slipped out of the hospital, keeping her head down in case anyone recognised her. The press had been lurking about, or so one of the cleaning staff had informed her. That had made her decision a lot easier to make. She was tired of living in a fish bowl. She was tired of being someone she wasn't, someone she had never been and never could be. The accident had been devastating but it hadn't been the catalyst everyone assumed it had been. She had already made up her mind that she could no longer live the life Javier had planned for them both. It didn't matter what his reasons were for marrying her, the fact remained that he didn't love her. He wasn't capable of loving anyone. And, while she loved him and would love him for the rest of her life, she could not continue living in hope that he would change.

A taxi pulled into the entrance of the hospital and,

once its occupants had settled up, Emelia got in and directed the driver to the airport. She had already booked the flight via the high tech mobile phone Javier had brought in for her. It was another one of his expensive presents, one of many he had brought in over the last few days: a pair of diamond earrings and a matching pendant, a bottle of perfume, a designer watch that looked more like a bracelet than a timepiece, and some slips of lace that were supposed to be underwear. She had received them all with a tight little smile, her heart breaking into little pieces for the one gift he withheld—his love.

The flight was on time, which meant Emelia could finally let out her breath once she was strapped into the seat, ready for take-off. She checked the watch Javier had given her, her fingers tracing over the tiny sparkling diamonds embedded around the face as she thought about him arriving right about now on the ward. He would be demanding to know where she was, where she had gone and who she had gone with. She could almost see his thunderous expression, his tightly clenched hands and the deep lines scoring his forehead. But, for some reason, instead of making her smile in satisfaction, she buried her head in her hands and wept.

CHAPTER ELEVEN

EMELIA had spent the afternoon on the beach. The walk back to her father's palatial holiday house at Sunshine Beach in Queensland was her daily exercise. It still felt strange to be on speaking terms with her father after all this time. But his recent health scare had made him take stock of his life and he had gone out of his way since she had returned to make up for the past. He had given her the house to use for as long as she wanted. He flew up on occasional weekends when he could get away from work and she enjoyed their developing relationship, even though they didn't always see eye to eye on everything. Emelia had even made a fragile sort of peace with his young wife who, she realised, really did love her father in spite of his many faults. In many ways Krystal reminded her of herself when she had met and married Javier. Krystal was a little naïve and star-struck by the world her husband lived in and did everything she could to please him. It made Emelia cringe to witness it, but she knew there was nothing she could say.

The one thing Emelia and her father crossed swords over was Javier. Her father thought she shouldn't have run away without speaking to him. In Michael Shelverton's opinion, sending Javier divorce papers three weeks after she had left was a coward's way out. He felt she should have at least given him a hearing.

Emelia was glad she had done things the way she had. She wanted a clean break to allow herself time to heal. But after a month she still had trouble sleeping in spite of the hours of walking and swimming she did each day to bring on the mindless exhaustion she craved.

She had covered her tracks as best she could to avoid Javier finding her. She'd gone back to her maiden name and only answered the phone if she recognised the number on the caller ID device. She had also organised with her father to have all mail go via his post office box address and he then forwarded it on to her.

She tried not to think about Javier but it was impossible to rid her memory of his touch. Her body ached for him night after night and sometimes when she was half-asleep she found herself reaching into the empty space beside her in the bed in the vain hope of finding him there.

Emelia came up the path to the front door of the house with keys in hand, but stopped dead when a tall figure rose from the wrought iron seat on the deck.

'Hello, Emelia,' Javier said.

She set her mouth and moved past him to open the door. 'You had better leave before I call the police,' she said, stabbing the keys into the lock.

He stepped closer. 'We need to talk.'

She tried not to shrink away from his towering presence. 'You can say whatever you want to say via my lawyer.'

'That is not the way I do things, Emelia, or at least not this time around. I made that mistake before. I won't be making it again. This time it is face to face until we work this out.'

Emelia tried to block him from following her inside but he put one foot inside the door. 'If you don't want to be visiting a podiatrist for the rest of your life, I suggest you take your foot out the doorway.'

He took hold of the door, his eyes challenging hers in a heated duel she knew she would never win. 'We can discuss this out here or we can discuss it inside,' he said in an implacable tone. 'I am not leaving until this is sorted out, one way or the other.'

Emelia let the door go and stalked inside. She tossed her beach bag on the floor of the marbled foyer and, hands on hips, faced him. 'How did you find me?' she asked.

'Your father gave me the address.'

Her eyes flared with outrage. *'My father?'* She clenched her hands into fists. 'Why, that double-crossing, lying cheat. I knew I shouldn't have fallen for that stupid father-daughter reunion thing. I should have known he would take sides with you. What a jerk.'

'He loves you, Emelia,' Javier said. 'He's always loved you but he's not good at showing it, much less saying it.'

Her hands went to her hips again. 'So now you're the big expert on relationships,' she said. 'Well, bully for you.'

'He wants you to be happy.'

'I'm perfectly happy.' She put up her chin. 'In fact, I've never been happier.'

'You look tired and far too thin.'

She rolled her eyes. 'You're not looking so hot yourself, big guy.'

'That's because I can't sleep without you.'

Something flickered in her eyes. 'I'm sure you will find someone to take my place, if you haven't already.'

He shook his head at her. 'You don't get it, do you?'

She stood her ground, reminding him of a small terrier in a stand-off with a Rottweiler. 'What am I supposed to get? I understand why you married me, Javier. I've always understood. I was an idiot to agree to it, but that's what people who are blinded by love do, stupid, stupid things. But things are different now. I left you before but the accident put things on hold. This time I am determined to go through with it. It's over, Javier. Our marriage is over.'

Javier swallowed the restriction in his throat. 'I don't want a divorce.'

She visibly stiffened. 'What did you say?'

'You heard me, *querida*.'

She screwed up her face in a scowl. 'Don't call me that.'

'Mi amor.'

Her eyes flashed at him angrily. 'That's an even bigger lie. I am not your love. I have never been and never will be. I can handle it, you know. I get it, *finally*. Some men just can't love another person. They hate being vulnerable. It's the way they are wired. It can't be changed.'

'On the contrary, I think it can be changed,' Javier said. '*I* have changed. I am prepared to let myself be vulnerable. I love you so much but I refused to admit it before in case it was snatched away from me. I have been lying to myself for all this time. Well, maybe not lying—more protecting myself, just as you described. I have always held something back in case I was let down.'

She stood so still and so silent, as if she had stopped breathing.

He took a breath and continued. 'I think I have always loved you, the *real* you, Emelia. You don't have to be stick-thin and done up like a supermodel to make my heart leap in my throat. You do that just by waking up beside me with pillow creases on your cheeks and blurry eyes and fighting off a cold.'

Emelia swallowed. Was she dreaming? Was she hearing what she wanted to hear instead of what he was actually saying? That happened sometimes. She had heard of it. She had done it herself, talked herself into thinking she had heard things, just because she hoped and hoped and hoped someone would say them…

'I have shut off my emotions for most of my life,' he said. 'Saying *I love you* is something I saw as a weakness. I guess I have seen any vulnerability as a weakness. That is probably why you felt you couldn't tell me when you weren't feeling well. I blame myself for that. I should have known. I should have looked out for you. Even Izabella has pointed it out to me, how closed off I am.'

'I'm not sure what this has to do with me now…' she said uncertainly.

'It has everything to do with you, *cariño*,' he said softly. 'I have loved you from the first moment you smiled at me. I can even remember the day. It was our first date. Do you remember it? Please tell me you haven't forgotten it. I would hate for you not to remember the one moment that has defined my life from then on.'

Emelia gave a small nod, her breath still locked in her throat. 'I remember.'

'You looked at me across the table at that restaurant and smiled at something I said. It was like an arrow had pierced my heart, just like Cupid's bow. I didn't know what had hit me. I hated feeling so out of control.'

She summoned up a frown, not quite willing to let go just yet. 'Your father's will,' she said. 'You can't deny that it had something to do with why we married in such a rush. You should have told me about it from the start. Finding out the way I did really hurt me. I felt so used.'

He pushed his hand through his hair. 'I didn't even know about my father's will until I had been seeing you for over a month. I had never considered myself the marrying kind. I had seen the way my father had ruined three women's lives. I didn't want to do that. I guess that's why he wrote his will that way. It was just the sort of sick joke he would have liked—to force me to do something I didn't want to do. Prior to being involved with you, I had always kept all of my relationships on a casual basis.'

His expression twisted with remorse as he continued. 'I should have told you everything about that damned will. Instead, I let Claudine get her claws in. The thing is, I didn't want my father's money for myself. I wanted Izabella to have what was rightly hers and I didn't want to lose you. Marriage seemed a good way of keeping both things secure.'

She still looked at him doubtfully. 'I don't think I can cope with living at the villa any longer. I know it's beautiful and grand and all that but it's way too formal for me. I feel like I am going to get roused on for bumping into things or if something breaks.'

He came over to where she was standing, stopping just in front of her. 'The villa needs to be a home instead of a showpiece,' he said. 'I can see that now. No wonder you never felt at ease there. That is another thing I should have realised. It needs a woman's touch—your touch—to make it the home it should always have been. Aldana has decided to retire. I have been a fool not to realise how difficult she made things for you. She didn't speak to the press—apparently, that was one of the junior gardeners—but she told me about the roses. She feels very remorseful about how she treated you. I should have told you myself why I hate having them in the house.'

She looked at him with a searching gaze. 'Did I know that before the accident?'

He brushed his fingertips over the gentle slope of her cheek. 'No,' he said. 'That was another vulnerability I didn't allow you to see. They remind me of my mother's funeral. Red ones are the worst. I can't bear the sight of them. I would have had every rose bush at the villa dug up and burned by now but my mother had planted them herself.'

Emelia felt the ice around her heart begin to crack. 'I didn't really want to leave you, Javier. I just felt I had no choice. And then the accident...' She gulped and continued hollowly, 'Maybe Peter would still be alive if it hadn't been for me.'

He gripped her hands. 'No, you must not think like that. I have heard from the police since you left. The accident was no accident. Peter's lover was being stalked by her ex. He was following you and Peter, mistakenly believing you to be her. He ran Peter off the road. Charges are in the process of being laid. You were not at fault.'

She put a hand to her head and frowned as the memory returned. 'I remember Vanessa. She was the best thing that had ever happened to Peter. They were so in love.'

He gave her a pained look. 'I know. I am ashamed of how I reacted to that ridiculous press story. I should have trusted you. You've had to endure similar rubbish and yet you've always trusted me.'

'Until that last time,' she said. 'The Russian singer.'

'Yes, well, that was perfectly understandable,' he said. 'You were in the early stages of pregnancy. I had never made you feel all that secure in our marriage. I was always flying off to sign up some big business deal. But all that has to change—if you'll only give me a chance.' He tightened his hold of her hands. 'Say you'll come back to me, Emelia. Come back to me and be my wife. Be the mother of my children.'

Emelia blinked back tears. 'We lost our little baby…'

He pulled her into his chest. 'I know,' he said, softly planting a kiss on the top of her head, her seawater-damp and salty hair tickling his nose. 'I blame myself for that. If you hadn't been so worried about me coming to terms with being a father, maybe it wouldn't have happened.'

She pulled back in his embrace to look up at him. 'You mustn't blame yourself. My father recently told me my mother had three miscarriages before she had me. I don't know if it's hereditary or not, but I'm sure we'll have a baby one day.'

'So you'll come back to me?' he asked.

She smiled as she linked her arms around his neck. 'I can't think of any place I would rather be than with you.'

His dark eyes melted as he looked down at her. 'I know someone who is going to be absolutely thrilled to hear you say that.'

She gave him a quizzical look. 'Who?'

'She's waiting in the car,' he said. 'She said something about BFF. What does that mean, by the way?'

Emelia's smile widened. 'It means best friends forever. She's really here? Izabella came all this way?'

His smile was self-deprecating. 'She didn't trust me to be able to convince you to come home. She said if I didn't succeed she would come in and do it for me. Do you want me to call her in?'

'Of course I do.' She ran to the window and, finding the hire car, waved madly to the young woman sitting inside chewing her nails.

Javier's gaze warmed as he came over and looped an arm around her waist. 'There's just one thing I need to do before she gets here,' he said, turning her around to face him.

'Oh,' Emelia said, smiling brightly. 'What's that?'

'I think you know,' he said and, before she could admit she did, he covered her mouth with a kiss that promised forever.

LET'S TALK Romance

For exclusive extracts, competitions
and special offers, find us online:

 facebook.com/millsandboon

@MillsandBoon

@MillsandBoonUK

Get in touch on 01413 063232

For all the latest titles coming soon, visit
millsandboon.co.uk/nextmonth

MILLS & BOON

THE HEART OF ROMANCE

A ROMANCE FOR EVERY KIND OF READER

MODERN

Prepare to be swept off your feet by sophisticated, sexy and seductive heroes, in some of the world's most glamourous and romantic locations, where power and passion collide.
8 stories per month.

HISTORICAL

Escape with historical heroes from time gone by. Whether you passion is for wicked Regency Rakes, muscled Vikings or rugg Highlanders, awaken the romance of the past.
6 stories per month.

MEDICAL

Set your pulse racing with dedicated, delectable doctors in the high-pressure world of medicine, where emotions run high an passion, comfort and love are the best medicine.
6 stories per month.

True Love

Celebrate true love with tender stories of heartfelt romance, f the rush of falling in love to the joy a new baby can bring, and focus on the emotional heart of a relationship.
8 stories per month.

Desire

Indulge in secrets and scandal, intense drama and plenty of si hot action with powerful and passionate heroes who have it all wealth, status, good looks…everything but the right woman.
6 stories per month.

HEROES

Experience all the excitement of a gripping thriller, with an in romance at its heart. Resourceful, true-to-life women and stro fearless men face danger and desire - a killer combination!
8 stories per month.

DARE

Sensual love stories featuring smart, sassy heroines you'd want best friend, and compelling intense heroes who are worthy of
4 stories per month.

To see which titles are coming soon, please visit

millsandboon.co.uk/nextmonth

JOIN US ON SOCIAL MEDIA!

Stay up to date with our latest releases, author news and gossip, special offers and discounts, and all the behind-the-scenes action from Mills & Boon...

 millsandboon

 millsandboonuk

millsandboon

might just be true love...

MILLS & BOON

MODERN

Power and Passion

Prepare to be swept off your feet by sophisticated, sexy and seductive heroes, in some of the world's most glamourous and romantic locations, where power and passion collide.